Trudy Jax

Beginnings

By

Hayden Pierce

Dedication

This book is dedicated to the love of my life. Your patience, understanding, and indulgence of my tangential mind continues to amaze me. Thank you for always being by my side, watching out for my best interests, keeping me on track, and just overall taking care of me.

Acknowledgments

To my high school writing class and college professors; you all are who have helped me to understand the power of the written word and the joy that can come from it.

About the Author

The author grew up in a region where snow wasn't just a seasonal backdrop but a recurring character—something that shaped both stories and sensibilities. With a lifelong fascination for suspense, crime, and the subtleties of human motivation, their writing blends the mechanical precision of a crime scene with the emotional resonance of lived experience.

Having spent time in both small-town classrooms and the quiet corners of libraries, the author credits their early writing mentors—from high school instructors to college professors—for encouraging a voice that values clarity, tension, and the power of atmosphere.

When not writing, the author can often be found chasing scattered ideas on backroads, tinkering with old stories, or simply enjoying long, quiet moments with the love of their life—someone who continues to provide the grounding and inspiration behind every chapter.

Contents

Prologue

The wind was moving the airborne snow around in swirls with brisk gusts. Four inches of fluffy white snow had already accumulated on the roadways. Two sets of headlights that were seen moving at a good pace down the road, heading for the bridge that crosses Carpenter Creek. It was a deep ravine that is thirty feet wide and about twenty feet deep when it was not raining and usually full when it was. The front set of lights was on a Lincoln Nautilus, black with chrome trim, all-wheel drive with sport rims, while the second set of lights was on a Chevy four-wheel drive Silverado, two-tone beige over brown with a fishing logo in the back window. With oversized fog lights mounted to a light bar on top, the truck had been lifted and had oversized tires with custom rims and a rumble, suggesting a non-stock exhaust and engine work had been done.

The Nautilus was approaching the bridge at about forty miles an hour, a bit fast if it were a Southerner who had not ever driven on snow, but Sarah Jax was no stranger to these conditions, having lived in the area most of her life. This stretch of road was familiar to her; she knew it like the back of her hand going to and from grade school as she volunteered time there often. She was on her way home after a meeting at the school, intently concentrating on the road ahead of her. Tightly gripped with both hands on the wheel, she did not notice the truck gaining on her at an unhealthy speed.

As she approached the bridge abutment, the truck driver contacted her car hard on the rear bumper, flipped his wheel slightly left, hit the brakes, and slowed. The police call it a pitman maneuver; it is used to send a car careening sideways, and this driver performed it flawlessly. Because of the snow, the out-of-control sideways skid was easy to accomplish.

The driver of the truck now had a front-row seat to watch the Lincoln turn slowly clockwise and slide, sending the driver's side door first into the menacing concrete structure on the approach to the bridge. The impact was colossal, brutal, and completely at the mercy of the speed, the metal, modern engineering, and the concrete bridge approach. The truck slowed enough to see the damage to the Nautilus that was quite literally wrapped onto the bridge abutment centered perfectly on the driver's door. He veered around the front of the totaled car, continued across the bridge, and disappeared into the night.

Chapter 1 - Beginnings

Trudy Jax's first step onto campus in Bloomington, Indiana, should have been one of the biggest thrills she has had to this point in her young life, but for Trudy, it was not. The thrill was not the newfound "freedom" that new college students must now learn to master. It was not the thrill of creating and implementing new time management skills of their own choosing; she was already well versed in personal time management.

As for the new crop of boys, she knew she was going to have fun, but they were secondary. Danny Veach from high school led the way to the things that taught her everything she needed to know about boys and sex. By the time they parted ways in his senior year, there was truly little, if anything, that had not been tried, perfected, and improved upon.

For Trudy, the true excitement was the adulthood of it all, the multitude of avenues that sparked in her inner core, the knowing and vision she had commanded herself to strive for, the power that she alone could wield for her. It was her: herself with all her goals, her timelines, her power of self, her knowing that the person within could not be held back, HER, her mind, her body, her glory - all working in calculated tenacious harmony.

She had been preparing for a long time for this last chapter in formal education. Trudy was one of those people who didn't see college as the great emancipator, an obvious time to go wild, but rather the path to finalize her earlier preparations and, to a lesser extent, acquire that overrated piece of paper that claimed the holder was qualified for whatever station in life they studied for.

She had already "made it." She already had a business sense that many would underestimate, but few who worked with, for, and against her would not forget too soon. She had been and would be a force to reckon with. Standing there, on the outskirts of the entrance to the campus where, she intentionally stopped to reset her goals with a smile, knowing the path for her future. A future she had been refining up to this point, a direction that most of her peers were only at the forefront of contemplating.

Trudy had her path mapped and polished; it was an afterthought. She wanted the college "experience" with all its trimmings. The boyish men, the female camaraderie, the fraternity and sorority of it, and the unknowns of college life. It was that very uncertainty that was part of what she would love about this first step, even though looking beyond college was a foregone afterthought.

The sun beat down full of its certainty and promises, warming her to the core from the deepest blue sky hanging over the campus that one could ever ask for. It seemed right, it felt right, and it promised a fantastic start to a new day, a new year, a new chapter to the book she alone was going to write.

She was free to be herself, her best self, the devilish angel that no one could contain. The best part of this newfound existence was that she understood no one could take any of it away from her. She had years to work and many years to plan; she had worked hard, invested, and planned well. A few "lucky" breaks and a few good sound decisions later, she was more than set; she was already self-made.

She had worked several jobs up until this point in life, even though she really did not need to. She was a diligent student and had easily made her way academically through school. Business-minded before she became a teenager, she studied prospectuses, invested wisely, and had prosperous results. Now, her personal bank account could easily pay for all four years of college without a dent in her checking account, all of this before scholarships, grants, and her daddy's college fund.

Her off-school accommodation, which also would serve as a home office, was solely owned by her. The price of the house and its remodel itself could pay for the full four years multiple times over. She kept it secretly and separately. As far as most people knew, she often house-sat for the owners who were loaded and traveled frequently; at least that is what she told her college friends.

TJC Investments owned the house, her quasi-glorified "office," as it was listed on the corporate taxes. She, however, officially lived on campus quite often during the first semester but by the second semester, she was there only one or two times a week, if even that. TJC Investments, her company, received snail mail that pertained to her at the house. Mostly, she did business with her business manager electronically and, whenever possible, face to face when he came from Evansville, Indiana, just an hour or so away, or in her office in Bloomington.

Her personal account ran well past seven zeros at this point, though only a very few select people knew it. Trudy was set, to say the least, and she was completely ready to use her self-gained power with the freedom to explore her desires and interests while sticking to her chosen path in academia.

TJ, as her college friends would come to call her, came from a speck on the map, really, a small town by comparison to the world lying at her feet. She already had her ticket in her hands, out of the farm fields, out from taking care of livestock, out of the sticks, so to speak.

Trudy knew that she owed her current place in life to residing in the middle of the farm "heaven," if you wanted to be a farmer, that is. She loved the farm, but she did not want to stay there. She really did like the advantages she had in her upbringing although it was without her mother. She would gladly trade it all for her mother back. She wanted more; that is why she had made a personal vow to never return to the outskirts of Eldorado, Illinois, for no longer than a visit, even though she knew there would be considerable assets there to contend with in the future.

For now, Trudy was miles away, both mentally and physically, soaking in her new home base, reveling in the whole airy feeling it gave her. She was glad to be on campus, and was looking forward to experiencing dorm life, sort of.

TJC Investments currently had interests in hotels, security, commercial cleaning, applications for computers and phones, and air travel. She owned a commercial, industrial, and residential cleaning products company. She had already funded several speculative apps that were now performing well in terms of financial returns. Her CEO had further extended her reach into business by founding Boutique Air, jets, and planes catering to businesses and individuals who had a need or want for the exclusivity of traveling in style. Her security division was at the forefront of the latest security scenarios for residential, commercial, and industrial clients, with a specialty in hotel management security.

Chapter 2 - About Business

With New York lawyer Kate Taylor's help, as well as a few others, Trudy was able to keep all her business dealings as an anonymous venture as far as her name was concerned. Only Trudy, Kate Taylor, Danny Veach, Amanda Parker, Sadie Taylor, Darell Cromwell, Fred Duersch, Cindy Matthews, Carl Wyn, and a couple of trusted others knew of the extent of her reach. Danny and Amanda, she trusted like no other; Kate was bound by confidentiality agreements, and Darell was paid well as the "CEO" of the investment consortium TJC. He orchestrated the running of all the businesses and how they interacted with each other to parlay the best possible outcome for advancing the financial abilities of the company. Fred paved the way for Athena Hotels to grow a bigger and better footprint. Cindy and Carl were brought into the fold by forethought, strategy, and little vision, but both were trustworthy and were also bound by confidentiality agreements for more than one reason. The Airline and management of all her businesses answered directly to Darell Cromwell.

Trudy knew Darell's life story even before he was employed as her face and CEO. She had him, and the other applicants checked out in a deep background check and personal footprint before they were called to be interviewed. Of the several candidates considered, she had been hoping Darell would be the one to work out. Given his past, she felt like his loyalty, once earned, would be unshakeable, and that was exactly what she was looking for: that and a sound business mind. She could not have been more right in her assessment.

Darell knew what discretion meant and what it meant to Trudy as he maintained her - really, their business well on her behalf in her absence. For now, he was at the helm, there to maintain and grow the business. The growth had been favorable in all aspects of their dealings. He knew Trudy would be playing a larger role in the not-so-distant future and was looking forward to it. When the time came for her to adopt a larger role, he would welcome her arrival, but for now, he ran the day-to-day.

The business was growing at a greater than-anticipated pace, and having easier access to his benefactor would be a most welcome change as she entered college compared to the sometimes-lagging responses he had from his high school boss. He maintained the direction of the company, even creating new avenues, but he also felt and understood the need to keep the owner in unity with the corporate proceedings.

Chapter 3 - Darell Cromwell

Darell Cromwell had grown up much like Trudy in the sense that he was from the countryside, out in the "sticks" really. He had what looked to be a promising future until his dad abandoned him and his mother when he was fourteen for a woman fifteen years younger than his mother. His "father" left his mother with the house and its mortgage, a stack of bills to pay and a meager factory job to pay for it all, and Darell. His mother was able to sell what they had and buy a smaller house on the edge of town.

Darell's mother worked hard, endless hours at times, but she was able to make it all come together, and in doing so, Darell learned many life lessons along the way. He helped where he could, working for local farmers seasonally when possible and the local IGA after school. He often did the shopping and a good portion of the cooking. He was bright and studious, well-liked, and outgoing. He focused his efforts on school and education with the sole intent to "get out" - out from under the paycheck-to-paycheck struggles his mom dealt with weekly, out from the grind that pushes a body to the brink, out from wondering if the bills were going to be able to be paid on time, out from under the hood of the old car his mother used to get to work - OUT! He did not know exactly how he would do all of this yet, but somehow, he was going to bring his mother with him as well. He had graduated summa come laude and, through his studious achievements, was invited to college in Bloomington, where the university gave him a full academic ride, a ride that he would not squander.

Chapter 4 - Good Ole Joe

While some of his friends at his college and other colleges also majored in party with a minor in studies, Darell majored in business and minored in more class load from his "free" ride. He excelled in the revered business classes there in Bloomington and was in the top ten academically. It was also at the university where he met the love of his life, Jenny Tines, late in his sophomore year.

In Darell's junior year, he had proposed down on one knee and had a three-quarter carat diamond ring that he had bought by working countless extra hours at the Kroger in Bloomington. He had been able to transfer stores there and asked for all the work he could manage during his off-school hours. Darell and Jenny were going to be married after graduation, and he was looking forward to the day. Together, they had been able to afford an off-campus apartment.

Late into their senior year, as the leaves were falling from the trees, he got ready to go to work; he kissed Jenny, told her he loved her, and would see her as soon as his shift was over. She hugged him tightly, kissed him deeply, and told him she could not wait. She looked fantastic! To him, she always looked fantastic! He did not want to go, but good things come to those who wait, right?

He had always thought that phrase was really a stupid concept for a much-revered saying. What he actually believed and felt was that, in the real world, good things come to those who are doers, those who go out and get, those who work to their goals and hustle. He was that guy. He was going to be that guy for himself and Jenny.

When he got to work, he realized from the confused, quizzical look of the manager that he had read the schedule wrong and was not supposed to be at work until the next day. The manager gave him friendly grief as he laughed at himself for being so absentminded, blaming it mentally on the class load and physical fatigue.

His thoughts turned to his Jenny and how he could now surprise her by coming home early and, to a lesser extent, enjoying a welcome break. He put together some pocket change and, with a broad smile, bought a single red rose to take with him and left the store.

When he arrived home, he quietly entered the apartment with the full intent of surprising his bride-to-be. He stopped dead in his tracks the instant he heard it. He had heard guttural moans from their bedroom. His face flushed red, and he felt the blood pressure build to an almost deafening pulse in his temples. Mustering all his self-control, he quietly walked to the wide-open bedroom door as he thought, *Why close it? I won't be home for another five hours.* Silently, he turned and momentarily watched as he moved forward quietly. He had slipped unseen into the room; both Jenny's and his neighbor's backs were to him, and the neighbor stood at the foot of the bed.

He thought he already knew what to expect; he had heard his lovely Jenny in the throes of passion with himself countless times, but seeing and hearing it all this way was almost more than he could handle. Darell had thought they really had a great sex life. They made passionate love; they truly had great sex, and lord, when they fucked, it was phenomenal. Now he was hearing all the same sounds, all the same moans, wondering why he had not been enough for her. Standing in a perfect position to watch everything, he was behind and at a slight angle, close enough to be a color commentator and be able to call the play-by-play if he had so desired.

There Jenny was - on her hands and knees doggy style, her beautiful, taut ass high up in the air as an open and willing receptacle, her chest crushing her incredible breasts low on the bed, facing the headboard being fuck-pounded stroke for stroke by the neighbor from the next door apartment.

He knew him - not very well, but he knew him. He and Joe had shared many beers and had great talks. He actually liked him, and they were becoming friends as they had many things in common. Now he could see they had shared one more thing.

He stood there and thought of what to do, what he wanted to do, how he wanted to do it, how to react, and which one he wanted to kill first. There was a buzzing in his body and brain as if something otherworldly was taking over. It was at that moment everything seemed to go soundless. He thought for an instant his ears had failed, but then he heard a distant buzz again that had been growing louder; then it began to fade again. Seconds later, the buzzing in his head subsided altogether, and he started to take in the scene more thoroughly and, oddly, more calmly.

Joe's balls were clearly, audibly, and unabashedly slapping her ass cheeks and making quite a rhythmic skin-on-skin smack. But the sound carried no weight for some reason, as if he should be there in the moment but just was not, not entirely, at least. The timing was constant and forceful, almost hypnotic.

It felt odd to him as he consciously just detached from it all as if he were watching through a window. The emotion of it all, the insanity, the sounds and smells, his outrage, all of it just somehow melted and faded away. He became a spectator with a growing inner clarity that was deciding what he should do for him. The detachment was an odd kind of a relief to him as it became much like watching a porno but up close and personal, where he knew the names of all the actors. He was so close to the action he might as well have been the director.

He stood there like he was on the front side of a TV screen and got to take in the scene, critique it, and yell cut, let us back up and do this or that again. He could have just as easily been alone on a couch with a remote in hand. He chuckled inwardly when he thought momentarily, if this really were a porno, I might be really into the action as it was quite good and intensely graphic. He thought momentarily that he could close his eyes and imagine fucking this hot girl hard.

It was just as if a rug had been yanked out from under him when all the RED in his brain came crashing back in like an avalanche because he HAD been fucking this girl, his girl. He momentarily thought of breaking the TV set into tiny pieces with his bare hands, but he strangled his emotions back into control once more as his mind went through how it was going to be played out.

He took notice of the curve of her back and studied it for a bit. He had always liked this view of her, her silky-smooth curves, her tight ass. For a brief second, he remembered how at one time, he had thought about actually trying to bounce a quarter off her ass. She had liked the compliment or at least the acknowledgment of her physique; they had both laughed when he got out a quarter and asked her to roll over.

For reasons unknown to him, he started to fixate on the cock that was being rammed into good ole Jenny harder and with more fervor. The smell of sex and sweat hung in the air as he began to clinically critique the scene.

He thought, *Hell, he must be doing well; she's dripping wet.*

Both had been beading sweat, and it had been dripping down their bodies. There was a wet spot of mixed juices forming under both, taking the rough shape of their glistening silhouette and creating a wet, shadowy outline on the bed.

In this detached state, Darell found himself inexplicably comparing Joe's dick to the mental image of his own for some reason. He mentally noted and realized that he had the longer cock and that he was definitely thicker, so it could not be about dick girth or stroke length. He almost had to stop himself from actually laughing aloud just thinking of it all in such a surreal kind of way. He concluded he obviously did not know her as well as he thought he did.

Still unaware of Darell's presence, Joe continued to stroke Jenny deep and hard like a champion race stud on a breeding farm, and while he stroked, he leaned back just a bit to accommodate a swing and fully smacked her hard on the ass. She moaned with delight. Taking her cue, he let loose a barrage of ass slaps that all had coincided between strokes. They were equally hard, loud, skin smacking, reddening slaps, beyond sunburn in depth and clarity; the redness in her ass had covered both of her ass cheeks and had spread out to the edge of her thighs. In one sense, Darell had been impressed. He remembered a couple of times he had seen light bruising on her ass from this exact position and how he had not thought much about it; now he felt like such a rube.

Jenny all but yelled, "Oh God… Fuck me… Oh God…fuck me harder!"

Joe obliged her. From tip to hip, Joe really drove forward with such intensity as if he were trying to spear her chest right up through her pussy. Joe's speed increased, and his thrust was so hard that Darell, still in his detached state, even wondered for a second what would happen if Joe slammed down on his own nuts. He almost laughed again aloud when he imagined the thought of them exploding everywhere.

His mind was spinning and numb and inventing shit along the way. He thought he was succumbing to the mental stress. This had been some sort of coping mechanism or just shock; whatever the hell it was, he thought he was really starting to lose his fucking mind. Silent and wordless, he just leaned against the wall behind them both and watched on.

What seemed like minutes later, Joe slammed in extra hard, arching forward, grabbing her long golden-brown locks, and violently, he pulled her head back hard to her moaning. Fully and without abandon, he rocketed his hips forward yet again as his body slammed with his full force up close to her ass, his hips straining forward still again and again. He moaned as he put forth a massive "HUUGHG!!"

His hips were still rhythmically trying to find deeper depths as his cock spasmed deep in her as her pussy flowed freely with the combined juices. His head bowed forward, and his body's tension began to release and fade; his thighs began to relax, and his posture began to indicate, at least for the moment, that his offering was spent.

She had been moaning. "Yes, yes, yes!"

She was orgasming right alongside his release, joining in the banter that surely had to be heard outside the walls.

To Darell, it was not the fact that Jenny was taking another man's dick; he was not the jealous type in that regard. To him, it was more about why he had been betrayed. He and Jenny, he had thought, had been honest with each other many times about sexual desires and had discussed the possibility of him and another guy with Jenny. Jenny and another girl with him, and several other combinations with fantasy positions and even exotic and not so exotic locations. They had even considered trying a wife swap eventually. If they were comfortable with that, try an orgy.

It was clear that there were possibilities that they both had entertained. Both felt, however, that it would be better to wait until after finals, after the wedding, when things had calmed down and expectations were easier to manage.

What was paramount to both he and her when they had discussed this at intimate times was how it would have to be open, honest, clear, and vetted - how each other's input and permission would be explicitly required. How it is a matter of trust and that this trust could not ever be violated.

He had seen firsthand his father destroy his mother's trust and subsequently her, and really, for a large part, Darell's world too, all over mindless sex. ALL that trust he had with Jenny had now just evaporated into the mist in mere minutes and two hard cums.

It was just at that moment Darell chose to speak up, "If you think I'm going down on you tonight, you're out of your fucking mind."

With that simple piece of verbiage, you could have heard an actual pin drop in the momentary silence. It looked like some mythical Medusa had turned them both to stone, but only for a split second. They both spun toward the sound as their bodies pulled apart. Joe's dick was still impressively hard and dripping post come, swinging back and forth. Jenny's pussy was flowing and dripping down onto the sheets and down her legs.

She said, automatically, almost robotically, "This isn't what it looks like…."

Astonishingly oblivious that it only looked like one thing: his future wife or, rather, his now ex-fiancé, getting railed by the neighbor. Though he had fucked her thoroughly and well, it was clear she had given what she got. Had it been a show, he would have not only been impressed, but he would have been as hard as a brick, but this was now his life. He had time to absorb it all, time to think it through, time to decide how to act.

Joe started to open his mouth, but Darell just put up his hand at a police action stop signal.

Darell said, "Don't just find your clothes; take your dick while you still have it attached and leave."

Joe found his clothes and started to straighten his underwear to put them on.

Darell said," Not here, fuck stick; take your fucking clothes with you and get out before I change my mind and hurt you."

Darell followed him to the door, where he opened it and pushed naked Joe, still firm-dicked, onto the outside landing, nude with his clothes in his hand.

Seeing Jenny getting slam-boned by another man, though unexpected, did not evoke the feelings of jealous rage he would have expected, though he thought maybe it should have. He had let the notion subside a moment as he thought, *What all have I been lied to about?*

The trust was now gone…completely. He thought in flashes about his dad leaving his mom over what ended up being a temporary piece of ass. He started to feel a loss of love, a smallness in his world, but only for a second. He had quickly steadied his head, recovered, and walked to her side of the bed and sat down.

Jenny was covering herself up with the sheet. He again almost laughed. "Really, modesty? After all we have been through, the thousands of times I've seen you naked, and now that I've seen you getting fucked by the neighbor…and you feel modest? I think we are way past modest here, so here is what is going to happen. I am going to get up, pack my clothes, pack my computer and books, and leave here. The apartment is in your name; you can have it. The utilities, internet, and cable are in my name, but they will be ended tomorrow by the end of the day. I will come back tomorrow and get the few things that are just mine; the rest you can keep. After that, you and Joe can fuck each other anytime you want. It is over… I love you, but it is over now." (Jenny was now crying) "All I want to know is how long I have been a fool?"

Jenny mustered up enough voice between her sobs and said, "It's only been two months… I'm so sorry…"

Darell cut her off and said, "Two months? I do not even get a parting. It was only this one-time lie; how the fuck did I miss this?"

He noticed their engagement ring on the edge of the bedside table and briefly thought, *Wow, how considerate; at least she thought of me enough to remove it!*

He pushed himself to his feet from the bed with the help of the edge of the night table, palming his ring discreetly as he went, afterward pocketing it. He packed his clothes without speaking another word, hardly looking in her direction again, even though she had regained her composure and was desperately begging him to stay.

As he left the apartment, Joe was in his open doorway, now dressed, looking like he was going to say something.

Darell cut him off once more by saying, "Don't! There is nothing left to say to you but thank you. Saved me a divorce later; she is your come dump now. Have fun!"

With that, he turned and walked away.

The next day, he came "home" midafternoon and cleared out several items left behind: toothpaste, his toothbrush, razor, and various other toiletries, including all the toilet paper and the last roll on the dispenser out of spite. His frat buddy Rick helped him with his recliner, and every picture they could find with Darell in it came off the wall. There had been one small dresser, his TV, and an end table. Darell's last thought in the apartment was, *Damn; those boys work fast,* as the power went out, and he left the key on the counter. He met his frat buddy at the truck they borrowed from Rick's dad. He looked in the back of the truck and realized all his crap, four years, really did not amount to all that much.

Rick looked at him and said, "Look, bro, less than two months until finals, then we are out of here; it's all good."

Rick threw him a beer as they both got in the truck and drove away.

Chapter 5 - Making His Way

Darell had graduated with honors and had been looking forward to entering the workforce enthusiastically; he was willing and ready to prove himself. He was even more eager to put the recent events behind him and concentrate on his future. Darell had varied options upon graduation due to several companies across Indiana and other states that were actively recruiting him and his fellow graduates.

It was a mid-sized company out of Evansville that had caught his eye for multiple reasons. Firstly, due to the size of the company, he felt there were opportunities to advance through expansion and product development. Second, the cost of living in the area was excellent in terms of value for the dollar, not to mention his starting salary was slightly higher than other qualified offers. Third but certainly not least, his mother was still living there.

She had started to date again when he had gone away to college. His mom had settled in with what was shaping up to be a long-term situation with a man, Jeff Rogers. He was also divorced and out of a relationship with a cheating ex-wife. He had full custody of his only son that he had raised by himself after the divorce when his kid was thirteen. David's mother rarely, if ever, came around.

As a gift to his son David at twenty-one, he had given him a Twenty-Three and Me DNA test to show him where his roots were from historically. The unexpected results revealed that there was no way that Jeff and David could be biologically related by genetics; both men were understandably upset. Four years later, Jeff and his SON were part of Darell and his mother's world. He respected Jeff deeply for his commitment to his son in the aftermath. Darell felt this spoke volumes about Jeff's character, more directly, the type of man sharing his mother's life.

Darell liked the idea of having a brother; he and David got along well, developing close ties and trust in each other. Even though there was a level of security in this knowledge of his mother's new and stable life, he had sworn to himself that his mother, who had taken care of him through countless sacrifices of self while he was growing up fatherless, would never have needed for want. He used that desire as part of his drive to succeed.

He started his first job working in a lower-level managerial position in a plastic thermoforming operation with high hopes and grand ideas. He had an endless amount of excitement at first when he started. This was to be his introduction to the adult working world, and he was looking forward to it. His first couple of months were an exercise in assimilation, which he deftly managed. The next six months were an exercise in frustration and disappointment. It was not turning out like he had hoped or imagined. It was even worse than could be predicted from the outside looking in.

He knew he was at the bottom of the totem pole, the low end of the food chain, so to speak. He was willing to prove his worth and earn his way up, but it was clear that this family-owned business, though prosperous, lacked the vision to take a mid-level company to the next plateau. There had been a little infighting between the controlling partners, who were brothers, and their three collective sons somehow managed to change priorities every time someone went on vacation, which was often.

This family treated the business like a personal bank, charging family trips and vacations to the business by making a visit to a local company under the guise of an investment opportunity or fact-finding mission. All these missions had names of places like Fort Lauderdale, New York, Puerto Rico, and Bahamas, some parts of the family were interested in Californian expansion, Canadian acquisitions, and the like. None of these little business jaunts ever bore fruit, and certainly, none of them lasted for less than a week and never failed to involve several members of their immediate respective families. This place, these people, these conditions were unacceptable, and the company was doomed to fail. Darell wanted to get out of there as soon as he could.

He knew he had to stay at least a year to not look like he was a job hopper, and now, being in that window, he was watching and searching Apps designed to network the working world and other professional publications for an opportunity worthy of his best efforts. It was clear that he was not appreciated as one of the tellers for this family's bank.

His break came as a potential match through an app designed to find and match employers and employees. What he saw was really an unassuming and vague advertisement looking for a CEO of a small but established business consortium. The online footprint of TJC Inc., the company in the ad was conspicuously lacking an online presence, but still, for some reason unknown to him, his interest was captured.

Chapter 6 - Trudy Jax

Trudy's mother was the only child of Italian immigrant farmers who had settled in southern Illinois. Sarah Mancine Jax died in an automobile accident on an icy road while on her way home from grade school. She had volunteered for a function and, on her way home, lost traction on a bridge approach when her car somehow slid sideways into the bridge abutment as if she had been t-boned by a car.

It would have possibly been better for Sarah to have actually been hit by another car; as vehicles move, spin, and deflect, they share the impact, but as the reinforced concrete of the bridge didn't flinch nor budge, the car she was driving, though well built, stood no chance for protecting her from an immovable object at the speed she was traveling. The sudden and abrupt stop penetrated the defenses built into the car and ended her life.

The firefighters took the better part of an hour out in the snow and the wintry weather to extricate her body, almost cutting the vehicle literally in two to do the job. The door and really the whole car frame caved in, unfortunately directly centered into the driver's door, causing colossal damage.

If there was anything even remotely good from any of this, it was when the coroner described the death as fast, if not immediate, and given the extent of the damage, more than likely she had felt no pain.

Trudy was a little more than twelve when her mother died. Instead of asking all the questions that a young girl beginning to burgeon into an adolescent woman would ask of her mother or be told of as the changes in her body surfaced, making the transition to adulthood more understandable, she was now looking at her mother's casket wondering why her mother had been taken from her. Her only questions centered on why she was now so alone. Her father, William Jax, did his best to console his little girl, held her through her cries, and hid his from her; he showered his adoring love upon her in the best way he could, though sometimes not understanding the needs of a tweenager.

He thought, *How could you plan on your spouse leaving you? How could this even be contemplated?*

Yet, here he was, struggling to come to terms with just that. He would struggle to raise his baby girl the best he could and still maintain the business of farming and all its constraints. He would make up for his shortcomings somehow, not knowing how that would be.

He was the father that every girl could have wanted or hoped for. He loved her deeply as he did her mother and held her close in his heart. He was a hardy man of infinite get-up and go, and just like his father before him and his father as well, he was always up before sunrise and bedded well after dusk. This was just what you had to do when you farmed.

Farming now was big business, not just a regional concern of yesteryear. His great-grandfather homesteaded two hundred and fifty acres of farm and woodland, pastures, and lakes. His son, Bill's father, would eventually add eight hundred and fifty more acres through well-placed acquisitions. Bill had learned well from his father and his grandpa the business of farming, and with much luck and success, Bill added several of the neighboring farms over the years as well.

As other families and their children lost interest in the land or hit tough times that they could not weather, often they were acquired by JAX farms. Bill was a fair man; he gave a fair price though he could have easily acquired them for considerably less, and for this dignified consideration, he was looked upon locally as a very honorable man and friend to all his neighbors and asset to the community. He provided several full-time jobs and part-time and seasonal opportunities at fair wages.

By the time of his wife's passing, JAX farms totaled a little over two thousand nine hundred acres. A little better than two thousand were tillable with corn, beans, milo, and wheat in the fields. The rest of the acreage contained over four hundred head of cattle, three hundred and fifty or so hogs, eight sizable lakes, clover, alfalfa, and hayfields, six houses, and a multitude of outbuildings and the corresponding staff needed to run the operations.

The house tracts that came with the acquisitions of other property were always offered at more than reasonable rent to the previous owners, usually at cost until they moved on of their own volition. The remaining houses he rented and maintained to and for several of his workers. There were three hunting cabins on tracks of feed plots among one hundred and sixty acres of woodland. The cabins were offered as rental retreats from the world in the off seasons, a rural bed and breakfast surrounded by nature, a place to unwind among the trees. When turkey and deer season approached, it was a highly sought-after hunter's paradise that had a waiting list to be rented out.

Farming for Bill was something he was very adept at running well, especially with his wife Sarah at his side. Now that his wife had died so unexpectedly, the things he had taken for granted, things his wife had done so seamlessly, he now had to do by himself, oftentimes with Trudy looking over his shoulder. He, nor anyone else, had not really understood just how much Trudy was absorbing daily or the effort she was making to understand the big picture of how the farm and its economics flowed. She absorbed her environment at a level beyond her years.

Bill loved his little girl to his core, as any father should, but the farm, his future, and hers commanded much of his time. The result of being pulled in so many directions was that Trudy had been afforded much free time left to her own devices, often supervised only by hired overseers who often had trouble keeping up or catching up with her. When it came to the intricacies of raising a daughter as a mother would, Bill often fell short on various fronts.

He honestly tried to make the farm and raising his daughter work in harmony, but he simply lacked the ability to do it properly because of a learning curve he had not been able to overcome. If it had a motor, was used on a farm, or could be used for fishing or hunting, Bill was your man. However, he had no inkling how to navigate pads, tampons, panties, and bras, much less how to give relationship advice with boys, crushes, petty loves, or, God forbid, sex.

He was often busy with the running of "Jax" farms, the fields, the livestock, and the hands on the farm; he simply could not be in every place he was required to be in order to be efficient and effective, cursing at times the shortfall he had with being there as he wanted for his daughter who often got less attention than he wanted to give. Running the farm was a tough business, and though her father was certainly up to the task, some things were less than ideal in the development of a burgeoning woman.

Trudy was a smart girl who knew how to take care of herself. She could make her way through the fields with ease and converse with the regular field hands and the occasional migrant worker, some of who stayed on and eventually taught her Spanish. Before she was in high school, she was fluent in Spanish and Spanglish and understood bits of Portuguese and a handful of other dialects that other migrant workers brought with them. She embraced the farm much like a tomboy, running tractors early, four wheelers and razors were a way of life. She was driving around the farm as soon as her feet could reach the pedals. She had fallen in love with mobility and the independence it afforded.

Trudy always was learning by listening to others and watching the actions around her. She understood how contractual negotiations played out by being in the room and was often overlooked because of her status and age. Whether it was hay, straw, cattle, beans, corn, rent or leasing negotiations, or dealing with dealers over the latest equipment, she was privy to it all.

Her father was well versed in ROI, and by proxy, so was Trudy, who was always dissecting the actual return on the investment. She had been absorbing this horse sense from a youthful age. She had figured out that the amounts of money that were being exchanged held a significant amount of sway. She had seen her dad use that power to the advantage of Jax Farms multiple times.

Trudy was now the twelve-year-old "woman" of the house; she had tasked herself during the summer months as the house's caretaker, just as her mother had been. She had taken on her mother's role even though there was now a paid housekeeper. She kept up with this routine only to feel closer to her mother as an odd legacy of sorts.

Every Tuesday was laundry day, and per normal, Trudy had readied the laundry in the washroom, loaded the front loader with jeans and work shirts and closed the door tight, put in the powder in its bay, fabric softener in its own, set the dial to permanent press, extra spin, heavy dirt, and hit the start button. When nothing happened, she hit the button once more with the same result. The washer and dryer set was about as old as she was, but the old front loaders had never failed, at least that is, until today. Not one to be deterred from her tasks, she called her dad on the phone. Her dad answered.

"Hello, sweetheart, what's up?"

"Dad, I have a problem."

"What's wrong?"

"The washing machine just gave up; I have tried several times, but it won't start, and I was wondering if you could send one of the guys to take me to the laundromat?"

"We can let this wait until I can have someone find out what the problem is, sweetheart."

"But, Dad, by the time you find out what is wrong, we will have a giant mountain of clothes that will take *forever* for me to catch up. I just keep thinking, what would Mom do? I am sure she would get the laundry done in town and tell you about it later. I would not have called you, but I cannot drive in town. All I need is a ride; I have everything else."

Beaming a smile at his little girl through the phone because he was so proud, he said, "OK, sweetheart, I'll send Sam to pick you up; he can do some running for me in town and take you back home after you're done."

"Daaad, he doesn't need to wait for me. I don't need a babysitter; I can call him when I'm done."

"OK, sweetheart, that will be fine. I'll call Sam."

Bill thumbed through his contact list, slowing down as he entered the 'T' section centering on Sam Taylor. Bill had been using Sam as his go-to on the farm. He was knowledgeable, dependable, and trustworthy. He saw great things in Sam and had been tasking him with the more important chores of the farm. If he asked anything from Sam, he could walk away without a second thought knowing it would get done competently within a reasonable amount of time given the task.

The phone rang on Sam's hip; he pulled it out of the carrier and answered it.

"Hello, Mr. Jax."

"Sam, how many times have I told you? Please call me Bill."

"Will do, Mr. Jax; how can I help you?"

Almost laughing, Bill said, "Hey, would you mind running up to the house and helping Trudy get the laundry into town? She said there was something wrong with the washer. While you're in town, you can pick up that list we have been working on from the Co-op. Grab the business card from the office and get what you can from there and the hardware store; we can get the rest from Lowes when we make a run to Evansville later in the week."

Sam knew that Bill liked to support the Co-op and the smaller stores in town whenever it was practical, paying up to ten percent more, if necessary, before giving his money to the big chains.

Bill continued, "After you get what we need, get back with Trudy and see about buying you two lunches if you would please. On me, of course."

"Yes, sir, Mr. Ja… Uhh…Bill. I'll get it done."

"Sam, Trudy says 'she doesn't need a babysitter' (Bill said with a cross of silly and sarcastic flair) and that I worry too much. She said she would call you when she is ready to come home. With that said, I would appreciate it if you were to stay in town. Please find someplace shady and cool; if *you* have any running there, go ahead and do that. I want you to stay close by if you do not mind."

"I will keep an eye on her from a distance, Mr. Jax; we can catch lunch at the Diner Bell; I'll make sure she gets home safely."

"Thanks, Sam." They both hung up.

Trudy had already placed the first basket at the top of the porch access steps when Sam arrived. The house itself had been built for Sarah Jax fourteen years ago, just after Bill made another expansion to the farm. At the time, the Jaxs were living in their home just down the road. It was rare that farmhouses were close enough to see each other, but because both houses were at their furthest corners of the respective properties, largely because of the terrain providing a good slope for a basement and storm shelter, making the neighbors well within eyesight of each other.

Dan Killian had lived where Jax's house currently is now. When he passed away at the age of seventy-nine, his "children' wanted nothing to do with the farm or the farming life. Bill gave a fair price for the property just as all his other acquisitions, and tore down the 1800s building that he felt was too small for his growing family. He had built the current house for his wife, who was carrying their first child when they finally moved in.

The house was constructed on the hillside and had poured walls for a basement with a fully encased concrete "safe" room for inclement weather. The main floor was a high ceiling open concept, with the main floor housing a mudroom laundry combination just off the three-car garage that connected through to the kitchen. A guest room in the distant corner with a full bath that had an entrance to the living room at the far end that served as the main floor restroom.

Upstairs was a master suite and a large bathing area; next was a central staircase that was bordered by a Jack and Jill set of bedrooms sharing a large bathroom between them. Beside the far edge of the staircase was a dumb waiter that Bill had the builder specially designed for housewares that Sarah thought at first was unnecessary and frivolous. As it turned out, with the laundry on the first floor, the dumb waiter became a well-used blessing because it held almost all the freshly folded clothes for the household on the first upward trip, saving countless trips up and down the stairs.

Outside was designed to be a respite if not an oasis, as the wrap-around porch sported a large screened sitting area with fans overhead and a patio out back that looked as if it had come out of the sample book as the over-the-top example meant to draw people in and entice them to lay their money down. Patio chairs, a screened-in eating area, a fire pit, and a grilling area with a hot tub on the near corner were all surrounded by a paver and block combination that tied everything to the house flawlessly.

Sam pulled up in a Chevy Silverado short bed crew cab to the front porch of the house, put it in a park, killed the engine, and got out to go to retrieve the first basket that was already sitting on the step just as Trudy came out of the front door carrying another large basket full of clothes. Sam met her at the edge of the porch.

"Trudy, let me take that from you. I'll put it in the truck, and you can go get the next one."

"Hey Sam, thanks. I'm glad you could come up so fast."

"I was just down at the red barn checking on a few calves, so I was close by when your dad called; dead washer, huh?"

Trudy disappeared and reappeared with another basket.

"Yup, the washer just quit; it was fine last time I used it, but now there is nothing…. Is everything all right down at the calving barn?"

Taking the next basket, Sam said, "Oh yeah, there are just two new calves that I wanted to make sure were still doing OK."

Trudy disappeared and reappeared again with the last basket that had hamper bags lying on top. Lights, darks, and delicate sheets mixed with towels were now all loaded in the back seat of the crew cab.

"I might go down there and see them later; they are so cute right after they are born, just learning to walk."

"They are cute," he said with a beaming smile, "but the bigger one down there had a little trouble coming into the world; she needed a little help. Doc Johnson had everything under control though…it's all good. If you do go down there, be sure to keep a close eye on the momma; she might be a little protective. So far, she's been calm, but you never can be sure."

Trudy climbed into the passenger seat of the truck.

"I'll keep that in mind."

The truck started and Sam put it in gear as the radio came to life with soulful blues.

"Hey, I like this music; I mean, I like rock and roll better, but sometimes the blues is just what a person needs, don't you think?"

"Yeah, I only listen to it occasionally; it kinda reminds me of my daddy. He was raised on the Mississippi Delta; it never was hard to find the blues anywhere you turned down there. My dad was a sharecropper; I guess that is where I got the love of farming from (he says with an appreciative smile), and he loved the blues. Now, every so often, so do I."

"So, did your whole family farm?"

"Well, not exactly," he said with a little laugh,

"His daddy before him was a sharecropper as well, but *HIS* daddy started out life as a slave, born on a plantation, until after the Civil War when good ole Abe freed us all. Even if some people around here did not get the memo."

Taken aback, Trudy replied, "I'm sorry to hear that; I didn't mean anything by it."

Sam laughed aloud. "Oh Trudy, don't you worry your little head; that was long before you and I were even dreamed of." He chuckled.

"Your daddy…he is a good man, values hard work, and I like working for him. He treats me…heck, he treats all his guys well. If there were more like him, slavery would have never happened," he said while ending in a chuckle.

"I guess I never really noticed it, Sam; I guess I should pay more attention to the world around me. I mean, I never see people that way. You are 'Black,'" she said with finger quotes.

"I'm "White" - finger quotes again - "The migrant workers that mostly come from Mexico, Guatemala, Honduras they are, for the most part, if I labeled them." Finger quoting again. "'Brown,' but I guess I really never noticed that kind of stuff out in that context. Maybe I should, but I really don't care what color anyone is or what language anyone speaks. It's not hard to tell if someone is nice or not; shouldn't that be what we consider? That is what I go by even though we have had some real assholes." Trudy caught herself, covered her mouth, and blushed, "Please don't tell Dad I said that!"

Sam chuckled. "My lips are sealed; I won't say a thing."

"We have had some bad people come through here; I have noticed they don't last that long."

"Yep, I think you're right, but for me and my family, some of the racial problems live right around town; we just can't get away from it unless we move. My Dad volunteered for the Army before he was drafted for Vietnam. His daddy fought in World War II for all our freedoms, yours and mine, but time seems to stand still in some corner places like our town except for islands like your dad's farm.

"I was always taught that the land is what it is about. Respect the land, treat the animals right, hunt, fish, and give back to nature when you can. Respect everyone based on their character and merits, so that is what I try to do. It is who I want to be. But sometimes that isn't enough; sometimes you have to watch yourself just because of where you are and just for being black. I mean, it is not everyone or every place, but sometimes, when and where you would least expect it. Sometimes, it is just a subtle feeling, but when it is there, it just nags at you."

"Your dad and grandpa were in wars? What did they do?"

"Granddaddy Taylor was a hoot. He died when I was about your age, but up until then, he would proudly tell us stories about flying with the Red Tails, the 'Tuskegee Airmen.' He said he was there when his squadron commander flew Mrs. Eleanor Roosevelt herself, even taking her for a midair loop at her request. She was the reason the black squadron was even deployed.

"Trudy, did you know that none of the bombers in World War Two wanted them to fly as escorts to protect them from the Germans because they did not think my granddaddies "Black" friends would be any good in the air."

He began to chuckle while talking, "By the time they flew their third mission, all the bomber groups were requesting them. Word had traveled fast about how they flew with such bravery and determination to prove themselves, fearless tenacity, skilled and ferocious. They lost fewer bombers consistently than any other flight escort wing. Even the Germans avoided the Red Tails when they could. I guess that might have been what inspired my daddy to fly helicopters in Vietnam. He was one of the first Black sergeants in the air and flew quite a few missions. Some of them were classified, and though he didn't talk about it much when he did, it sounded quite hairy. After all that they gave, their kids are still sometimes dealing with racism here in the good ole U.S.A. at times."

"Wow, you must be so proud of your family. I heard my dad say you served in the Army, too. Is that true?"

"Yes, I was in for four years as a helicopter mechanic, and both of my brothers are still in the service, one is a Navy Seal, and one is an Army Delta Recon. Two Army and one Navy family reunions are fun; Isaac would say two Army guys might stand a chance at stopping one Seal if he were wounded or something, and Thomas would invariably ask what a squid is again? Oh yeah, I remember, fish bait." Trudy laughed at the joke and was still absorbing Sam's story, "To tell the truth we are all close. And if my sisters do not keep us in line, mama could level the lot of us with a look. I really think Uncle Sam ought to hire mommas because, after all that training, two of the deadliest men on the planet can be taken down by my mother's sideways glance." Trudy and Sam had laughed aloud as Sam mocked a sideways motherly glance at Trudy.

"What does your dad say about it?"

"He passed a few years back from cancer. We never could pin it outright on Agent Orange, but we think that is where it got its start. Mostly, I think he was just proud of us all, even when he would say stuff like." With quick finger quotes to get his hands back on the steering wheel, he said, "'He and Grandpa knew how to fly; I guess you boys just can't handle the hard things to do.' It was always a fun time when we got together."

"So, were you always close like that?"

"We all fought like cats and dogs the way brothers and sisters do, but God help the fool that would try to pick on any one of us; if you weren't family, the rest of us would come crashing down on them like a sledgehammer." Laughing, "Everyone knew that you just don't mess with those Taylors; they're all half crazy."

"What do your sisters do?"

"Julie was a nurse practitioner, now she's becoming a full-fledged doctor; she is in her last year of residency and wants to eventually become a trauma specialist, and Kate is a lawyer in New York, corporate law, I think.

And as exciting as all that may sound, I'd rather be right here in the dirt where I am."

Sam beamed a smile, saying, "It's MY passion."

"I would love to meet them sometime."

With the blues on the radio playing Lie to Me by Johnny Lang, the truck slowed and made the turn into the parking lot and came to a stop in front of the "Wash Tub" laundromat; Sam killed the engine and helped Trudy put the baskets in roller carts at the front of the building.

Sam commented, "Looks like they aren't very busy." Sam gave a small laugh, "Good for you, yes? I am going to do some running for your dad. I should be in town for a while; your dad wants me to make sure you get lunch. I'll stop back in a bit to get something to eat with you before I head back if that's OK. We can…" With finger quotes again and a laugh, he continued, "'Do lunch.' I'll have my people get in touch with your people."

She laughed at Sam's playfulness. "OK, funny man, I should be throwing things in the dryer by then; we can go eat between the cycles."

"That will be just fine," he said.

"Thanks for your help, Sam; I'll see you soon."

Sam turned to leave when a man with a woman and two loads of laundry entered and 'accidentally' bumped into Sam.

The man of the couple said, "Oh, excuse me, B-o-y. Didn't see you there."

Sam gave the man a stern face and looked him up and down with a piece of shit sneer. Trudy's brow furled as she now blatantly saw up close what she had not been seeing along. She was about to say something, but then she caught Sam nodding her off.

"I'll be back later for you, Miss Jax." Sam had said it loud enough to make sure the couple caught the last name. With that, Sam walked out, got in the truck, and drove off.

Trudy finished separating the piles of laundry into the appropriate piles for colors, brights, and whites. A few minutes after Sam had left, the door opened again, and a sturdy but aging-colored woman came through the door with the first of three baskets of laundry. As she looked around as to where to call 'home,' her eyes met with Trudy, and Trudy spoke up.

"Excuse me, ma'am, but there is room on the benches here by me." She shot a sideways glance without moving her head to the only other bench by the rude man and woman. Sadie saw and seemed to understand as she spoke up.

"Thank you, young lady; it would be nice to have someone to talk to for a while."

She moved her laundry basket to the empty bench next to Trudy and, without a word, returned to her car for the next basket but didn't have to worry about the door as Trudy was holding it open for her.

"Thank you, young lady."

"You are welcome, ma'am, I'm Trudy… Trudy Jax, ma'am."

"Is that so? With manners like that, I suppose it runs in the Jax family, which does not surprise me one bit. I am Sadie."

She sat down basket number two and headed to the car for number three.

"Your daddy wouldn't be William Jax now, is it?" She went out for the last basket.

Still holding the door, "Yes, ma'am, it is. Do you know him?"

"No, not formally but I did know your mother, sweet, wonderful woman… So sad to lose her so young. She was such a wonderful lady. She helped my boy get a job several years back. I miss her, I cannot imagine it has been easy for you without her either."

Caught a little off guard, Trudy said, "No, ma'am, it hasn't; I really do miss her a lot."

Both ladies turned their attention to the laundry before them as Trudy started to load the appropriate washers with their respective loads. She had taken out a five-dollar bill and fed it to a change machine. After collecting her quarters, she fed the washing machines and started their respective cycles.

"So, Trudy, why on Earth are you here at the Wash Tub? Surely, you have a washer and dryer at home. I just hate carrying my stuff in here all the time."

"Well, the washing machine just died today. I am sure it can be fixed, but right now, everyone is in the fields, so the easiest thing was to bring it here and hope that the washer can be fixed before next week. My dad had one of his guys bring me in: Sam. My Dad says he is a good hand, and I like him too. He was fun to talk to on the way here, so the drive was not bad, but carrying in all the clothes, well, that is not so fun."

With a warm smile, Sadie said, "Well, I'm sorry your washer broke, but I am glad you had good help; it IS so hard to find good help these days. It warms me to see you so involved with running your house; I think your mother would be very proud of you."

"Thank you for saying that; I hope she is smiling when she looks down."

"So, young lady, tell me about you; how are you doing? How are you getting along in school?"

"I'm doing well in school. It's actually been easy for me, but since it's summer break, I keep busy at home trying to keep things caught up in the house; I never knew housework could be so overwhelming."

Sadie chuckled just a bit. "It can be a lot of work to keep a house clean. You're trying to do all of this by yourself? That is a lot of work."

"Dad has hired a housekeeper, but ever since… Well, ever since mom died, I like to do some things just to feel like she is with me. It seems like more and more; I wish she were here. I guess that sounds a little bit weird. I wish I could ask her all kinds of questions, things she knew but Dad doesn't. I just wish I could call her…."

Trudy went silent for a long pause and looked both ways as if to make sure she was not overheard, and Sadie could see on her face a slightly twisted, lost look that was trying to express itself. Upon a brief reflection, a single big tear boiled out of her eye as she tried to control and hide it; she wiped it away. Regaining her composure, she addressed Sadie.

"Would it be too out of line to ask you a few questions, woman to woman? I mean, I know we don't know each other very well, but I have very little contact with any other females I can talk to except at school, and they are all my age."

Seeing Trudy struggle with her internal conflict, she smiled and said, "Let's see if I can help…" After a long pause, she continued, "Woman to woman…."

"It's kind of embarrassing, but I know that things change for girls my age, and I know my mom was going to teach me through it; I… I know a few things because she told me as I asked, but now there are some things that I'm really not too sure about."

"Oh, sweetheart, you can ask Momma Sadie anything you want. I have two daughters, and I know that your mother would have helped them if they were in your shoes. So why don't we start by you telling me what it is, you know, and I'll try to pick up where your mother left off and fill in any blanks you have."

"I really hate to trouble you, Sadie, but you are so easy to talk to." Sadie smiled.

Trudy began to shyly tell Momma Sadie in a lowered voice about how her body was starting to change and about hair growing where there used to be none, how her shirt was now starting to gain distance off of her belly, and how some of the girls were having a period thing. Momma Sadie pulled young Trudy to her side and gave her a warm, reassuring hug. She relayed to Sadie everything her mother had told her and sheepishly waited for a reply.

"I am confident we can get you through this with no problems. Now, there might be some things that will sound odd at first, but we will get you the information you need to make this bearable. You will be able to manage right along by yourself soon, I promise. And if at any time you are not sure about something, I am sure we can find a way to talk if that is what you want, OK?"

"I just feel so overwhelmed over little things. I am not even sure how to pick out a bra, much less pads. Tampons? Wings or not, how is it all supposed to work?"

"I know that it can be overwhelming for a young lady, but that is OK; life sometimes is not as easy as we would want it to be. That's when you reach out to the people around you and find the ones who care that will help guide you. I will do that for you if you would like?"

"It just feels like I have known you forever. Thank you, Sadie."

"Come here, Trudy..." Sadie gave Trudy one more big hug. "Sometimes it just takes a simple act to let us know we are not alone. A mother knows when a child is in trouble or hurting; it does not matter if it's your child or someone else's; you help when you can if they let you. If you need some help or advice I'm here to listen and help anytime if you want me to be. I know someday there will be a time that you will be able to help someone else, your way to pass it on, and when you do, you will smile and remember today. I promise."

Sadie and Trudy were well along in their conversation about 'everything,' getting to know each other better, and sharing their life's details when Sam arrived back at the laundromat. Sam half laughed, and half smiled at Trudy.

"I see you have met my momma." He stooped down a bit to hug Sadie.

"Mom, would you like to go to lunch with us?"

Both Girls were finishing loading a wall of dryers and had just fed them an hour's worth of coins.

"Absolutely! This lovely young lady and I were just getting to know each other, but I could eat something. What do you say, Ms. Jax?"

Smiling at her new moniker, she said, "Yes, ma'am, I would love to have lunch together; I'm starving."

"Well then, I'll walk both of you beautiful ladies across the square to the Diner Bell; I think they've got pretty good food there."

"Sam, your mother is just wonderful," Trudy said, quickly putting together what she knew of them now and winking at Sadie. "She was just telling me how she had three sons, two she liked and one not so much; she has to be talking about you." She said this with a chuckling laugh, which also drew a laugh from Sadie.

Pulling Trudy in a one-armed sideways friend, a reassuring hug, Sadie said, "What do you say we let this handsome young man take us to lunch? Hmm?"

"Yes, ma'am, that would be just fine with me."

Sam held the door for both women as they headed across the square to the diner. A turkey club with chips, a home-grown Cobb salad and ranch, and a pepper jack burger and fries rounded out their orders. After they finished, Sam paid the bill.

The Diner Bell was truly a great spot, with open windows, cozy booths, and standalone tables dotted throughout. It had a good variety of food, homemade quality, and very reasonable prices. There was a help-wanted sign there that caught Trudy's eye. After lunch, Sadie and Trudy walked back to the laundromat together. As Sam was leaving, he told Trudy he would be back in an hour to see if she was ready to go and headed to the Farmers Co-op to finalize his part of the trip.

An hour passed with both "mother" and child talking about life, getting to know each other more intimately, more closely. It was easy to tell that Sadie is relishing the role of "the mother to ask." The ease of conversation made it so that Trudy felt safe to ask Sadie some very personal questions, the kind that makes a young girl blush, but the kind that needs real-world solutions and answers, along with some intimate descriptions of how exactly things are supposed to work.

Their tit-for-tat conversation drew them deeper into each other in a way that is normally reserved for mother and daughter. Being able to replay the part of "mom" for Sadie was both nostalgic and uplifting, glad to be able to serve like this once again since her daughters had moved away. It was clear that these two "need" each other at just the right time.

In the brief time they spent talking, a firm bond had been forged between the unlikely duo that would prove one of the best strokes of luck to date in Trudy's young life.

Likewise, for Sadie, it felt great to take on the motherly role once again; she was more than happy to do so. Sadie is warm, caring, and approachable, with a well-rounded view of the world. No nonsense, practical, and efficient in her approach to accomplishing things that she wanted to get done. Sadie is realistic about the world around her and wary of how other people are and act.

She happily took young Trudy under her mothering wing, becoming a surrogate of sorts of all things womanly. Trudy took this all in and began to incorporate what she had learned into the way she is living life and forming opinions. The level of the conversation was surprisingly on an adult level and impressed Sadie. Trudy was more mature than most of the young girls she has seen and heard in passing around town. She took Trudy into her heart deeply.

Sam arrived outside the laundromat just as both "women" were finishing the folding. Sam started with his mother's baskets and placed them in her back seat. Afterward, he carried Trudy's burdens to the truck. He hugged his mother once again and told her he would see her later for supper. Sam turned back to Trudy and followed her around to her side of the truck and, with one fluid action, opened the door and mockingly bowed and said,

"Milady," He directed her to the seat with a splayed-out arm. Laughed with Trudy and stood up straight to see his mom backing out laughingly shaking her head. He walked back around the truck, hopped into the driver's seat, strapped in, and started the truck.

Music in the background. "Did you have any troubles with the laundry?"

"Oh no, and with your mother there, time just flew by. I really like her; I'm going to be seeing her off and on. She has invited me over any time I want to visit. We had a good talk."

"Oh, really about what?"

"Oh, a little of this and a little of that…" With her eyes wide and spaced out, purposely bugged out in a stare at Sam, she said, "A little about you."

She started laughing a bit. "Actually, it was mostly girl talk and a little about my mom, too. Your mom and mine worked on a few projects at the school together. It was nice to learn about my mother that way."

"That does not surprise me one bit. Mom has always been around when us kids were in school; nobody messed up or else…" He laughed a bit. "But even that did not stop us from getting in our share of scrapes and scraps.

"Football, baseball, volleyball, tennis, wrestling, and swimming - somebody was always doing something, and somehow, we all made it to each other's games and meets. It seemed like Mom and Dad were always there for us. You know, in all that time, I don't think we have ever heard talk about winning but rather making ourselves proud. It didn't take long for us to figure out that meant sportsmanship and giving our all. Not even practice was halfhearted; it was ingrained, instilled, and expected of us. To this day, the Taylor name is all over the walls of the high school. We also had our fair share of detractors, but they knew to leave our clan be…"

Laughing a bit, he continued, "It was kinda like throwing rocks at a hornet's nest. You might get away with it once or twice, but when the hornets find you, you get stung multiple times from all directions. School for us was just a wonderful place to be; I learned a lot there and not just from classes."

Mentally reminiscing musingly, he continued, "It seemed like momma was always there at the school in one way or another."

They arrived back at the Jax home and Sam helped unload the baskets onto the porch for Trudy to take inside. She thanked Sam for all his help and asked him to tell Sadie that she enjoyed meeting her and was looking forward to seeing her again.

Trudy laughed when, less than a week after the washer breakdown, she was instructed by her father to schedule a time to be at the house to let the "servicemen" in. What that meant was that in conjunction with her dad and Sam, who undoubtedly had advice from Sadie, had purchased the latest and greatest set of front loaders to replace the old ones. They were high-capacity, highly efficient, wonderful works of art.

Not much more than two hours had passed as she saw the two old machines leave and two new ones get installed, a clean cycle initiated, and the servicemen take their leave. She had signed the invoice when they left and saw what it took to buy the set and what it cost to have them installed. She understood the cost of things. Moreover, she understood how the numbers worked together and how you could work the numbers to your advantage.

She liked how the whole bargaining through delivery worked and how you could take control in certain areas to get your best value. She paid attention to these little things; she understood how they worked together. Through this understanding, her dad had no problems explaining his deals to her as she picked it up readily, and they bonded over these seemingly small events in life. She was gaining valuable knowledge, and he liked watching her absorb the information and ask quite astonishingly poignant questions about the deals and the manner of the purchases.

Seventh grade flew by, as did eighth, while she was simultaneously learning from the sources around her. Business and working relationships with her dad and life's other surprises from Sadie that her dad was not proficient with. Trudy was now very much a young woman, fully five foot seven and weighed in at one hundred and twenty-five pounds soaking wet. Slim, pretty, athletic in build, and with all the attributes of a young woman developing nicely for her age. She was now excited and looking forward to high school. As high school approached, she often was found at Sadie's house for hours on end. The two had a bond that was unorthodox, but they both made sure it worked for them.

The family bond between the Jaxs and the Taylors became deeper with each passing day. Sundays had become a ritual reserved for a morning time together after church for Sadie and Trudy, mostly to talk about the week, learn a recipe or two, and put together a lunch for the guys while enjoying girl time. Bill Jax had been especially thankful for Sadie and how wonderfully his daughter had taken to her, more directly the immediate access to a "mother" for the things that a father "could" do but is often best explained by a womanly figure and woman's touch.

It was even better for him to see that Sadie was there out of true love, care, and concern. She was a no-nonsense, get-it-done, high-expectations type of woman, like her son. Bill saw this can-do spirit rubbing off on his daughter through her actions, and he liked that notion immeasurably. It was reminiscent of how his wife approached things, making him even more thankful for that aspect of their relationship.

Trudy was frequently over at Momma Sadie's, not just for questions but to visit, feel a motherly touch, learn to become a better cook, ask a question or two about her studies, and sometimes just to hang out. She was also keeping up with her "duties' in her own house, though she really did not have to.

She helped on the farm as often as school and chores would allow. She always had great time management skills, often leaving her father wondering how she managed to keep abreast of it all and being even more proud because of it. Trudy was so self-driven in all the right ways; her father loved that, too.

Winter always arrived with its set of challenges, not difficult in its nature, but this was when the real deals for the farm were made. Whether it was procuring seed for the spring plant, trading in tractors or combines or implements, or adding to the "fleet," or buying the next needed thing. She watched her dad maximize his dollar and influence.

There was always one more meeting to attend, one more price to rethink, one more quality report to consider, but it all had to be done before breaking ground in the spring, and through it all, Trudy was there asking, poking, and prodding her father who feigned being exasperated with her endless questions all while being so proud of her level of understanding.

The one single thing Trudy took time to understand and grapple with was scale. The scale of the farm, the scale of the people it took to make a year pass profitably, the scale of the numbers in terms of the money flow, and the scale of the power that this much acreage yields in the business world.

Whether it was cows or hogs going to slaughter or the fields being brought to market, she understood its power, saw firsthand, and grasped that the number of zeros behind the number often evoked the power in front of the number. JAX farms certainly had a number on both sides of the column to make any business doing business with the Jax's pay attention to the details.

If you lived in the city, they would call it street smarts, but here it was simply good fashioned horse sense, well, horse sense with a whole lot of horsepower behind it. Trudy saw firsthand how that influence could be used in a positive way.

Bill Jax loved his daughter, and his love was often expressed in constructive short shopping trips to stores and occasionally a mall for the essentials where he usually stayed in the truck. He knew his daughter to be reasonable and knowledgeable when it came to understanding the difference between want and need. She seldom spent frivolously, and when she did, it was more rare to be for herself.

She had already demonstrated many times that she understood quality and how buying once at a slightly higher cost was more beneficial than buying lower quality twice, even at half cost. The quality item more than likely would outlast both cheaper items combined from the get-go with less operational headache.

His love often came with dollar signs attached, not as a buy-off but as his expression of love. Jax farms easily was a multi-million-dollar enterprise, so he rarely balked when she asked for money to purchase a desire or need. To be fair, he noted, she scarcely ever had asked for extravagance or big-ticket items, so when she did, there was usually plenty of leeway.

Bill's attention was constantly turned toward the farm, the fields, next year's crop, John Deere's latest wares, and how many miles were on his trucks. He knew well how to love; she could see it in his passions, how he had always doted on her, and the way he protected her and made her feel safe. Trudy could also see that when her mother died, part of the light went out in his eyes. She knew she was loved and felt his love every day, but equally, she also was a spitting image of her mother, a constant reminder of loss that, at inopportune times, haunted him.

Trudy was not sure which was the worst part for him, the isolation from losing his wife or the accident itself burnt in his memory, but the end effect really was the same eventually. Trudy dearly loved her mother, but since it had been a few years since her passing, she had hoped that her father might find love again for himself someday if for nothing more than for him to be more balanced, though he rarely ventured far from his surrogate wife, the farm.

Early on, even in grade school, Trudy exhibited a keen intellect for her age, a knowing or direction that the majority of her peers did not have. She had a drive from watching her father tirelessly operate the farm; that drive was pushing her to excel from within herself. She felt this self-imposed narrative, a drive from seeing everything work in harmony, stemming from her dad's work ethic, and she used that drive to make herself excel. She knew she would need to be self-reliant or otherwise allow herself to be a victim of the world around her. She had decided early on that she would be no one's victim if she had any say in the matter.

Survival was in her grain, and she knew that education would play a key role in years to come, not just in books but in the signs and indicators surrounding her. She understood that education is not a thing that just lived in books; it was on the street corners, in the hallways, and at the purchase counters. This education had been ingrained in the fabric of life, and she had the uncanny ability to see it with blinding clarity. Things that most kids looked past or failed to see at all, she soaked in and learned from it all. Be it successes or failures from everyone around her, there was a lesson she could learn from almost any situation if she dissected it.

These were the lessons that had been laid at her feet, she was learning from all of it. It was more than fair to say that she had gotten very good at reading people, their drives and what motivated them, their vices and their downfalls, what buttons to push, and when all timed to exact a tap or nudge to obtain a general direction. It was not quite manipulation, more like a hypnotic suggestion, an intricate and delicate form of power that she was already becoming quite good at. She also had an uncanny ability to hone in on the things with depth, more than a surface type of importance, the things that truly matter when trying to accomplish tasks or projects.

She was not above having fun; she was, in fact, very likable and had many friends in and around school. She soaked up her environment and made it work for her, not in a bitchy sort of way but rather with that X factor that had people wanting to help her because of her presentation, even early on in high school. Whether it was her fellow students or her teachers, she had the ability to work her environment well to the desired outcome.

Trudy was able to see through the visual noise the audible confusion and hone into the heart of the matter that drove the individual, and she did this all with a non-malicious and smooth application of self-directed will. She had been able to capitalize on this form of currency, whether it was information or the presentation of an opportunity.

She often was able to augment behaviors to affect a favorable outcome for the benefit of her friends and teachers as well. In doing so, the recipients always felt compelled to help her out with whatever the situation called for. They often did this not out of a sense of 'they owed her,' but because of the manner she was able to help. It begged them to want to give back without the perceived obligation that others expected with their tit-for-tat. For whatever reason that often was unrefined, they all knew they wanted to be a part of her success somehow. It was the elusive "IT" factor that no one could readily explain.

Babysitting had been her first actual job; she liked kids well enough, but equally, this helped her see the commitment it took to raise a baby and take care of kids. She decided then, and there that child rearing would need to be considered heavily as the toll it took on the body was only surpassed by what it did to the mind. She had seen the struggles that were involved in trying to make it work through the eyes of her employers. She had also seen the blinding, unflinching love as well and decided that for her, at the right time, it would be a good thing to have children, but it would have to be on her schedule.

As she began her freshman year in high school, she could see how the newest crop of girls was often not much more than the targets of all the boys. She saw when a few of her friends became teenage mothers at this young age how, they limited options for their worlds.

Early into the first semester, she had sat down with Sadie and tried to gently wade into the birth control discussion, and in true form between the two ladies, Sadie yanked the bandage right off the tender spot, so to speak, and asked the real and tough questions. She cut to the heart of the matter as to whether she intended to talk to her father about this and whether she was sexually active or had plans to be anytime soon.

Sadie told Trudy, "Sit down here with me, and let's talk. If you and I are going to have this discussion, we are going to have a very adult discussion with all the possibilities and sides being talked about, understood, and explained. You need to be able to explain yourself to me, to yourself, and to your father with clarity.

"Don't get me wrong, I have definite ideas on what I want to tell you, but I want you to think this through and understand it for yourself first. What do you know, what do you want to know, and are you ready to discuss it all with me?"

Drawing in a big breath, Trudy said, "Well, I can tell you what I have read and what I have personally seen; I mean, I live on a farm, I've seen the cows with the bulls, the sows with the hogs, I get how babies are made in that sense. To directly answer your question, I'm not sexually active, but I have seen a boy or two I would be interested in dating. I've seen firsthand how a lapse in judgment has affected some of my classmates, and because of that, I have no plans for sex right now. I do, however, sometimes have a pretty rough period, and I know that the pill can help regulate some of those aspects as well, so I was thinking two birds, one stone.

"Now, on the subject of sex, I have read a few things, and, honestly, with the internet and smartphones, it's not hard to get answers to questions that might be uncomfortable to talk to anyone else about. I do want to be sure that what I think I know is true and correct. I don't want to hide from the truths of it all. I don't want this to be some taboo, silent, un-talked mystery, but rather a facet of life. I see it all around me, and I know I'm just at the beginning of it all. To that extent, I know I'm a bit naive, but I just want to cover all my bases before a time comes when I wish that I already had. You can't imagine what I've heard at school from some of the other girls. I know they're dead wrong, yet they believe what they are saying themselves is actually true. I think what they believe is really scary, momma. I want actual facts, relevant knowledge, not some idiotic made-up truths."

With a big warm smile, Sadie replied, "Trudy, you know I love you, and child, I do love how your mind works. I'm not the prude I bet you think I am. All my girls were on the pill before the first day of high school. Not because their father and I didn't trust them, but being young and frankly hormonal, and all things new that you have now seen being thrown at you, with boyfriends starting to pop up, peer pressure, and bad facts, it just made sense to protect their future, to protect yours as well.

"That is not to mention that the minute any girl hits high school, she becomes a conquest for every boy there. My daughters, much like you, were asked by me why they should be on the pill and what they knew about sex and sexuality, and they answered in the exact same way as you did. That is to say, in an intelligent and adult-like fashion. They, too, had a lot to learn about relationships and the world around them, just as you do. They were trying to be responsible just as you are trying to be, and for that, I was proud of them, and that is why I'm proud of you.

"Knowing yourself from within and starting to envision your dreams unencumbered by a fleeting lapse in judgment. Being your own guide while making informed, good decisions. Ultimately, all of this will be exactly what YOU make of it. It is what makes me truly proud of you."

"Will you help me talk to my dad? I'm not sure how to approach this with him without him making a leap beyond what I'm really wanting to accomplish. I am afraid he will see this as me simply asking for a license to have sex. That couldn't be further from the truth. I just don't want to make a mistake down the road that I think I would regret."

"I will gladly help you; I will pave the way, but you will have to be the one to tell your dad. You will have to keep him in the know just as you would have with your mother. It will be difficult at times, especially with your dad instead of your mom, but as a young adult, you have to know that this is a part of being a grown-up. An adult conversation with adult eyes and adult consequences."

When the ladies arrived at the main barn, which also doubled as the head office for the farm and the main mechanical warehouse for cleaning, servicing, and repairing all the equipment, Bill had a most inquisitive expression on his face. He had gotten to know Sadie on many levels and was extremely happy that his daughter had a woman to talk to on all the womanly things in life, so when Sadie and Trudy arrived together, he was most attentive.

Sadie stepped into the office by herself as Trudy wandered down the row of equipment, stopping to look at a broken cross brace on a three-bank wide disc set and milled around there as Sadie and Bill talked. When Sadie emerged from the office, Bill gave her a most uncharacteristic hug, and then he stepped back a pace.

"Sadie, I can't thank you enough or express how much I appreciate what you bring into Trudy's life, and mine means to me; it truly is a blessing to us. Thank you!"

"Bill, you have an amazing young woman there; being here for her is easy; she makes it that way, and besides, it helps me feel young again."

With a small chuckle, he said, "I'm not sure how that works, but I could use about five gallons or so of that; it just seems like I just feel older every day. Again, thank you so much for all you have done."

With that, Sadie turned to wink at Trudy with a reassuring smile; she turned and walked on out of the doorway.

"Sadie says we need to have a discussion that I need to pay attention to. I have got to say that I am so glad she is here for you, and I'm glad she is here for me as well. What is on your mind, young lady?"

With that, Trudy hugged her dad as he hugged her back.

"I wish Mom was here…."

With a very stunted chuckle, "So do I, sweetheart…so do I." The second part of his statement was half taking on a whole new meaning.

"So, what's up with you?" Trying to keep it open and light.

Trudy drew a big breath and started talking to her dad in the office while they were both sitting in comfortable high back office chairs. Bill listened to his daughter intently as she once again rehashed the pertinent parts of wanting to see a doctor, the whys, and the reassurances that she was indeed still his little girl. Talked about her fears and of some of the mistakes of some of her classmates. Bill ignored his office phone blowing up and turned down the ringer while listening simultaneously, fully turning off his cell.

By the time Trudy had finished, he could not help but hear his late wife in his daughter. He stood up as she did when she had finished talking; he hugged her and thanked her for telling him. And agreed with her reasoning to be on the pill. He let her know how much he appreciated her being able to talk it through with Sadie and then himself. He told her how much of a beautiful young woman she was becoming, how much she was like her mother in the way she thought, and how she, like her mother, had always seemed to have matters in hand.

He also told her how he had noticed her grades, the compliments from her teachers, and how he always let them know that this was all Trudy. She smiled and hugged him again, and with a kiss on the cheek, she told him she was going to set up an appointment after she got to the house. They parted ways, and he went back to his desk, turning on his phone and cell. He stopped for a bit to relish the moment with a smile. She was becoming more than just a young woman, although deep inside him, she would always be…his little girl.

Trudy was on the pill long before her first real interest in boys, and that thirty-day pack became her go-to before the true start of every day. The pain of the difficult periods had become more regulated and considerably less. Being on the pill comforted her to a degree when she watched the slow-motion train wreck that a few of her classmates were experiencing because of unintended pregnancies from not taking precautions. The thought of being protected from at least that facet eased her mind.

Between Trudy's 7th and 8th grade years, she noticed a change on the farm. The shift was subtle and natural, but Sam was now working side by side with her father much more often than he had in the past. Instead of running the fieldwork constantly, he was now shoulder-to-shoulder and helping make decisions with her dad.

There came a time when she was hovering, and to be honest, she was halfheartedly snooping; it was when she realized her dad was grooming Sam to manage the farm. Sam was being asked to make critical decisions and price calls that normally were in Bill's wheelhouse and domain. Sam's instincts, as far as she could tell, were spot on and in line with what she would have anticipated from her dad. She concluded this was going to be a good fit. It all made sense as the Taylors were more and more a part of their family lives as well as in their farming lives. She had already spent countless hours with Sadie, and from what she could tell by watching Sam and her father, it was going to work out well.

Chapter 7 - Transitions

All was fine on the farm until early in the spring; sometimes in the night, it was not. Sam's Truck had been given a new impromptu paint job. The truck was parked in front of the Taylors' house, and in bright colors, there were now racial slurs and white supremacy slogans that were emblazoned across the truck's bedsides, doors, hood, and windows.

There had been some hints of racial troubles before - some blatant, some muted - but never like this. There had also been an uptick in comments in town and mention of some of the higher-ups visiting the small chapter of the Ku Klux Klan that still held a footing in town.

Old man Wilhite made it no secret what he thought about different races in his neck of the woods. His son and, to a lesser extent, his grandsons were very much on the same path as him. It was not hard to see that this posturing was part of a show designed to impress both local sympathizers and national leaders. An impression had been made that would have long-term ramifications, or so it was thought.

The next day, Trudy was clearly emotional when talking to her father about it, and Bill was clearly just plain disgusted. He let Trudy know there was a change in the works that would only help part of the immediate problem. But he had no idea how to change the hearts and minds of a small minority of the population that made up the bigots. Bill called Sam to the office and had him sit down to have a talk with him.

Bill asked, "How is your mother, Sam?"

"She is a little shaken, a lot angry, and plenty mad. I put out a call to my siblings to let them know what was going on, and they were all understandably pretty upset, too. There is a plan to come together soon, as soon as we all can make it happen."

"I'm sure Sadie will be glad to have her brood home. I hate that you two had this happen, but I called you here because I wanted to talk to you about something else that I had been wanting to do for a while now. I have been watching you - how you run things, your decisions, and the way you interact with others - and I think it's time. What I'm saying, Sam, is I think you're ready for a promotion of sorts. I want to make you the general manager of Jax Farms.

"I will still be very much involved in the day-to-day in terms of getting things done - spring planting, fall repairs, and the like - but I will be taking a back seat, looking over your shoulder instead of you looking over mine - that is if you want the job.

"Along with the position, there will be a significant jump in your pay structure, bonuses linked to profits, and the Barn House down from the pasture is yours - again, if you want it. That includes the guest suite house. I am hoping that Sadie will have a mind to join you — again, if that is acceptable to you and her.

"Most importantly, I want you to know that the business with your truck has nothing to do with this, but it would seem to be good timing. Wait…that sounded really shitty; good timing of sorts, if that's possible, given the crap you're dealing with from last night.

"I guess, however, since it did happen, I could point out that it is obvious the Barn House is deep onto Jax Farm property; I'm sure no one would venture in that deep, so you won't ever have to worry about your mother again. There is no rent, no lease, and it comes with a company truck."

Sam had been diligently saving, watching Bill, and learning the trade and the ins and outs for a long time. He had not really been cognizant that Bill was giving him the access that he was getting. He realized that, in retrospect, it was unprecedented to have the access he had been given. He had been learning from Bill, and as it turned out, Bill was a particularly good teacher. Sam had wanted to learn what he could, and afterward, at some time, step out on his own, buy a piece of property, and begin growing it just as the Jax family had. But now this offer was changing his thought processes as he could see some alternate possibilities.

"Bill, I do believe I would like the opportunity to have my hand on the helm. I have been watching and learning from you for quite some time - contracts, salesmen, and people; I think I'm up for the challenge. I am happy to accept your offer.

"As for the house, I really appreciate the offer, but I don't think some backwoods bigots are going to do more than puff out their chests, so I don't think there is a need even after," he said with a smile, trying to be lighthearted. "The truck was given its new paint job that moving would be needed."

"Sam, I don't think you understand what I am saying. This has nothing to do with that; the two aren't related in any way. Why do you think I had you on the far side of the farm for the last four weeks? Sure, we had some drainage issues that the dozer and track hoe crew were fixing, but I could have easily had someone else go direct and supervise that, keeping your true talents up here in the office.

"If I had done that, you would have seen the remodeling crews. I didn't want you on this side of the farm because I wanted this to be just right - a surprise. I was going to make you this offer, which includes the house when they were done. The remodel crews just finished their last punch list yesterday. New roof, reinsulated, new high-efficiency furnaces for the house and the suite, new cabinets, new appliances - hell, it's all new except for the bones. So, what do you say?"

"Well, OK then. I guess there is nothing left to say for me, but yes, thank you. I'm going to have to talk to Mom about her part, though." Sam stuck out his hand to shake Bill's hand; both firmly shook with a smile.

"Don't thank me now; we have spring planting yet to do…boss."

"That feels a little weird; I don't think I'm ready to go that far yet," he said with a prideful, muted chuckle.

They were still in the office beginning to talk about the transition and expectations of each other when they noticed dust trailing from a car; they stepped out and watched it arrive. As it approached, two bubble gums became visible on the top of the roof, though they were not flashing. The sheriff pulled up to the office parking area and got out; they were there to greet him.

Roger Burns was a big man, mostly muscle and two hundred and forty pounds, with arms that strained against the officer's short-sleeved shirt openings. He stepped out of the cruiser that yielded slightly higher on the driver's side as he departed the vehicle.

Roger was technically a transplant to the area; his wife was the one who originally had ties to the community. He met his wife in his college days and married her shortly after he had taken a law enforcement job in Mt. Vernon, Illinois. Several years later, he took a deputy job out of Carbondale to be closer to his wife's ailing mother. He liked the area, as did his wife, so he stayed there after his mother-in-law passed away. He ran for sheriff the next year to affect changes he thought needed to happen. His platform was a transparent inclusion for all, the law available equally for everyone was the main vibe. He won in a landslide victory and ran unopposed for the last two election cycles after that.

He was well-liked and a steady pillar to the community, levelheaded and calm, cool under pressure, and fair to all under the law. This was now his permanent home, and it showed by how he made a point to service all the county's communities by staying in touch with all the local concerns and following up where he could to affect change for the better.

Roger approached them. "Hey, Bill…Sam." As he took off his hat and palmed it in his left hand, he continued to say, "I have been meaning to have a word with you both; it's just been so crazy around here lately. Sometimes, it's hard to keep my head from spinning completely around. Sam, I'm sorry about what happened this morning; I have a good idea who is behind it, but as of right now, no proof. When I get any proof at all, I promise to act on it."

"I appreciate that. I have been able to get most of it off with a high-pressure washer, but there are some spots that are going to require a little more work than that."

"I really wanted to see how your mother was holding up. With the troubles in town and now the truck thing, this shit makes me sick."

"Wait, what troubles in town…with my mom?"

"So…I guess she didn't tell you? You know she is really a tough ole bird, and I say that with the utmost respect for her. For the last couple of weeks, there have been some disturbing comments and harassment involving people of color in town, mostly from the Wilhite boys. They made it a point to be in your mother's way; she backed them down fairly well. Honestly, I think they are scared of her. Hell, I don't think I would ever want to get cross with her either, to be honest."

"That sounds like my mom."

Bill interjected. "Their daddy wouldn't be Tom Wilhite, would it?"

"The very same guy; why do you ask?"

"Nothing really, but I remember my dad telling me Tom's old man fancied himself some sort of white Messiah, you know, the kind, white power, the better race, claimed to have held a lynching."

Bill shook his head in disgust. "My father said he would rather deal with herds' worth of fresh cow patties than deal with the Wilhites for anything. Apparently, from what you are saying, those apples didn't fall far from the tree."

"So, Bill, what else do you know?"

"What do you mean? Am I missing something here?"

Roger began to fidget somewhat, and Bill could tell that he was pussy footing around something. He knew Roger to be fairly direct, but now, for some reason, he was being vague, and his posture was a bit structured, tight, and even tense. It was clear he was hemming and hawing, but for what wasn't yet obvious to him.

Bill spoke up. "OK, Roger, spill it; I've known you far too long for you to dance around the subject with me. What's going on? And don't tell me nothing; you look like your wound tighter than a hot spring. You're more nervous than a long-tailed cat in a room full of rocking chairs. What's going on?"

"Now, hold on, Bill; I'm going to tell you everything I know about it; I just wanted to know where to start. I think you have answered what I needed to know. Along with their comments and harassment in town, the Wilhite boys have been mouthing off about how…" He looked at Sam's eye to eye, then said, "Sam, these are their words, not mine; I hope you know me well enough…" Turning back to Bill, he continued, "They were mouthing of how they know exactly what happened to that nigger lover Mrs. Jax."

Bill was taken aback; then he flushed red.

"So, it made me think one of two things: either they love to hear themselves talk and stir the pot, which I am sure that they do, or maybe your wife's accident wasn't entirely an accident after all. I had my lead investigator open your wife's file again and look at it with fresh eyes. I asked him to look for anything out of the ordinary. It was a mess that whole damn thing, shit you know, the car was literally torn in half and cut again in two. It wasn't the condition of the car that caught Mike's attention, though; he apologized and apologized again because he felt that he should have noticed it the first time when he was summarizing the accident. He even offered me his resignation…which I refused.

"Bill, really, we had no reason to suspect foul play given the conditions and the circumstances, but now, after reviewing all the photos again, Mike saw what appeared to be a large scrape across the back bumper. I'm guessing you wouldn't have let your wife's car look like that, winter or not, would you, Bill?"

"Going into winter? Not a chance; her car was fine; it had just been serviced before the snow and was in pristine condition before the wreck. You're telling me that you think those boys had something to do with my wife's death?"

"No, they were too young to drive at the time. I mean, it's possible they could have been out on a four-wheeler and saw something, but I don't think so. I think we may have missed something else altogether. It had to be a car or a truck that made that mark on the bumper. And being in the back of the car, it wasn't part of the actual collision. So, I started a search with the local body shops and worked my way outward from there. I was looking for anyone that had any type of bodywork done shortly after the crash's time frame, more directly, any bumper work being done."

"And?"

"Just one vehicle that had only bumper work done around that time. It was a Silverado four-by-four owned by Tom Wilhite two weeks after the crash that had a bumper replaced. The body shop said their records show that the bumper brackets were bent, and one of the pushers on the front was missing. They repaired it a week later after they got the parts in.

"I'm telling you this now because I don't want you to hear rumors about this; I wanted you to hear it directly from me. Bill, we have looked at every angle we can think of for usable evidence, but there is no earthly way we can prove what we think we know. Even though he still has the truck, your wife's car has long been crushed and recycled. I'm sorry, Bill, but I think we really dropped the ball here. I wanted you to hear all of this from me."

He turned to look at Sam, then said, "And as for your mother, Sam, you need to at least tell her some of this; these boys might be more dangerous than they seem. At the bare minimum, they are out to prove something. With the head 'Dragon' coming to the Wilhites' homestead for a recruiting drive two weeks from now, things just might get worse. I've already stepped-up patrols and authorized overtime for a few days before and after this asshole gets here. My guys are happy to work the hours; they don't like what is going on any more than I do.

"And Bill…Bill, I need you to just leave it alone. It is only a matter of time before they truly implicate themselves or their dad or both. I'll be waiting for them when they do. Please, just let me handle it. I don't want to have to arrest the wrong person. I can see you're angry right now, but I promise you, it will not be forgotten."

Bill looked up skyward, trying to strangle back emotions flooding to the surface. His face had already flushed red, his temples were pulsing visibly, and his jaw was tightly clenched and set. It was plain to see his blood pressure was off the charts. Grabbing a deep, ragged breath, his fists had already balled up, and his arms were tensed. He tried to maintain his composure, but then he sternly asked, "Exactly how are you going to handle it, Roger?"

"Now, Bill, I could lie and tell you some bullshit about how I can fix all of this and make it right, but the truth is, it is going to take some time - more time. I know this isn't what you would want to hear, and it is a lot to process, but I have to follow the law regardless of how I feel or what I think I know. It comes down to what I can prove. We dropped the ball once; I can promise you it won't happen again. I know you're going to rethink all the possibilities ten ways from Sunday, but I need you to leave it alone and trust that I will not let it go undone."

"HOW MANY FUCKING YEARS DO YOU THINK THAT'S GOING TO TAKE, ROGER??!!"

Bill turned around, clearly fighting frustrations and emotions; he stormed back into the office, reliving that awful day in his mind as he went. The door slammed, and shortly after, a loud, guttural, frustrated yell came. Roger and Sam could see through the window as the first desk inside the office space left the ground. Bill had grabbed the edge of the desk and, as a vent of his anger and angst, ripped the edge violently upward, giving the whole heavy wooden desk a three-quarter rotation fully in the air before it crashed back down on the floor, bouncing once and settling upside down on the desktop. Sam had never seen him like this before, nor had anyone else; Roger and Sam collectively looked at each other in pensive astonishment as an inquiry to each other as to what they should do now.

Sam broke the silence between them. "I'll keep an eye on him for a little while. I have never seen anyone this angry; I'll hang around until he cools off and calms down. I'll have that talk with momma after I leave here. Thank you for letting us know what's happening. Let us know if anything changes?"

"Of course, of course, you know I will. Please let Bill know I will keep him apprised of any changes as well. Sam, let him know I'm truly sorry for everything, but I promise I won't let it rest."

Half an hour later, without a word, a calmer Bill tries to turn the desk back over and asks Sam to give him a hand at righting the desk if he could. Upon doing so, Sam relays the shared information to Bill. After they get the desk sitting on its feet, it is clear that the desk will never be usable again for its intended purpose.

"I'll order a new one tomorrow, Bill; why don't we stop for the day? Go be with Trudy; I have to have a conversation with momma. I'll see you tomorrow morning."

The two left the office, going their separate ways. Bill found Trudy and relayed the events of the day, leaving out the acrobatic desk and the anger. Sam found out that the Wilhites had been much worse than even the sheriff knew, Sam was deeply angered and outwardly angry at Sadie for not letting him know about the problems she was facing in town. Sadie made it clear that it would take a whole lot more than two peckerwoods to stop her from doing as she damn well pleased. But after Sam rehashed the conversation with the sheriff, Sadie had fresh new eyes as to his concern and promised to be more vigilant and to let him know if there were any other problems, no matter how small.

Sam let the air clear for a while. He took some time and relayed his concerns to his sister Kate in New York to get it off his chest and to keep his siblings in the loop as well. Kate promised to touch base with the others and let them know how their mother was doing.

After an hour or so, Sam brought a little light to their day by replaying the job offer and his acceptance to Sadie, who was duly happy for him. He meagerly approached the idea with Sadie about living in the guest house near him, fully expecting serious pushback about the plan. Sadie caught him totally off guard when she told him she thought it sounded like a wonderful idea. She liked the idea of being closer to her son at work, to Trudy, and to their extended family. Besides, who wouldn't want all new everything at least once in their life? It was still close to town and out in a much more peaceful setting, noting at her age, the simpler that things in life are, the more enjoyable they become.

Almost two weekends later, the last of Sadie's furniture was placed in the suite just as she wanted.

"It is a real special treat," she said, "to have a new everything and everything new."

Sam, Bill, and Trudy were all happy. Sadie made meatloaf, mashed potatoes, and sweet corn with iced sweet tea as the first lunch cooked from her new kitchen. It was great home cooking that came with an extra spring in Sadie's step; everyone was equally excited to see how happy Sadie was with her new surroundings.

Sadie told them all, "I am looking forward to having everyone here this next weekend; it has been a long time since everyone has been together at the same time. It will be so nice, even if you all are coming together just to check on me." She gave Sam a half-stink eye, "Bill, I can't thank you enough."

"Don't thank me; it is all Sam. I can't run this farm without him." He jokingly corrected himself immediately, saying, "Well, I guess I could run things without him; I just don't want to."

Chapter 8 - The Gathering

The weekend arrived, and the sheriff, as well as all his deputies, were on high alert. Deputies were pulling around-the-clock patrols, and the "Dragon" and his "Second" were now out at the Wilhites farm with a gathered small audience.

A makeshift podium had been set up on the back deck, and twenty-five chairs for the new potential recruits were on the lawn looking up at the 'podium.' Old man Wilhite and his son Tom presumably were to announce their guest as they were standing slightly behind the leaders. Eighteen of the chairs were occupied as old man Wilhite stood behind the podium and announced his guest and stepped around his guest to make way for him to address the crowd and stood a few paces behind him. Tom, his son, stood behind the "Second" just a few paces to the right of the podium, just like his father with the Dragon. Both Tom and his father were in their respective places to honor their guests as dutiful sponsors. All the while this was happening, and concurrently with their stepping behind the guests of honor, there was unseen activity about half a mile away.

First man: "Range 850 yards, low tailwind value, locked in."

Second man: "Agreed, waiting for alignment."

First man: "I've got good alignment."

Second man: "I've got good alignment."

Second man: "Ready to engage?"

First man: "Engage."

--

Second man: "On my two, five, four, three tw…."

A singular shot rang out before the word "two" had been fully articulated, and almost a full second later, four men were violently heaved backward in a jumble on top of each other in two bloody, nonmoving masses.

The spectators were not quite comprehending what had happened until they heard the report of a gunshot as the sound caught up with the bullet. The whole crowd hit the ground as soon as they realized what the sound they heard was.

First man: "Break down exfil; move on the quiet."

Over a mile through the woods later, a GMC crew cab Denali truck exits slowly onto the main road from an oil well side cut out in the woods. There are two large Black men in the cab.

The truck traveled about twelve miles down the road in no particular hurry until it pulled into a dirt lane and continued to the Wabash River edge. Both men exited the vehicle. As one man set up an old log he had picked up from out of the bed of the truck, he retrieved both gun barrels from the floorboard of the cabs' seat in the back, now detached from their respective breaches.

The other man lit up and adjusted the cutting tip to a small set of oxy-acetylene torches. He is wearing cutting goggles and begins to waste the barrels away to molten slag with the cutting tip of the torch. Less than ten minutes later, the only thing left of both barrels was a pile of granulated metal droppings, which the man who had not been using the torch picked up with a shovel from off the ground and flung deep into the water. The torch was shut down and left to cool. Afterwards, it had been stowed back into the toolbox in the back of the truck. The cutting log was rolled into the water; both men silently watched as it drifted away.

Afterward, both men reached into their pockets and pulled out one spent policed brass casing and unceremoniously chucked it out to the middle of the muddy water. They turned without a word and made their way to the cab; they both got in, the truck started, and they headed back to the main road as if nothing had happened.

It was a joyous occasion at the Taylors' house for Sadie even with the reason behind why they all had come together. Her boys, Isaac and Thomas, were due to arrive at any time. Dr. Julie Taylor had arrived two days prior, and Kate had arrived with her boyfriend, Kevin Stephens, earlier in the day.

Kate was inwardly excited and had wanted to see how long she could go before anyone noticed she was engaged. She had only made it to the top of the porch steps before Sadie homed in on it and hugged Kevin to welcome him to the family. Kate asked her mother how she knew as she had barely gotten out of the car.

Sadie laughed and said, "You can't hide a glow like that. The boys you had gone out with in high school never had this effect on you."

Bill and Trudy were also present at the reunion, and besides an obvious complexion difference, they intermingled with the group as part of the family because, in essence, they were. Sam introduced them to Kevin after shaking his hand as his second dad, Bill, and his littlest sister, Trudy. The rest of the Taylors were already in complete agreement with that years ago. When the slick new black on chrome, fully decked out GMC Denali arrived with Isaac and Thomas inside it, the reunion was complete.

Eight full racks of baby back ribs were already done but still in the smoker, waiting only to get a healthy slathering of barbeque sauce. There was cross-talk throughout the living room, everyone catching up with everyone else. Julie was dating, but it hadn't gotten too serious yet. Kate and Kevin rolled off the tongue nicely, and everyone loved the sound and flow of it. They were planning a late spring wedding and wanted to keep it simple and small, and after a brief look around, suggested, maybe here at the farm? That idea landed favorably with Sadie and the rest of the gang.

Isaac was dating a woman that he felt might be the one, but she was sorry she could not make it as there were other plans that she could not cancel. Nonetheless, he assured them all that she very much wanted to meet everyone as soon as time permitted. Thomas was not sure if he would ever settle down; an Army wife's life could be a lonely and scary proposition, so he thought it might not be in the cards for him.

Someone had noticed and commented that there was dust coming down the lane. The car had bubble gum flashers on top of it, which were the first visible parts of the vehicle; slowly, the whole car came into view as Roger pulled to a stop in the drive. He originally had planned to go to Bill's house, but he saw the gathering of cars and altered his trajectory for the Taylors. The men stepped out to greet him.

When Roger arrived on the porch he was met by all five of the men. Kevin had squared up beside Sam and Isaac, followed by Thomas and Bill.

They were lined up in a lazy semi-circle shoulder to shoulder to shoulder like a formidable front line on a football field. No man was under two hundred pounds, all of them together like this was a wall of weathered muscle.

Roger was a big man himself and had never feared any man but thought to himself, *Damn, I would hate to be on their bad side.*

Roger knew the family was closing ranks around Sadie, and he knew why; he really admired their solidarity, but even so, he had a job to do.

Bill was the first to speak, "Good morning, Roger, what's up?"

"I'm sorry to intrude on your gathering," he said, looking to Sam, "but I'm investigating a quadruple homicide that happened just two hours ago."

"Oh my God, Roger, was it anyone we know?" Bill replied.

"It was George and Tom Wilhite and their two guests, the 'Dragon' and his 'Second.' It has the earmarks of a very professional hit. It would appear by all accounts that one shooter was able to kill four people with one shot. Almost magical."

Looking at Tom standing next to Isaac, he said, "Tom, I was wondering if you or Isaac could lend me some insight for my investigation? I mean, what does it take to hit a target roughly half a mile away? At least, that's all we can figure out in the preliminaries based on the impact and time-lapse of the shot report. What kind of skill set would be required for two shooters to pull a trigger simultaneously and hit four targets in one cold bore shot?"

Isaac took the lead. "On a day like today? Hardly any wind; I would think that anyone worth their salt with a decent rifle could do it at that distance easily. The right weapon, the right ammunition, all the right conditions, piece of cake."

Thomas chimed in. "Deltas would wash out any sniper that couldn't do that before the end of the first week on the range; the conditions right now are more than ideal for a pro. Do we have to worry about a killer running on the loose now as well?"

Roger replied, "No, I don't think so. Honestly, I was going to ask where you two were a few hours ago, but clearly, you guys are clueless as to what happened, right?"

"Three hours ago, Isaac and I were driving on our way here….together."

"Any stops on the way?"

Thomas looked at Isaac; Isaac interjected. "Other than gum and gas In Mt. Vernon, Indiana, nope." Furling his brow, he said, "Wanna see the receipt?"

"That won't be necessary; I believe you."

"Sheriff, I assure you we are here just to visit our mother and make sure she is safe. Have you been able to have a word with those boys we heard about on my momma's behalf?"

"No, Isaac, I haven't yet, but something tells me I'm not going to have to now. I wonder if I came back with a warrant, it would do me any good.

I wonder just what I'd find?" By the intonation of the question, it was clear he knew what had happened and was fishing for an answer.

Thomas answered him blank–faced: "If you are referring to any evidence…" After a brief yet eternity-long pause and an eye lift, he continued, "I can assure you there is no evidence that exists to be found here, but feel free to check; you don't need a warrant, look anywhere you want… Now if you like…"

After a long, exaggerated pregnant pause and slowly glancing between each of the brothers and gauging the resolve on their faces, Roger knew he was looking into hardened, unremorseful, battle-tested eyes.

"Humph, no need." He bit his lower lip briefly. "I have all the information I need. So, when do you boys head back to, uh…well, work."

"I'm heading back to the Evansville airport next Saturday; Thomas is giving me a ride, and then he's heading on as well."

"Well, you two have a safe trip."

Bill piped up. "You wanna stay for lunch? Ribs and everything that goes with it?"

"Thank you, but I have to be going; this is going to be a long day. I need to go and gather what information I can for our investigation. Bill, Sam, I'll keep in touch."

Sam replied, "Thanks, Roger; you let me know if there are any troubles for my mother's sake, won't you?"

"I will, Sam, I will for sure if I hear anything at all. And hey, before I forget, and I really mean this," Turning to face both men, "Isaac, Thomas," he said, shifting his weight and pivoting to include Sam in his gaze. "Truly, thank you for your service to our community and the country." There was clearly more to this thanking than gratitude for their service deeds. "Be safe."

With a nod, Roger put his hat back on and paused.

"I wouldn't be surprised if you don't hear from the FBI soon; they are getting involved with their hate crimes unit. They wouldn't stop the Wilhites and their friends from gathering over First Amendment issues, but now they sure as hell will make a show out of trying to find their killers; just a friendly heads up."

Roger walked back to the cruiser, got in, started up, and headed out, disappearing into a cloud of dust. There was an air of knowing in the round from the non-participants, an unspoken moment heavily shared. Breaking the silence and changing the mood by coming out of the door from behind them all.

"Ribs, anyone?" Julie exclaimed, drawing everyone's attention back to the house and to the kitchen where she had been expertly doctoring the ribs to completion.

Sadie had been looking forward to this day for a week with great anticipation and had outdone herself. The food fare on the table was promising to lead them all to fallow. Besides the ribs now stacked high in sections of four on the center of the table, they were surrounded by fried okra, green bean casserole, pasta salad, a zucchini-squash-onion and potato dish that by itself was heaven, corn, and homemade rolls with butter for both. The first round of plate wrestling was interrupted twenty minutes later by a half-loud, half-excited call out from Julie.

"Who wants cake and who wants pie? Momma, you have outdone yourself again."

Kate chimed in sarcastically. "Whatever you do, don't eat the peach pie; it's horrible… Kevin and I will take it home with us just to get rid of it…y'all might want to try the cake…" she said, not containing her laughter.

Sadie interjected. "You know I will never forget… Katie, I made two peach pies," she said with a beaming smile, "one just for all of us and one just for, uh…Kevin to take home; you'll have to see if he will share."

Kevin beamed a smile directly at Sadie and said, "One slice….maybe two if she is nice to me." Sadie smiled warmly back at him. He took that as a general approval of his hostage negotiation declaration.

Isaac, Tom, and Sam took a short walk with Kevin while letting the food settle, and they made it clear that they all liked him. Kevin worked on Wall Street and could provide for their sister well as if she needed that given her position and steady advancement in her law firm's partner tract.

Equally, they made it clear that they knew that life sometimes takes unexpected turns, and should things ever get bad, he needed to understand raising his hand to their sister wouldn't be tolerated. The message was well received, not as a threat but as a piece of valuable knowledge, which it was intended to be. They individually welcomed him to the Taylor family with a firm handshake, which he impressively returned. Kate and Kevin left to go back to New York mid-week. Julie left the day after.

Late the next Friday afternoon, the three remaining Taylor men were nursing Busch lights while walking up the road to the office to meet up with Bill. Upon arriving there, new cold soldiers were retrieved from the office refrigerator. Bill took a back seat to Sam as he was going through a recap of what was being accomplished on the farm, the way the cycles repeated themselves yet were always new, and how all the entities played together. By the way, his brothers were listening; it was clear they were impressed by Sam and his orchestrated working knowledge of such a large enterprise. Bill himself felt even better knowing that his semi-retirement could go full time at any time should he so desire without a hiccup to the business.

Bill had asked the brothers if the cabins were in decent shape and if the Razors, which they both were using as transportation back and forth, were in good working order. They both were happy with the arrangements and said that everything was good in that regard. Bill verified turkey season and deer season "reservations" as both "boys" enthusiastically verified their desires. The Taylors always had the first season in any of the cabins they desired. And though the cabins and hunting areas were a premium pay for rent, the boys never had seen an invoice and never would.

Bill looked tired when he spoke. "Well boys, I'm heading up to the house, Isaac, Thomas, I'm sure you know, but if by chance you didn't, Roger believed that Tom Wilhite may have had a hand in my wife's death. Now, I'm not one for violence, but I must admit I have had several sleepless nights trying to come to terms with that. I have concluded, without a doubt, that there are some people in this world in need of killing…." Looking back and forth between the two soldier brothers, "I too want to thank you for your service. You always have a place here if ever you need it," With a smile that was joined with Sam's smile when he said it, "That is if you can work for the boss without fighting."

After a small chuckle, Isaac and Thomas thanked him; he also thanked him for their mother's new environment, and Bill made sure the boys knew that it was all Sam's doing.

"Boys, you have at it, I'm going to turn in. You both have a safe trip home."

Within a few short weeks, the atmosphere in town clearly had shifted; an air of freedom, decency, and ease flowed. It was as if the main pot stirrer for the town was now gone, and no one really had the gumption to assume the cause. Tom's boys were no longer the boisterous bully boys they had been; they were more characterized as being castrated and clearly guarded.

Within three months, Jeffery and Donnie Wilhite were already trying to settle their father's estate. They had to sell the farm because they couldn't afford to run it and had squandered any chance of learning how to run a business due to their own selfish concerns taking precedence. There was only one offer to come in for the farm. The offer was a rock-bottom price offer levied from a law firm out of New York. The offer was approved by the boys and paid out. At the closing of the property for the former Wilhite farms, one Samual Taylor, on behalf of Jax Farms, signed the deed of ownership.

Both boys moved on to Mt Vernon, Illinois, where six months later, it was found out that the youngest of the two brothers had been killed in a stabbing at a bar's back alley over some comments rumored to be about another man's colored girlfriend. Copious amounts of alcohol were involved, and the exact motives surrounding his death could never be confirmed or denied, as there were no arrests in the case. The oldest brother was in jail for theft, awaiting trial.

Chapter 9 - Trudy's Start

Trudy had been watching her father for years making deals, evaluating seemingly unrelated occurrences that eventually came to influence each other. She watched how her father could work the money so the money could work for him. That apple did not fall far from the tree.

When her mother was alive, Trudy had been given an allowance, it was an allowance for chores and activities, money she dutifully saved. She could balance a checkbook by the time she was eleven, and her balance was starting to amass to a very tidy sum. When her mother passed, her allowance somehow got quadrupled; it did not take long for her to figure out that her dad knew she was receiving an allowance but had no idea how much, which, given his grasp on the farm's finances, actually bewildered her. She soon after realized that her mother had overseen her allowance, so why would her father know or care how much she had received?

Regardless of how it came to be, her allowance was amassing itself at an even faster rate, coupled with what she would come to realize as some sort of makeup for time lost payment or perhaps guilt for being pulled away from her, but four to five times a year her dad would literally hand her a wad of cash for clothes and as he said, "Whatnot." She was given instructions to let him know if it was not enough, it always was about six times too much so most of it went straight to her account.

When she was thirteen, she had asked for a new computer to which her father barely blinked when he bought the latest greatest tech so his daughter could do her homework. She did, in fact, do her homework on it and a whole lot more. She started to study the markets and do research on the avenues that interested her. She eventually began to invest, mostly in the tech sector, focusing on APP startups.

Trudy had inquired with a local bank manager under the guise of a class project on how a person could get involved with startups. Much like what she had seen on the Shark Tank, she was interested in venture capitalism on a small scale. She had asked him how a young person could break into investing. He was all too happy to change his routine for the day, even if it were spent explaining to a young girl who would not understand half of what he was talking about if that much.

It was a good mental exercise for him and a welcome change to the monotony of his normal day, so he brought out the deluxe package to fully impress her. Little did he know that the sponge before him had not wasted a word that had been said. She had heard how, when, why, and more importantly, retained the names of several "startup" hopefuls that he flippantly mentioned as a means to further impress her; she had voraciously absorbed his knowledge. His examples were low-key investments with enormous upsides if they became viable vehicles for electronic traffic.

She began to delve into macroeconomics, microeconomics, the world of investing and any book with investment strategies and advice. Used the internet to go beyond the average interest of the typical investor to create a detailed synopsis of the prospectuses she had been studying. She had decided there was a good opportunity in a social platform in the area in the form of a photo manipulation app.

With the APP, anybody could elongate a face, stretch a smile, and add a third eye if it were desired, as it had promised to have some very intuitive and quite original algorithms. The programmer had enthusiastically returned her email and invited her to invest as he had a basic framework but needed a cash inflow to be able to devote himself to full-time development. Originally, she had proposed investing eight thousand dollars for twenty-five percent of the business. The developer agreed to the percentage and terms. With a valuation of thirty-two thousand and being his only investor, she felt as if she might come out favorably in her first attempt at the world of investing.

Not long after that original investment, she was contacted by the programmer saying he was making substantial progress and even sent along a demo that was truly shaping up as promised but still had a few bugs and glitches to be worked out. He was inquiring as to whether his investor would be interested in owning fifty percent as an equal partner. Trudy thought about that for twenty-four hours and decided she liked what she had seen in the sample. Given the amount of time her friends had spent on social media, at least an even return minimum sounded very plausible. She updated their contract and wired eight thousand dollars more. The programmer was very thankful, saying this would allow him to continue his work, which he felt he was getting close to completing.

One week later, he had messaged her with an update: most of the glitches were gone, the app had a good flow and was easy to use, which was promising. There were still a few refinements that still needed to be ironed out, but the programmer seemed very capable. Along with the update, he asked if she was interested in twenty-five percent more of the business. His personal life had taken a slight downturn in the form of needing to install a new engine in his car as it was his only means of transportation, and he needed to be able to get around. He felt eight thousand would allow a mechanic to do the work with enough left over to provide the living expenses for completing his work. Trudy contemplated this for a bit, weighing the pros and cons as she told herself, in for a penny, in for a pound. She agreed to be the seventy-five percent share owner.

Again, the contract was updated but this time with a clause of her being able to actively test the APP for viability and likeability. She paid to have the APP copyrighted which really was not that hard to do by herself. She sent out a "beta" version to the web for a trial run. She was looking forward to the rating section populating as feedback about the general perception and likeability of the APP.

Love, like it, more more, the most entertaining app in a long time, and many more encouraging replies with very few detractors. Within three weeks, several thousand hits were recorded on it. The feedback that had been directed to her site was phenomenal.

She had not heard back from the programmer for four weeks, which she thought was odd, so she had reached out with the full intention of updating him with the good news on how well the APP was being received. When he finally contacted her back, something seemed off in his reply. It was as if he had almost lost interest in the project.

Trudy asked him point blank if he had finished the program. He said he had poured himself into the project from the start in earnest but, due to financial decisions, had taken a position at a tech firm and had put the APP on the back burner. She asked if he was close to finishing, to which he said yes, but his new job was capitalizing all his time. She was infuriated as she felt like the programmer had duped her. Thankfully, it was electronic communication because if it had been face-to-face, she thought she would have ripped his face off right then and there.

She gave herself some time before she replied. After regaining her composure, she asked him if he was interested in selling her the last of the interest he held in the project. He said he would be more than happy to, but his priorities were currently elsewhere with his new job. When she offered a two-thousand-dollar bonus for a completed project and all intellectual permissions and ownership if he completed the work, the programmer's interest was piqued. She felt like he must need money, or the APP was closer to completion than he let on, either way, her offer was accepted within seconds of her last send. She said she would wire the remaining balance of ten thousand on delivery of the final product and that she would have her lawyer write up a finalized contract and bill of sale with all terms included.

After all the negotiations were made and accepted, a simple, innocuous email from a law group representing a social platform that was interested in entering talks for buying the complete app popped into her email out of the blue. Trudy quickly made an indication that talks would be a welcome development, providing they had mutually agreeable terms and that she would be in contact after apprising her team of lawyers.

Directly after she had pressed send, she picked up the phone and called a New York number from her address book. It was Kate Taylor's cell phone.

Kate answered, "Trudy? It's good to hear from you. Is everything all right?" There was a mix of inquisition and a part or two of fear.

"Oh no, Kate, there is nothing wrong, quite the opposite; I do, however, think I need a lawyer in a good way, and I was wondering what it would take to hire you."

"Now, wait a minute. First, you're family; you won't need to hire me. Second, what is this about."

"Well, I'll tell you all about it, but first, you have to promise this is between us only. I figured you would help me for free, but if I at least pay you something after that, I'm a legally confidential client, right?"

"Well, if it is that serious, I will bill you one dollar. Is that OK?"

"How about this, one dollar and one percent?"

"Trudy, just what have you got yourself into?"

Trudy took the necessary time to explain how she had gotten the money, how she had invested, and how she thought she was going to lose her investment entirely. She also relayed how she believed they were on the verge of making this APP really work. She continued through the release of the beta version and how she had been contacted by a tech firm on social media to buy the App. After she was finished with everything she could remember in chronological order, she asked Kate once again if she could help.

"Well, Trudy, one dollar and one percent sound really good now," she said with a chuckle, "Yes, I can help you, and yes, I will represent you. First, let's start by finalizing your complete ownership of the APP. That is an easy sales transaction; we will get all rights and permissions and prevent any claims to the piece as well."

Kate had an airtight contract ready in noticeably short order for the programmer, spelling out what he was selling and for how much, with final payment due on delivery, how his intellectual considerations were no longer valid as Trudy would be able to do what she pleased with the APP.

Kate and Trudy were both sure all the programmer saw out of it was a quick cash infusion. Just as the three times before, the money was going to drop into his hands after the deal was done. He signed an E-contract in seconds, downloaded the form, and wet-signed it. The wet copy was still required by the agreement and would be overnighted to Kate's office. His current signatures were enough to ready the payment for sending when the final product was complete.

Four days later, Kate had a fully signed contract. Three days after that, a fully complete and refined project had been sent to Trudy in its fully functional form. The beta version offered a capable sports car for anyone to use; it was now being replaced with a fully functional, fully loaded Lamborghini. After Trudy had pushed send on her end and the payment was completed and verified, the programmer thanked her and wished her the best of luck.

The application was then uploaded to Google Play as an update that replaced the Beta version. The last version was incredibly well received and was trending on its way to going viral. Within a week of updates and even more downloads on thousands of phones across the world, the accolades were flying in. Her biggest delight came as she heard, daily, about how it was being received by her peers at high school. What made it even sweeter was that no one knew she owned it, and it made it possible for them to use it. Nine days after the download update, she received an updated offer from the social media platform, which wanted to acquire all rights to the APP immediately.

They sent a tentative offer of eight hundred and forty-five thousand dollars. She told them she would be turning the negotiations over to her legal team and that they would be hearing from Kovach Associates out of New York City soon. She called Kate immediately; she was excited and full of good angst. Kate could feel her energy through the phone and was equally excited on her behalf.

Kate calmed her down a bit and told her, "I have been involved in several of these types of acquisitions, and the original offers were often lowballed offers just to see if they can pick up a superior product at bargain basement prices. With your permission, I'll get to work on it and see where we can go."

Trudy gave her free reign but reminded her, needlessly, that she wanted to remain fully anonymous.

Kate had made a counteroffer of five and a half million dollars cash and six percent of ad traffic, citing the exponential downloads since the beta went live with a full program. The offer was immediately countered with three million cash and 1% ad traffic; this was countered with four million five hundred fifty thousand and five percent. The offer was countered with four and a half million and two percent of the ads. After a back-and-forth multiple times and refining the tip of the pencil, Trudy was to give up all rights to the APP and relinquish all rights to the programming with its source code. It was to be unlocked for their programmers to use and alter as they saw fit, in exchange for four million five hundred fifty thousand dollars cash and four percent of ad traffic revenue in perpetuity regardless of the changes to the APP. Trudy also retained the use of the programming structure for future considerations.

The ad traffic conditions were the greatest points of contention as this money had been anticipated to be north of three hundred and sixty thousand yearly, potentially more for Trudy's part alone. Upon a verbal agreement, a contract of acceptance had been drawn up and all parties had signed it. The deal was done, and the initial payment was received in three weeks.

She thanked Kate for her diligence and protection and for helping her to stay anonymous. Kate told Trudy it was she who should be thankful as this deal, in and of itself, the app sale, had helped to bolster her partner tract bid. The current partners were more than aware of the perpetuity clause and how it would be bolstering their bottom line moving forward.

Trudy Jax was now a millionaire and then some to boot, completely anonymous, and now with ample legal representation. It was suggested by Kate, the lawyer, that she get permission from her father, in writing, to start a small business LLC and all that entails to make it indisputably legal. Trudy did as Kate suggested, and under the guise of a class assignment on the ways of the business world, her forms were completed. Bill hardly even looked at what he had signed, anything for his girl.

She was now a registered business owner, sole LLC owner. She was now fully legal, and with an enormous amount of seed money for the future, all before the summer, she could legally drive. She would soon call through the switchboard at Kovach Intellectual Partners asking for Kate Taylor's assistance on a purchase as the partners managed real estate law and corporate law and clearly were well versed in intellectual protections as well.

Growing up on a farm had certain advantages; one of them was the freedom to roam. Roaming on a farm the size of the Jaxs', meant work trucks and tractors, side by side and four-wheelers, just to get around and to perform tasks around the immediate area. Trudy had learned to drive four-wheelers and side by sides early and was driving a truck the summer of her fourteenth year after a growth spurt had enabled her to reach the pedals of an old farm truck.

It was not uncommon to find her stopping just short of town in the old Chevy flatbed four-wheel drive. It was a comfortable ride; Bill had "forgotten" all about it when it came to farm duties, knowing full well it was becoming Trudy's transportation for local errands. The truck he referred to as a beater was actually one of the most well-maintained vehicles on the property; he made sure of that.

Any time that Trudy even mentioned a rattle, bump, or bang, it was checked out. During the summer months, if she were not visiting Sadie down the way, babysitting, pulling a shift at the diner, or doing housework, she often would be found bringing sandwiches and cold drinks to the field for the workers.

More times than Bill could count, she would find him on the back forty and chase him down for lunch. It was always in the middle of a workday; he would always feign complaint but relished every time his little girl found him.

The Sheriff, on occasion, would see this unmistakable vehicle parked on the outskirts of town; he basically knew what was happening but chose not to investigate further. Her access to town was secluded, and it could be considered more of an access road than an actual county thoroughfare. He had, on occasion, purposefully watched how she handled herself in the truck from afar and was impressed, noting that there were several in the county who had been driving for years that couldn't drive as well as her. He also knew that Bill would not hesitate to make any damages, should it occur, whole. The rest was up to Bill and his insurance, so he opted to stay out of it.

On occasion, she would only be about a mile from Jax Farm's property, parked close enough to have a short walk into town should she have a need to. Roger also noted that if she was shopping in town, at the grocery or hardware store, or at the diner, pretty much any time she was going to need to be several places in town or multiple stops in the immediate area, someone else of age from Jax farms would be driving. On occasion, it was Sam who drove her in when he could break away from his now all-encompassing duties. Roger had suspected that when he saw Sam playing chauffeur, this was just a 'break' that Sam felt he needed at times, be it mental or physical. He appreciated how Trudy's travels were managed.

Trudy worked in town for tips as a waitress at the Diner Bell when she was fifteen, largely as a way to keep up with the latest in town. She liked to meet and greet people and to be unaccountable as far as her time in between the farm, school, and work. This enabled her to have a large amount of freedom to do things she wanted to do. As a bonus, she liked people in general, well - most people anyway.

Her ride to town often was the school bus as high school started around seven o'clock and was too far across town from her "parking" spot to walk. Some things could not be avoided. Until she received her license at sixteen, if she could not bum a ride, she either rode the bus home from school or went to work and called home for a ride at the end of her shift. About eighty percent of the time, she found a way home from dinner as she was well-liked by many of the regulars.

When she had turned sixteen, the truck was exchanged for a Jeep Cherokee four-wheel drive. It was almost a new car with a blown-up engine that was the result of an ugly divorce and a mishap involving sugar in a gas tank. Bill picked it up for a song, dropped the gas tank, put in a new one, rebuilt the engine, and gave it to his little girl. The whole rebuild took less than two weeks to pull the engine and put the engine back in and ready to run, including the three days of waiting on the rings and bearings, a rod, and some other mechanical things for the engine rebuild. Bill had told her what each part was, but she was not a hundred percent sure as to their exact function.

During the repair of the Jeep, she was there to hand him the wrenches when needed. She knew how to change her own oil, change a flat, and, at a cursory level, diagnose a problem beyond the thingy went kerplop or would not start and made a whining noise. There really was not a need to know much more beyond that, as the refurbished Cherokee was solid in every way.

Being able to accurately describe the issue and know vital terms were ingrained into her, as her dad had emphasized, "It may save you a lot of money if some mechanic is trying to take advantage of you." Even though she could not rebuild it, she did know what made it run. The day she was given her new keys was a good day indeed.

She started investing and was doing surprisingly well. Her gains after taxes were easily enough to pay for her college in a few years from then without dipping into the original investments. The money notwithstanding, Trudy was bright and studious, a natural in class, and by the time she graduated, she would have an academic full ride. Through grants and scholarships that she had been applying for since her freshman year, she had amassed enough to pay her own way. All of this still did not even take into account what her dad's love was going to pay for.

Her plan for college had real traction, though you could not tell it, as the only thing anyone knew, including her dad, was that she was getting scholarship help. She was truly looking forward to stepping away; she was prepared, financially armed to the teeth, and ready for the time to come.

High School was not the dreaded monster for her as it was for many of her peers. She was a good student, a good student taking tough classes, advanced classes, classes that cost her the Valedictorian moniker. She did not care about a title as her course was already set; she would, however, note that the "Valedictorian," though bright, all but refused to challenge herself with mind-expanding courses; rather, she took the easier line. Trudy wondered if it was a lack of concern for her educational future or if the fact that her parents were wealthy was in play, but in the end, it did not matter to her because she was leaving this all behind.

The future for a sizable percentage of her classmates would be less than fifty miles from the epicenter of their high school. Of course, there would be several that would make it hundreds of miles from here with free lodging in a locked-down fraternity. The state had only a few prisons, and none of them were nearby. She was sure that some of her classmates would be making reservations for themselves. She had acknowledged that the area might be a part of the bible belt, but apparently, quite a few of those bibles ran on methamphetamine. It was apparent from the local news that a person can only sell meth so long as a dealer before a friend of a friend needs to get out of a ticket or legal pickles and would be happy to sell out their supplier for a deal.

By the time she graduated, twenty girls would easily have dropped out to raise a child. It would be fair to say that out of a class of one hundred eighty-three, eighty-five percent would graduate, thirty percent with grades of a B or above, and ten percent would go on to finish college. She was determined to be one of the ten percent. She would be even more resolute to be one of the five percent of them who would not come back home to stay.

Dating for her in school was an experiment in learning, to say the least. Her first crush and heartbreak was from Bobby Johansen in the seventh grade. She also learned that a chuck on the shoulder, a lift of the chin, and a hug from Dad saying it was his loss was what she would get at home when it ended. This prompted her to rely even more heavily on Sadie as their friendship continued to bloom. She resolved to learn quickly and ask a lot of questions of momma when she could for no other reason than self-preservation. She was thankful that she and Sadie could talk with ease to each other about all kinds of subjects.

In the end, momma, Sadie, and reading proved to be her best teacher. Trudy was rarely found without some sort of book near her. Her guilty pleasure for fun was racy romance novels. By the time the first call to love hit her, she had a self-taught yet vague idea of how the whole thing worked between boys and girls. She had thought she had understood what she needed to know right up until she read her first erotic story. It had opened her eyes to a whole new world.

She learned quickly there was an entire world out there that had its own terms, its own meanings, its own vibe, and all this excited her. She looked forward to the day to learn and do firsthand what it was she was reading about. Trudy's bra size was morphing at what seemed a weekly rate at times as her curiosities grew along with them accordingly. Boys started to notice her and her changes; she was starting to get more curious about them as well.

Her first introduction to what she considered actual sex was, at best, described as awkward, fumbling, and eye-opening. It started with the first real kiss as a freshman late into the school year. She had fallen for first-year football linebacker Greg Bitzman. They "dated" for a while and kissed many times, sometimes passionately; it had excited her enough to finally know what her books meant when they said odd things like "her sex flowed hot and wet." She almost laughed aloud when she soaked her panties for her first noticeable time. Greg had convinced her to let him caress her bare breasts; she felt like she was on fire from the inside out. He thought the giant smile she was wearing, along with those soaked panties, was about him, and to a point, she guessed some of it was. For Trudy though, it was mostly about the understanding of the mechanics and emotions involved. She now felt normal and understood her body's biological feedback. The lack of knowing the why's and how's was gone, and it felt good to her.

It was less than a month later that Greg had one of his fingers in her. It felt gloriously rough and mechanical, but in the clumsiness, a fire had been lit as well. Merely a week later, she had a grip on his rock-hard penis, and after just a few caresses and not that many strokes at all, he had come all over himself and her hand. His come was hot, slick, and white as it shot from his beltline to his chin, crossing her arm and landing unceremoniously across his tee shirt with a few more ejaculations that ran down her fingers to his balls.

With summer break nearing, she had taken one more step toward applying her knowledge about sex. She was hesitant because of the lack of actual experience but she had read all about it several times and thought she was ready to put what she read into action. She had decided to try and give Greg a perfect blowjob. The problem with her plan made itself evident quickly. Greg did not last nearly as long as all the men she had seen in the videos that she had watched. When he came, it was in a truly short amount of time, and when he came, he came fast and hard without warning her, and by all appearances, it was mostly a surprise to him as well. Trudy vomited down the front of his jeans leg before she could manage to get outside of his car, where she fully heaved. She had felt incredibly embarrassed and inadequate, but then again, she felt like, to some degree, she was learning.

When she heard gossip talk around school about her failure in the blowjob department the next day, she knew he had failed in his promise of confidentiality to her, on top of being broken-hearted. He had talked, more accurately, bragged about how he was getting some. He failed to describe his premature rendering along with it. Beyond that, she learned that, according to Greg, things had progressed much further than a blowjob and that he had apparently had to teach her how to become a woman. In any event, she was embarrassed to the core and hurt. Greg was left with just his right hand to date when she broke up with him that same day. She thought he was such a dick to violate her trust and vowed to guard herself better in the future.

Chapter 10 - Meeting Danny Veach

A week had passed when the diner's entrance bells rang as the door opened and closed. A young man was standing in front of the wooden podium with a sign reading, "Please wait to be seated."

Trudy approached. "Hey, hello, Danny. Welcome to Diner Bell. Is there more coming, or is it just you?"

"Hey, Trudy. No, it's just me."

"Would you like a table, a booth, or a seat at the bar?"

"How about the corner booth over there," he said, pointing to the left corner.

Trudy led the young man to the booth. The diner was a corner storefront with four-seat tables across the front windows, booths set up along the inner wall, and a counter bar with fixed swivel seating. It was not much different from any small-town diner—it was tidy, clean, and had excellent food with a broad selection of options.

The diner had several customers at various stages of their meals but was not too busy.

"I'll get some water and be right back."

"Thanks."

She returned with silverware rolled in a napkin, a menu, and a glass of water, placing them in front of Danny.

"Here's a menu, or do you know what you want already?"

Danny looked up with piercing gray-blue eyes, making contact with Trudy's. He gave his best boyish smile. Trudy was momentarily taken aback as if she was looking at him for the first time. She quickly regained her composure, hoping it was not obviously noticeable. Danny smiled just a hint bigger.

"Just you on a piece of toast, a date later tonight, or a Diner Burger with cheese, dressed, and a side of fries—whichever is on the menu."

Trudy started to blush as she began to fight back with a big smile.

"So, a Diner Burger with cheese and fries. American, Pepper Jack, or Swiss?"

"Whichever you recommend," he said, smiling even bigger. "And ketchup for the fries."

"So…Pepper Jack. The ketchup is on the table," Trudy said, pointing at the inside of the booth. Danny had not taken the time to notice it. She looked at him with a warm smile that was, this time, shared between them.

"It's not too hot, is it? The cheese, I mean."

"It could be, depending on your personal tastes, but cheese isn't my thing," she said with a lighthearted, sheepish chuckle before walking away toward the order bar.

She brought the burger and fries to the table and set them down in front of Danny.

"I'm sorry. I should have asked earlier—do you want a drink other than water with this?"

"No, water is just fine. I just might need it to put out the flames."

"You just never know."

They shared a laugh before Trudy walked off to take care of other customers. Near the end of his meal, never letting his water get more than half empty, she brought his ticket to the table. The ticket had her phone number and a note that said:

"I'm not a major fan of sleeping on toast, but I get off work at 8:00 p.m. We could discuss it then if you like?"

Danny paid his bill and, half stating, half asking, "I'll see you later…?"

"Looking forward to it."

Trudy saw Danny's truck parked at the curb as she walked out of work. She smiled, and he got out and approached her.

He addressed her, "Would you like to go for a drive or something?"

"That would be great. Where to?"

"No place in particular unless you have something in mind."

"How about going over to the lakeside park?"

Danny smiled. "Sounds good."

With rock and roll playing low on the stereo, he pulled out of the parking lot and headed toward the park.

"How long have you been working at the diner?"

"I've been there for about a year. I like it—it's laid back, and the Murphys treat me nicely. People are fun to listen to and see. It keeps me up with all the latest gossip. It's amazing what you can hear if you just listen. I've heard all about almost everyone in school except you for some reason. I don't think I've heard anything more than a mention of your name. I thought all you boys had a need to be known."

Danny chuckled a bit. "I'd rather stay quiet and keep things close to the vest. I'm not like some of these dumbasses out there talking about how hot they are and who, where, and when they've been with someone—both the girls and guys. I'd rather just be a little more secretive than that. Besides, it gains you nothing to be a blabbermouth and get that kind of reputation— if you intend to keep dating, that is. I hope you don't mind me saying it, but you were so right to drop Greg like a hot rock. He is such a dick. Not all guys are like that—just thought you'd like to know."

"So, you heard all about that, huh? I'm apparently exceptionally good—just ask Greg. He taught me everything I know." She laughed as she said it.

She continued, "Hmm, so you're secretive? You have big secrets, do you?" she joked playfully.

"Oh, you haven't a clue. I'm incredibly good at keeping them to myself. You haven't heard about any of them at the diner, have you?" He laughed with her.

"Well, I'm just glad to know that taking a drive with you now isn't going to turn into us doing it all night long at school tomorrow." She laughed.

"Oh no, you will definitely be famous by the end of the day," he mockingly replied. "I promise."

Danny put the truck in park, overlooking the lake, with the moon reflecting off the still waters.

He continued, "I would never do that, even if it were true and even if I were mad at you. I value privacy and discretion too much. My bragging about you would only serve to belittle me, so NOOO, thank you."

She lightheartedly acknowledged, "That's good to know; I feel the same way."

She continued, "I can't believe freshman year went by so fast."

"I can't believe I'm going to be a junior already," he added.

"So, what do you want to do after high school? Are you going to stay around here, or do you have bigger plans?"

He was quick to respond. "Oh, hell no. I'm going to college for business and then on to culinary school—far away from here. Things are much too complicated here. I want a wide-open, clean slate to be me."

"How do you mean?"

"There's plenty of time to talk about that later," he half-nervously laughed. "It's a secret, remember?"

"Business and culinary school? That's an odd combination."

"I love to cook. I love creating something new, and I want the freedom to set my own menu, my own business—my restaurant." Exaggerating, he put his hands over his mouth. "Oh no, you know my deepest, darkest secret. You're a trained spy, aren't you?"

She laughed at that as he continued.

"So, I guess you'll have your hands full with learning to run a farm? How are you going to handle that?"

"Actually, I'm going to go to college and start my own business as well. Sam, my dad's farm manager, can oversee the farm. It's not my cup of tea. I'm going to own hotels, communications, and technology—and dabble in shipping. Who knows, maybe you'll come work for me."

He laughed lightly. "Well, you've got it all figured out. I guess I have to warn you that I'm not your typical guy. I won't come cheap. I'm a real quality person here, and I have needs as well."

Both laughed even more now, amused with each other—neither knowing that the other had a much deeper connection with their statements than they had let on.

"Besides, I'm going to own my own chain of restaurants. Nice places—things we don't have here. I'll put my restaurants in your hotels, but you'll have to beg me for them first."

She laughed with him.

They talked into the night until eleven o'clock when Trudy told Danny they needed to get going because she had an eleven-thirty curfew and didn't want to cut it too close. Danny took her to her car, waited for her to start it up, and waved as she pulled away. Both teenagers were smitten with their night.

The next two nights were a repeat of Tuesday night. They both had an ease with each other that they couldn't readily explain. It just felt good—fluid, smooth, and weirdly, confidentially comfortable. They both felt as if the other could be trusted with their secrets.

They kept ending up at the lake after driving around a bit; they always talked late. The comfort and desire culminated in a date planned for the movies in Carbondale on Friday night.

After the movie, when Danny dropped her off at home, he walked her to the door, said goodnight, and leaned in. He gently kissed her lips briefly, a smallish peck. As he pulled away, Trudy stopped him from turning and landed a heavy kiss—longer and with just a hint of wanting more.

She pulled away. "What are you doing tomorrow?"

"No real big plans. Why?"

"Bring a swimsuit, and I'll give you the grand tour of the farm. We can swim in one of the lakes—or fish, if you'd prefer," she said with a light laugh. "Or both. Say around nine? That'll give me time to clean up the house and gas up a razor."

"That sounds like fun. I'll be here. Trudy, I had a fun time tonight. I'm looking forward to tomorrow."

"Me too. I'll see you tomorrow."

They both smiled and took a moment to look at each other again, breaking hand contact—fingers sliding through each other to the last fingertip touch. Danny turned and made his way to his truck. With a big smile, she turned to go inside, pausing to watch Danny's truck disappear into the night—watching his taillights fade into the road dust while reliving her night.

She opened the door and stepped inside. Just as she closed the door behind her, her father spoke up.

"He seems like a nice boy."

"Daaad…really?"

"Wait, wait, wait. It's not like that. I was in the kitchen getting a drink and heard his muffler. He's going to need a new muffler pretty soon. I just walked to the living room," he said, winking. "I didn't see you kiss him or anything. In fact, I was on my way to bed."

"Daaaaad," she replied, exasperated.

"Trudy, sweetheart, it's OK. I'm your dad. I'm not blind. You're growing up—you're not a kid anymore but a young woman who, I think, is well aware of the world and how it functions. I know how it all works, too. I was a teenager once upon a time. I kissed my first girl when I was fifteen. I remember how awkward it was. And when I kissed your mother for the first time, she was sixteen and a half, and I was seventeen, as I recall. I remember some things. You just remember that you have Sadie and me if you have any questions," he said with a laugh, adding, "Mostly Sadie. And me, too."

Trudy understood his squeamishness.

"Now, I'm going to bed. Don't stay up too late. Love you."

"Thanks for trying to make that cool, Dad. Cool and weird, but cool. I love you, too. Goodnight."

"Trying?" He feigned disappointment.

"It was really close. Not quite there, but…" Overacting, she searched her memory and reevaluated it visually on her face as a joke, scrunching her face mockingly. "Well, it was close," she acknowledged.

Her dad turned and headed upstairs, laughing.

Saturday morning came, and Trudy started early by making breakfast for her dad. She had carefully watched the diner cook many times when he prepared bacon, eggs over-easy (or any way you please), toast, hash browns, pancakes, waffles, and ham. He had taught her the efficient way to slam out a hot breakfast on the griddle over the course of her tenure. She could, if pressed, fill in for him if necessary.

Now, she used her skills to plate breakfast at home for her dad just the way he liked it, as she understood from the countless times he had ordered the same thing when they went out to the diner. If nothing else, when it came to breakfast, he was easy to cook for.

She cleaned up the dishes, and the kitchen was spotless—tidied up with everything in its place, along with the rest of the house—all before eight-thirty.

She walked over to the barn, fired up her favorite Razor, drove it over to the filling tanks, and topped it off. Afterward, she drove it to the front of the house and parked it by the porch.

As if on cue, Danny's truck rolled up the driveway. Trudy let out a small audible laugh as she realized that, indeed, Danny was going to need a new muffler, as she, too, heard him well before she saw him. She made a mental note to make some kind of comment to her dad just for the fun of it. Danny parked alongside the porch where Trudy was waiting for him.

Trudy watched Danny get out of his truck and took a moment to drink him in. Danny was a bit taller than her, maybe five foot ten inches. It was simply perfect for her to look up slightly and kiss him, but not so tall that she had to stretch. His boyish features were fading but were not completely gone. She suspected that a good portion of it was how he carried himself rather than physically maturing, although he had a good bit of physical changes well underway as well. He did not play sports for the school, but his physique suggested he would have been well-suited for it. At about one hundred seventy-five pounds, he was cut and sturdy. His arms looked as if he had worked out—not that she had ever seen him in the school weight room—but he was solid and manly.

She could tell by how his shirt hung across his shoulders that not only were his shoulders a bit wider than most guys his size but his chest was also developed. When he rearranged his shirt getting out of the truck, the lower half of his abdomen was visible, and it promised a full washboard. His strong thighs filled out the cargo swim shorts he was wearing. All in all, she was pleased with her view.

She was a bit curious as to how the rest of him looked, and based solely on his tight ass, which she felt was perfectly formed, she surmised that she would be happily rewarded. His facial features were strong, and his mustache was well-groomed, though thin. His shoulder-length sandy blonde hair was trimmed and well-proportioned to his face. His piercing grayish-blue eyes, just as before, drew her in and melted her inside.

She had already caught herself getting more than just a little damp the night before when she let herself get lost in his eyes. She had not let on through the previous night's or last night's date and was sure he had no idea how deeply he had affected her. Today was no different for her, as his lasers cut through her to her inner core. He had a grace in his movement, a flow that sent an air of confidence that completed the ensemble. She smiled wide and big and gave him a small peck on the lips as he stepped onto the porch and set a small cooler down.

"What did you bring?"

"Just some Cokes, ice, and some water."

"I guess great minds do think alike. I made some sandwiches for lunch. I hope you like ham and cheese?"

"I do like ham and cheese—well, depending on the cheese," he ribbed her a bit.

"Pepper Jack, of course. I heard you like things hot."

"Ouch, I thought you didn't gossip," he jokingly complained.

She just laughed at his over-the-top act of disappointment.

"Do you still want to load up the Razor and get going?"

Snapping out of it as if nothing had happened, "Absolutely!"

They loaded up, hopped in, and belted down. She took off, touring the fields and backroads, crossing through the various pastures and pens, skirting the fields on service roads and tractor trails. The ride itself was fun, especially since she knew where all the good mud holes were and which ones to avoid.

After their adventurous morning, things slowed down as Trudy made her way to the back cabin built by a six-acre lake with a beach on the front side of the porch.

The cabin was meant to be a self-contained oasis and had all the amenities of a home. Tucked back into the woods, the summer retreat that doubled as a hunting cabin was about as isolated as you could get. Other than hiking in, there was one way in and one way out on a gravel, dusty road. She knew there was plenty of warning time should anyone decide to invade their slice of escape because of the dust trail that could be easily seen minutes before anyone could arrive.

She chose this location for exactly this reason, though there were several other options available that were similar in nature. Ultimately, the lake being so close to the cabin was the deciding factor for this particular location.

Trudy parked the Razor near the beach, got out, and grabbed one cooler as Danny grabbed the other and the beach bag. When they got to the edge where the manicured grass met the sand on the edge of the beach under a large oak tree, Trudy pulled out a blanket from the bag, spread it out, and set the coolers on the edge before sitting down. Danny joined her as she opened up the cooler with the food in it.

"It's been a while since I went for a ride like that. That was pretty fun. I hope you liked it too?" Trudy asked.

"It was a blast. I didn't realize your place was so big. There are a lot of fields here. How big is it—do you know?"

Chuckling, "The whole place is a little more than three thousand acres. We just went around about a third of it. There are seven more lakes besides this one, several more fields, and three more cabins. This is my favorite one out of all of them, though. A person could get lost around here if you're not sure where you're going. Altogether, I think there are like fourteen farm places that are now Jax Farms."

"You get out our drinks, and I'll get the sandwiches finished. Do you like lettuce, tomato, pickles, ketchup, mustard, or mayo?"

"I like all of that except no mustard, and really…there has never been a good use for mayo, ever," he said with a sly laugh while getting out two sodas. "Coke or Sprite?"

"Sprite, please." A short pause later, "I'm not so sure about you now. Really? No mayo? You have clearly gone mad," she laughed as she handed him a paper plate with a fully assembled sandwich made to order. She then sat her plate in front of her as well.

"It's nice being out here with you. I'm glad I came. It's a wonderful day with good food—my compliments to the chef, by the way—and being here with you makes for the best Saturday I have had in a very long time. I'm glad you invited me out."

"The chef?" Laughing, "Store-bought ham, lettuce, tomato, and bread do not make a chef. However, the ham company is one we sell our hogs to—full circle, field to plate. My dad says the ham came from here, most likely. So, I will take part in that compliment on behalf of Jax Farms." She splayed her arms open wide to encompass the landscape with a laugh.

"Wherever it came from, you put it together just for me. I really like that, so thank you. The 'chef' is also a great driver, fun to talk to, and very pretty. There is something about you that just puts me at ease. I can breathe around you; honestly, that doesn't happen too often for me. It just feels good."

Trudy had already slipped off her shoes and, while Danny was talking, laid back, bridged up, and slid off her shorts, revealing a bikini bottom. She stood up and pulled off her shirt to reveal her bright orange, red, blue, and yellow tiger-patterned swimsuit. Danny noticed firsthand how well it fit her.

Trudy was trim and fit—thirty-six C, with ample breasts—and he could not help but notice that her nipples were trying to make themselves known to the rest of the world but were also muted by the swimsuit fabric. She had a body that a mid-thirties woman wanted back: firm, tight, and standing proud in all the right places. She just turned and ran to the water, giving Danny a full-on view of a perfectly rounded ass, cupped just so— also firm. He noticed a little bounce as she ran.

She made her way to the water, and while crossing the beach, she showed graceful athleticism—muscular and solid yet feminine at the same time. She was not the gawky sixteen-year-old he was expecting but a maturing, well-put-together, hot body. His penis twanged uncontrollably just for a second.

He watched as she ran into the water until she was a little more than knee-deep and then dove under, only to come up about twelve feet off the shore, standing on a sandy bottom in neck-deep water. She resurfaced, threw her hair back, and brushed the water from her face.

"Are you coming in?"

"Absolutely!"

He hurriedly kicked off his shoes, pulled his shirt off, and headed to the beach at a trot. Trudy noticed she was spot on with her guess. She liked the view of "her" washboard as he was entering the lake and disappearing under the surface of the water.

Trudy felt a hand touch her calf and another slide up her other thigh, and as Danny's head broke the surface, both of his hands firmly came to rest on her ass cheeks. He cupped them momentarily as he stood up and pulled his hands free to clear the water from his face and pull his hair back.

"Two things—thank you for lunch, and I think you are beautiful."

She cupped her hands around his neck and jumped slightly underwater to pull her legs up and around his waist.

"Two things—you're welcome, and I think you are gorgeous."

The water was perfect for swimming and frolicking, so that was exactly what they did for the next twenty minutes—splashing and touching, floating and treading water off and on until they came together just as they started.

They both were amazingly comfortable with each other. There was an ease that flowed between them. As they came together for a hug, they both noticed, even through the cool water, that they could feel each other's body heat.

"I'm not used to being this comfortable with someone else," Trudy bluntly told him as it came out as a declaration. "The last time I was, well, it kinda bit me. But on the upside, apparently, I'm extremely good in bed. Just ask anyone."

She laughed as Danny joined in.

"Greg is an idiot—and an asshole to boot. I would have never done that to you or anyone else. I like to think that I know how to be private about that kind of thing. Lord knows I have my secrets—probably more than my fair share."

"Oh really?" She laughed. "Do tell. You said you had a ton of secrets? I can keep a secret. How about sharing?"

"I never said a ton of secrets, but I bet you are good at keeping things to yourself. It's just that the secrets I do have might change how you look at me and what you think about me. That is one thing I do not want to happen. I'm enjoying this too much."

"Give me just one secret, and I'll give you an opportunity to hold my trust, too. Or you could use it to destroy that trust and me in the process—that is if you want to take the chance. You just might find that I'm better than you think. Besides, you might be surprised by the few secrets I have of my own.”

He looked deep into Trudy’s eyes and held her close.

“Have you ever really had sex with anyone? I mean, I know what Greg was saying, but no one believed him. So, let’s start there. Have you ever really had sex before?”

“Well, that would be a matter of degrees, I guess. I know what sex is, but if you consider a hand job and a blowjob sex, then yes. But if you’re asking if I have ever had intercourse, then…” She sheepishly paused. “Well…no. To be accurate, three hand jobs combined may have lasted five minutes and about a minute and a half blowjob. Greg came quickly compared to some videos I have seen. I have done my homework online—it’s easy to find videos. So no, in that regard, I have never had sexual intercourse. How about you? Anything to brag about?”

Standing there in the water, Danny felt himself get full—not hard, but full—and he knew it was an auto-response from just talking about and thinking about sex.

“Yes, I have had sex—sexual intercourse and more. You may not believe this, but I have been having sex since I was fourteen. Since then, I have had sex with six different partners. To be honest, I have had a lot of sex. I’m not sure if that is really good or really bad. In retrospect, some of it was confusing. I’m not sure about telling you all of it, but for some reason, I feel extremely comfortable around you, too. Does hearing that I have had sex change your image of me?”

"No, it doesn't change how I see you. But I wouldn't have suspected, in passing, that you would be so experienced. Would you tell me about them…? I mean, I don't need names, just…well… 'ABOUT' them. I am interested in hearing about it. I promise you can trust me—it goes no further." She smiled. "What is said at the lake stays at the lake, I swear."

"I'll tell you some of it, but I'm not sure you would like it all, and I'm not sure how to, well, describe it. Some of it is, well, a little wild—and in some circles, to say the least, probably kinky in others."

"Now I definitely want to know!" She laughed but was clearly just as serious.

"OK, here goes nothing. My first time was sort of natural; it just kind of happened. I was in the woods exploring with a neighbor girl, Britany, as we often did to kill time. We were good friends next door, bored and looking to just play outside, but then we found a hardcore skin magazine on the roadside. We both looked at it, and we both had questions back and forth. One thing led to another, and there was a version of show and tell of sorts.

"There we were in the woods, checking out each other's bodies, touching and feeling, and asking each other questions about what felt good and what didn't. Shortly after that, I was going down on her; she was going down on me, and we both loved how it felt. We had no clue how to do things right, so we just experimented. We were barely past puberty. It was dumb luck that she didn't get pregnant because we ended up having sex all the time—sucking and fucking whenever we had free time. Both fourteen and no supervision—God, we had a lot of fun.

"In retrospect, that was either the greatest thing or maybe the worst thing ever to happen to me. Honestly, I still don't know for sure. But what I do know for certain is that it took the mystery away, and it gave us a sort of freedom. When we hit high school, the pressure to get laid just wasn't there. We were secretly having a lot of sex, getting laid anytime either of us wanted—it felt great. She could keep a secret, and I could keep a secret, so things just continued. I would hear about guys trying to get laid and the lies they told to try to get into girlfriends' pants or the liars describing how wonderful they were in bed.

"I knew better because I really knew. All the lies just to be cool—I knew by what they were saying that they really had no idea. That's why I knew Greg hadn't had a clue about what he was bragging about and how.

"I also heard the rumor mill in high gear around the locker room. It seemed like no one had a clue how to keep their mouth shut about conquests, real or imagined. I figured it was best to keep my mouth shut. That paid off well for us. She appreciated my silence, and we continued to fuck all the time for about half of that year. She moved away because of her dad's job. That really sucked. We both knew what we were doing and how to do it by then. We had A LOT of fun. It seemed like hundreds of times.

"I bet if I told that story in the locker room, they would all think that I was the one lying. It is all true, all real, and all incredibly great for us at the time. Does that shock you too much?"

"Well, starting at fourteen caught me off guard, but it's nothing too far out there. I'm glad it was a good experience for you. My shining moment was gagging and vomiting down Greg's leg. I certainly don't have anything close to your experiences."

"I hope you know that I have no expectations of you. I just want to be your friend, and you want the same. You know, in some senses, I feel a little twisted on the inside. It took a while to come to terms with myself. It sucked to have to get over the loss of a sure thing," he laughed nervously. "I liked her well enough, but we both knew we were just using each other for our own satisfaction. There was no love, but there was a whole lot of like—all the time—and that was great for experimenting. If either of us heard about something or wanted to try something different, like a new position, all it took was a call.

"I learned a lot but also found out shortly after that I had a whole lot more to learn. All in all, it was—or rather, she was—she was really a lot of fun and nice to talk to as well."

"I would have hated to be number two. I mean, not knowing your past, you had to have been heavily disappointed in your next encounter. Someone like me, not knowing a thing? I mean, really…!"

"That's funny because I was thinking the same thing at first, but the first time for my second person, Karen—well, it wasn't her first time either. I got the impression that I may have been one of her early guys, but she certainly had some experience. I mean, not as much as mine based on the things we did or the things I had done to that point, but she knew what she was doing.

"We only had sex four times. It felt like I was more of a conquest on her part rather than being a partner." He feigned disappointment. "I felt so used," he playfully smirked. "It was fun but fleeting. Three months after we had parted, she got pregnant by someone and dropped out of school. Are you sure you want to hear about all of this?"

"That's one reason I'm already on the pill. You would think that if she were going to be having sex, she would have been more cautious. And absolutely, yes, keep talking. I want to hear it all. It will stay right here…. I promise. I'll never breathe a word without your permission first."

"I am trusting you here, Trudy, but if you really want to know, here goes. Number three was the hardest for me in retrospect. I dated Kelly Clemming a couple of times. We went out to the movies, we went out to eat, but it just wasn't a fit. We never even kissed."

"I know her from class. I don't get it. How is she number three if you never even kissed? What am I missing here?"

He half-giggled. "She was into all kinds of clubs at school, always staying late. It was hard for her to even find time to go out on a date with me. She was nice but totally immersed in one project or another. I think she liked to be able to tell her friends she was dating someone. That is how I got to meet her mother, Denise."   Trudy's eyes opened wide for a moment.

"We really hit things off quite by accident. She had been divorced for about four years at the time. She had Kelly when she was seventeen, but she still managed to graduate college. She worked remotely from home half the time; the other half of her work was at her office in Carbondale. She was able to have big blocks of free time on her hands because she had been working from home. It was relatively safe because her daughter always called before she left school for home, like clockwork. Almost.

"I was supposed to meet her daughter at their house. Kelly told me to go on in because the house was empty; her mom was at work in Carbondale, and she said she would be there in a little while. I went on in mostly because I had to use the bathroom and walked in on her mother getting out of the shower. I wanted to look away, but I just couldn't. She jumped back into the shower, but when she did, she stepped on the shower curtain, bringing the rod and curtain down. I smiled at her, and she half-smiled back. I stepped forward and grabbed a towel. I was about to give the towel to her when I looked her straight in the face, trying hard to ignore her naked body, and asked her if she would like me to dry her back.

"She turned her back to me. Why? I still don't know, and I really didn't care at the time. She just stood there in front of me, stark naked, while I started to dry her. I towel-dried her from top to bottom, and I may have accidentally kissed her neck long and soft in the process. She tilted her head back and let out a quiet moan. I took that as a sign to keep going, so I kissed her back high on her shoulder, then her side, right on her ribs by her elbow, and I moved to the side of her right breast. She turned toward me slowly…I kissed her nipple, and my hand started to roam. Well, one thing led to another right there in the bathroom.

"Her daughter and I broke up the next week and just became friends. I always parked down the street when I came over, which was often. Her mom, Denise—now SHE really liked to fuck. Honestly, I really think a big part of what she liked about me was my youthful stamina and enthusiasm, and I liked the way she wanted and the things she wanted to do. To be honest, it was thrilling to be getting laid by an older woman. With her maturity and experience, she became the best teacher any boy could want.

"She taught me how to go slow and take time to make it all better, how to be passionate, and how to find what she wanted. She showed me how to fuck and how to have sex, and how to be sensual and soft. She had a wild, kinky side as well. I liked that a lot. She taught me about all kinds of kinks too—the positions she liked, the things she liked, and the things she wanted to try. She was into toys, ropes, whips, cuffs, and all kinds of battery-operated devices. It turned out that I liked a lot of that stuff as well; most of it felt good, if not incredibly good.

"She was fit and built, and I was, well, horny, wanting more all the time. I liked her touch, her finesse, her willingness to take, and the time she took to teach. I learned more than just sex from her—a whole lot more. Lord, some of the things I've tried…Some things were erotic and fantastic, others not so much. I really learned a lot about my body and hers—really, women in general."

"What happened to her after that? I mean, it sounds like you both had a good thing going. Why stop?"

"As I said, her daughter always called before coming home—until one day, she didn't. We nearly got caught in the middle of a very wild blowjob. There I was, hiding in a closet with my hands tied with ropes and leather-strapped restraints around me. I was trying not to make a sound or even breathe, and Denise was hurriedly putting on a bathrobe under the guise of getting ready for a shower while talking to her daughter, who was on her way down the hall, heading for the doorway of her bedroom. From the time we heard her to the time I was getting into the closet, thirty seconds had passed. It was really close. My clothes happened to be on the other side of the bed, just out of sight, thankfully.”

“So, you broke it off since you almost got caught?”

He let loose a half-embarrassed laugh. “Oh, hell no. Denise closed her door after talking to Kelly a bit, turned on the shower, opened the closet, untied my hands, and finished blowing me right there. I think it was one of the hardest comes I’ve ever had—the excitement of being caught and hiding. I’m not sure what made it so good, but it was intense. The narrow escape definitely made it feel spectacular for both of us.

“She swallowed, wiped her chin with her palm, looked me straight in the eyes, kissed me deeply, smiled at me, and turned to go take a shower. I redressed and went out the window. We both mutually ended it three months later when she said ‘yes’ to her boyfriend in Carbondale and moved in with him. They were married late last fall. Kelly never knew.”

“Oh wow. That had to be exciting.”

“Absolutely. After her, I didn’t have sex for about two months until I went to a party with David, a friend of mine. It was a mixed crowd. I met a girl there who came on to me. It had been a while, so I figured, why not? We ended up in her dorm. It turns out that Kendra was a college junior and a full-on freak. We fucked long and hard, off and on, for about two months until she wanted to see where I lived.”

He laughed playfully. "She had a full-on come apart when she realized I was still in high school. She never asked, I never said, and I guess because of the things we did and what I was doing to her, she figured I was older. She noped right on out after that, but it was fun while it lasted."

"I have zero experience, comparatively speaking. It is a bit intimidating hearing you tell me all of this, but thank you for trusting me."

"You are easy to talk to. You make me feel like I could trust you with anything."

"Thank you for that, but after hearing all of this, I'm not sure how anyone would or could measure up to that."

"Well, that's the thing that I've learned from all of this. It's not like that at all. It isn't about someone measuring up. Everyone is so individual. I learned that we all have our thing, and that thing has no comparison to anyone else's thing."

"I went out with a girl a few months ago, Amanda. We hit it off, and she initiated sex, so I took my time and realized that she was just trying to be needed and loved. She wanted to feel like she mattered to someone in a heart-to-heart kind of way, and I fit the bill. Yes, we wanted sex, but it was the connection that was best for us. She mattered to me in a different kind of way, and I guess it showed. Things were strained for her at home, and I was a breath of freedom. She could do as she pleased around me, and I think it really suited her. In the end, there were a few things that we differed on and couldn't get past, so we broke it off.

"Even when we broke things off romantically, we were and are still great friends, but we just didn't work out as boyfriend and girlfriend, so to speak, and that was OK. It was an epiphany about understanding myself and, to an extent, others.

"I decided to just take things slow, but then, well, you happened. I saw you and wanted to know more, so I waited until the diner wasn't too busy, and I came in for supper. I don't care what we do or if we do anything at all. I know now that it's about truly getting to know someone. I finally know myself for the most part, and because of that, I genuinely want to appreciate someone else for who they are.

"So, I'm here because I like you and want to get to know you. I would be lying if I told you that you didn't turn me on. Regardless of whether we continue from here, I'm truly enjoying getting to know who you are. I know that has to sound sappy, but it is how I feel."

He nervously asked in earnest, "What do you think about all I've told you so far? I mean, really, I feel like I'm a bit exposed here, wide open and naked, telling you all my secrets, but I wanted you to know me. So, what do you think of me now? Has what I said made a difference in how you see me?"

Trudy had always found something special in nature, a oneness that really could not be equaled—her version of a church. That oneness she felt in nature was now spilling over her, with Danny telling her his deepest secrets. And as secrets—wow, she thought.

What Danny had told her was initially shocking to an extent, but to her, there was a visceral openness he had shown her. That openness appealed to her on a baser level. She knew she would never, could never, violate his trust in her. He had given her something of himself, raw and incredibly personal and, to a degree, socially dangerous in a sense. She liked the fact that he had placed his trust in her hands with a secret that she would never retell.

Just hovering around his body for the last ten minutes, talking about his inner secrets, she felt him get full, then firm but not hard, multiple times, off and on, while relaying his exploits. She realized that while he was talking about his sexual encounters, he was clearly re-experiencing pieces of it. Though she had never sought out his cock with her hands, there in the water, against her legs and stomach, and occasionally her ass as they hovered around each other, a story was being told without words, and she liked it.

She did not know if it was the act of someone trusting her fully or if it was hearing things she herself wanted to experience that was driving her forward, but she knew that she liked Danny. She wanted him. She had wanted him from the first time they had met at the diner.

There was something about him that she could not identify—a confidence and presentation that begged her forward, a sense that she wanted more with him, much more. She wanted to open herself completely on several levels, to give him something of herself that only he would have, to let him know just how much she liked him.

She was ready to trust him with her greatest leap of trust—something that, if he were careless, could hurt her deeply. She had wanted him from that first moment, and now she wanted him even more—without barriers, without inhibition, on a raw, carnal level.

She kissed him softly on the cheek directly after he had asked her what she thought about everything he had said. He was clearly pensive and nervous as he waited for her reply. She turned away at that moment and, without saying a word, made her way to the beach.

He stood there, wondering what was happening, and began to suspect the worst as she made her way out of the water toward the Razor. He stood watching as she hit the sand. She pulled the top string of her bikini top, reaching around her back while walking, and pulled the bottom string of her top as well.

By the time she got near the blanket on the beach, she had pulled both side bow strings of her bottoms, dropped both pieces to the ground in the middle of the blanket, and continued to the porch of the cabin. She strolled bare-assed, nude, and full of confidence in herself and within her own resolve.

She hit a few numbers on the electronic keypad and opened the door halfway. She turned to look at Danny, who was still standing there in the water in awe and disbelief.

She was a vision of fitness, bronzed tan, and tight-bodied.

Looking directly at his face, she said, "Well?"

She just left the question hanging in the air. It was as if the question floated through the air over to him and slapped Danny in the face, who fielded the question easily.

He slowly walked up out of the lake, and by the time he passed by the blanket, he had already loosened the drawstring and the first two snaps, dropping his shorts there in mid-stride.

She noticed he was firm, and his body was almost mesmerizing—simply wonderful to look at. His dick was right at five inches or more as it hung there, firm.

She knew Greg was about three and a half firm and not a full five when he got hard. Greg's hard state had not been nearly as wonderful to look at as Danny's firm was. She really wanted to see Danny hard and tried to anticipate his size like that.

She all but needed to see him hard, knowing she was the reason.

She could see he was obviously thicker than Greg had been, and his balls were spectacular in comparison. He was circumcised and beautiful. One word came to her as she stood there, stunned. Her body had been drying as she left the lake in the warm air, but Danny's presentation—really his walk, his body, and her wanting—all of it was blending together, getting her completely wet in a totally unique way.

For his part, he had noticed her breasts, once firm under the bikini, now bare, standing pert and tight, with her nipples perking out like two medium-sized thumbs. They were begging him forward, driving his legs as if they had no choice in the matter. He knew she was highly aroused; he could clearly see all the signs, but he vowed to himself that, for her first time, he would only follow her lead. He truly meant it—her friendship meant more to him than any roll in the hay could when he had all but said it earlier.

When he arrived at the door, she took his hand, pulled him close, met his lips with hers, and kissed him long, deep, and hard. She tasted like nothing he could readily describe. If raw desire and wanting had an actual flavor, he could not imagine it being anything else. She turned and led him across the cabin floor to the cabin's bathroom shower. The water was turned on, and the shower was adjusted for warmth. She pulled him in with her and began washing his hair, with no complaints from him.

She foamed up a scrunchy, turned him away from her, and washed down his back—half scrubbing, half massaging. He let out signs of enjoyment with her every touch as she moved on to his arms. There was a little extra time spent on his ass, to both his and her immense enjoyment. The scrunchy was re-lathered, his chest washed and then set aside as she finished washing his cock with her soapy hands.

He had now grown to the full length of her hand, and then some, and his thickness was a good handful—a throbbing handful—as she felt him go full-on hard. She loved his girth in her hand. She knew it was majestic by feel alone, though she had yet to see him fully engorged and erect.

She turned to rinse the soap, and while looking into his eyes, she melted into a watery kiss. She pushed him backward slightly and looked down, taking in his wholeness. She was not disappointed at all as her right hand found his undershaft, supporting his cock gently. Her left hand carefully and completely circled the bulbous head, which she could feel straining against its dermal confines with every heartbeat and throb. She wanted to kiss it but was immediately distracted by a foamy scrunchy now washing her back.

Danny stooped down just enough to reach her ass cheeks and cupped them in his hands, washing them as he raised up. He kissed her once more, then washed her breasts. He was not sure if a woman's breasts got tighter with wanting, but he knew their nipples did. As he passed over each rock-hard thumb, she gasped a moan of pleasure from his touch.

Turning her away from him to rinse her chest, he set the scrunchy aside as she did and cupped both of her breasts from behind, leaving her nipples peeking out from between fingers that he ever so slightly squeezed. She arched back into him, wanting him inside her as she pushed into his chest. He sucked gently on her water-splashed neck, the heat of his lips ripping clean through her.

While still holding her left breast and nipple with his left hand from behind her, he gave up completely on washing the body before him. He caressed the water across her belly, on down to her well-trimmed mound, where he cupped her sex with his whole hand, pushing in only as far as to force a deep gasp from her. He pulled his hand up ever so gently over her wet mound and found the waters parted for him, inviting him within her deeply.

He let one finger gently slip inside her soaked crevice as she arched into him hard, pushing into his hand, clearly wanting more. He kissed her neck once more and gently removed both hands.

Lost in the bliss of it, she had not noticed that he had turned off the water until the curtain opened. He stepped out, lifted a towel from the holder, and beckoned her out.

He took his time drying her from her feet up, taking even more time to completely dry areas of great concern, and met with her muffled moaning approval. Her hair was dried as best as a towel could do.

She took the towel from him and started on his back, high on his shoulders, down his spine, clearly taking time with his ass and continuing down his legs. When she got to his feet, she gently turned him around and started up one leg from the front, then the other. His cock was now standing hard and proud from her soft touches.

He was fully six and a half, maybe seven inches long, and with considerably more girth than Greg—just as she had expected. She leaned forward and took him in her mouth, but only halfway. She started to pull back, but when she arrived at the tip of his cock, she sucked herself back down onto him and cupped his soft balls.

Danny was definitely bigger than Greg, and she liked it.

She pulled herself off him as he groaned a guttural moan. She dried him up to his chest and, as he had done, took time and care to dry his hair.

She could feel her heart pounding—her every beat was evident, but not only in her chest. There was also a throb with every contraction of her heart muscle that was being directly felt deep in her pussy and on the tips of her nipples. She felt like she was truly going to explode.

She noticed one other thing. At first, she thought he had missed a spot while drying, but she quickly realized she was now dripping wet with wanting desire, and it felt glorious.

Chapter 11 - Virginity Lost

Trudy took Danny's hand, led him to the bedroom, pulled back the covers, and laid across the sheets sideways, pulling him in with her. They began to kiss deeply as their hands freely roamed each other's bodies. Danny could feel how wet she was when his hand made a cursory pass across her swollen mound. He looked her in the eyes and asked,

"Are you sure you want me as your first?"

Trudy just kissed him harder and pulled him on top of her as she rolled onto her back.

Danny positioned himself between her legs and half-supported himself with his elbows, all while looking into her eyes.

"I'll go slow, but it may hurt some. I'm a little bigger than most of the other guys at school."

Trudy just smiled and moaned as the head of his now raging-hot cock touched her outer lips. She could feel his heartbeat through the head of his dick, her vulva, and inner labia, begging for more information and recording every sensation, staining it deep in her brain. Her excitement and anticipation had been growing at an exponential rate.

Danny carefully worked inward—just a touch and just a little side to side—making sure she was in an acceptable position to receive him. He began to push forward as she half-gasped, half-moaned, so he stopped right there, the head of him fully engulfed in her throbbing, tight pussy fire. She was wet and slick, but her inner walls were tight, and her muscles fought to surround this new invader, pulsing against him—wet yet unyielding.

Trudy reached both hands up to cup his ass cheeks and very gently pulled him forward, maybe an inch. An inch of ecstasy with some discomfort but really no pain like she had heard about from other girls in school. She had wondered who was lying and who had useful information. At the moment, she did not give a damn.

There was a lot of resistance between her thighs—a wonderful, wanting resistance. She could feel her tightness against the girth of his shaft and exactly where inside her, her pelvic muscles were waging war with his cock's head. This was an ongoing, delicious fight inside her, so she pulled him forward maybe half an inch more.

She felt incredible, he thought—tight, wonderful, slick, and searing hot. Her muscles were straining to eject him, pulsing around his shaft, squeezing him so incredibly tight. When her fingers dug into his buttocks and pulled him in a bit more, he gasped and groaned, whispering, "Oh God, Trudy, you feel incredible."

Trudy smiled. She smiled for many reasons—not because he was pleased, but because, though the pressure was heavy, this nuclear-hot contouring of her inner being was heavenly. His cock was giving her all the sensations she fantasized about. He was halfway in her now, and his body was shaking from restraint. Every fiber of his being wanted to be within her. God, he wanted to be lost completely, deep in her.

He had heard of several guys from school who claimed to ram home with other girls in some feeble attempt at domination. His initial thought was that it ruined the experience for their partner and themselves. That, to him, was not only counterintuitive but incredibly ignorant.

He let the burn wrapping his member begin to scorch a place deep in his mind—the fit, the heat, the wanting—all but mentally begging Trudy to want him more. She did not disappoint when she suddenly rolled over. He followed her roll as if he were welded to her, now looking up into her beautiful face, holding as still as he could as she sat on him.

She leaned forward through the awkwardness of his half-entry and kissed him with her tongue deeply. When he thought she was finished kissing, she kissed him again—deeper and more passionately—as she purposefully began sitting down on him slowly, without breaking lip contact.

She sat all the way down on his rock-hard cock and just sat there, lip-to-lip, gasping for breath, moaning, and to a small degree, wincing. It was all so damn erotic. His dick pulsed once uncontrollably, swelling inside her briefly, to her delight. She had felt his twitch and, with a gleeful moan, leaned forward more and kissed him hard again.

He was now fully in her, motionless, being squeezed by her vagina like he had never felt before. Her pussy was trying to crush his turgid shaft, and the mutual fight—the war of their sexes—was the most incredible feeling that either of them had ever had.

Trudy pulled away from his lips and told him while sitting up, "I want it all."

She fully sat up and committed her full weight upon him, sitting flush on her perch, skin to skin, triumphantly in her accomplishment, until Danny grabbed her hips and arched up into her, stealing half of a spectacular inch more.

This time, it did not hurt her at all, but it did send a wave of ecstasy coursing through her as she audibly and loudly moaned with pleasure. Danny just smiled and went back to absolute stillness, savoring her quivering cunt pulsing on his invader deep within her.

Danny said, "Don't move from there—let me."

She smiled, quizzical but also knowing. He changed the direction of the thrust. She hadn't anticipated this nor fantasized about it either, but one thing she knew for certain—given his fullness and her uncontrollable clenching at this time—she hadn't thought that the discomfort, almost at the edge of pain, would recur.

But the change of direction pulled at her deeply in the most wonderfully stinging kind of way.

It did not last for long because Danny had stopped moving for the moment, having only withdrawn about an inch. The direction changed again slowly and methodically, her muscles re-familiarizing themselves with the head of his penis deep inside her, slowly making headway forward again, and it felt great.

The amount of discomfort was less than half of the first assault, and when he gently arched up into her, fully to his depth, the only thing she felt beyond a glistening pleasure was her body's release of more fluids. She was beyond wet—she was flooding in the most fantastic fashion.

He stopped again at the end of his journey and waited a full count of ten seconds, but her mind only registered a partial movement in time as he started to withdraw from her while gently lifting her hips from underneath.

Two inches this time—for what felt like a whole three feet inside of the two inches.

Her body barely complained.

He was going to again give her body time to realign itself, figure out its protest, and how it would present itself, but as he let loose of her ass, Trudy herself changed direction and steadfastly, yet slowly, sat down on him. She planted him deeply within her furrow and pulled him tight, savoring this glorious fullness that was pulsing with his every heartbeat.

Danny grabbed both of her ass cheeks and rolled once again, welded to her, this time at the hips. He again supported his weight and slowly changed directions, easily pulling three inches outward as he moaned, and she continued to get even wetter. He pushed in fully with just a little perceptible increase in speed. Trudy moaned and met his hips with hers. Changing direction yet again, Danny pulled out to the very end of her tight tunnel this time, leaving just the pulsing helmet inside her.

This was now his very own pussy, fit just for him. She felt great, and better yet, he had been right about taking his time as she pulled him into her while their bodies again reacquainted with each other into a glorious, perfectly contoured fit.

He obliged her direction by slowly plumbing to her depth. When he bottomed out, she hugged him tightly and once again rolled their welded bodies one more time, triumphantly mounted deeply on her perch once again. She slowly raised her hips and gave notice to her vaginal muscles. Her pelvic floor had closed the complaint department. His shaft filled her completely and fully; he was apparently built for her pussy, fit for her pussy.

She pulled up with determination and just a bit more speed, testing whether the complaint department was truly out or just out to lunch, but there was no bad feeling, no discomfort, just wonderful wetness. She sat on him at equal speed with the same result. He rocked upward, hips colliding gently as they bumped together.

Trudy leaned forward and kissed him on the mouth, and moved down his neck to his chest. When she got there, she kissed and sucked on a nipple. He was just about to react when she dipped her hips upward and pulled off of him at a wonderfully mind-boggling slow pace.

His body tensed as she let go of his nipple, and with both hands on his chest, she began to work her hips into him, onto him, around him. He felt good to her. It all felt good, and she was feeling even better as her pace slowly increased.

He writhed under her as her body moved up and down on him. Her muscles may have forgiven the intrusion, but they were not going to give up a close-quartered conversation. With every stroke, there was a new comment on structure and size with every recurring cycle. It was searing his mind. She was racking his body, and his whole being was on the verge of teleportation. It was almost indescribable.

Trudy pulled up to the top of his glans, and she could feel his pulse through his dick. Because she was curious, she pulled up slightly more, her tightness almost squirting his bulbous head out. His dickhead came to rest, wrapped in labia. He was out of her for the moment, and she did not like it.

This was her dick, and she wanted it back deep within her.

Trudy struggled just a bit with alignment and logistics, but in short order, she learned how to best align herself and pushed onto him again. It was almost driving her insane to think that every entry, every inch, felt much better than the first, and it came with a hunger, an unforeseen desire, a wanting, as she impulsively and all but involuntarily dropped down his shaft with graceful precision.

As she landed, it felt more like she slammed into this incredible stopping position. Something with the breath of a whisper at first changed inside her.

She had felt herself before; she knew where her clitoris was, and it admittedly felt good to be rubbed, but this was different. She could feel her clit pulsing with her heartbeat, but most notably, she could feel it was swollen like it had never been before.

The whisper that she felt before was now gaining a voice, pushing to get out from inside her, struggling to surface, to free itself. She pulled herself up his shaft to the top near the head and accelerated downward, bumping hips with Danny and awakening something in her clitoris.

It was no longer imperceptible. It had status, it carried a report, and the report asked for more information.

She pulled up again, not feeling any pain. There was no discomfort, only bliss, and after an accelerated pace downward, their hips crashed wantonly. The only message she received from her clitoris was to do it again but with more determination, please.

She pulled up faster and literally slammed down, half-yelling out, "Oh God," getting wetter as she went. She unleashed an all-out onslaught on his cock and balls, a torrent of thrust and pull, with every stroke encouraging her until the report just did not matter anymore.

She was being driven by pure code from her pussy that was stuck in a cycle of repeat, repeat, repeat. Her clit drove her and her hips on, commanding slam upon slam relentlessly in its own bodily directorial debut.

Danny was writhing under her body, holding onto his come with dogged determination. He was watching her lose control while enjoying him. He was feeling her buck into him with an already learned hip tilt at the bottom for maximum depth, with the added bonus that it rubbed the clit in a most pleasurable fashion against his pelvic bone.

He had seen that many times before in his learning stages with Denise. He knew Trudy was on the verge of exploding into a serious orgasmic event, and he was putting forth his best effort to help and join her.

As she thrust, readying the hip tilt, he thrust into it hard. She was audibly losing control of her senses, but Trudy could have cared less at that moment. Something lit on fire from deep inside her. It had started at her soaking wet clitoris, and it grew from there. It was gaining in feeling and starting to control every fiber of her being. It was rocking her body beyond delight. She could not believe her senses at first. She couldn't believe that it was possible for Danny's rock-hard cock to get bigger, but it was beginning to.

She could feel it swelling, and every slam downward met a new size that somehow managed to trigger a more profound understanding of detachment, a total, involuntary release rising inside her. An animal growled from underneath her; Danny was letting out a guttural, animalistic moan as he lifted her fully ten inches higher with the arch of his back, forcing himself to the complete and total possible depth. She felt his hot, torrential release inside her. His first spasm shot against her cervix with a delicious, hot poke at her inner walls.

She would have stopped to ride out the sensation with him, but she could not. Almost simultaneously, when Danny pulsed his biggest and released his seed, she felt a match light a fuse. The fuse set off the dynamite sitting at every one of her nerve endings inside her, all in milliseconds of uncontrollable elation; it grew from there. He arched up, she arched down, and she lost herself. Exactly where she was had her confused now, but she did not—really, could not—care; her pussy was convulsing, forcing her body to pump into him, which only caused the last result to recur again and again and again. Her mind was tumbling and spinning, and all that could possibly be said about it was that her body was on full tilt.

She was fucking downward uncontrollably. She barely remembered thinking there was no way anything could escape their tight connection, yet they were soaking each other. Her mind could not hold onto any thought for more than a second. She began to come in waves. Waves upon waves. She could not understand it; she could not figure out how these waves were overcoming her since she could no longer even move. The only thing with any movement at all that her mind could register was her pulsing pussy, and she just could not care beyond that incredibly euphoric release.

From somewhere hidden inside her, a blinding binary fission was trying to escape, but it was masked with a new horrendous wave that she welcomed with screams of pleasure. Somewhere in her consciousness, it came to her, and through tightly squinted eyes, she was able to only glimpse downward to see Danny stroking her hard, furiously, and deep. He was pounding her pussy. Had the orgasmic phasing in and out of reality not felt so indescribably good, she would have thought he was punishing her.

Danny was slamming into her hips, grinding at the bottom, and sending her clit further and further into the stratosphere with every contact, which was happening at an astonishingly blistering pace. She could not understand how this could be. Hadn't he come? Wasn't he supposed to be done? She was on the verge of questioning it more when the next wave, more intense than the last, washed over her. She could have been sitting in the middle of a bonfire, and she would not have noticed. She had a personal bonfire fully ablaze. She had not realized she had been begging Danny to fuck her harder and harder.

Danny was absolutely pounding her for all he was worth, with his full force upward, hips tilting for the last millimeter of distance on every stroke. Though he had already come, he was not like some other guys he knew; he had no refractory time. He was hard as a brick and stayed that way until well after he was done using his dick for however long that was. Danny was in excellent physical condition, and as soon as his sensitivity had subsided, he began to fuck Trudy in earnest; she had been begging him for more and more, so he fucked doggedly on.

Every sensation was incredible, Trudy's body begging for salvation, begging to be set free. He had felt the beginnings of the end; his second coming was about to arrive, and when it did, it just so happened to coincide with the next full wave for Trudy. Her mind-altering, utter confusion set in, brought on by Danny's hot prick once again swelling deep in her wonderland to meet his release. When he came, at the moment his next shot pulsed out of his shaft, Trudy arched backward uncontrollably, laying back on his raised knees, hips thrusting, begging him onward and inward.

She was crying tears of delightful exhaustion as she fell forward and lay across his chest. Her body was not cold, but she was shivering, truly quivering, spent, breathing hard and deep. Smaller waves cascaded through her and caressed her; she wanted to close her eyes and drift aimlessly away with any breeze that came along, without a care in the world as for the destination.

He was still hard when she came to, still hard when she lifted almost off him, still hard when she let their combined juices slide her back down fully, still hard when she pulled herself reluctantly off him, spent and weakened. Still hard when they finally made it back to the shower ten minutes later. Both were weak-legged and totally spent. There was an incredible physical and insanely powerful thirst.

They took turns washing each other once again, but this time, it was more utilitarian and fun than sexually inquisitive. Trudy pulled the towels from the rack, and Danny helped her strip the bed. They collectively put the linens in the small laundry room.

Still completely naked, together they walked out across the sand to the blanket to find their clothes and to get a drink. Trudy picked up Danny's now-dry shorts as an hour and a half had passed, and without a word, she offered a leg hole for Danny to step into, holding them while in a kneeling position. She held still as both legs found their mark separately.

She pulled his shorts up onto his legs, bare-assed naked in front of her. She stopped pulling when the waist of the shorts met his ass, held them in place with one hand, and cupped his balls and now-deflated dick with the other. She kissed the head of his dick. She stood up and helped his shorts over his hips and carefully caressed his dick and balls back inside his front. Trudy finished pulling up his shorts and snapped the snaps on his fly.

She cupped his complete package and closed her eyes for a moment, as if she were reliving the whole experience in one moment, smiled, and opened her eyes.

Trudy turned to get her suit, but Danny stepped up from behind, cupped both of her breasts and half-sucked, half-kissed the nape of her neck.

"Are you OK? I mean, this has been incredible, but are you OK with everything that happened today?"

She leaned back into him and savored the feel of his strong hands cupping her breasts.

"I'm a little sore, which I suspect might get a little worse by tomorrow, but I'm so glad my first time was with you like this. I can't imagine any other way that losing my virginity could have been better, and I have you to thank for it," she said thankfully.

"I can't wait for next time…? But—"

"But what? Did I do something you didn't want to do?"

"No, no, nothing like that, God no."

"That's good, but if not that, then what?"

"Well, uh. I'm not sure how to express this."

"Come on," he chuckled, "With all that we have shared today…what?"

"Danny, I really like you. You're smart, you are…well, hot. I like talking to you, and," she chuckled, "out of all the guys I've had sex with, you are definitely the best, but I have a hang-up that I'm not sure how you will feel about. I don't want to be exclusively boyfriend and girlfriend with you or anybody else, for that matter. I'm not staying here. After high school, I'm going away to college. After that, I'll be commanding my vast empire!" She chuckled at the duality of her statement. "I don't want to be anchored to anything until I get to where I want to be."

He kissed her softly on the neck as he pulled away. She turned to face him, still bare to the afternoon sun, and he smiled big.

"You're in luck, and really, I was afraid of how this would play out as well, but I feel the exact same way. I really like you, and yes, yes, yes, if you will let me be with you for a second time, it will be on my mind all night. I'll be dreaming about numbers three, four, five, and ten if you have me. You're incredible, beautiful, sensual, and damn, your body is—" he leaned forward and kissed her neck, upper chest, then sucked a nipple into his mouth for a wet kiss.

"You are all I could dream of, but I am not going to stay either. I have two years left here, after college somewhere, culinary school, and then I'm off to the working world as a chef. I agree on not being tied down, but wouldn't it be great to be able to have easy access to someone you really like to have fun with, be with, and hang with without having to set stakes and boundaries? A friend with benefits but more? I could enjoy you without being hurt or jealous if you went out with other guys. Can you do that too, or is that too much to put up with?"

Trudy closed the distance between them and looked him straight in the eyes while grabbing his cock and balls through his shorts.

"There is a version of that in my head that tells me we are thinking pretty much the same thing. Really, the only thing that could ruin it is if you forget how to do what we just did." She gently squeezed his now firm dick.

"I don't think I'll ever forget today; you were fantastic, Trudy," he said with a boyish smile and a joking manner.

"By the way…uhm…what are you doing tomorrow?" He broke into a laugh while saying it.

Trudy busted up laughing and said, "Laundry…uh, towels and bedsheets."

She bent down to pick up her bikini bottoms and tied the sides. Danny plucked them out of her hands and kneeled to let her step into them, then pulled them up her legs, stopping at mid-thigh. He let them go and wrapped his hands around her ass, plunging a tongue deep into her crotch.

Trudy involuntarily ticked forward as his tongue parted her labia. He pulled back and finished pulling her bottoms up. He looked up at her,

"Turnabout is fair play, yes?" He beamed a smile.

Danny stood up after grabbing her top and stepped behind her to drape the "bra" over her chest, then began to fumble as he tried to tie the strings. Trudy laughed and told him she had it, spun the strings to the front and tied her bow to her specification, spun the suit back around to cover her breasts, and asked for help tying the top strings, which Danny expertly did this time, tying them like his shoelaces but only on the back of her neck.

Trudy turned to Danny. "Now that we have our own secret to keep, maybe we can talk about those other secrets of yours…in a little more detail sometime? We could even re-enact some of them if you like?"

"Maybe…we'll see." He was smiling ear to ear.

"How about you pick up our stuff here, and I'll go start the laundry."

It was late afternoon when they arrived back at the house where Danny had parked. They had seen Trudy's dad go inside from the front porch as they approached. Trudy parked the Razor in the barn, and they unloaded their stuff and headed to Danny's truck. Danny had dropped the tailgate, and they unburdened themselves on the metal shelf of the gate. Trudy hugged him tight while she stole a glance at the porch door and kissed him with an enthusiastic, short kiss.

Danny turned and picked up Trudy's wares and headed for the house door.

Chapter 12 - Meeting Mr. Jax

"Where are you going?" She had expected him to mount up in the truck and leave.

"To meet your dad, of course. We know he's home. I would be a total dick if I left now."

"Are you sure you want to meet him now?"

"If I plan on being around for a while, I'm guessing he would want to know who I am. Besides, the longer it is before we meet, the more anxiety that will build all the way around. I would rather face everything head-on if you don't mind."

Bill had been within earshot of their conversation, half eavesdropping and half walking through. He had seen their kiss and felt this was someone Trudy really liked, as she was not flippant about this type of thing. She had always been more discreet, if not secretive.

He knew that on a bright day, looking up at the porch windows was like looking into a dark hole. He could have been a scant few feet from the window or door, and they would not have seen him. He retreated into the living room, turned on the television, and acted as if he was none the wiser, though he was impressed with Danny's resolve.

The door opened to the side entrance off the porch.

"Dad!!??"

"I'm in the living room, Trudy!" he said back in a raised voice.

Two people entered the living room. Bill acted as if he was caught off guard and stood.

"Dad, this is my friend Danny Veach. He wanted to meet you. Danny, this is my father, Bill Jax."

Danny offered his hand and advanced to meet Bill's open hand. "It is really nice to meet you, Mr. Jax."

Noticing and liking that Danny had a good, firm grip and had made eye contact the whole time they were shaking, Bill appreciated that the handshake had just the right amount of pressure and duration before they released each other's grasp.

"Had I known you were coming, I would have had my shotgun out just for you." He had a big smile while looking at Trudy, then let out a small chuckle. "Ahh, I'm just kidding. Is it Danny or Dan?"

"Mr. Jax, I have always gone by Danny, but I was thinking that when I left for college, I would arrive there as Dan. I don't know many adults that go by Danny—everyone just shortens it."

"I see. Well, Danny, you can call me Bill. Did you kids have a fun time today?"

"Yes, sir. Your daughter was able to get me all muddy, yet she managed to stay totally clean in the process. She showed me all around what I thought was the whole farm. By the time we made it to one of your lakes for a swim to wash off my mud," he smiled at Trudy "I told her your place was fantastic. She told me I had only seen about a third of it. It really is a beautiful place."

"Thank you, Danny. A lot of hard work went into it, and it still does every day. I'm sure Trudy will get around to showing you more at one time or another. Just remember to stay out of the corn rows and beans and watch out for the bulls, and you will be just fine."

"Yes, sir, Mr. Jax. This might be the wrong time to put this out there, but if you ever need help here on the farm, I'm always looking for work. Besides, I was told I apparently need a new muffler."

Bill looked inquisitively at Trudy, who was beaming a smile that was trying not to become a laugh.

"There is always something going on here. Next week, we are putting up four hundred or so bales of hay and capping eighty or so round bales after moving them into their winter home. I'll have Trudy take you by the office to meet Sam. If he has the work, I'm sure he could use you—if you're up to it."

"Thank you, Mr. Jax. I am interested in knowing if you can use me. It was nice to meet you, but I better get on home before Mom sends out a search party for me."

"Drive safe, Danny. Go easy on the washboards."

Danny and Trudy turned and headed for the porch.

"Will do, sir." They walked out to the truck.

"Your dad seems nice."

"Most of the time, he is, but I've seen him mad a time or two, and you don't want to see that side of him. It's scary."

"My guess is that he is fair but direct and takes no crap from anyone—just a feeling I get even though we just met. It just kinda feels that way. Do you think he was serious about helping put up hay? I really could use the money."

"If you are serious, I'll introduce you to Sam next week, but I warn you—they will expect a strong work ethic. That's the best way to get into everyone's good graces around here."

"I'm not afraid of hard work," he said with a smile at the door of the truck.

Trudy kissed him again as he got in the truck. He shut the door, powered down the windows, and leaned out.

"Whatcha doing tomorrow?"

"Tomorrow morning is breakfast with my dad, and lunch is with Sadie—always the same on Sunday. Before you ask, that is my thing. I'll share that in my own good time." She beamed a smile at him.

"You wanna hang out at my house tomorrow around two or so? A friend of mine, Dave, is coming over, and we are going to kill some people," he said, beaming a smile back at her, "Call of Duty."

"I may need to clear it with Dad, but I don't see why not."

Sunday morning followed the routine that had been established for quite some time. It was rarely changed unless it was a version of it where breakfast was enjoyed at the diner.

Today, it was bacon—ultimately from Jax Farms—and eggs over easy from the Millers one farm over. White toast, milk, juice, and coffee—black with two tablespoons of honey, locally sourced—topped off with dollar pancakes and maple syrup.

Trudy had always made enough to feed Sam as well in the event he came up, which happened two out of three weekends. If he did not come up, it was breakfast for lunch, which she enjoyed as well. Today, she saw Sam walking up the road, across the porch, and in the door. He had not knocked in quite some time, nor was he expected to.

Sam sat down without a word, as was custom on Sunday morning. It just was not good etiquette to speak or, for that matter, elicit actual words— just short of the house being on fire—before the first cup of joe was officially dead and its replacement had been sought out.

Bill had waited for Sam to reach for the decanter before he spoke. He knew Trudy had already started number two somewhere between flipping the dollar flapjacks and locating the syrup.

"Good morning, Sam. How are you this morning?"

"I'm a little slow going this morning. I was out a little later than normal last night. How are you?"

"I'm well. It was nice to sleep in a little this morning."

Bill was usually up around five a.m. but had slept nearly until seven, just as he had for the last month of Sundays. Trudy was always up around six unless she had been out late or was not feeling well. She had heard her dad start to stir around, so she had begun breakfast.

After a sip of coffee, Bill asked, "Out late? Problems?"

"No problems, a date. Jessie and I have really hit it off." Sam smiled big. "She just might be the one, Bill."

"Jessie, huh? Well, good for you."

"Uh, Dad?" Her question trailed off, her meaning floating just a bit.

"Yeah, yeah, I didn't forget." He looked at Trudy, then at Sam. "Trudy's boyfriend, Danny, might be looking for a job. I told him we were putting up hay next week and that he should talk to you to see if you needed a hand."

"We can always use a hand with the hay, especially at the barn. Nothing better than to have enough guys to rotate out of the loft when it's hot out. Have him come down Monday morning around eight. I should have everything up and going by that time."

"I'll let him know this afternoon. I was going to hang out with him and his friend Dave. Is that alright with you, Dad?"

"That's fine, but don't be too late." Bill turned toward Sam. "Just because I like this kid doesn't mean he gets a pass. If he isn't working out, let me know, and I'll handle it. How's Sadie been?"

"She is good, but I've noticed she is slowing down a bit. She is still as rambunctious as ever, though. I saw her light come on while I was walking up here. Church at nine every Sunday. I think I'll give her a ride today if she wants one."

Trudy spoke. "Would you tell her I will be down for lunch?"

Sadie would know to translate Sam's prompt of her arrival into I am coming down to fix lunch. Sunday was a clockwork event that was rarely missed.

Trudy continued, "Chicken fajita wraps. And if you two are nice, I might make a few extras."

They both knew that this translated to Do not show up until after we are completely done cooking, which meant right after twelve-thirty and not a minute sooner. But they also knew not to wait too long after, or their plates would morph from good and warm to barely warm or even cold if it was still too much later. There was a balance to showing up.

This gave the girls much-wanted time to catch up and do their girl thing, which both women looked forward to with much delight every Sunday, as it always resulted in a fantastic lunch.

Chapter 13 - Sadie Knows

At eleven o'clock, Trudy arrived at Momma Sadie's guest house. She had two grocery bags filled with food and drinks—rice, beans, chicken breasts, peppers, spices, Verde, guacamole, tomatillos, and salsa. Sadie had already set out most of the bowls and pans she anticipated would be needed.

"Chicken fajitas? It has been a while since we fixed that. It made my mouth water just to hear Sam say that."

Suddenly, Sadie stopped dead, leaned back just a bit, and drank Trudy in. She approached Trudy, who had set the bags on the counter and gave her a long hug.

Trudy inquired, "Is everything OK?"

"Everything is just fine, unless—"

"Unless what?"

"Unless he hasn't treated you with respect. Has he?"

Trudy went cow-eyed with a how-the-hell-did-she-know look.

"How…uh, how did—"

"Something changes in a girl—an air, a glow, a pace that sells them out. I knew just by looking at you. He treated you with respect?"

Blushing red, Trudy replied, "He did, Momma. He asked several times if I was sure. I pursued him, but he was very gentle. He kept asking if I was OK. I really think, compared to stories I have heard, that it was exceptional in the way he treated me. Do you think it is wrong that I didn't wait until I was married? Are you disappointed?"

"Everyone and everything has a rhythm and a flow, child. I have been watching you because I knew that you were going to be you on your terms. Just as long as he treats you with respect and doesn't ever hurt you."

"I don't think he is capable of being bad to me." She was now smiling at Sadie.

"Just keep your head about you. And remember, if you ever need to talk about anything—"

"You would be my first stop. Oh God, do you think Dad knows, too?"

"Men are clueless. I think they just make an assumption around eighteen or nineteen, but even then, they are lost."

Both women chuckled at that.

"Danny met Dad yesterday. He wants to meet you, too. I may have mentioned you once or twice, so he wanted to meet my mom."

She looked at Sadie with a warm, loving smile. Sadie hugged her again—tight for a little extra count—and as she released her, she asked,

"You want the chicken or the rice?"

Both women set about making fajitas in a manner that would make a mother in the heart of Mexico City proud. After the veggies were chopped and the sautéing was completed, the chicken was sliced and seasoned just so, married to a light coating of Verde and a dollop of guacamole spread along the chicken's length. They assembled the montage into extra-large fajita wraps, tightly sealing them up. They put them in a skillet to brown the shells and melt the cheese internally. Sadie made a point to make seven, which confused Trudy, but Sadie was Sadie, so she continued.

Sadie and Trudy had finished their fajita wraps and had been waiting for about five minutes when the boys showed up. Bill followed Sam inside, and both men sat in front of a plate with two wraps apiece, with large glasses of tea behind them. Without asking, they knew the tea was going to be perfectly sweet, but both were taken aback on their first bite, savoring the incredible taste. They would have expressed their delight more verbally, but it was hot and incredible. There was no good reason to stop for anything other than a sip of tea sporadically until each wrap was gone.

As per the norm, the guys finished their lunch and expressed how great it was. After excusing themselves, they both made their way to the office, where both women knew they would plan the next week of work to be accomplished, rehash the month out, and beyond expectations. She knew well that it would involve a beer or three.

Sadie wrapped number seven in aluminum foil along with several layers of napkins, put it into a paper bag, and handed it to Trudy.

"You're seeing Danny when you leave here, right?"

"Yes, ma'am, I am."

"Make sure he knows you made that. I can see your eyes light up when I mention his name, and he will always be somewhere in the back of your mind—just as Dwight has been in mine. He was a good man, too."

"You still miss your husband badly. I can always tell that. I can see your eyes shine when he is talked about."

"I do miss him every day, so much, even now. But, Trudy, my husband was Earl."

Dwight happened two years before I met Earl." She winked at Trudy with a slightly devilish smile. "Now, you go tell him lunch is at twelve-thirty next week. If he isn't sure how it is supposed to work, he can meet the boys in the office before." She tilted her head toward the door with a smile. "Now, get out of here, young lady."

Laughing with Sadie, "You never cease to surprise or amaze me." She leaned forward and kissed her on the cheek. "I love you, Momma."

She turned and left.

When Trudy arrived at the Veach house and knocked on the door, a lady with beautiful facial structure and well-managed hair answered.

"You must be Trudy. Danny said you were coming by. They are in the living room playing that damn Xbox again," she said with a laugh. "Actually, I watched them play for a bit. Other than all the killing, The Time of Duty, or whatever it is, it is addicting if you're good at it. It's addictive if you just watch it, too. I'm Mindy Veach, by the way."

"It's very nice to meet you, Mrs. Veach."

"It is nice to meet you as well. Don't let them get too lost in the game. They are both fairly good, judging by other online scores. They get tunnel vision when they get on a roll. I'm going shopping in Evansville with some friends. I'll be back around eight or so. There are leftovers in the fridge.

Other than that, you're all on your own for supper. That is if you can tear them away from that game."

"Yes, ma'am. It was nice to meet you. Uh, have I got you blocked in?"

"Oh no, you're fine."

There was a brief honk of a horn.

"There's my ride now. You kids play nice."

She laughed and stepped out the door.

Trudy stepped around the corner where two guys were playing Call of Duty. Danny smelled food in the air, looked at Trudy, and pressed pause on his game.

"That smells great. What is it?"

"Homemade chicken fajita. Sadie wrapped it just for you. Uh-oh, Sadie told me to tell you that lunch next week will be at twelve-thirty and not a minute sooner. If you want, you could come up with the guys who will be waiting in the office as well.

"You should know that it is rare to get an invitation to our lunchtime. Honestly, it sounded more like an edict than a question of whether you could make it." She laughed just a bit.

"Let's see what you got there." He unwrapped the fajita and sniffed it in awe.

"Dave? Are you hungry?"

"No, I'm good. I ate before I came over. What time is it?"

"About two forty-five."

"Shit, dude, I've got to go. I told my mom I would be home around three." He shut down his game and logged out.

"You must be Trudy." He looked her up and down. "Damn, Danny, you didn't tell me she was this hot." He laughed and looked at Trudy. "Actually, he said you were gorgeous." He had been trying but failed to embarrass his friend.

"It is nice to meet you. See you around sometime. Later, bro." Dave stepped out the door and was gone.

"Did you just plan that?"

"And what if I did?" He was battling a mouthful of fajita. "This is really good. I'm going to need the recipe for my book."

"Your book?"

"Recipe book. I'm collecting great food fare recipes. When I open my own place, I will have gone through them, put my personal touches on them, perfected them to my standards, and made them mine. Except this—damn, it's good—it will stay the same if I can steal it from you."

"I'll give it to you, but when you're up and running, you can never charge me for any meal. Ever. Deal?"

"If that's the price of this recipe," he said, finishing the last bite, "it's well worth it." He laughed.

He grabbed her hand, led her to the couch, and sat down with her. He was almost finished with the last of the fajita bits and was working the remnants from the corners of his cheeks and teeth.

"Do you want to play Call of Duty or something else?"

"What I really wanted when I came over here—before your mother answered the door and probably before you and Dave even started playing this game—was, well, you.

"You on your couch, you on your floor, you in your bed… How do you feel about kitchen tables?" she said with a laugh.

"Tables? They are great for eating at, so maybe we will get back to that. I haven't had time to vacuum the floor, and the couch has chip crumbs in it, but I think I can make my bed work. I thought you might be a little too sore, so I have made zero plans in that regard."

"I really had no plans, and yes, I'm more than just a little sore, but halfway over here, something changed. I started to think about yesterday. I started to think about you.

"I think you may have created a monster."

He smiled, looking deep into her eyes. "Let's see what we can do about that."

He grabbed Trudy by the hand to help her up and into him as he made contact with her lips, and they began kissing passionately. He led her to his bedroom and very slowly took off both her and his shoes. He then removed her shirt, revealing a comfortable but lacy bra, and pulled his own shirt over his head. She watched as his washboard abs transformed into pecks.

He changed the order by taking off his jeans and revealing men's bikini briefs. They were bright and colorful, which made her smile. He wrestled her jeans from her hot, supple ass. They were almost painted on, leaving little room to work with, but he finally managed to free them and slide them down her legs. Being at floor level, he pulled off her socks and then removed his own as well.

"This isn't hardly fair; you have on more clothes than I do," he said.

Trudy reached behind her, and in one deft movement, her bra was undone and sliding down her arms.

He barely heard her say, "Fair is fair."

Directly after the bra came off, he was mesmerized by her incredible, firm, and perky breasts. Her nipples stood straight out as if begging him to suck them—so he did. With one of her breasts encompassed and caressed by his free hand, the other nipple was shrouded in his hot, moist mouth, his tongue lashing the tip as if punishing it—yet achieving only pleasure. She moaned with excitement and drove his head harder onto her breast, smashing her resilient mound delectably inward.

His other hand roamed downward, slipping under the hem of her panties. He wanted to get her wet—moist, at least—because he wanted to enter her without causing any more discomfort than the day before. He was much too late, as he felt her panties already wet on the front side of his fingers. When he slipped a finger inside her, it was clear there would be no issue. She moaned, arching into him, writhing as she did. He somehow willed himself to pull back from her nipple.

She was a vision once again—glowing skin and a radiant smile. When she moaned and audibly begged, "Please," he thought he might come right then and there.

He pushed her back onto the bed. She sat down and was then pushed backward. For a second, she had a perfect view of his ceiling fan, but when he stuck his tongue as deep as he could into her hot, dripping-wet slit, she involuntarily closed her eyes tight. Her mouth had not received the message and had no intention of staying silent—it moaned helplessly as her body was driven to a place she knew yet was new to her all over again.

Arching into his face, she could feel his hands digging into her ass from underneath; given the space, she couldn't help but give. She began to writhe, trying to find a modicum of control to enjoy the incredible, heavenly sensation—but then he moved. She thought about complaining when her hips were thrust higher still as he encompassed her clitoris with his lips and sucked it hard and passionately, circling with his tongue and sending her to new, instant heights.

She came with a rage and a flood as Danny smiled. Her hips thrust forward with every tongue flick. She came hard again, soaking his face. He kept her there for another round, driving her nearly crazy. He loved cunnilingus—eating pussy was at the top of his best-things-to-do list. As she was coming down, he had her hold onto his neck and dragged her like a bulldozer to the head of the mattress. Still breathless and spinning, she closed her eyes, which only intensified the effect of everything all over again. She didn't mind—it was a great feeling until something started to change.

She was about to open her eyes and begin a rudimentary investigation when she felt the head of his cock parting her, spreading her, entering her. Unlike the day before, he never stopped, gaining speed for his entire length. She wriggled and writhed the whole way as he delivered the full six-plus inches. It was a single, stabbing assault—precision bombing at its finest. No sooner had the head entered her than he stroked inward, violently deep and hard, with a binary push that culminated in hip-to-hip contact and remained there, as if they were glued together. She gasped hard and deeply, moaning her pleasure loudly.

The flame ignited through his cunnilingus, which had begun to smolder, reignited like a bonfire fed pure oxygen and gunpowder. Every cell in her body desperately tried—but failed—to defray the flames. She simply lost her mind. Now audibly screaming in pleasure, she didn't even realize she had begun to fuck him of her own volition. He hadn't moved until she did—but that's when Danny put his youth into overdrive in such a way that even a jackhammer on full tilt would have been envious and proud.

He started to pound her, and with each successive stroke, his thrusts landed harder—over and over again.

Every thrust brought her to new heights, and when he bottomed out inside her, those heights gave flight to what was left of her mind. He pulled out and dragged her to the edge of the bed, rock-hard, barely swinging due to his turgidity. Grabbing her ankles, he lifted them, walking them above her body, spreading her wide. As he approached, he dipped forward and planted his rod deep inside her, burying himself to the hilt with a hip tilt, desperately trying to find even more ground with every stroke.

This position was new to her—and simply glorious. He stroked her hard as she whimpered and flailed helplessly at his pleasure and her own. She liked this position a lot, but then he suddenly dropped her ankles and pulled out again.

He spun her over, lifted her up doggy-style, and entered her from behind. Trudy loved this position too, but not as much as the last—until he pushed her head down to the mattress, changing the entry angle by lifting her ass in the air.

Somehow, he found another brush pile out there in need of burning and scorched it to the ground. She might have filed a complaint, but the only sound she was capable of producing was loud moans and a strange little screech—some basis in an unknown foreign language, completely unintelligible, though she verbalized it often.

She hadn't seen much of anything for the last ten minutes, but she felt as if she had learned an encyclopedia's worth about her body—and Danny's dick.

She thought she was on the verge of mastering this new epiphany, this magical experience when he really let loose. Danny was fit, and now that her ass was up in the air like this, she was at his perfect height. Looking at her perfect ass, seeing her tight, perfect breasts and nipples attempting to sway but holding fast with their perkiness, he became inspired and truly began to fuck with purpose and intent, pounding fully into her. His cardio ability was just wonderfully sinister. She had been set out on a cloud and had no recollection of how she got there. There was nothing but pure, unadulterated pleasure. She had no idea that forty-five minutes had passed.

Stroke after stroke plastered a new layer of ecstasy across her body. She had lost track of coming and was working on an out-of-body experience when he thrust inward so hard that he pushed her ass upward six inches or more and roared out a come at the apex with such a release inside her that she felt it. The thrust was commiserated with his effort. She felt the heavenly swell, and it intensified her orgasm as she continued to come. They both collapsed forward in a sweaty mass of tangled bodies. There, they lay silently still for ten minutes, trying to recover enough to function properly.

When they had caught their breath, Danny rubbed her back gently, lovingly, gaining the same pleasure he was giving her through his fingertips. He had not known her long, but her touch had a most hypnotic effect on him.

"Come on." He helped pull her reluctantly upright and to her feet, then led her to the bathroom. It was a nice bathroom when considering its size, but the furnishings were clearly an ode to a guy by the way things were arranged and the items left out. He started the shower and warmed it—a touch too warm.

Trudy stepped into the water stream. "Whoa, hot, hot…"

"I can turn it down. Sorry, I thought you liked it hot."

"No, I'm getting used to it, and it feels pretty good on my back."

Danny stepped into the shower in front of her and hugged her under the water flow. He picked up the shampoo and put a dollop on his hand. He leaned her back to soak her hair, and after she wiped her eyes clear, he applied it to her hair. He took his time, wordlessly massaging her scalp and lathering her hair lightly, letting his fingernails pull furrows through her hair and down her head. Trudy thoroughly enjoyed his treatment. He rinsed his hands under the stream and lifted her head to let the water play with the suds while he lightly, and still wordlessly, kissed her lips.

When her hair no longer held evidence of soap, he gently turned her around, letting the water roll down her back between them both. He lathered just his hands and began washing her neck, chest, and breasts. Her nipples still stood hard and defiant, but it was hard to tell if it was remnants of the previous hour or the heat of the water. He washed them well but did not hover. He made his way down her torso, loving her every curve and washing all of them with his caress. Holding one of his hands in front of her face just inches away to mock-block her vision, as she was not supposed to see what he was doing, he sent a soapy palm down between her legs and, in earnest, lathered and rinsed her. He wanted to dwell but forced himself not to.

When he got to her toes, he changed direction, moving up the back of her legs, only to be slowed by the roundness of what he thought might be the perfect ass. He took his time kneading and washing her cheeks, then made his way to the small of her back. He scratched lightly up her spine and across the whole of her back, which caused her to cave her chest forward like a cat fully stretching its back. Then she released, with all hints of tension gone.

He gently and carefully washed her face. She wiped the water from her eyes, and he pulled her backward just a bit, pulling the curtain around as a corral for the water. He reached for the towel rack and retrieved a towel for her. She had felt the poke and the bludgeoning of his dick—hard still—flailing aimlessly against her legs while he washed her. She had wanted to wash him in return, but he had handed her the towel, and it smelled like him, so she took it and stepped onto the bathroom rug.

He washed himself in short order, but by the time he was drying off, she had already dressed and was lying on the bed beside a spread-out towel. She was admiring his nakedness as well as his confidence as he walked nude into the room and started to get dressed. She lifted the towel from the edge in a triangular movement.

"So, this is what the jokes about sleeping on the wet spot are about?" She was smiling broadly at him.

"Sorry for that."

Joking playfully, he said, "No, you're not!"

She looked him straight in the eyes. "You're right. I'm not sorry—not sorry at all."

"Probably a good thing I'm doing laundry tomorrow, huh?"

"Well, you better be done before seven-thirty if you want to meet Sam at eight."

"Shit, I almost forgot. I guess I'll strip it now and put on the clean ones, then do laundry when I get home tomorrow."

"Sounds like a better plan."

They both stripped the bed and put the new sheets in place. They had a small argument as to whether the pillowcases were to be changed. Trudy won that argument and had a promise that he would always change them with the sheets every time. After making the bed, they both jumped into it, hugging and rolling a bit to make sure it looked like it had been slept in so his mom would not be suspicious. He followed her to the door, where they kissed long, slow, and deep for about thirty seconds. Then she turned to leave.

"See you tomorrow. Uh—jeans and a couple of T-shirts, you are gonna get soaked. And if you bring some trunks for the lake after?"

"I'm all over it!" he said with a huge smile.

Chapter 14 - The First Workday

Trudy had turned in early, noting to herself that sex could really take a lot of energy out of you. She relented a bit and conceded that it might be a function of an orgasm; she was not sure which. She had fallen asleep before she had time to begin to dissect it. When she woke at six-thirty, the tables had turned. She knew her dad was up and out and probably had been for the better part of an hour. More importantly, she knew there would be hot coffee on the warmer waiting for her in the kitchen.

She dressed and began her much-needed assault on the coffee machine. By the time Danny arrived, she was alive and well, ready for a new day—give or take a well-placed yawn. She walked with him down to the office, which was about a football field away. It was almost dead center between the old house and the new. Sam was just getting off the phone when they walked in at seven fifty-five.

"Morning, Sam. How are you?"

"Just fine." Looking at Danny, he added, "And you must be—"

Cutting him off, she said, "Sam, this is Danny. Danny—Mr. Taylor. Sam."

Both men shook hands. Sam was equally impressed as Bill had been with Danny's poise.

"It's good to meet you, Danny."

"Likewise, Mr. Taylor."

"Let's get off on a good foot here. It's Sam—just Sam, OK?" he said in a friendly voice.

"OK, Mr.…uh, Sam."

"I'll see you around?" Trudy looked inquisitively at Sam.

"Three-thirty."

"Three-thirty it is. I'm going to walk down and see if Sadie needs anything. See you all later."

When she rolled up in the Razor at three-thirty, she could see Danny was beaten and tired, but he still wanted to take a swim with her. Cooling off might just be the ticket. It was about a ten-minute drive across the fields and down the lane to "their" cabin. Between the hum of the motor, the whine of the tires, the sway of the Razor, and how he was tucked into the bucket seat with the music on the radio, he was deep and fast asleep when she turned off the motor next to the lake.

The dusty rooster tail from the lane had all but disappeared by the time she had the blanket out. She had laid her clothes on the corner for handy access and gently shook Danny to wake him. When he opened his eyes and became human again, he started to smile widely as he looked at her heavenly, stark-naked body. His inner animal wanted to come alive. His cock had twitched somewhere in his sweat-bound jeans, but his mind just could not connect—he was truly tired. She coaxed him willingly out of the seat and onto the blanket, undressing him fully. He had no objections to being naked, but he just wanted to lay there for a bit and rest. He promised to get moving in a minute or two, but for the moment, his sore muscles just wanted a break.

He relished the deep massage he was getting on his back and buns and felt that he would have trailed off to sleep again had Trudy not found banjo strings for muscles in his back and laid into them with her strong hands. She had him wincing a few times as she dug her fingers into his back.

"Damn, you got strong hands."

"Exercises brought to you by the Delta-Seal workout."

"What is that?"

She explained it to him. "Every time either Isaac or Tom came home, the class was in session, and movements and exercises were expected to be completed before they returned the next time they arrived. It really is great fun, and I have learned some good moves.

"Not really a structured Taekwondo or Karate of any sort per se, but a practical guide and motions for in-the-field type assault. Both are basically my bigger brothers, and both are combat hand-to-hand instructors. They have assured me that if I'm ever behind enemy lines, I'd do just fine. Tom has said I'm better than half of his troopers with twice the training time and that I'm a competent and potentially deadly learner. In short, I'm apparently a badass."

"I believe it," Danny joked.

"Turn over and let me see that chest. I told you today was going to be hard work."

Danny obliged her by struggling to roll over. She brought out some groans when she dug deep into the muscle. When she tailed off the deep course of massage and started a gentler and more smoothing caress, she saw his eyes flicker and literally saw his eyeballs roll back into his head. He was fast asleep once more.

She looked down at his manhood and smiled. Naturally dressed left, she noticed with inner delight. She gently cupped his balls and began to caress them in her palm. There clearly was a connection and correlation between his balls to his flaccid penis because she could directly see the cause and effect she was inducing on her sleeping boy toy.

There was a stirring that was all of its own accord, an inflation that became more prevalent every time his heartbeat. She could feel his pulse in her hand and see the blood flow fill his now half-standing cock. When she gently caressed the head of his member, the whole apparatus flinched and twitched away from her as if it were trying to escape her touch.

Danny slept on; it looked as if he were deeper still into sub-consciousness. When she had him full-on hard, she stopped, admiring her work. It was a splendid cock that had a life of its own, pulsing as if it commanded the heart. The bulbous head was beautiful, and the blue and red veins running down the length of his shaft were gorgeous. She could almost remember how each contour felt inside her. This only served to hitch and change her every breath.

Trudy leaned forward and very carefully and gently sucked the head of his dick into her mouth, going as far as she could down on him and back up. Her tongue swirled around the edge of his helmet, which was starting to turn a marvelous color of light purple. Danny began to moan lightly in his sleep and slightly writhed, slightly arching occasionally. She could tell she was the catalyst for fueling a great dream for him.

She lifted her head free from his cock and gently, ever so carefully, straddled him. She was wet just from undressing him—now, partly from sucking him and partly from desire—she was drenched, slick, and wanting. She lined up carefully over his iron rod and sat slowly down onto him, deeply. In his sleep, he let out a long and slow, barely audible, and satisfying moan.

She was sitting fully down on his shaft and was making sure not to put too much pressure from body weight on him. It was just a wonderful tango of pulsing, hard dick and clenching, hot, wet vagina that drove her excitement. She moved with clock-like precision—relaxed on her way down and clenching on her way up. The motion she was implementing was like an exquisite hand jacking him off, except this hand came with a searing body heat and hot, slick, full-contact, all-encompassing personal meat locker.

She moved up and down slowly for about thirty seconds from one stroke until its completion. She was keeping her body aligned to not put any weight on him yet, feeling his every inch and pulse push against her inner walls. She was wet and flowing heavily with every stroke as she had trouble maintaining her resolve. She had used a vibrator before, but this one had a pulse and marvelous veins that sent glorious sensations through her spine to her very being each time her labia tried to smooth them down.

Trudy had an elated smile when she felt him enlarge as she was still moving at an iceberg-slow speed up and down. She could feel his cock gaining girth—Danny was close to coming but still dead asleep. She had begun to come herself as her twat started to convulse, almost sucking his shaft with rhythmic fluttering, coaxing his head to explode deep in her of its own volition. She had just bottomed out, juices flowing, pelvic muscles flinching and tightening around his shaft when his head was involuntarily swelling up. She reached back and took his balls in her hand.

Two things happened simultaneously—his balls tightened up, and he came. When he shot his load in her, she felt it like no other time because of the slow, determined movement, and he sat bolt upright while moaning out a grunt. When he collided with her breasts and felt her hard nipples on his cheek and face, he woke from a most incredible dream that turned out to be real. With his head now shoved between mountains of warmth, he half hugged her, half pulled her down, and finished his come through the spurts and pulses.

Six glorious and ball-draining spasms later, he was able to sit back on his elbows and enjoy the wondrous view in front of him, riding out the most satisfying and complete come in the most wonderful way he could think to experience it. Trudy just smiled at him.

She feigned her best innocence. "I'm sorry I woke you, but you were out so deep and looked so good. I just couldn't help myself from playing, and your body all but begged me to continue. I really hope you had a good nap, though."

"Sweet Jesus, Trudy, you have my permission to wake me like that anytime. I had the most amazing, vivid dream, only to wake up and see that it was all real. That was incredible."

"So… I did OK then?" she asked sheepishly, all innocent-like.

"You're amazing, Trudy. Just amazing."

"So, you think you can make it to the water this time without falling asleep?"

"Well, I don't know. If this is the punishment I get, if I don't, I might not want to."

"I could have just as easily painted your finger and toenails if you want?"

"No, no…nooo, I think I can make it to the water."

They walked hand in hand, both naked, down into the water a little more than waist deep. Turning around to face the cabin, they stood there, and then they both just fell backward into the lake.

Skinny-dipping never felt so great—the hot and humid day retreating, a slight warming breeze under blue skies, water flowing freely around their body parts, feeling glorious. They soaked for half an hour, which consisted of hugging and kissing each other. It was soothing and welcoming.

Trudy dropped Danny at his truck, but not before a deep, long, and passionate embrace. He jumped in the truck, started it, and drove away as Trudy was taking the Razor to the barn.

It turned out that Danny was indeed a good worker. He learned quickly, was able-bodied, and was not afraid to get his hands dirty. Bill had reserved judgment until the end of the week, at which time he expressed his findings.

"Trudy, your boyfriend—"

"He's just a good friend, Dad."

"Your boyfriend is a solid young man. I've seen him work his ass off when I was around. I thought some of that was to impress Sam and me, but later in the week, when we gave him some crap jobs to see how he performed, well, he seems like he is a better worker than most." He joked, "I will allow you to keep him around. We always can use a good hand."

"Well, soon enough, you can only use him on the weekends. School starts in two weeks. This summer has flown by."

"All joking aside, he is a good worker. I would hire him any time. You can let him know I said that—without letting him know I said that—can't you?" He smiled at her.

"I will let him know somehow," she replied with exasperated undertones.

"Are you two going out tonight?"

"Yes, Dad, we are. We don't know if it's dinner and a movie or just driving around. I heard there is a party on the Johnsons' back forty, but we're not sure what we're doing yet."

"He won't be paid until next week, so here, take this." He handed Trudy two hundred dollars. "We'll call that a headhunter's fee—you can take him out. Will that cover dinner and a movie these days?"

"Dad, you know it will, but I thank you just the same. And to think I was going to ask Sam to adopt me. Good thing you turned out so cool." She followed by giving her dad a hard bear hug. "Thank you, Daddy."

Bill loved it when she called him "Daddy." It usually came when he went over and above, or found the correct "Dad" groove, or in general, noticed her excelling at anything. It was all good as long as he heard the words.

Chapter 15 - Timing Matters

Sunday arrived with a blink. Danny pulled up to the guest house porch and got out of his truck at twelve o'clock straight up. He was excited to see Trudy coming out the door to meet him. He was confused for a spell when she said nothing and just pointed to the office barn. He started toward her.

"Hey, Trudy, I hope I'm not late."

Trudy did not even acknowledge him—just took two steps sideways, turned, and extended her arm once again, pointing toward the office. He finally got it and realized she really meant twelve-thirty to eat, but he could come early and visit with the guys if he wanted. Without a word, he turned around, got back in the truck, and headed to the office. He parked out front and entered.

"Man, she was serious about not showing up until twelve-thirty, wasn't she?"

Bill and Sam replied in unison, "You didn't go over there, did you?"

"I did, but Trudy wouldn't even talk to me. It was only for a minute. Why?"

Both men shook their heads in a form of disgust.

Sam piped up, "Thanks a lot, Danny. Have you no remorse?" He was half-joking, half-serious.

Danny was wide-eyed. "What did I do?"

"You got us all in a pickle now. I hope you like to dry."

"Wait, what? What just happened?"

"Oh, you'll see soon enough."

At about twelve twenty-five, the men started walking to the guest house, Danny trailing behind after retrieving a bouquet of flowers from his truck. They arrived at the porch at twelve thirty-two. Sam looked at his watch.

"We're good, I think… or do you want to wait?" Sam inquired.

Bill replied, "Let's give it a minute. We might get a pass since he's new, but I don't think we should push it."

Danny was looking at both grown men, trying to figure out why they were scared to go in too soon. Catching the phrase "he's new, we might get a pass," he realized it was all about him.

"What did I do?"

The men opened the door to the most wonderful smell in the world. Both women were already sitting and eating their plates of food.

Bill asked, "Trudy, Sadie, it smells wonderful. What's on the menu?"

Sadie replied, "Broiled pork chops, homemade cheesy potato au gratin, green beans, and corn. For dessert, homemade peach pie."

There were already three places set with tea waiting for them. As they started to find their seats, Sadie stood, looked right at the newcomer, and spoke.

"Danny, is it?"

"Yes, ma'am, I'm Danny Veach."

"Come here, and let's have a look at you."

Sadie met him halfway along the dining table and stopped. Danny, unsure what to do, just stood there.

"So, you are the one to catch my Trudy's eye." She eyed him up and down. "You'll do," she said, half-joking, half-approving. "Just remember, if you hurt her, I will find you. Just so you know."

"Yes, ma'am. I would never hurt Trudy."

"That is the right answer."

She continued, "Tell me, have you been working with Bill and Sam all week?"

"Yes, ma'am. One or the other, and sometimes both. Why?"

"And did you tell them you were coming here today at any time during the week?"

"Yes, ma'am, I did. I wanted to know if there was anything I could bring, but they said that you and Trudy took care of everything."

"Is that so?"

With those three little words, both men knew they were completely sunk. One was looking down at the floor, shaking his head, while the other was looking to the heavens with a wincing stare upwards. Both knew that Sadie had just put the blame squarely on their shoulders.

"I didn't feel like I could meet you for the first time and not bring you something, though. These are for you—Trudy mentioned you liked daisies."

"I do like daisies! They are beautiful. Thank you. You can call me Sadie."

She took the flowers, stole a hug from Danny, thanked him again, and took the flowers to the sink. She chopped off the last half-inch, put them in a vase, and returned with them to the table, giving them the center location of honor.

The boys were in various stages of eating or loading their plates. There was plenty to eat, but everyone saved room for dessert. The peach pie almost melted in their mouths. Sadie was unequaled in her pie-making skills—except for Trudy, who had often helped her make them and learned directly from the master.

"Trudy? How about we go find the swing?"

Laughing a bit, she replied, "Sounds good."

Both women got up to head out back, and Danny got up as well as if he were going to follow.

"Where do you think you're going?"

Danny stopped and looked at both men with a question in his eyes.

"We have food to put away and dishes to do by hand."

"Can't we just use the dishwasher?"

"We can't, but they can." Sam just let the statement hang in the air.

"I guess I'm missing something here. Why can't we just..." That's when he got it. "I arrived before twelve-thirty??!!"

Bill said, "Yup. And we let you do it. No one messes with girl time without paying the price. Like we said, I hope you like to dry."

The boys worked well together in a good team-like fashion and finished the cleanup in forty minutes flat. Both girls could have finished the same task in twenty, but they were still impressed when they met out back to report on their penance.

"Dad, I was going to go to Danny's and meet up with Dave to play some online games unless I need to do something here?"

"I don't need anything, so—" He looked at Danny. "Drive carefully."

"Yes, sir, I will."

Both he and Trudy joined up side by side as if to go.

"Sadie, that has got to be the best lunch I have had in a very long time." He briefly looked at Trudy. "Short of last Sunday, this makes me wish I was here for that one too. Thank you for having me out."

"It was nice to meet you, Danny. We will see you next week."

"Yes, ma'am, if you'll have me."

Trudy hugged Sadie, and Danny told Sam that he would see them tomorrow at seven. They turned and left as the three discussed Danny. It turned out that all three liked him for independent reasons.

They heard Danny's truck start and saw it make its way down the road, kicking up dust. Danny had called Dave and let him know he was heading home and would meet him there at his house.

Chapter 16 - Danny Revealed

When they arrived at the Veaches', Danny's mom was again getting ready to head out with the girls to do a little shopping, as was her ritual—her sanity check with her friends, she had said. She was almost ready when Dave arrived. Danny already had the TV on, and the game cued up, almost ready to go online. They had gotten an adult bean bag out for Trudy, and she had just settled in it on the floor in front of both boys, who were directly behind her.

Mrs. Veach told them that if they did not like the leftovers, then they were on their own for supper. She told everyone goodbye as her friends honked from the road to let her know they were there.

Ten minutes later, the boys were immersed in the game. Mrs. Veach had been correct when she said it was addictive even just to watch. Trudy had been engrossed in the action on the TV. The surround sound was booming all around them, and the stunning visuals splayed out across the screen were so incredibly vivid. She had not noticed Danny's avatar was not moving, as Dave's man was in an intense gun battle that he was winning quite skillfully.

Five minutes had passed before she realized Danny's man was still at a standstill on pause, so she turned around to ask him what was up.

When Trudy turned to look at Danny—being in the middle of the two boys in a bean bag on the floor and lower than the couch—she was looking directly at Dave's shorts and underwear on the ground beside his feet. Danny's face was over his lap, sucking on Dave's hardened root.

Seeing Danny down on his friend's dick caught her off guard for a moment. He was all the way down, deeper than she had ever had a dick in her mouth from a guy, even Danny. He was deep-throating Dave and was physically, enthusiastically enjoying himself in doing so.

She obviously had not noticed Dave removing his shorts and briefs and guessed he had just arched up to let Danny do that—all the while gaming. She certainly had not heard Danny's enthusiasm as he had been sucking him for a little while.

She watched Danny for a while as he pulled Dave's dick up and out of his mouth, only to catch a breath and guide it back in and down his neck. Dave was not as big as Danny and not quite as long either—close in both regards, but not quite.

Danny sucked Dave's hard cock for several strokes and would come to the top of his manhood, bobbing and orbiting around the head, rotating it in his mouth and tongue as he went. He adoringly sucked in Dave's manhood much like a person holding a cherry stem with the cherry dangling in front of their lips, sucking it in gently to get it completely in their mouth through the gentle force of suction—pulling it in with a ghost force almost, divine in its sensation.

It appeared to her that Danny was really sucking Dave well. Dave was clearly enjoying the attention his cock was receiving.

She also noticed that watching this action was getting her sticky, and sticky was quickly becoming wet. Her close-up voyeurism was turning her on immensely. Her nipples were suddenly sensitive inside her bra, and her panties were wet with desire—a wanting, a need.

Watching was getting her hot and starting to burn inside her brain with an increasingly uncontrollable desire. She looked up to see Dave, who was staring at her, almost evaluating her as if to gauge her reaction.

Dave and Trudy locked eyes for a moment, and then he smiled—both with his mouth and his eyes. Trudy smiled back. His eyes lazily rolled back as they closed, enjoying his fellatio with a total lack of concern for who could see them, occasionally now moaning his approval of Danny's efforts as a sign to Danny that she was watching.

She did not notice that the speakers had gone silent, nor that Dave's avatar was now paused too, nor did she care any longer. She did, however, notice when Danny went past his mouth and down his throat with the turgid man meat—Dave all but shuddered when he did.

She knew that she, too, wanted to learn how to deep-throat someone. She wanted to do this to Danny.

Danny knew at some point that Trudy would see him sucking his friend off—he had planned it, and Dave was game, so here they were.

Danny was getting lost in feeling Dave's glorious six inches or so sliding in and out of his mouth. When the inch and a half or so in diameter went into his throat, he had an indescribable amount of ecstasy washing over him.

His pleasure was now audible with every stroke. It was physically causing the twitching of his own shaft through his jeans. He had not expected to feel Trudy unzipping his pants from behind and beginning a struggle to remove his jeans, but when she dropped the jeans to the ground and went back for the underwear, he was so temporarily lost in his own pleasure that he didn't seem to care.

There he was, sucking his friend—sucking him deep, hard, and well. He was going balls deep with every face push-down, feeling the straining veins on the sides of Dave's shaft, tracing them as he went down and up with his tongue.

To top it off, Danny was now being grabbed by his 'girlfriend.' He was hard already, but she was making him harder with her every touch.

He continued to suck Dave with grace and smoothness—expertly—from the tip of the dick to his belly, with audible moans of satisfaction and desire mixed with hunger coming from both of the guys, one or the other bucking uncontrollably when the right combination of tongue location and depth was achieved.

Trudy knew Danny was truly sucking him well by the expression on Dave's face. Dave had been very nonchalant at first—gaming while being blown—but now she noticed that he was concentrating on how well Danny was engulfing his member, how wonderfully his tongue was circling the ridge of his head, and the glide of his tongue on him.

Danny's tongue almost cradled his undershaft at times, creating a sensation that really could not be adequately described, and when the head of his cock passed from mouth to throat, he arched backward a little uncontrollably, moaning in pleasure loudly.

Danny would let loose a "Hmm" and a groan of desire as he moved about the dick.

She had seen Danny's face when he was fighting to hold back a huge come—it was the same look that Dave was struggling with now.

Every slide into Danny's mouth made it harder to contain his resolve and composure.

He wanted to explode down Danny's throat, and he would eventually, but he was determined to hold it off as long as possible.

Danny, on the other hand, was sucking him so expertly that holding down that commitment was slowly becoming a losing battle.

Trudy had freed Danny's cock, held it firmly in her hand, and gently pulled forward on the shaft with great delight. In doing so, she felt and saw a huge boil of fluid pushed out, so she captured it along her finger, looking Dave in the eyes as she sucked her finger into her mouth, savoring Danny for Dave to see. This turned Dave on even more as he gasped for control.

Danny had felt Dave's manhood swell just a bit and knew the meat he was servicing would not last much longer. He was trying to make Dave explode. Dave was still fighting off his soon-to-be-exploding come as hard as he could. Danny sucked his root-like he was on a personal mission to drain him completely, lapping him in and stroking his face down Dave's length faster and faster with wanton abandon.

Trudy wondered how it would all take place, but she didn't have to wonder for long. Danny had pulled completely off Dave to catch a good breath, and as he went forward to take Dave in again, she saw firsthand the head of Dave's throbbing cock swell, convulse, and pulse.

Dave could only manage a "Uurrhhggh" as his first shot of spunk landed on Danny's cheek, lips, and face in a long, singular spasm.

In the middle of Dave's second uncontrollable pulse, Danny had the head of his dick in his mouth just in time for his cheeks to gently push outward as if a pressure hose was ballooning his mouth. Danny knew it was going to be a heavy load and managed to eagerly swallow while pushing forward, all the while giving off tones of satisfaction as Dave was coming into his mouth.

Danny got the shaft well down his throat for the subsequent pulses and, between pulses, jerked up and down by an inch or so, moving the shaft in his throat—sending Dave off to even more in-depth sensational heights between spurts.

There were many pulses that Dave had produced and, in doing so, had a sort of slamming against Danny's face many times, arching into Danny's lips, trying to steal just one more millimeter in depth. They were both lost in each other.

Trudy was still slowly pumping Danny's man muscle with her hand. Danny was moaning with delight, a hum of pleasure—a humming of this wonderful engulfment. She realized that the act of Dave coming in his mouth and down his neck was turning Danny inside out with pleasure.

It was only when Trudy abandoned her hand job and lay sideways on the couch that Danny once again realized she was even there. She sucked his cock into her mouth sideways, with much pre-cum leakage on the first draw down his dick.

His leakage might have been mistaken for a come due to the volume, as sucking Dave clearly was creating a pre-cum flood. It was thin and sweet, not milky thick, but Trudy eagerly stole it just the same.

When Danny pushed her away, she was confused at first but soon understood without words being spoken.

Dave had left the couch, and Danny was now on his back, lying across the overstuffed leatherette arm backward—his cock pointing skyward, begging for attention, and his mouth upside down, now open, awaiting Dave to take his spot.

Dave stepped up to the couch, aligned his meat with Danny's mouth, and slowly, fully inserted his cock into Danny's mouth and down his neck. Danny moaned in wanting delight when Dave was fully in him.

He pulled out slowly and entered the same way once again. Danny was getting harder still with every stroke from Dave. This went on for several strokes as Trudy watched the play-by-play, getting more turned on as she went.

Dave was fucking Danny's mouth and face.

Danny was purring and humming with excited delight, his audible, low-toned humming clearly rocking Dave's world.

Trudy's personal scene-to-man-on-man porn unfolded in front of her. As it progressed, it was getting her even more deliciously lubricated.

Trudy was shedding clothes as she watched the action. Now naked, her crotch was all but dripping wet, bare, and longing among two writhing men she was getting ready to join in on the fun.

Dave was now stroking fully and frequently down Danny's neck in smooth, complete tip-to-nut motion.

Danny was being face-fucked in the literal sense and was moaning in ecstasy while Dave was stroking.

Her "boyfriend" really was into this beautiful dick.

It only got better when she took Danny into her hot, wanting mouth. She had been watching Danny and started to mimic his earlier actions.

Her saliva was flowing, occasionally dripping with a full mouth. She felt she just had to try it.

She sucked her way down Danny's dick to the back of her throat, and just as Danny had, she drew a deep breath around the mouthful of dick and forced herself to push forward, deeper, fully taking him in her neck.

She started to gag at first, pulled up to gain her composure, then pushed herself over him again.

She now understood that this was a game-changer because as the head of Danny's cock started its journey down her throat—even with Dave fully in Danny's own mouth—Danny still arched and moaned with unparalleled delight.

His satisfaction was turning her on and turning her inside out.

In his arching and moaning, she got it. She understood.

And what's more, it was now captivating her with strands of grandeur and elation.

The deeper she went, the more she wanted to go.

She loved the feeling of being full in her neck. She loved knowing her every twitch and move was sending him further and further over the edge.

Trudy was loving Danny's cock deep inside her and down her throat.

She wanted to milk him orally.

And if it were possible, she was going to suck him inside out.

Trudy started sucking him like she had never sucked him before—up to the head, teasing and torturing it with her tongue, then moving on to his full length.

First, she circled the glans.

She traced a vein down or cradled the underside of his shaft with her hot tongue, slowly sliding her tongue up the whole width of him, causing him to shake minutely with uncontrollable shudders.

She continued her glorious torture, and randomly, she would push his shaft fully down her neck until she bottomed out and kissed his belly.

She picked up speed and more personal satisfaction and delight as she went.

She was able to understand the gag, breathe around it, and, best of all, send him arching skyward into her mouth with her every wanting consumption.

She was now full-on face fucking him with her own face, and he was losing control. Danny was sucking Dave; Dave's every stroke, mixed with every thrust of Trudy's face, was separating Danny's mind and body. Just as Danny was sure that there would be two separate entities lost and looking for the one corporal place that they were supposed to be in the mystical ether together, the two distant factions reversed course and came barreling back together at light speed reuniting his burning mind and now epically euphoric body. His balls massively imploded, releasing a torrent of his juice down Trudy's neck with his almost mind-numbing thunderous explosion. He bucked wildly and moaned with even greater ecstasy to the two connected by his body.

Dave was quickly approaching a come, and Trudy was already coming in a wild self-induced gratification. Trudy never realized that her satisfaction through satisfying someone else could give her an orgasm in and of itself. She felt herself explode more and more with Danny's every jolt of his nuts pushing through the man-goo that was shooting down her neck. Trudy pulled ever so slightly up and down just as Danny had for Dave. She pulled up to catch him in her mouth; he tasted wonderful, and she wanted more.

Danny pulled Dave up and out and pulled his cock out of Trudy, the last of his offering stolen as he pulled his still-hard cock from her lips. She smiled at him and leaned forward as if to kiss him but turned to the side just a bit and licked a large dollop of come off Danny's cheek and shared it with him through a deep kiss. Danny wasted no time as he moved from the arm of the couch and directed Trudy to the seating surface on her back, angled off the couch with one leg on the couch and half her ass and the other leg off it. He reached under her thighs and hauled himself between her slit, she was dripping and creamy. When he sucked her clit in, she had a micro-orgasm almost immediately; she knew when he dove deep between her legs that there was another more pertinent, more profound come to be coaxed out.

Dave watched her pussy getting eaten for a bit and really enjoyed his view, her body tight and beckoning; his cock was coming back to life from a brief under-inflation. Danny was, as Dave noted, expertly and aggressively eating her out; it was hot to watch. Danny was lapping her pussy like a thirsty dog at a water trough, long deep laps, and Trudy was almost bucking upward with every micro fight he had with her clitoris at odd intervals, they were both enjoying each other immensely. Danny was licking and lapping, delving as deeply as his tongue would allow, and Trudy was arching into his face with his every tongue thrust; she realized she had Dave's glory in her hand. He was standing hard and wanting. Trudy did not want to leave him lonely, so she pulled him alongside Danny, who stopped to watch as Dave's cock went into her mouth slowly and fully. Danny went back to sucking her clit. Her clitoris was straining now, and his every coaxing brought her to new heights. Her fleshy thumb was bright red and swollen from the exquisite abuse. Every little touch, every slight breeze from a breath, set it to higher plateaus.

Trudy suddenly felt the need, or maybe it was a want; at this point, she did not care, but she did, however, take charge and direct what she felt ought to be happening. She gently stiff-armed Danny off her crotch and pulled Dave out of her mouth yet held on firmly to his straining manhood. Trudy slid off the couch and guided Dave to a sitting position against the arm of the couch with a wonderful view of the room. Trudy got on her hands and knees, looking Dave straight in the eyes. She smiled at him as she centered up her mouth and wrapped her lips on the bulbous head and sucked her way down deeply, and began to suck Dave methodically and fully. He was not as big as Danny, but she did not care; it was a beautiful dick, and it went down her throat much the same, with the same enthusiasm. She loved his vein structure, the ridges of his shaft, and the hat on its head. Dave was being consumed and sucked in the most pleasing way; he could watch her every move, and he concluded that her moves were incredible.

She had not paid attention to Danny, she figured he would get the hint and figure out where she wanted him, ass up and soaking wet, waiting for him to get the drift, and he did. There she was, bobbing and sucking on Dave when suddenly she no longer had to bob. His first entry almost smashed her face into Dave's now-straining cock. From then on, Danny's thrusts in her were propelling her forward with his every stroke. Stroke after stroke, she was thrust forward and down on Dave's cock; Danny controlled the rhythm for all of them. All three of them were in tune with this orgasmic overture. She felt Dave gaining in size and realized he was going to come soon, hopefully with a big load, as she wanted more than a mouthful, nothing her neck could not manage. She also felt Danny swell directly after Dave did. Trudy was regulating her pelvic wet clench with her suction via her kugels edging Danny on, using her mouth, neck, and pussy to bring them both as close to simultaneously releasing an orgasmic cacophony of mingled sex juices as one entity; she was almost spot on. Danny was the first to come, and when he did, Trudy's core felt his swell and release coupled with the last desperate thrust that touched something just perfectly deep inside her, and she orgasmed both physically and audibly, the vibration of her audible moaning mouth tones sent Dave over the edge, and he came hard. Dave's prick had been straining in her mouth, balls flooding in pulsing thrust-laden hip tilts. A glorious train wreck was set in motion.

She let Dave get two spasms out and pulled up enough for him to finish in her mouth. His love juices were just as sweet as Danny's; she orgasmed again, just savoring it all. She loved it and could tell there were absolutely no complaints from the two lovers connected through her as she swallowed and licked what she had missed from her lips.

When they both had arched forward simultaneously, she had been almost crushed between two hard cocks, but she did not care as this was the catalyst that set loose a primal and brutal orgasm within herself; it just got better from there. Trudy rocked uncontrollably for a while, unknowingly pleasing both men. Dave was being consumed on a plane that would not easily be recreated, all the while she treated Danny's hard cock with a vaginal walled straining orgasmic spasm. The coat of hot, slick meat wrapped around his spent cock pulsing on his shaft uncontrollably felt beyond amazing. Danny almost yelped from a type of sensitivity overdrive, his body convulsing as the head of his cock sparred with her inner regions that just kept jolting around inside in waves for what seemed like a decade. They all pulled free from each other and laid as one body in a sweaty, sticky heap on the couch, well satisfied and spent for their collective worth.

Dave was the first to move as he scooted out from under Trudy. She and Danny could hear him start to shower and bathe. When he was finished, he walked out of the bathroom, mostly dry, still dick firm. He picked up his clothes, now strewn about, dressed, bent down, kissed Danny on the forehead, and said, "I'm going to go. Call me later if you need to."

He looked at Trudy. "I'm glad we finally had some time to be together. Maybe we can do this again sometime soon?"

Dave smiled at her, turned, and left, leaving Trudy and Danny both still spent in a partial heap on the couch.

She looked at Danny. "Call if you need?" She had a long pause. "Dave is the number six you didn't want to talk about."

"Yes."

"If that is the case, number five—Amanda? She found out about you two?"

"Actually, Dave was number five, and Amanda number six. She had come over for 'game night,' just like you did, and watched most of what you saw, but she did not have any desire to join in. Not that it was expected, but she took it all in and gave it an honest review. She said she was not ready to share me like this. She knew that I couldn't give the one-on-one commitment that she wanted. Obviously, she was not equipped with what I needed from time to time.

"We are still good friends, and occasionally, we talk—but just as friends. I cared about her and still care about her, just as I care about you. I don't want to hide from the ones I want to share my world with. Just the same, I am not out advertising either because people can be serious assholes. She promised to hold my confidence close to her heart.

"In all actuality, I think you would like each other, given what I know of you two."

Trudy acknowledged, "I do know her as well. We are friends. Now I know why she has asked about you a couple of times in passing. I told her we're just friends, but I thought you were doing well. She was asking about something else. This kind of changes things a bit."

"She is genuinely a nice person, but this was more than she was ready for at the time.

"This is me, Trudy. All of me. It is who I am, and as much as I care about you, and the deeper my feelings become, I feel like you need to know—there is a place in me that, on occasion, wants a cock in my mouth, that wants to taste the flood of come, and wants to feel things that a woman can't totally give me.

"I don't want to hide it from you, just as I didn't want to hide it from Amanda. I don't want to lie to the people in my life that matter to me. I would rather risk a friendship and lose you by telling you the truth and trust my secret is safe with you rather than deceive you by omission or hiding the truth.

"I used to feel all twisted inside and had a tough time understanding it myself. Now, I'm finally good with myself, even though, at times, I still struggle with pieces of it. Believe me when I say I know it's very confusing.

I still struggle with a few aspects of it myself, so if you can't get past this for any reason, if you must distance yourself, I will understand.

"All I'll ask is that you hold to 'What is said at the lake, stays at the lake,' so to speak. No one except Amanda and now you know at our school. Dave has his secret at his school, so that part works out well for both of us.

"I didn't want to get so far in a relationship with you that when you found out, you would feel like I lied to you. That's the last thing I ever want to do. My thinking was that by showing you this side of me earlier, it would be easier to try and save feelings if it all goes bad instead of later when you might be more deeply committed and get hurt deeply.

"Does that make any sense? I hope I'm making some sense here. I really want to know what you think about it, even if you're pissed or angry with me."

"I'm not pissed, and I don't think I'm angry, but I might need a minute to articulate what it is that I feel.

"How did you meet Dave, anyway? And how long have you known you are bisexual? How did you two come about?"

"I met Dave at a mutual friend's pool party cookout. I was in the pool, and so was he. It wasn't some bullshit, romantic, across-the-way, we-locked-eyes kind of thing. He was in the pool, backed up against the corner, watching everyone splash around.

"I didn't even know he was there. In fact, my back was to him as I backed up to the pool's edge. My hand palmed his junk for a long second before I realized there was someone behind me."

I turned and was like, "Shit, man, I'm sorry."

He halfheartedly said, "It felt good. How was it for you?"

I said, "I'm guessing the girls like your size," kind of as a joke, kind of to defray things, but he said, "Why? Don't the girls like yours?"

He reached forward, grabbed my balls and dick, and held them for a very long second—long enough to feel me start to get hard. I liked his touch, and it confused me a bit. He said, "Imagine how that would feel in my mouth."

Can you imagine me tongue-tied? There I was, getting harder by the second and at a total loss for words.

He reached forward again, but this time, there was no doubt. When he grabbed my hard shaft, he held it long enough for me to feel the heat from his hand and get even harder.

He said, "I think I would like to feel you in my mouth."

I was starting to freak out. I mean, we were in the corner, talking low, and no one could see. He grabbed my hand and put it on his hard cock. Freaking out, trying to make sure no one was seeing us, I just pulled away and spent the next twenty minutes well under the water.

I noticed it took some time before he got out as well. I left shortly after I was able to get out of the water, but afterward, I got a call from him that night. He got my number from our friend at the party.

He said that he was sorry if he had made me uncomfortable but couldn't resist saying what he said because he had always had a weird fantasy about another guy. He asked if I would please keep this to myself, as he had never done this before and wouldn't get the nerve to do it again. No one knew his desire except, obviously, me.

I told him that his secret was safe. I only knew a few people from his school, and I didn't see them that often, but I promised I would make sure I steered clear of this subject in general if I was around them. He thanked me profusely—I could hear a sort of controlled panic in his voice.

Two days later, I called him back.

He said, "If you're calling to give me a hard time, I would appreciate it if you lost my number."

I told him that I was calling to give him a hard time. "In fact, I want to feel the hardness that I wanted to give you in my mouth."

I just blurted it out because I didn't want to overthink it. He thought I was joking at first, but I assured him I was not.

When we met up at my house because Mom was shopping, I conjured up every blowjob I had ever received and compiled the best things list in my mind. Then, I proceeded to give him the best of what I got from all the girls who had blown me.

He watched me, partly in disbelief, I think. I don't think he had expected to come so hard. I really threw myself into it and almost pulled a Bitzman moment when my mouth got full of him. I just swallowed, and I was delighted by the whole thing.

He went down on me, and I watched. He said he mimicked me the best he could. I had no complaints. When I came, I came hard, but he swallowed my every drop.

I'm his first guy, and he is mine.

He likes girls too, but when one or the other of us is in the mood—the mood best described as "only a dick would do"—well, it's mutually fantastic. We keep it to ourselves and have an agreement that, should either of us want to sample another dick, they must let the other be aware for safety reasons.

So far, for me, it's his dick only. I think his dick itself is perfect for me. I love him as a person, but I'm not in love with him. There are times, though, that I love his cock—it's almost a cock-worship thing.

This is why I said I don't want to be strictly a boyfriend-girlfriend thing, but I do want to keep my circle small. I want you in that circle, so if you have any questions, I'm an open book.

If you decide to go and want me to leave you alone, I will accept that too. I wouldn't like it, but I would leave you alone. I really would understand because I've been here before, and I have had time to think it through instead of having it sprung on me like I did to you.

However you want this to go, I will respect and follow your lead."

"Well, it did catch me off guard to turn around and see you deep-throating him. Jesus, you were all the way down. I can see you are passionate about it.

"You do know that girls have the internet as well, don't you? We also surf porn for many reasons. I may have watched one guy or two suck off another guy—just while passing through some sites that aren't exactly mainstream.

"I may have watched and even touched myself while doing so. I'm not saying I did—I just may have. It may have turned me on watching you suck Dave. I loved the way you were driving him wild with your mouth.

"It may have inspired me to deep-throat you. That may have been the very first time I've ever deep-throated a guy. I might have loved it immensely."

She feigned innocence through her teasing.

"Danny, it did turn me on, but I don't think I want to do this all the time—although I thought Dave was cool about helping you out with me. I almost wanted to fuck him too, but your tongue had me so captivated, and, as it turns out, he was a bit too busy anyway.

"I hope you didn't mind that I was sucking him. I mean, I wasn't sure what you would think of me, but I was caught up in the moment and really was enjoying everything.

"Soo… there.

"Did watching you suck Dave catch me off guard? Yes. Was I able to get past it? Yes. Did it turn me on? Definitely!

"It inspired a thought or two that I may want to explore in the future— some of them might involve Dave if he is willing.

"There are a couple of combinations that I think would be best explored while fishing in the back cabin.

"You think Dave likes to fish?"

She continued with a halfhearted laugh.

"As for your secret, it is safe with me, and it always will be. I promise. And soon, I want to share something with you—a secret that only a few very select people know—and you will be one of them. I will, however, be calling you my boyfriend because, technically, you are a boy and a friend," Trudy lightly joked. "But if you think you are going to tie me down for a long-distance relationship, you're wrong. I'm not a one-guy girl, and it's all your fault."

"You give a girl an orgasm like you have given me, and you expect me to wait for months at a time for some dick? It is simply not happening. So you're gonna have to get over yourself because I'll be dating other guys."

"So, you are good with this as long as I'm not too needy?" he asked lightheartedly with a smile. "Seriously though, are there any questions you want answered? I mean, you can ask me anytime, but right now—if you have a concern?"

"In fact, I do have a question you can answer for me." Trudy mustered the most serious face she could. "Are you washing my back first, or am I washing yours?"

She got up with a smile and headed to the bathroom for a shower.

Following her, he said, "I can't believe that was the first time you ever deep-throated. It was fantastic—and bonus—you didn't puke on me."

They both laughed at the joke.

"I think Dave would like to be involved in a threesome occasionally. We get together on Sunday evenings for game night. Occasionally, we hit pause, so thinking we do this all the time would be a misunderstanding—just so you know.

"You think you could show me that deep-throat thing again?" he inquired, earning her stink-eye look and a smile back.

"Shut up and get into the shower." She reared back and smacked his bare ass.

Getting in the shower and clearly pleased with her ass slap, he quipped, "Promises, promises."

They showered, and afterward, Danny took her home, walked her to the porch, and gave her a spectacular kiss goodbye.

Chapter 17 - The Beginning of an Empire

Trudy had been walking on a virtual high for quite some time—four and a half million dollars in the bank with royalties yet to come, a boy she liked who was not full of bullshit and knew how to deliver mind-bending orgasms. Things were going great at work, and the farm was helping deliver unseen pleasures. School was about to resume, and she was not worried about a thing. And to top it off, she was about to get her license to drive…legally.

While the deal for the face-altering app was in motion, Trudy was already thinking ahead to what was next. She had halfheartedly dreamed about getaway weekends before coming into such luck and thought if she owned a hotel, she could get away any time she pleased. She began to peruse business opportunities. She had already invested in no less than twenty new app startups in less than a year of royalties when a simple ad caught her eye.

A hotel chain was in bankruptcy and was trying to liquidate. However, it was obvious that there were serious upkeep issues with several of the buildings inside the sale—all of them. She was not sure how to go about estimating the refurbishing costs or whether the operating income would be sustainable. After all, they were going bankrupt. It occurred to her that she had potential resources she might be able to rely on if she found the right person. She started a search within the business community apps, looking for a retired hotel owner, manager, or controller to use as a consultant.

She had stumbled across Terry Wise and his bio. He had retired a year ago. At one point, he had owned a small chain of hotels that were bought by a larger chain. They had kept him on as an operational manager and liaison to make the transition from his chain to theirs as seamless as possible. After three years, he had slowly phased himself out, and both chains were thriving well. Trudy thought it was a perfect combination to assess whether the conditions were salvageable and if the return was favorable.

She called him on the phone, introduced herself, and explained why she was calling. Not giving her age and knowing that she sounded young, she made it clear that even though she was young, she was serious. She explained that an investment had really come through for her, and she wanted to have her money work for her and her future. Trudy asked him to name a price for assessing the whole setup. She explained that she knew it would take some time and some travel, but she was committed to financing anything he needed to properly go through the properties.

Terry had said that she had called him at a perfect time. He had really liked the idea of retiring and being able to see his grandchildren more often, but school was starting again, and he was frankly getting bored in retirement. Working was in his grain, and it wouldn't leave him alone for more than a short stretch of time. They agreed to a price for his time, which was reasonable. She arranged for a credit card from TJC that would cover all travel and expenses. She arranged for Terry to have a complete look at the defunct chain's books and access to all the sites. Terry felt that he could give a proper assessment in about three weeks.

True to his word, three weeks later, he was ready to send Trudy an assessment report but wanted to talk to her first in person if possible. She had already gotten her license, and her Cherokee was running like a diamond, so she agreed to meet him in Evansville near the site of one of the offerings. They were to meet at the coffeehouse nearest the airport.

When she arrived, she could easily pick him out because it was the middle of the day on a Saturday. It was not a premium time for the older set to be hanging out. She introduced herself to Terry, who was taken aback as she looked noticeably young. Trudy laughed it off, saying, "I get that all the time."

Terry started by saying, "I have reviewed the books extensively, visited all the sites, and I'm ready to give my recommendations, but I felt that a face-to-face conversation was warranted to best express my thoughts."

He told her that the books told a story of financial hardship on the surface, but when he dug into it, the main problem was ownership. The original owner of the chain had started with one hotel and built up the business to what it was now. When the original owner had it, it was easily turning a handsome profit. He knew how to run a business and clearly knew how to run the hotel business.

"He died three and a half years ago, leaving the business to his two children. Adults as they may be, they couldn't manage to get along. They had been advised to hire management but wouldn't. They wouldn't pay for necessary maintenance and improvements, and the business went into disarray in less than two years. Fighting over money, they let everything fall on its face and die."

Terry leaned forward. "Trudy, if I were ten to fifteen years younger, I would buy this business if I could, because I think that somewhere around seven hundred and fifty thousand dollars would restore them to their former glory and become very profitable within a year.

"It's a shame what those 'kids' have done to it. Their father left them an income that would have ensured they wouldn't have had to work a day in their lives if they didn't want to. If only they had made a few key decisions, which they were clearly unable to make.

"It sounded to me like they would entertain less than they are asking for if they could make the sale soon, as the hotels have been on the market for about a year. It is ripe and well worth the effort with the right leadership."

Trudy was listening intently. "I want to move on this quickly if I can line up the right people. Are you by chance thinking of coming out of retirement? I need someone with valuable experience and know-how."

"I'm not ready to come out of retirement, as tempting as it may be. I would, however, consider overseeing the renovations and maintenance to get things back to where they need to be. I can do that as a part-time consultant and still have a lot of my time freed up, if that is of interest to you. Furthermore, I have a name that I think you might want."

"I would be interested in you overseeing the hotels back into decent shape. I think you are uniquely qualified to oversee that aspect. If we can work that out, I am all for it. Who is it you think I may want to hear about?"

"His name is Fred Duersh. He was my operations manager before I sold my hotels and was exceptionally good at overseeing all aspects of operation. When I sold, they kept him in his same role. He doesn't have a lot of upward mobility in their structure, and Fred wants more—looking for more of a challenge. I don't think you will find a better, more capable person than him out there. I would be happy to make an introduction if you would like."

Things moved quickly from there. Trudy called Kate Taylor, who walked out of an internal meeting to answer her call. After Trudy had explained her last month to Kate, she was equally excited and impressed with her prowess. Trudy gave Kate complete freedom to barter on her behalf, expressing that she hoped they could do well given the report from Terry.

Kate had made a ridiculously low offer that, had it not been a legitimate business deal, might have been looked upon as stealing. She waited for the counteroffer to see where common ground would lie. When the counter came back, it was less than two hundred thousand higher than their offer. Two dickers back and forth, and a price was agreed upon that was ninety thousand more than the original offer. After a quick call to Trudy, both women felt it just might be the deal of the century. Two days later, a contract had been signed by both siblings, and the deal was in motion.

Trudy had become the owner of a hotel chain that she had decided to call Athena Inns. For about ten cents on the dollar, she had paid cash to secure the deal on what would become her hotels.

With Kate's help, TJC set up a line of credit for two million dollars through Wall Street banking, and Trudy set Terry loose with a mandate that he understood—to make Athena Inns high-end of midscale, low-end of upscale, with the proper amenities to support it. Given the freedom to act, he went about his work as if he owned the Inns and watched the money carefully in that regard. He would prove himself by coming in under budget and over quality. Fred would be just as pleased as Trudy, maybe more.

Trudy had met with Fred Duersh in his home in Louisville, Kentucky. He and his wife, Mary, invited her inside to meet their two children. They talked a bit about life and goals and where they wanted to be in five years. It was a good meeting for the family. One boy and one girl were both in grade school. Mary was a nurse, and Fred felt he was ready to be a CEO of a chain. It was clear that they gelled well with each other.

Mary commented, "You look noticeably young. What's your secret?"

Trudy promised, "I'll make my secrets known just as soon as I can."

Everyone laughed at that.

Fred suggested a quiet bistro to talk and get a handle on what was happening and the expectations before he would consider accepting the position. After Trudy had explained her beginnings, how the complete process unfolded, how Terry had faith in him, and that she had hired Terry to oversee renovations, all this gave Fred a good feeling.

They discussed pay, which would start at about twenty percent more than he was currently making. His benefits would be started as soon as he was able to get HR up and running and find insurance and investment advisory representation for 401(k)s.

Fred said, "I'm looking forward to collaborating with you, and I'm up to the challenges ahead, especially since Terry is teeing up the whole platform for me to begin with."

Trudy was excited and could tell Fred was looking forward to beginning.

"Fred, I want to offer you the position, but there are a few things we must do. First, there is a non-disclosure form about me, as I intend to be anonymous as far as the outward-facing part of the company goes. There are a few other things you need to know as well. If you want some time to read this," she laid out the forms, "but I assure you that it just demands your silence if you decide to reconsider working with me."

"I see no issues with that." He signed it without delay.

She began, "I want you to tell your wife my secret. I am sixteen years old—I just turned sixteen three months ago. I am trusting your expertise to run this enterprise, though I fund it. I will monitor things through your eyes, through the accountants' eyes, and through occasional visits. So, I want to know if anything I just told you is going to be a problem."

"Wow, that's quite an interesting bomb you just dropped, but it does explain a few things. Will I have free rein to act if a situation demands it? Or will you be intimately involved?"

"I will be intimately involved with high school, and yes, I would expect you to manage all aspects of the business, assuming that you will know if and when I need to be involved with a decision. Your bonus and pay are going to be tied to the success or failure of the hotels. The better I am doing, the better you will be doing, and vice versa. I see that as a wonderful check for you to maintain vigilance and act appropriately in that regard.

"The only thing is, as far as my business is concerned, my lawyer, you, your wife, and soon my best friend are the only people who are aware of how old the owner of the company is and what my finances are. People tend to discount teenagers, so I don't plan to tell anyone else unless I feel they need to know.

"So, what do you say? Are you hired?"

"Ms. Jax, I will be honored to be in your employ, and I think we can turn this into something big. I will make sure you never regret hiring me. As for your age, I don't think it should matter—you seem to be a very down-to-earth, confident, intelligent woman. I'm looking forward to working with you and getting started."

Two months later, the first Athena Inn came online. Much of the same staff had come back to nicer digs and a better working atmosphere than they could ever remember. They were up and running with a well-balanced price per room versus atmosphere and offerings.

The restaurants were a local draw at most locations within a month with their restaurant bars. Occupancy was better than half throughout the week and almost full on the weekends, ebbing and tiding with local events and seasonal changes. Clearly, the right combination had been dispatched.

Chapter 18 - Danny in the Fold

The next weekend, Danny had redeemed himself by following the no-interruption protocol and joined the guys at the office. They all migrated to Sadie's at the proper time. Lasagna, hot garlic bread, and German chocolate cake were delectable—they all ate well.

There were no issues this time, but almost all of them looked at Danny funny when he asked for his 'cake in a bowl with a touch of milk in it as well. They were ratcheting up the rhetoric to give him a hard time about being so weird—until, of course, Sadie followed suit.

She moved places to sit by Danny in solidarity and even mentioned how some people had such small minds and empty palates, not once mentioning a name. Bill and Sam grimaced at the playful fun it was intended to be. Danny and Sadie bonded over the proper way to eat this type of cake in particular. They even reveled in the stifled opinions just a bit.

Danny was careful to minimize his input, lest he get stuck cleaning the hog pens later.

Chapter 19 - All About Trudy

Trudy and Danny took the long way around the farm to avoid being seen by anyone. They made their way to their favorite cabin by the lake. Danny had brought along a duffel bag that occasionally clanked in a muted way when it was jostled. He had also brought a small ice-filled cooler but would not share what was in either one with Trudy. He promised that when and if she saw it, she would like it.

After they parked the truck on the side of the cabin, Trudy entered the door code, and the door swung free. Danny stopped her from entering, reached into his pocket, pulled out a black piece of cloth, and had her turn her back to him. When Trudy's head and body were turned away, he hugged her closely, then swung the cloth in front of her face and pulled it up to her eyes, blindfolding her.

Trudy stood in the doorway, blind, acclimating to the sudden darkness as Danny took her hand and carefully led her into the front room and across the floor to the kitchen. Trudy strained to use all her other senses to compensate for what she could not see. She was led to a dining room chair that she knew was solid and comparatively heavy—all wood and amazingly comfortable.

Danny instructed her, "Sit."

She obeyed. Still straining for audible information, she heard echoes from the bedroom, the duffel bag unzipping, and rustling noises, as if someone were digging through a drawer or a bag. When he returned, she felt cool metal touch her skin, followed by a series of clicks as a bracelet was fitted to her arm loosely. There was another series of clicks on her other arm. When she heard a combination of clicks and vibrations on the spindles of the chair, she realized she had just been handcuffed to it.

She feigned protest. "Danny, what is happening?"

Danny leaned in close, his breath warm against her ear, and whispered, "All you need to say is 'Danny, please stop,' and it ends. Or 'Danny, more, please,' and I will continue. Do you understand?"

Trudy acknowledged she did.

"That is good to know," he replied.

"What do you have in mind?"

"Shhh," was all she heard.

Danny stepped behind her and, from behind the chair, cupped both of her breasts with his hands, caressing her. She pushed forward into his hands.

All her subsequent questions were met with silence. Her ears strained harder to adjust, but she only heard him walk away, followed by little rustling noises in the distance—probably in the duffel bag.

A not-so-distant humming started, as if someone were busy with a task and enjoying themselves. She could tell the sounds were a bit away from her, down the short hall. It seemed like five minutes had passed before she sensed someone near her again.

This time, she heard him coming much earlier—her senses were coming alive.

Sensing motion to her left, she felt a tug on her left arm, heard a click, and felt the shackle release, dropping loosely by her side. She felt and heard a matching sensation on her right side.

Then, suddenly, she was pulled upward by the metal tethers attached to her wrists. She had no choice but to follow the urging.

As soon as she was standing, the shackle from her left wrist was captured and hauled behind her back as if she were a prisoner. Danny clasped both of her arms in his strong hands, pushing her forward and to the right, out of the dining area.

She could tell by the echoes becoming more refined and the new smells that they had just left the dining area.

She felt the light leave her skin and, by the air changes, suspected they had entered another room. She was almost certain it was the bedroom based on the direction of travel.

She had been correct in her assumption.

Danny guided her carefully down the hall and through the door without speaking or bumping into anything until she reached the edge of the bed. She stopped with the front of her thighs touching the mattress.

There was a fumbling and a ratcheting sound again from her left side— then from her right. She correctly guessed that it was the free ends of the cuffs being latched again, but this time to each other.

Her arms were still free, hanging straight down.

Trudy stood there passively, dutifully, questioningly waiting for the next movement.

Danny was happy to see that Trudy had indeed worn the outfit he requested for her to wear to Sunday lunch. He had made a point of requesting it, as he had bought her the complete ensemble as a gift for no reason at all.

It was a welcome gift, even if unexpected.

The clothes fit her well. They complimented her body and were all the right sizes—from the bra to the panties to the shirt and shorts. She felt good in them, partly because it was her style and partly because Danny had impeccable taste.

He was hoping she had followed his instructions to the letter and wore the bra and panties he had bought her as well, though it didn't really matter at this point because he wasn't going to stop his plan, which he had worked out days before—unless, of course, he was asked to stop.

Trudy felt hands on her hips, turning her one hundred and eighty degrees, facing her directly toward him. With her back now to the bed, she was gently pushed into a sitting position.

Her right arm was pulled to the side, causing her to lean slightly sideways on the bed. She heard a metal-on-metal clipping.

Danny crawled past her on the bed.

She could smell him—his pheromones were clear, and his light personal musk mesmerized her for a brief second as she inhaled him.

He advanced across her to the other side of the bed. He grabbed the other cuff, capturing her left arm, and hauled it with him.

She made a few adjustments with her body, scooting her butt as best she could to keep up. He had been just a little rough but had made no apologies for it. She almost liked being handled by him this way.

There was a realization that she had just traded a chair for a bed when she heard the same faint, singular snick that she had heard with her right side. Through her perceptions, the motions, and the sounds that the cuffs had made, they were acting as the binding ring, and she was now captured to something that moved quietly but had a metal clasp binding her down.

Trying to join her hands, she felt the cuffs snug up at about eight inches of movement in total, and in doing so, she found her unspoken belief to be correct.

She was busy trying to determine the extent of her movement capabilities while blinded when she felt a strap loop around her left ankle, pulling it outward. Another snick followed. She anticipated and received similar treatment with the other leg.

The resulting clasp sound left her able to partially bend her knees, but she was unable to join them together. She had been silently trussed to the corners of the bed, spread eagle, and fully dressed.

Her body was coming alive as a version of flight or fight began to well up in her. She felt her left sandal loosen and fall. Her right followed suit after being pulled free.

She had been thinking ahead of Danny, convinced that his plan was going to fall apart. She waited for him to catch on to how he had messed up. Her shirt, her pants, bra, and panties required individual freedom to be removed.

She may have been bound to the corners of the bed, but he was royally screwed if he had planned to have his way with her.

No sooner had the thought run through her mind than she heard an odd sound—sch sch sch sch.

A series of the sound repeated. Sch sch sch sch.

She had heard it before but was struggling to place it. She was running the sound through her mental comparisons when she felt her shirt lift. Sch.

Still mentally comparing known sounds, she felt the fabric of her shorts rustle, then another sch sch.

She heard something with some weight—possibly metal, maybe plastic—being placed on the dresser. She felt Danny sit on the bed at her mid-waist.

He lifted her shirt at her waist, and she heard it rip, followed by a rush of cool air against her exposed chest. That was when she placed the sound.

It had been scissors.

He had started a cut at all the key places of her outfit while she had been internally laughing at him for not thinking it through.

She now realized bigger issues lay ahead—he had, indeed, thought ahead, at least this much. She began to wonder how diabolical he could be.

Her anticipation grew. Her other senses went on high alert, making up for her faux pa. He ripped the fabric up to her neck. She felt him turn away, then a pull on both sides of her right leg, followed by the tearing rip as her leg was exposed.

Now she understood, at least this part—he was ripping her clothes off her.

By the time he reached for her left leg, her nipples had responded, and her crotch moistened.

This was turning her on immensely.

Danny had ripped her clothes to their reinforced banded hems, collectively at the neck and waist, where the tearing stopped. The bed swayed slightly when he left it. She heard him pick up the shears again and return wordlessly.

She felt her ragged clothing being pulled away gently as the sch sch sch sch cut what remained from her armholes and neckline.

She half flinched, half shivered when she felt him drag the cold steel down her belly to her panty line, followed by a few sch sch sch later, leaving her panties exposed.

This time, she arched up as the heartless metal made a slow, tantalizing trudge up her belly to her chest. She felt the blade turn sideways, coaxing its way under her bra straps.

Sch…

Followed by the chest strap, joining between her breasts.

Sch…

The other strap.

Sch…

Almost all her clothes were now in pieces.

Danny started high, working his way low, pulling material free from around her and under her.

Her shirt was in pieces. Her bra was crippled and totaled. Her shorts were pulled free, leaving only her panties to protect her.

The panties were lace—an off-pink thing that he really liked. Delicate and soft to the touch, sexy and beautifully crafted, crossed with an ivory sheen. He knew they were perfect for his endeavor and delighted in his purchase at the lingerie store in the mall.

Trudy had really liked them. They were a thing of art, and when she had tried them on for him, a few things had happened. He had gotten hard very quickly just watching her, and she had been delighted at how wonderful they made her feel. The panties, coupled with Danny's jeans-straining prick, got her wet. He had made her take them off quickly before she had to wash them. He made her promise not to wear them until he specifically requested them.

The promise had not stopped her, however, from making him stand with his hands flat against the wall, back straight, unmoving, as she drained his balls with her mouth.

She loved Danny's dick coming in her throat, and if she could not wear the panties that felt so good until he specifically asked, then she would take what she wanted on her terms in retaliation.

Danny had not complained about his punishment. It was these very panties defiantly blocking him now. Or so she thought.

His strong fingers dug into the leg hole, and he heaved them apart, ripping the panties free from her leg as she gasped uncontrollably. Trudy was no longer just moist.

With every sense she owned now on overdrive, straining to seek knowledge, to help get a handle on the situation—to no avail—she felt her pussy starting to flash wet in the growing excitement of it all.

Her crotch had flooded wet. Trudy nearly came when he treated the other leg hole with the same animalistic abuse. She was in a highly euphoric, delightful place when she felt his hands by her hips. She wanted him like never before. She anticipated the final release that would complete her disrobement. But it never came. Instead, he lifted her ass upward, pulling on the remaining waistband like a handle. Her hips arched upward for him. Her labia lips parted, and deep between her thighs, his face met her belly just long enough for him to feel her with his tongue.

It went deep within her.

She arched even more, involuntarily, as her now-standing baby's thumb met his lips. He sucked her clitoris into his mouth and scolded it heavily for moving without permission. She came.

And when she came, it was intense and violently hard. She had not realized that he had ripped the remnants of her panties free from around her waist until she came back to earth from her orbit.

Still panting.

Still flowing.

Still wanting.

Her senses were screaming, straining, tingling, begging for input when she felt him leave the bed and retrieve something from the dresser, she longed for a glimpse of the dresser and what all he had brought. She knew he had brought things to torment her, she wanted a clue to how to weather her gathering storm, none was given. She felt something spongy, almost stretchy on her belly. There was poking of sorts between two of his fingers. She felt him post his fingers around three inches apart, she could feel and sense something between his fingers was close but not quite there. Her muff convulsed when she felt the snap just below where her panty line had been. She knew instantly it was a rubber band by putting together the clues, and he had just snapped it on her belly.

It had a direct line of communication with her pussy walls and apparently it had requested the great flood. His fingers moved upward only fractionally, and she felt him pinch outward again, this time it was not as long to wait for the snap, nor was it as intense, his fingers found new ground. There was another pinch and a longer delay and a hard snap, she realized that the timing was quickly becoming the key to anticipatory waiting, she knew the longer the space between the pinch and release the harder the snap and the higher the band had been drawn. He again found new ground and repeated his torture leaving little red birds feet walking around her belly slowly moving northward.

Every snap had been varied, Danny knew what would be more tender than something else and snapped accordingly as he drove her inner self to the edge of sanity. When he reached the base of her tits one fractional move at a time, a new conversation began with her, one of great concern. The singular thought of that scorched feeling on her nipples was easily going to cause her to end it and tell him to stop. She would have no part of that! For now, she soldiered on. When Danny stretched his finger out on the side of her breast there was a greater awareness, a more tangible feeling, and she could tell the band was about an eighth of an inch wide. The next time she felt the release a new sensation greeted her, two snaps. He had pulled both sides of the band this time and this was a new sensation altogether, the first with a micro sting that landed lightning across her peaks, the second milliseconds later almost had a numbing effect …. almost, and it was spectacular.

He was now on the bottom side of her left breast and gave a small pop, he orbited sideways and higher and issued a double pop with greater magnitude. She was writhing with every pop, snap, and burn. It seemed as if Danny was enjoying her destruction, teasing it on and it was driving her mad. He lifted and moved to the other breast just as high up and issued a barn burner. It had to be a tall pull because it was a long gap, when the double snap landed it roused a deep single ignition in her body. Lift off was approaching and he had not even touched her clit beyond a small licking. He had not really touched her pussy at all yet, but she was burning just the same as if he did.

Who knew no sight would drive her beyond the ability to think and form actual words freely? The sensations Trudy was now experiencing were staining her mind with pleasure deeply, writing over the one simple thing she had to remember to end her suffering, all she had to conjure up vocally was Danny stop please. She knew he would comply.

He reached her nipple on the left, she could hear the bands strain between his fingers twanging in their stretch as both sides of the band now straddled her straining nub, he had planted his fingers down opposite sides of the slope with the bands directly over her nipple, holding the areola from lifting and flying away, now vulnerable and exposed. Her nipple was unprotected and alone pulsing with her every heartbeat, threatening to go nuclear if prodded in any way as a means of self-preservation. She felt his fingers of his other hand dig for both sides of the band and capture them, she wanted him to definitely stop, she definitely did not those bands brutalizing her peaks. She did not want him to lash out on her nipples, she was struggling to get the halting words out, tongue twisted she fought to articulate the protest by finding the right words, but it had been too late. She had not realized the amount of time there had been since he had captured the straps until the time she registered a need for a response.

Time halted, stopped dead, refused to register any increment of a chronological advancement in the midst of the aftermath. It was brutal, sadistic, perverse, excruciating, agonizingly wretched. She almost screamed out while load testing the restraints, hips bucking wildly writhing in captured pain, she heard someone scream DANNY MORE PLEASE! Her pussy exploded as she felt the walls deep within her pulsing, empty but full, untouched but slammed senseless. She had no idea who was yelling but it was clear that a request for a repeat had been made.

She had separated into a writhing mass in the middle of a torrent convulsion and an unfeeling bystander enjoying the show, blinded and vulnerable and yet still hearing someone begging for more please. Danny had already moved to her other nipple, she hadn't felt the bands lay over the tip of her nipple, she didn't feel his fingers spread and travel down the sides of her breast, therefore she couldn't tell his fingers were spread a bit further down the sides on this tit. It had in fact been much further down than he had been on the other side.

Had she felt his fingers dig for the straps she would have staged a protest, but she was in another world. She had just barely begun to come back to this reality. She shuttered uncontrollably when without any discernible warning, a singular snap directly on top of, and massively delivered to the tip of her nipple had been unleashed. It had morphed instantaneously as it became a mind-numbing crash that tore through her being. It was set off by a simple touch, an explosion on top of this unencumbered nipple up until then.

The impact inexplicably set her crotch on fire as the rubber band whipped through the air breaking through the sound barrier and collided with her nipple at approximately Mach three. The singular strap had landed its blow and what seemed to be an eternity later the other side of the band crashed home as well. She momentarily visualized a ticket counter with some random nondescript voice saying passport please. She had just checked herself into another dimension.

Arched up as high as she could go, trying but failing at pulling the bed posts inward in an attempt to crush the wood into relenting. In the middle of the whole explosion, her sugary walls released a most glorious treat, she came and came and came again bucking upward in waves. The fire in her nipples had not relented, both nipples had joined forces and combined with their collective complaints. As they both connected with each other for a check on unity, from down below, deep within her from a place that she did not know existed, an epic volcano was now flowing freely. The bed was drenched with her fluids alone, there was not a wet spot, there was a wet area, and it was getting wetter. The shadow of her lower hips and crotch was a dark patch extending outward past her sides.

In the middle of her heavenly escape from the wonderful pain, she had not noticed Danny had moved from the bed and was already returning, she had not heard the cooler open and close, she did not feel the little pink curvy start up. She did not know the selector had been ratcheted up to the highest intensity. When the curvy's mock suction cup wrapped around her entire clitoris and pulled at it in pulses, she came and flowed hard once again. She screamed out in ecstasy. Multiple orgasms on multiple orgasms had removed all contact with reality. That was when it happened.

It had occurred all at once and in one fluid motion, just as her hips flailed and pushed upward Danny inserted a piece of fire deep into her vagina, deep amid her confusion, and it just sat there doing its thing. It was on fire, screaming hot, her inner flesh screeching in protest, fighting through the wetness, and then it morphed. The glass dildo that had been submerged in ice all this time at thirty-two degrees had announced itself in a crossover mind altering flash. It stayed there unmoved for what seemed to be about an hour or more but thirty seconds after it was inserted, he pulled it free and plunged his seven full turgid hot inches deep and did exactly the same thing. He remained unmoving, absolutely still, glued in place, as his fire burned through the ice, and she bucked wildly yanking against the cuffs and straps coming violently with such insanely passionate rapture. He pulled out of her and her walls clenched shut in a beautiful longing protest. Fire and ice never had more meaning.

Trudy felt her legs being messed with and heard a snick twice and then her arms as well along with two more snicks, she still could not move on her own. Danny rolled her over to her stomach and started at her legs with two more snicks, her arms again followed suit. This time she had enough space to kneel but not much more than that. She could rock and move her hips forward although her legs were still captured. She could rock and move backward but this would leave her in doggy position, ass up as her arms would be pulled from the front, she was helplessly still trapped.

She felt Danny fiddling with her nipples, but she was still delightfully blind. Suddenly her left breast caught fire as a clamp of some sort was slowly tightened. Her right side joined the fight moments later. Danny must have used her protest hidden inside a wincing moan as a sign of acceptable tolerance because when he was through, her nipples throbbed fighting their captors in such a delectable way.

He pushed her upper body to the bed leaving her pussy sky up and accessible, an access he would soon use. She heard Danny back at the dresser and felt an object against her side, it was soft and pliable. He slid it up her body and gently pressed it against her lips. Trudy parted her lips and received the head of a dick, a life like glans, a veiny cock. He slowly pushed it in until it was down her throat and pulled it out just as slowly, she loved it. When it had come to life she realized that the realistic feeling dick had a vibrator in it, its head was big but not bigger than Danny, and when it went in her cock trap smoothly, she could tell the shaft wasn't as big as he was but it was long and he plumbed her depth with it fully, resting it just below her G-spot. She was not sure if she could take any more if the two ever connected.

She felt a ball touch her side, it pulled up alongside her cheek and was pressed against her lips, it was a ball on a shaft but directly after, her lips were touching another ball, he pushed a bit more and now she had a ball connected through a shaft to another ball but her lips were against yet another ball, he pushed just a little further with just enough distance to tell that this ball was bigger, he pulled back to the previous ball, it was obviously smaller by just a little bit, he pulled out yet again to the last ball that was clearly just fractionally smaller. She had never seen this kind of vibrator before, but she was certainly intrigued. She heard Danny make a bit of noise, there was a pop of a cap of sorts and a clip of a closing cap and shortly after she felt it. The cock in her was whirring away and feeling beyond great and building to a delight within her. There was pressure on her anus, and she knew right away what was now going to happen.

She had never had anything put into her ass and was not sure if she wanted him to push it in, as it turned out he did not. It was as if he had read her mind and only just put a heavy pressure on her ass. As her pussy throbbed, she pushed backward just a bit, and the first graduation was in by her own volition. She moaned when it popped in. There was a tightness there but also a rising good feeling. When Danny had pushed and pulled just ever so slightly the two sides of the two adjacent balls, one in and one out, the feeling was stirring something powerful inside her. After a minute or two, Danny's rocking back and forth on balls had stopped and there was a pressure again that Trudy now understood this was under her control. She eased back into it spreading just a little wider to accommodate. It was deliciously incredible, glorious, and exquisite all at the same time. It was all being coaxed on by the whirring deep in her pussy, she was feeling absolutely full and was loving it. There was more pressure and her push twice more that began to stretch her in an intensely, delicious, and insanely wonderful way.

It changed once again as a switch was thrown and the balls came to life inside her. Her pussy pulsed around the faux dick and her ass pounded on the door as if to say I am working here, please shut up. An argument ensued within her and both factions were becoming more animated in their resolve for dominance. She was absolutely roiling in the dark, blind, and still unable to move much, unable to remove one thing or the other and being caught in between two now warring factions, both threatening nuclear proliferations. Neither side would get to have a say in the matter as the torturer Danny would remain in control.

She had not noticed between the heavenly distractions that Danny had once again left the bed and already had returned, she did, however, feel his presence as he dragged something soft, well soft-ish, across her back. She could feel him beside her when she heard a "haawhip" as something very audibly with a snap that put the rubber bands smack to shame. It had landed in his palm near her ear, sharpening her every sense. The sound was so abrupt that her pussy and ass clenched unintentionally pushing each other to the edge of the precipice.

Danny started between her shoulder blades and drug it down her spine slowly to the base of her pelvis, it went up and over to her left ass cheek. Danny laid it there across her back, she could feel the handle and the length and its outline searing its way into her memory stores emulating this device to what she imagined would feel this way. This shape was oddly familiar, but she was having trouble placing it. Suddenly she realized it was a riding crop and that gave her chills. She heard a rip, a tearing but had no clue as to what it could be, nor did she care anymore when the instrument of her imminent destruction was lifted from her back.

She was writhing much more now, the war inside her was now fighting each other on another front for complete undivided attention. Outside her, her inner legs were wet halfway down her thighs and her legs were beginning to quiver as never before. Her mind excused itself and checked out as her animal instincts took over with the first "thaaawap." The crop landed a perfectly luscious and savagely brutal blow to the sweet spot on her ass cheek.

Her mind left and her body became its own living being in that instant. Trudy did not hear herself yell, "Oh god Danny more please," and other than a negative connotation Danny would not have cared anyway. He began to methodically wear her ass out with the crop slowly and deliberately. He alternated ass halves back and forth and landed blow after neighboring blow until two patches of her ass glowed red. Trudy was begging for more but had no recollection of how she was even able to speak.

Danny dropped the crop and gently removed the balled ass destroyer from her and lined up his cock in the same hole. He would not enter her; all he had to do was just push forward to introduce some pressure. He did not have to contribute more than that as she pushed to him and he sank inside her, she pulled forward just a bit and shrieked in delight and sank him back into her more fully. After that he took over and slowly stroked a full length, her ass was convulsing and her pussy was pulsating and quivering, he could feel the vibrations through the separations inside her and was loving it. She was now fuller than she could have ever believed possible, Danny's enraged hot cock and the fleshy substitute competing for space in such a way that she was losing all semblance of spatial reality.

She came in waves, there were no longer separate entities but a continual release coming hard and soaking the whole area. He was close to coming so he pulled out, when her ass relented, she began a new round of coming hard once more, the glorious stretch released to a wonderful respite. Danny moved forward and removed her blindfold and as she watched, pulled of the condom he had been hammering her with and offered his cock to her.

She looked at him and said, "Yes please." He knelt in front of her and arched slightly forward as she took him in hungrily and fully resting her face against his belly and back up again. He was straining hard, and she knew he was on the edge so she half face fucked him as he half face fucked her. She could taste herself from earlier and found she was sweet but his pre-cum took over heavy and runny.

She knew in tormenting her, he had tormented himself to an explosive point and was lining up for a horrendously large release. He did not disappoint; she took the first two full pumps of his balls in her mouth and almost gagged as she choked down his convulsing meat, but she managed to get him fully down her throat for the remaining expenditures. There were many pulls from his balls this time, if a guy could have multiple orgasms like she did, she thought this would be it. His pulses lasted longer than ever before as she felt his juices shoot down her throat walls deep in her. She savored the come she had purposely left in her mouth and licked a heavy dollop off her cheek as best as she could without the use of her hands. He had pulled out of her and moved in close to lick the remnants of his spunk off her cheek that she could not get to and let her steal it from his mouth though a long enthusiastic kiss.

He un-snicked her wrists and moved downward and extracted the dick that was still purring away from within her, she shuttered uncontrollably when the head of it cleared her gash. Trudy would have balled up for an intense cry had her legs not been captured, when Danny un-snicked them as well, she did exactly that.

Crying, convulsing, not wanting to be even touched, her every molecule was vibrating at light speed. Danny covered her gently with a sheet and lay dutifully beside her quietly taking real care not to touch her, waiting for her to regain her sense of self. He was absolutely beaming as he knew he had destroyed her in such a glorious new way. He loved satisfying his Trudy.

This was the first time ever—the first girl ever—that made him feel like he belonged, had a purpose, was not defective, and liked him back without condition. He knew he was going to miss her when he left for college. This was the same reason he wanted to please her in every feasible way.

For now, he just watched her shudder occasionally and was pleased when she curled up like a satiated cat. Half an hour had passed before she stirred to life with an incredible thirst. Danny welcomed her back with a Cheshire cat smile.

"Good afternoon, Beautiful. Are you OK?"

"More than OK. I'm wonderful—sore a bit—but wonderful. That was… well, I'm not sure what that was. Shit, Danny, a whole new side that I had never considered. I think you have ruined me. I really liked that a lot." She beamed a smile at him. "You wouldn't have happened to bring something to drink? I'm dying of thirst here."

Danny looked down at the lower part of the bed and spoke. "I'm pretty sure I know why."

Trudy looked down and saw that the lower third of the bed in the middle had been soaked. She began a half-embarrassed laugh.

"I have bottled Starbucks iced coffee, 7UP, or water?"

"Starbucks, please."

"I thought as much. I brought you two."

They both drank about half of their bottles and mutually decided that a shower would be best. They walked to the bathroom; Trudy was still a little unsteady. Danny started the water, getting the temperature to the level Trudy liked—a bit warm for him, but he would settle into it.

He washed Trudy as if she were a prized possession—slow, gentle, methodical, and thorough. He loved her curves and how the soap on her skin let his hands glide smoothly. Her breasts, neck, back, and legs, the curves of her ass—all supple and firm, taut and muscular in a feminine kind of way that all but screamed, Look at me, I am well put together. He delighted himself by making sure there was no patch of her body left untouched.

Trudy laughed when he again shielded her eyes as he washed her single hair patch and the extents of her heat. He was so stupidly boyish in his playful mock concern that it was tantalizingly cute.

On her part, she loved when Danny washed her—with or without the sex. He simply made her feel like no other person existed in the world except her and touched her in such a way that it was almost indescribable. Yet, it felt as if he were painting her with love, a tenderness that, even with the water and soap, could not be removed.

It was as if he were giving of himself in such a way that it could not be duplicated, copied, edited, or otherwise replicated. It was an invisible layer of armor that he pulled from himself as a gift.

When Danny had finished making sure she was spotless, she returned the favor with much the same sentiment—the same care and patient control as she navigated his body with her hands and soap.

If it were possible to fall asleep while standing in the middle of a shower, the care and manipulation she was giving his scalp as she washed his hair almost achieved it.

When she moved down his chest, she playfully and artfully made sure each nipple, in turn, was completely and thoroughly clean, exfoliated in a loving, palmed manipulation. She returned the mock eye covering so Danny could not see his penis being cleaned.

Trudy loved cleaning his member after sex because he was usually still hard or at least firm. It had been an easy half an hour or more, and he was still a far cry from flaccid—firm, almost full, but just before it got the notion of standing up to look around. That was how her hand had experienced him this time.

Trudy loved to draw her hand down his shaft in a slow, teasing way, threatening to reignite his problem but deftly stopping just short.

His fullness felt wonderful in hand, and the distance up one side and down the other simply delighted her.

She had made a conscious effort not to envision him sliding into her, as this might be cause for round two—a second round she did not think she could survive.

They had just finished two and a half hours of pure bliss—a bliss that required no immediate sequel, as everything that could have been done in this episode had been done, and done well.

She continued with the rest of his body, slowing for his ass just for her own enjoyment.

She liked his body—it just fit hers so perfectly.

She liked his person—honest and straightforward when needed but coy and shielding when it was called for, with the intelligence to know when to employ the nuances required to make a cohesive interaction with just about everyone.

Trudy knew she was going to miss him when he went away for college. One of the best reprieves that she would take comfort in was the fact that Danny would not have a need for want.

She had planned to make sure his every financial need—from freshman year in college to graduation day and on through culinary school—was taken care of through his fortunate landing of the T.J. Consortium Scholarship.

A scholarship that he had not applied for or even knew he had won… yet.

It was a full ride to any college of his choice.

When they had finished drying each other, they went to get dressed. That was when Trudy realized that her clothes were in pieces.

She had a towel wrapped around her when they arrived at the bedroom.

"I guess we have a problem here."

"What do you mean?" Danny asked as he put on his underwear and began pulling on his socks.

"Well, scissor boy, it was really fun and exciting at the time, but I'm not sure my father is going to appreciate me showing up wearing nothing but a towel."

"Humph. That is a real problem, isn't it? What do you plan on doing about it?"

"What do you mean, what do I plan to do about it? You caused this. What do you plan to do about it?"

Danny just pulled up his jeans and hopped a few times to get them seated on his hips.

"Well, let me put some thought into it."

He walked to the other side of the room, picked up the duffel bag— one of the same ones he had all his surprises in—and handed it to her.

"I asked you to wear the outfit I bought you so I wouldn't feel bad about destroying it. Also, so I knew exactly what you would be wearing."

Trudy looked in the bag and saw duplicates of everything she had been wearing—from the underwear up.

"Now that's sneaky smart. You never cease to amaze me. I'll almost use the word impressive, but before I do, we have to be outside so you don't have to squeeze your head out of the door."

She laughed while she said it, as did he.

"I was hoping that you wore at least the pants and shirt. The rest we could get away with. But you had worn everything requested, so no, I don't feel bad about destroying anything. It was a lot of fun being in charge that way. It was incredible watching you strain to figure out what was going to happen. It turned me on quite nicely.

"Thank you for playing along."

Trudy dressed herself under Danny's watchful eye. He was clearly enjoying her body as she began to cover it with the second set of garments he had brought along. When she was fully dressed, Trudy began to strip the bed.

"You want to give me a hand with the sheets? We can strip the bed and put on the extra sheets from the linen closet, get these in the wash so I can dry them a little later."

"No problem. I'll clean up our mess in here, get fresh towels in the bathroom, and get the wet ones to the laundry."

By the time Danny had finished, Trudy had already stripped the bed and was in the process of putting the fitted sheet back on when Danny came to help her in the bedroom. He immediately went to the window, opened it fully, and left the room to open the living room windows. When the second set of windows opened, there was a slight breeze pushing the curtains with a gentle cross flow. He returned to the bedroom.

"When I came back in here, it smelled like heavy sex. I'm guessing it would be better to air the cabin out before we left, yes?"

"Absolutely. Now give me a hand with the sheets."

They both worked well together, played off each other's cues effortlessly, and completed what the other was moving toward without asking. From the outside looking in, they were a couple. From the inside looking out, they were truly two great friends—comfortable with each other and the way they moved. It was as if they had an unspoken language that transcended words. They were both simply great around each other.

When they had finished, Trudy sat on the end of the bed, wrangling her smartphone, and asked Danny if he would sit next to her. He complied and parked himself in a half-turned position to see her better.

"I have wanted to tell you something for a long time now, but we have been so busy and around everyone else that I didn't feel like we could have the time to discuss this without being interrupted."

"Uh-oh. Discuss what? What did I do this time?"

She laughed. "It is nothing like that. I told you I had a secret that no one knows around here, and I want to let you in on it. You would be the fourth person in the world to know it."

"OK?"

"I have told you that I am going to go to college for business. I have told you that I want to become a force to reckon with and make something of myself."

"We all want to do some version of that. So, what is your point?"

"Well, that's my secret. No one around here knows anything about it, but I have already made it. I own a company called TJ Consortium."

"Who is the TJ Consortium? What do they do?"

Trudy began by explaining how she had been saving cash for as long as she could remember, how she invested in the app startup, and how it paid off. When she told Danny about a four-million-dollar-plus bank transfer into her account, he was dumbstruck. When she continued to describe how she had invested in a defunct hotel chain and revived it, he was amazed.

She told him that, according to everyone involved—from her hotel manager to her accountant, the realtors, and Kate's assessment—she estimated her net worth to be more than fourteen million dollars and climbing. She went on to explain that she was getting ready to expand even further into the service sector.

Danny sat there in awe.

She went on to tell him that she knew he would not like this next part, but it was something she just had to do.

"What do you mean? And what has this got to do with me? I don't see my connection."

"I have instructed my lawyer to establish a scholarship for a full ride to an accredited educational forum—whether that is college or some other specialty school—once a year for a deserving student. It starts this year and goes forward into the foreseeable future. I also have it on good authority who is going to win the scholarship this year, and you haven't even applied for it yet.

"You are going to have a full ride that includes books, housing, tuition, and a monthly stipend for incidentals. It will all be a legal charitable write-off for me, which will help my balance sheet per my accountants."

"I can't let you do that. Don't you know how much that is going to be? I would feel guilty taking your money just because of our friendship."

"That is exactly why you shouldn't feel bad about it. You never knew, never asked, and did not care whether I had money or not. You just liked me for who I am, and because of that, I would feel simply great to be able to make your life easier.

"You and your mom won't have to worry about financing, and you won't have to wonder if you can even afford it. You will graduate with absolutely no debt on top of it all."

"I'll never be able to pay you back. I would feel like I owe you all the time."

"You would owe me. Furthermore, I intend to collect—not just from you, but from every other recipient of the scholarship.

"As payment, I will require an equivalent grade of B-plus or better, ninety percent attendance or more, and after graduation, a non-binding commitment to give five percent of the amount of scholarship used back to the scholarship fund.

"Your donation will be spread out over whatever amount of time you deem affordable. Rest assured, no one will ever try to collect. It is an honor system that will be strictly voluntary on the recipient's part. I am hoping that everyone who benefits will want to help someone else benefit as well.

"So that is the payback expected. I think it is a doable penance, don't you?"

"It is very doable, and I would think that any deserving person would strive to excel to those conditions based on common sense alone. That still doesn't mean I will like it as far as our relationship goes."

"I thought it might be an issue with you, but it really shouldn't be. If you were loaded, would you help me out?"

"You're damn straight I would."

Then it sank in.

"Shit. OK, OK. Thank you. I can promise that I won't waste the opportunity."

"I already knew that. I wouldn't have made the arrangement if I thought otherwise. However, there is one thing that will require payback, though."

"What's that? Just name it."

"If you think you can blindfold me, have your way with me in any old fashion you dream up, and think there will not be repercussions, then you are sadly mistaken.

"After that little performance, I believe when I dole out my version back on you, you're gonna beg to do my bidding."

She started to laugh, and Danny joined in.

"There will be a payback for sure."

They both finished cleaning the area, closed the windows, and started the laundry. Trudy made a mental note to return in an hour or so to switch the laundry to the dryer.

Chapter 20 - Meeting Amanda

The next Tuesday at school, Trudy turned the corner and bumped into Amanda. They had always been friendly, if not friends, so she took a moment to see how she was doing.

"Sorry about that, I wasn't watching where I was going," Trudy said.

Amanda replied, "No worries, I wasn't watching either."

"We haven't caught up in a while. How have you been?"

"I'm well, thank you. Trying to keep up my grades. I think Calculus and Advanced Chemistry might have been a bit too much. It's killing me, but I'm managing. How are you doing?"

"I'm struggling with Physics, but for some reason, I get Advanced Chem. It just kind of clicks. I just wish some of my other classes were that way."

"If you understand Chem, maybe I could give you a call if I'm having issues?"

"Sure, that would be no problem. I'd be glad to help you."

"I wouldn't want to cut into boyfriend time, though. I've noticed that you and Danny have been hanging out a lot."

"That wouldn't be a problem at all. Danny is pretty understanding."

"He is a great guy. I like talking to him. He isn't like the other guys around here—kind of down to earth in a special kind of way. Are you two doing OK?"

"We get along great. I mean, he's just like any other guy. I had to train him, of course, but by and large, he is a fast learner." She laughed.

"Most guys are trainable." Amanda laughed with her.

"I hope you aren't angry at me for anything. I found out recently you two had dated for a bit. I had no idea until a bit after we got together."

"Oh no, I'm not angry at you at all. How could I be? I called it off between us. I may have been premature in ending it, but that is on me—nothing to do with you at all."

"What do you mean by premature?"

"Wait, that sounded wrong. I'm not secretly hoping you two split or anything. I just meant we had a few issues that could have been discussed a little better, but instead, there was a thing or two that kinda got sprung on me, and I wasn't prepared for it. In retrospect, I think we both could have handled things differently. But I am happy for you, though—both of you."

Trudy stepped in closer to Amanda, whispering after checking their peripheral surroundings, "I know about the bisexuality." She backed out of her personal space. "And how it had been sprung on you. Game night?"

"Yup. Game night."

"Kind of a shocker when you're not expecting anything, right?"

"Oh wow, yeah. But you must have handled it differently than I did. I wish Danny would have introduced his nature in a smoother fashion. Things may have been different."

"It was a bit abrupt, for sure."

"For me, there I was, the daughter of a fire-and-brimstone preacher, and suddenly everything was turned on its ear. The whole thing made me reevaluate what it is I honestly believe. Danny isn't the Devil as I was taught. On the contrary, he is the nicest person I have ever met.

"I was happy when you two found each other. You're a good person too—a good fit. I am glad for you both."

"Well, since you know and I know, I'm guessing you will understand this. We aren't 'dating' each other. Everyone thinks we are, and we are OK with that. We are just extremely close and trusting friends." She gave a sheepish smile and raised her eyebrows. "With benefits."

"Oh wow, you two aren't exclusive? How do you guys manage that?"

"Honesty, really. There is no way I would expect exclusivity. I simply don't have the right equipment." Both girls smiled a knowing smile. "We hang out, and we are honest with each other. If there is a desire that needs to be filled, we help each other fill it."

"I'm curious, if you don't mind me asking, when you found out, what did you say to him? How did you handle it?"

Trudy gave a devilish smile and raised an eyebrow. "I didn't say a thing. I joined them." She tilted her head as if questioning. "TMI?"

"Holy shit. No. I thought about doing the same thing. I mean, I just wasn't ready for that. Dave is a nice guy and all, but my mind was reeling. I wish I could have brought myself to stay. I just wasn't ready for that leap."

"What about now? If you had to do it all over again, would you join in?"

"Well… uh."

"I'm sorry. That wasn't a fair question, and it's really none of my business. I was just being nosy. Forget I asked."

"No, no, no, wait. It's not that. The question isn't too far out for me. I'm just not sure if you would like how I want to answer it."

"What do you mean?"

"I told you that if I had enough time to think things all the way through, I might have had a different response. I say that now because I have had the benefit of thinking about it all the way through—as well as many other possibilities that I have only recently considered.

"My dad is a preacher, and what Danny does should be a one-way ticket to hell, right? But the thing is, Danny has always been better to me than any other guy I have dated—both before and after we parted.

"I have had a long time to think, and I have watched you two closer than you think. I have made up my mind about a few things. But—"

"But what?"

"Well, I can give you a comprehensive answer, just not here in the open."

She grabbed Trudy by the hand and dragged her down a locker corridor that dead-ended with no cross-traffic as the late-for-class warning bell sounded. In a lower voice, she continued.

"I have thought about it many times, and frankly, now when I think about it, I get wet. Given another opportunity, I would fuck them both at the same time.

"I want them both in many ways.

"I'm positive my father's head would explode if he ever heard that or found that out. In his book, I would be going straight to hell.

"But Danny is a good person. Dave is too, from what I know. So yes, I would handle it much differently now.

"Hindsight is a bitch.

"I see you and Danny and can tell you two are just wonderful together. So why would I want to hurt either of you?"

"Oh wow, I wouldn't have guessed that you would feel this way. I thought you were just too prim and proper to make room for other possibilities. I hope we don't make you feel bad when you see us together. That would be the last thing Danny or I, for that matter, would ever want to happen to you. He really values your friendship; he has told me this on many occasions. I have always liked you, so I'm sorry if our being together has made you feel bad in any way."

"No, no, it is nothing like that at all. I look at you two, you're happy, and I'm happy for you both."

"Thank you. I'll tell him that. I think he would like to hear those words if it's OK with you?"

"That would be fine by me. I really mean it. There is one more thing… I am happy to hear you say that you two aren't exclusively attached to each other because… I'm not sure how to say this."

"If you want to ask him out, I really am OK with that. I won't be angry, I promise."

Amanda pivoted to be directly in Trudy's space, reached up with both hands, gently cradled her head, and looked deep into her eyes. Then, she leaned forward and kissed her full on the lips—first with her lips and then deeply with her tongue.

This caught Trudy off guard for a moment as she received Amanda's tongue and kissed her back, long and deep. The class bell rang as Amanda released her grip and ended the kiss.

While turning away, she said, "How about a movie this weekend—Friday?"

Trudy was dumbstruck, blushing, and now unexpectedly wet. "Uhh… ye—yeah, yes… call me, OK?" A weird confusion set in.

The rest of the day passed in a blur for Trudy, as she had never considered being with a woman before now. It consumed her and was all she could think about.

She had no concept of the passage of time and could not recall if she had spoken to anyone whatsoever after the kiss. She liked the kiss—it was warm and inviting, soft, almost dainty, with a serious undertone of wanting and desire.

If a soft, warm, inviting embrace was actually a feeling, she had just discovered it and liked it very much.

When she finally gathered what she needed to go home at the end of the day, she headed for her car. As she approached, she could see Amanda already waiting there for her. Trudy smiled, opened the back door, set her books on the floorboard, and stood to meet Amanda.

"Trudy, I am so sorry. I shouldn't have done that to you. I don't know what I was thi—"

Trudy all but full-on assaulted her, reaching up under her blouse with one hand and finding the lower wire of her bra. With one deft movement, she worked her hand under the wire and over her breast while her other hand half-supported, half-grabbed a full handful of Amanda's hair, pulling it back, tilting her head as she kissed her neckline and around up to her ear.

As she released Amanda's hair and her head dropped earthward, she engaged her in a long French kiss. It was deep, wanting, and sensual, while she simultaneously felt the nipple in her hand harden and stand in her palm in direct response to what she was doing.

As abruptly as she had begun, Trudy pulled away just far enough to be on the edge of Amanda's personal space.

From a distance, all one could see was two people talking closely. Parking in the back row had its advantages.

Up close, if a person were allowed to check, two hormonal teenage girls were deep into each other, and both had nicely damp panties to show for it.

"Apology accepted."

Amanda was almost breathless and blushing red. "I want you so bad right now it hurts. I want to caress your naked body, kiss you all over, breathe you in, and eat you to insanity. I was so afraid to tell you how I felt today. I was afraid of what you might say or do, but now I'm so glad I did.

"You make me weak inside. You just wreck me.

"If I were not expected to be home in half an hour, I would be trying to find a place for us to get to know each other better."

"I think I would like that a lot. Can you talk later tonight?"

"Do I want to? Yes. Will I be able to? It's hard to tell right now because my dad doesn't allow talking on cell phones after eight-thirty, and he is always over my shoulder all the time for one reason or another. He has been so controlling since the divorce, so I may not be able to tonight, but I'll try."

At eight-thirty, Trudy received a text that read:

"See you tomorrow."

Her phone chimed again, but this time it was a picture file.

When Trudy saw it start to load on her phone, she was immediately captivated. It was loading from the bottom up, slowly, like the internet had just gone into hyper slow-mo. But even at this pace, as every pixel found its place, Trudy got wetter.

Amanda's legs were crossed comfortably, yet in a provocative, almost parted pose. Her toenails were a crimson red, and one foot was resting as if it were floating, with both of her calves in a strain.

Her legs were sexy in a way that most women wanted but very few had, bronzed to just the right shade of tan from the sun.

Her legs were silky smooth and toned with the physique of an athlete. As more of the picture came into view, Trudy could see a beautifully trimmed patch of pussy hair and the hint of lips lower that were, to her, tragically obscured from view.

There was just enough for her to want a whole lot more.

Her belly had a woman's six-pack—toned, shapely, and inviting, with the cutest innie belly button.

She wanted to kiss that belly button—all around the rim of it—and made a mental note to do just that at one of the earliest opportunities possible.

When the pixilation cleared to reveal Amanda's breasts, Trudy thought they were spectacular.

Gorgeous and pert, caught somewhere between a C and a D—thirty-four or thirty-six.

Her nipples were standing tall on top of a tight lily-pad areola, inviting anyone to come have a look.

Her neckline and face snapped into view and stunned Trudy.

She had never thought of another woman as a sexual being in this way, but in this context, she was hot and wet with wanting.

Amanda's face was heavenly—beautiful proportions, perfect symmetry, and glowing like the sun.

Immediately, Trudy now understood the allure of crimson lipstick that men had always praised. She wanted those lips now, and when she closed her eyes, she could remember their taste.

She wanted to taste her as she lay there.

Her arms were comfortably hugging herself, fingernails matching her toes, and her lips tying it all together.

Trudy was not a hundred percent sure how, but she wanted to absolutely devour Amanda.

She wanted to fuck her into oblivion, though she had not actually worked out the mechanics of it yet, but she knew she wanted Amanda in a primal manner.

She envisioned Amanda in every way possible and was soaking herself with every new position she could conjure up.

The thought of lying naked and exploring each other's bodies was dismantling her mind.

Trudy texted her back.

"You dropped a book insert and left class before I could catch you. I would like to give it to you in the parking lot tomorrow. I usually park in the back row on the far left under the trees. I have a heavy class schedule tomorrow, so please try to come early."

Trudy knew she had said enough to Amanda about her intentions. She also knew that her dad, if he were truly over her shoulder, would only see class-related conversation. She knew that the picture lasted just long enough on Amanda's phone to complete a send and had immediately been purged afterward. She had carefully word-smithed her reply for prying eyes.

Trudy was wearing a skirt and loose blouse combination with flats. She saw Amanda approaching, wearing a light, airy jumper. The sight of her warmed Trudy inside as she simultaneously felt her labia engorge. She was getting wet from fifty feet away, and it felt beyond great.

Amanda was happy to see how Trudy had parked because it was in the furthest corner—no area behind for traffic—and overall, it was secluded.

The night before, she had masturbated to the thought of Trudy's touch, achieving the most satisfying release for herself. Seeing her standing there reignited those same thoughts.

She felt that Trudy was gorgeous—amazing, really—and was beyond happy that her advances of yesterday had not been rebuked or scoffed at. She felt herself getting wetter with every step as she approached to stand close to Trudy's body.

"Good morning. How are you today?"

As she said this, she stepped in close and put her right hand on Trudy's side just above the waist of her skirt.

When Trudy captured her wrist with her left hand, Amanda immediately thought she had overstepped her bounds, but she was thrown completely aback when Trudy not only pulled her closer but also slid her hand into her bare inner thigh and leaned forward to kiss her.

They kissed—hard and deep, passionate and loving, gentle yet firm. When Amanda's hand met Trudy's panty-less crotch, it ventured inches more into her pussy lips as they both gasped.

"Good morning. I hoped you had received my true intent last night. I really do want to give you something here in the parking lot."

She smiled big, then suddenly gasped again and rocked forward just a bit when she felt a finger go inside her. She rocked further still and gasped deeper when the second finger joined the first. She could feel a micro-flow meeting her heat's acquaintance as her clitoris jumped straight up in sensory overdrive. Her body was loving its introduction to Amanda's hand.

"Good morning to you. And you should know that my dad thanks you for looking out for me. He wanted to make sure you gave me what I needed, so he dropped me off early. He thinks I should have more friends like you."

She smiled even bigger than she had been smiling because of the playful word deception.

"Do you have what I need?"

Both girls smiled broadly at each other.

Amanda continued, "I think there is something you should be aware of."

She leaned forward and embraced Trudy again with a slow, sensual kiss, almost begging for a deeper venue.

"I don't really know what I'm doing. I'm just acting on how I thought I would like for this to go—my fantasy, in a sense. I have never approached a girl before but have wanted to let you know how I felt for a while now since I had been watching you with Danny."

She pulled her fingers out of Trudy, stared her straight in the eyes, and put her fingers in her mouth. As she sampled Trudy's juices, she closed her eyes and hummed, "Uuu mmm," clearly enjoying the taste.

She removed her fingers from her mouth, and as her eyes opened, she saw Trudy coming in closer to kiss her passionately. They French-kissed, sharing themselves. Both girls were deeply enjoying this incredible new sensation together.

Trudy told her, "I think I really like your touch."

She gasped deep and hard when she realized that Amanda had gone back under her skirt, put two fingers inside her, and rested her thumb on her clitoris before beginning to massage it.

"I like touching you. God, you are so wet, and all I can think about is either kissing you endlessly or kissing your clitoris. I feel it standing there. It is so hard right now."

She roughly crossed her nub at the same time, causing Trudy to get momentarily weak in the knees as she orgasmed.

"I think I really like touching you a lot."

Trudy sheepishly pulled Amanda's hand out, licked her finger and thumb, and kissed Amanda hard and deep. She then stepped to the side and put her hand up the loose leg of her jumper, sliding under her panties that she could tell were outwardly wet. She sank three fingers in a triangle of sorts and began to knead the inner walls of Amanda's pussy, causing her to moan and arch into Trudy's hand.

She had a tough time containing herself audibly when the thumb was brought into play. Trudy had returned the orgasm in kind with a glorious inner launch and gave Amanda a little time to enjoy the gift.

When Amanda opened her eyes moments later, she felt Trudy pull her hand out of her convulsing walls. She saw Trudy take her fingers to her mouth and savor her work as well, and again, they kissed.

Amanda quipped, "This is possibly the best start to a Wednesday at school I have ever had," she said jokingly as both girls giggled about it.

"I am not sure if I can make it to Friday. If I could strip you right here, I would. I would lay you across my hood and lick you until you screamed. I want you. Your taste is incredible. I want your body next to me, on me."

Amanda flushed. "Oh God, you have no idea how hot you are. I want to fuck you right here and now too. I would skip classes and find someplace to be with you today if I didn't have two major tests. Friday can't get here fast enough."

Trudy opened her back door and pulled out a package of handy wipes and a roll of paper towels. "Never leave home without it. You never know when they might come in handy."

Both girls snickered.

After rudimentary cleanup and drying off, Amanda pulled out a roll of breath mints from her purse, broke the roll in half, and gave a half to Trudy.

"I keep a toothbrush and paste in my locker. You never know when you might be kissing the boys," she said, beaming a smile at Trudy. "You can borrow it if you want to."

"No need. I have one too, for just the same reason."

Both girls laughed.

Trudy reached into her purse, pulled out a pair of panties, carefully stepped through them with her heels on, pulled them into place, and started to adjust their fit.

"Would you like some help with that?" Amanda offered while she smiled.

"Sure, if you have decided to skip those tests, because we are going to have to miss school if you touch me again."

Both girls were clearly smitten with their newfound relationship.

"Fine, I'll leave you alone—for now."

"Speaking of leaving things alone, would you be offended if I suggested we ignore what has happened between us while we are inside the school? I mean, we don't have to avoid each other, but no kissing and touching. I really don't like other people in my business here or anywhere."

"Oh, thank God! I have been thinking the same thing. I just wasn't sure how to bring it up—I didn't want to offend you. I know you can keep a secret, as can I, but if this gets out, some of these ingrates here wouldn't let it go—not to mention my dad finding out—so I completely understand. That doesn't mean I can't text you though, does it?"

"Right now, I'm thinking of wrapping my arms around your thighs and burying my face in your pussy. So, if I'm going to have that on my mind all day, you are going to hear about it too." With a huge smile, she added, "But no texting after you go home because your dad might talk to mine."

They both laughed.

After the second period of classes, there was a buzz on Trudy's phone, as silent mode was required in school.

Amanda texted, "I can't quit thinking about seeing you naked, laying down, and having you sit on my face while I lick you into a new orbit."

Trudy replied, "I have thought of that position and a few others already. Just so you know, I'm going to be your FF."

She quickly followed the text with another. "Your face fuck. I am going to ride you until your ears are wet. I have already had to get out an emergency pad to keep my panties dry just thinking about you."

"FF—friends forever? Or face fuck? Hmm, I like your version best."

"Get to class. Good luck on your test. If you get an A, I promise to lick you into a most wonderful release after I spend some time on your beautiful nipples."

"You're on."

She followed the text with a big smiley-face emoji.

When the last class rolled around, both girls were hot and bothered, wanting the one thing they could not readily have but maintained their agreement with only furtive glances in the hall and an occasional "Hey, how are you?" vibe as they interacted in passing. It was strictly publicly platonic.

Amanda texted, "I really hope you like my pussy because I aced both of my tests today. I can see myself pulling your head deeper into me. I want you so bad right now."

"Would you like a ride home after school?"

"Absolutely. See you at your car?"

"I'll be waiting."

When Amanda arrived, Trudy's car was running, and the radio was playing soft rock music. She put her backpack on the back seat and got into the front with Trudy. They wanted to embrace each other badly, but the traffic was prohibitive, so Trudy made her way to the park with every intention of parking to have another talk, as she was liking this newfound relationship with her friend.

When they got there, the park was vacant. When they parked in the back section at the far end of the park, there was not a soul in sight. They both moved their packs to the back area of the Cherokee so they could have more room in the back seats to sit comfortably.

Trudy was about to start a conversation when Amanda put up a singular finger to Trudy's lips, as if motioning her to say shhh.

She reached under her skirt and clamped the edge of Trudy's panties with her pinky, beginning to pull them downward. Trudy remained quiet and lifted her ass off the seat to give her better access. Amanda pulled them off her hips, down her thighs, past her calves, and freely tossed them unceremoniously in the seat.

Amanda looked Trudy dead in the eye as she smiled the biggest, warmest smile Trudy had felt or had seen in a long time. It felt good inside.

Amanda slowly turned her head through the arc of possible foot traffic and car movements—the area was devoid of distraction.

She turned back to the skirt and began to hike it up. Trudy lifted her ass once again, letting her skirt turn into an upside-down lampshade. Amanda caressed her skin gently, causing Trudy to lay her head back and lazily close her eyes in satisfying delight.

When she felt Amanda's tongue on her muff, she almost came from the sheer novelty of it. But her body decided not to allow it—it demanded that a penance be paid through hard work and determination instead of any prize being arbitrarily given away.

There was not a large issue with the hard work and dedication required for the endeavor, as Amanda's tongue began to massage her inner and outer labia in loving, mind-boggling, ever-increasing, wonderfully gentle strokes.

Trudy's clitoris was standing as hard and tall as it had ever done before. She had been gone down on by Danny many times—and by Dave as well, for that matter—and felt as though their efforts were of professional grade, but this was a different story, a different category altogether.

There was a difference in Amanda's touch—an electric silkiness to it, a softness of a woman that was all but devoid of the mechanical clumsiness that men had. Amanda was lovingly taking her in, taking her own sweet time, and her body was responding in kind. The response was just the same as ever before but, somehow, it was all that and more. She thought it was the tenderness of her lover or the way her lover was anticipating her every want, coupled with a desire to please. She realized motivation was partly the key—Amanda was giving to her what she herself wanted in return. In her offering, Amanda had given her an almost magical moment of unadulterated bliss.

Her morning release that Amanda had given to her with her hands was but a simple prelude compared to this. It was fantastic, as every orgasm was, but just as no two orgasms were the same, the way she had gotten here—the journey itself—was in a class of its own.

When she felt the welling inside her, the glorious build-up, it carried with it a completely different, phenomenal promise that began as a whisper heard deep in her being instead of in her ears. When the whisper started to grow and pronounce itself more intelligibly, her body began to tense. She could not understand why she had not released yet, but still, the same voice grew louder. Her body became even more tense.

It was as if a cloud of perfect wanting, perfect giving, perfect knowing, and total bliss had been unleashed across her aura in one singular, deafening roar. The release happened with an almost mystic depth and clarity, unrivaled in its completeness—cataclysmic—a oneness that had washed over her as if a warm embrace was slowly hauling her in, freeing her earthly bounds, and inviting her to lay down weightless, surrounded by heavenly, timeless clouds.

Several minutes had passed before she realized she had soaked the seat.

Trudy had just regained her composure and had begun to think about how she could return such a wonderful experience when she felt Amanda's head lying on her stomach. When she looked down through her short auburn hair, she could see she had been crying.

"What's wrong, Amanda? Did I do something wrong?"

"No… no. That was something so beautiful. It was so alive, natural, and full of light. You are so beautiful. I lost myself for a moment or two. It was an unbridled freedom, like my body had become weightless. I was just so lost in being a part of you, part of your world, that it felt like we had a oneness, as if I was really a part of you. You were loving me and letting me love you. It was just so special that when you came, I had the most wonderfully powerful orgasm as well. It was indescribable and so calming and open in a sense. Thank you for allowing me in. I really am so grateful."

There was a long silence before Amanda continued.

"I really like being around you. I like lying here just feeling you with me. I know it kind of sounds a bit crazy—out there, in a 'zentopia' kind of way—but I can't describe it completely. It just felt... rather, I just felt like I was a part of something much bigger for just an instant. I am so sorry if all this sounds too weird. Really, I'm not crazy or obsessed or anything like that. I just don't have the right words."

"Actually, it sounded—you sounded—wonderful. I guess it could be twisted and misconstrued if a person wanted to, but I understand what you mean. I have felt that way before. It is a great feeling. You sound stark-raving mad if you try to describe it to anyone, but once you have felt it, the words that fail to come help describe it better, and THAT is crazy. But I do get it."

She joked, "Now, if you get all crazy-eyed and start to stalk me, I'm going to have to drop you like a hot rock."

They both laughed.

After kissing a bit more in the park, Trudy took Amanda home and dropped her off.

On her way home, her Bluetooth phone rang across the car's system. It was Danny.

"Hey, Tru, how are you? I haven't seen much of you at school the last couple of days. Is everything all right?"

"Everything's fine. I've just been a little preoccupied with a few tests. It's all good now. What's up?"

"Well, I was calling about tomorrow."

"I was wanting to talk to you about tomorrow as well. I know we usually go out, but I am going to have to cancel—unless I've forgotten something important?"

"I was going to cancel on you as well. What's up with you?"

"I ran into someone, and I wanted to do a little catching up with them. I didn't want to leave you in the wind, but it sounds like you have other plans as well?"

"Yeah, there are a few things I'm trying to iron out. I think if I had a few hours Friday, I could get it all where it needs to be."

"Anything you want to talk about?"

"No, not really. We can talk about it Sunday if that's OK. Saturday is going to be a long day working with Sam, so we can catch up later?"

"Sure. How about the cabin after lunch Sunday?"

He chuckled a little. "Absolutely. I would really like to catch up with you at the cabin. Can't wait."

"You are just so easy. That might be why I like you so much. I will see you Sunday if I don't see you around the farm Saturday."

"Looking forward to it. Bye."

Chapter 21 - The Date

Friday at school, it seemed like the whole school itself was vibrating. The clock would wind backward for a while and then teleport forward. Time was relentlessly teasing both girls. They had planned to see a movie together and have a girl's night out. Both had cleared it with their fathers to be out as late as eleven thirty. The last bell came about fourteen and a half hours into the seven-hour school day, and a breath of fresh air washed across the whole campus when it finally rang. Two girls could not have wanted their freedom more.

They had made plans to meet with their friends and go out for pizza and catch a movie. Although it was true that a group they knew was going out and eating together, and it was also true that they were all going to a movie, the part that was a little less known was that both Amanda and Trudy were not eating with them. They had already seen the movie and could easily pass a quiz if questioned. The two of them were going to get some fast food to go and be off by themselves.

Trudy had watched a few videos—some off Pornhub and a few from YouPorn—all depicting utopian sensual lesbian affairs that she knew did not really happen in the real world. She viewed them because she figured that much of it was using bits and pieces of actual encounters. The moves themselves were mostly what Trudy had envisioned, just in the most unbelievably effective way.

There were, however, some bodily contortions she had not logistically thought about, and she wondered if it was just the porn flair or inspired by real life. One video incorporated a few toys, mostly of a variety that she already had experience with through the many wonderful sexcapades with Danny and Dave.

She could not speak for Amanda, but every time she barely thought of anything intimate with her, she flushed hot and dampened. The long anticipation was stirring something deep in her, and it had made her restless. When she got home from school, she groomed herself, making sure the parts that were shaven were silky smooth and the parts that were not were well-defined and properly trimmed. She had laughed when she realized that she was prepping more completely for Amanda than she had ever done for Danny.

That thought perplexed her just long enough for the water to pull through the system and get hot. She stepped in, showered, and lost track of her thoughts altogether.

She dressed in what she felt was her best and sexiest bra and panty set. Danny loved them, as had Dave on the game day that she took over the proceedings shortly after Danny's mom left. She had put on a strip tease act for the boys that ended up with her well over thirty dollars richer. She had told them to have bills on hand as they would need them if they wanted to pay for play. It was an immense amount of fun that resulted in a sweaty mass of bodies and intermingled juices.

She wondered if there was really such a thing as lucky panties and bras and laughed inwardly when she realized that both boys certainly would agree.

She had considered a fishnet kind of thing but reconsidered and changed over to thigh-high stockings with a matching garter set. She hid it all with an above-the-knee plaid schoolgirl number and a complementary top that drew your eyes to her breasts. It was form-fitting and tailor-made for her, as if someone had tastefully painted it on.

She adorned her ears and fingers with just the right amount of bling and completed the ensemble with a diamond necklace. She stood back and admired her work, mentally noting that, given what she saw in the mirror and possibly because she felt so hot and sexy at the same time, she felt sure that she would want herself if there were two of her.

She turned, shut off the lights, told her dad goodbye, and set off to meet the girls at six. She met up with Amanda, who was waiting inside with the other girls. Her dad had dropped her off as the others were arriving as well. The deception was complete.

When Amanda saw Trudy arrive, she stepped out to get picked up at the front door, out of the eyesight of everyone else. Since no one was expecting them to join their group, no one missed their presence. When she sat in the front seat and adjusted herself, belting in, she looked at Trudy.

"You look amazing!"

"Thank you, so do you."

"No, really, you are naturally good-looking, but right now you are above and beyond. You are gorgeous."

She reached over and ever so slightly, ever so lightly, brushed her hair back with the back of her hand, letting her fingers glide downward as she cleared the hair from her neck. She leaned over and dropped a butterfly kiss on her neck that sent a telegram straight to her pussy, flaring her inner walls to life.

"Where are we going?"

She had noticed that they were headed away from the nightlife and outward to the edge of town.

Trudy beamed a smile. "I know a place where we can talk uninterrupted. It's not far from here, and it's fairly secluded."

"Secluded is nice. It is always nice to get out from under a magnifying glass. I am so happy to be here right now. I have been thinking about you all day—what I wanted to wear, how I want to be, what I hope you will like. I have to tell you, you have been in my thoughts all day right up until now. I want to hold you so tight."

They turned down a country lane.

"I have been doing the same," Trudy admitted. "I want to kiss you, taste you, be close to you. I can hardly wait."

The whole time she had been driving, her neck and cheek had been lovingly caressed. The side of her breast felt the heat of knuckles passing along them. An adventurous hand would occasionally find new fields to comb. It was a battle to keep her concentration while driving.

When she had finally put the car in park and killed the ignition, a blazing hot kiss ignited on its own accord, landing passionately on Amanda's wanting lips right there on the front seat.

"Where are we?"

"It is a hunting and retreat cabin on the back side of our farm. Danny and I have used this place often. I think you will like it… Uh, I hope I didn't just make you uncomfortable talking about coming here with Danny, did I?"

"No, not at all. I mean, I have dated around and have found out, as far as sex is concerned, it is difficult to beat Danny's touch, but he is yours now. I respect that."

"That's just the thing. Like I told you before, he is not mine. We are just 'together.' So if there were a moment that you wanted to relive or wanted to have with Danny, I wouldn't be offended. I would encourage it. Part of our little pact is that we let each other know about any extracurricular encounters for safety's sake. And telling each other about it would be like a voyeuristic fun time."

"I might think about that later, but right now, I'm right where I want to be."

She kissed her one more time, and both girls got out and walked to the door. Trudy entered the code, and the door swung free.

"Come on in. The living room is right here in front, the bathroom is behind the kitchen to the left, across the hall from the bedroom."

The door swung shut and latched. There was an ambiance throughout the cabin as little nightlights gave off a surprising amount of light. Trudy gently took Amanda's hand in hers, held it over her shoulder, and led the way to the bedroom, stopping in the doorway to give Amanda a chance to get the lay of the land.

Standing there in the doorway, Amanda lifted her hand free and palmed the side of Trudy's face, gently pulling her back with delicate, soft hands into an embrace that was half a hug and half a pose. With the pose, she sucked her lips onto Trudy's neck near the shoulder of her left side and gently kissed her way up the curve until, multiple soft velvety kisses later, she arrived at her hairline.

Trudy turned around, and they hugged in a warm embrace.

The embrace they were giving each other was long, tender, and special to both. If there was such a thing as girlfriend virginity, they both realized this was as close as it would get as they hugged each other—not just out of friendship but with longing, loving overtones. Sensual and sexual for the first time, without a care about anything.

Their embrace had given them both a lightheaded, airy feeling—an experience that had been savored for what it was, for the first, complete, real time. Both women only interrupted their embrace, backing off ever so slightly to look at each other without fear of capture, and then kissed as passionately as they had ever done before.

It was better than being with a guy for this first time, as they had an unspoken understanding that just came to them naturally—a soft meeting between them. The primal wanting gave way to melting, which in turn reestablished a wanting as they ever so slowly kissed each other inside their embrace while slowly moving over to the bed.

Trudy kicked off her heels and landed two inches lower, in perfect alignment for them both to see eye to eye. As they gazed deep into each other's souls, the small fire that had been keeping them both at a simmer was fanned, and the flames began to pick up intensity.

Trudy began to unbutton Amanda's deep blue blouse and, as she did so, slowly revealed a wonderfully fitted, delicate black lace bra. She could envision her spectacular breasts from the picture she had received on Tuesday, but the picture did not do them justice whatsoever. The specimen before her was a goddess, and she yearned to know more.

She had been slowly kissing her as she unbuttoned her blouse, and when she reached the beltline, there was a pleasing gasp and a moan.

She knew Amanda's eyes were closed, as she could tell her head was tilted back in bliss. When she drew her nails up her back while rising back to standing, she could feel her become breathless. When she stepped behind her, she realized at this point she could do anything whatsoever, as Amanda was leaning back into her in the most trusting way.

It was an odd feeling for Trudy to remove another woman's bra, and for an instant, she felt sorry for Danny and all those times he had fumbled with the clasps. She found herself unaccustomed to this task as well, from this side of the garment. It both invigorated and frustrated her at the same time, but she managed to unhook the hardware in short order.

Her hot skin laid bare into Trudy's chest. Even covered with her shirt and bra, she could feel the body heat searing through the fabric, rekindling the flames in a new place entirely. She dropped the bra free as she crossed her arms, hugging her, cupping both breasts in a gentle but firm embrace.

Trudy's crotch went hot in an instant. She had felt her own breasts before, but this was something different—something more, something special, and titillating. It felt so good, wonderful, and loving. They both softly gasped as she captured both nipples simultaneously and encapsulated them with her thumb and forefinger.

It was heavenly exquisite, primally alive, and fantastically exciting. She focused on a singular desire—to kiss one of her nipples. All she wanted was a single nipple in her mouth, an opportunity to express to it how she felt.

She slowly spun Amanda, who was half lost in this incredible feeling of a warm embrace mixed with hot desire.

When Trudy's mouth closed around her nipple, Amanda arched back and unconsciously raised a hand, gently pulling her head toward her breast deeper. Trudy's lips explored this protrusion, which was connected to every fiber in Amanda's body. As her tongue explored the extents of her hardened nub, the body gave away its secrets, as her flesh seemed to shiver and shake with each carefully placed tongue lashing.

When she sucked in just the nipple and let her tongue glide carelessly across the top of it, Amanda's hips arched forward uncontrollably. Trudy kissed her breast—all of it—leaving no patch of skin unpampered. It was an unequaled delight to Amanda as well.

Trudy moved from one breast to the other but recaptured the nipple with her left hand as she did so. Kissing her way up to the crescendo at the top of her other straining areola, a neo thumb adorned the top, waiting, straining, begging for her.

When she sucked in this nipple in a low-vacuumed, hot, wet, almost erotic way, she gave a pinch to the other restrained nipple and let the two micro-explosions collide with a verbal, pleasing moan and an air of begging for more—an audible longing.

Amanda pulled her head inward much harder this time, and when she did, Trudy bit with just a slight amount more pressure, equaling the applied pressure with her fingers on the other breast, unleashing an animalistic moan coupled with a "God, yes" from her.

It was delicious to hear.

Trudy squatted down and placed a hot, wet, slow kiss on the edge of her exposed belly button. Just as she had promised herself, she accosted the edges with no complaints from its receiver.

When she stood, Amanda was waiting for her with a warm reception and a deep, heavenly kiss. She felt her crotch become increasingly engorged with every tongue-on-tongue escapade.

Together, they both knew how to kiss in such a passionate way that it transcended the two bodily entities that were meeting, really for the first time, unencumbered. It became more of an introduction to each other's desires.

When Trudy's blouse dropped free, Amanda was delighted to see the wonderful, lace-adorned breasts. She wanted them and wasted no time with the clasps as she removed the bra while in a hug, face to face. She nipped at Trudy's neck as she let the bra fall freely to their feet.

She stopped and stepped backward a step.

"God, you're beautiful. I could look at you all day. I like boys, I liked being with Danny, but looking at you right now, there is nowhere I would rather be. I want you!"

She stepped forward once again and felt for a zipper as she was kissing her way down Trudy's belly. She found the tang of the zipper and grabbed hold of it as she worked her way down. Halfway to her belly line, the skirt fell victim to gravity.

Trudy stood before her in garters and thigh-high stockings. Amanda found this to be highly erotic, but Trudy had not noticed because of the tender kisses and loving caresses as Amanda moved about her body. With her eyes closed, gleefully experiencing the moment, she did not realize that Amanda had worked her way behind her until she felt hot, warm lips on the back of her neck. She was about to gently lay back into her when a hand cupped her sex, forcing an unexpected arch forward and backward, rocking her in the sweetest bodily argument ever conceived.

Pleasure was washing over her, and it was having a terrible time finding where it should land, as her whole being—her every fiber—begged for attention. It was moving her body in ways she could not control. Her head was being pulled to the side as kisses floated down to her nape. Her breasts could feel the gliding heat of Amanda's palms, and when the nipples tried to identify the intruders, they were met with the desire to see the two interlopers again, to make sure the culprits were properly accounted for.

When her thighs started to feel breezy, she realized that the garters had been tampered with in the loveliest, most sinister way, causing the stockings themselves to migrate in a shimmering mess down her legs of their own accord. They had neared her ankles when a purposefully slow-moving Amanda let her hands meet with her upper thighs. Using the legs as a road map, her hands slowly made their way down to help liberate the nylons. The touch—the soft, loving glide, the heat of her hands—set Trudy ablaze.

When the leggings had been summarily dispatched, she expected a loving return up her legs. It did not happen as she had anticipated. Rather, she felt a hot embrace on her thighs—Amanda had a hot mouth on her sex from the outside of her panties. She could feel every flaming breath as it made its way across her inner thigh, parting between her legs in a deliciously soothing breeze. Amanda could taste her—she was wet, her panties were soaked, and her arousal was pushing right through the silky lace fabric. She loved her nectar; she loved even more the fact that it was her who had gotten her to this state to begin with. She wanted to give more.

With an iron will, Trudy beckoned Amanda to stand—partly because she wanted to disrobe her, partly because if Amanda had stayed any longer, even over the panties, she was going to have the most delicious orgasm, and she did not want to have it alone.

When she got Amanda standing, she worked her way around to the back of her, kissing a path of fire droplets as she went. When she centered herself on Amanda's spine, she worked her way down to kneeling and, from behind, unbuttoned her slacks, deftly hooking her thumbs to pull them down.

She was not content with releasing just the slacks—she also hooked her panties as well. All of it came down as a unit. She coaxed each leg from its prison and drew her hand up the outside of her right leg. In one deft motion, she stepped to the right ever so slightly, and as her hand started to pass her thigh, it veered off course, and two fingers lost themselves inside Amanda, who arched heavily into and away from this unexpected atomic visitor.

She thought her sex was going to explode as her pussy responded to every micro-movement. Amanda willed herself to straighten and turned toward Trudy, where she pushed her forcibly back onto the bed. Amanda all but ripped off her panties and pulled the remnants of the garter off. She was breathing raggedly and commanded Trudy further back onto the bed.

"I'm sorry, Trudy, this part isn't what I envisioned at first, but I realize, there is one thing we have to do right now."

She moved to the head of the bed, climbed on, and straddled Trudy while crawling down her. When she had aligned her pussy with her face, she dipped her hips toward Trudy, who not only received her but captured her ass with her arms, pulling her in deep.

Trudy's tongue entered Amanda's wet, hot longing. Simultaneously, Trudy felt a tongue enter her as if it were choreographed timing.

Both women were so worked up that there was a parallel drenching. It was an orgasmic cacophony that resulted in multiple rolls across the bed and back, a humping and a muted face-pounding from both women, and an orgasmic, multiple release—fluidly recurring for both.

Their wanting had presented itself in a manner that was all but primal now. It was calling to them as they rose into a skittering, shaking, shimmering mass of legs and torsos, all straining for a oneness of being.

They barely had the energy to realign themselves after they fell breathlessly apart together, spent and ragged. When they finally did manage to get face to face, they kissed passionately for a second, then intertwined their arms and legs within each other, lying there in an afterglow they had constructed for each other. It was an incredible after-blaze bliss.

They slowly came back to a cognitive reality state, still riding a breeze inside themselves as they untangled their arms and legs to get to a better face-to-face position to apprise each other's condition and mindset.

Trudy was the first to talk.

"That was incredible. YOU were incredible. I had a whole agenda I wanted to go through—how I wanted to touch you, where I wanted to touch you—but I was so close to coming just from being here with you. When you took charge, what you did was so right. It was fantastic."

"I know, right? I had the same thing in my mind. I wanted to do a whole checklist of things as well. I had thought about this all day. I wanted to please you so much. I was going to ask you for a whole host of things if you hadn't already, but I just couldn't do it. I wanted you so badly it hurt. Somehow, it's you that makes me want you so badly. I just can't explain it."

"I was thinking just the same thing. I'm lying here with you, and I can't imagine a better start for us. But for now, I'm just lost in my mind, thinking."

"Thinking about what?"

Without another word, Trudy rolled up on her elbow and leaned in for a kiss. It was a long, passionate, full-tongue kiss that invited comfort, delicious wanting, and an acceptance that warmed the two of them.

She broke free and started to kiss down Amanda's neck. Simultaneously, she slid across her firm abs and ended up cupping her vulva with her whole hand.

Amanda drew in a heavy breath and arched slightly upward. Trudy took her time getting to the nipples, and when she found the first one, she unleashed an oral attack that culminated in a severe tongue lashing, as if for some unimaginable slight. She moved on to punish the other nipple and breast, all while her hand was working inside of Amanda, feeling her become wetter and start to flow again once more.

Her hand remembered how to satisfy herself—how to work over her clitoris in just the right tactile pressure—but now, for the moment, it was on someone else's body, and that somehow made it all that much better.

She felt like the detachment from the personal sensory feedback was strange. For a brief moment, a newfound respect for Dave and Danny's efforts flashed through her mind.

Her fingers alone in this wilderness began to act autonomously, and when they did, somehow touching this hot, wet muff also connected to her own clitoris. It was as if it were feeling every circling and battle with Amanda's nub by itself as well. It had begun to drive her on with deeper commitment and fervor.

She had worked over both breasts orally with equal longing and desire and moved down to her belly. As the kisses were laid from one side to the other, she reached a point where the bed would allow her to go no further. Amanda laid on her side, exposing the tender, soft curve of her back meeting her ass. When the trail of kisses was impeded again, one more twist was made, making the rollover fully complete.

Amanda was on her stomach. The kisses found their way along her hip line and onto her supple butt cheeks, all the way down to the sensitive lower curves of her flesh meeting in with her thighs. Both sides of the bare skin had been equally toured, almost acting as a primer.

Trudy stopped and totally broke all contact with her, letting the night calm settle in wordlessly, silently.

Just as it seemed there was too much time-lapse to bear, with the backside of her fingers ever so slightly making a breath of contact, she started with the curve of her ass where it met the spine and dragged her fingernails almost invisibly and ever so lightly over Amanda's now dimpling skin. The only sign that she was still touching her was the uptick in breathing and the breathy soft moans of delight.

Amanda arched forward, willing the touch to be more tangible, but Trudy stopped once more and let the air calm her.

Both hands lifted, she landed both downward with an unexpected smack of palms on both ass halves. They connected in an electrified snap that brought a rush of cooler air in front of her palms, spontaneously combusting as the palm met buttocks, culminating into a heated whirlwind.

Amanda moaned loudly, arched upward again—but higher—and Trudy grabbed her writhing body by the hips, pulling her up to doggy position and putting a thumb deep within her.

Only seconds had passed, but it felt like a wonderful eternity.

Her thumb now in her and fingers massaging her labia, her clitoris, and really the whole vulva, the feeling was leaving Amanda to feel like she was slowly being unhinged by a wonderful outside force.

She had been wet before, but now a new complement of lubrication was rushing out to greet her wonderful assailant.

Minutes later, Trudy extricated her fingers from Amanda's quivering body, as it was clear that the treatment she had been given was fantastically familiar. She knew what had to happen next.

Trudy pushed her forward to the headboard. When Amanda arrived facing the headboard, Trudy turned over while lying down and slid on her back under Amanda, between her unsteady thighs and legs.

When she captured her hips with her firm grasp, she hauled her honey pot to her mouth and pulled her in tight. It was clear that her body was very receptive to her exact position, as the arch was now pushing downward, begging inward.

As she sucked her clitoris gently in, the rest of Amanda let her know that every fiber within her was on the same page. Through moaning and hip tilts and the flow of her want on her face, Trudy knew her reception was indeed being well received.

Amanda started to hump forward uncontrollably into her lips—it was clear that she was getting closer.

Trudy was happy about this because, in one of her daydreams, she was right here and knew exactly what she wanted and what she was going to do.

When Amanda came, it was a cross between a beginning whimper and a half-muted roar, accompanied by a flood. Without control, she was humping, screaming, trying to retreat but hopelessly locked by Trudy's arms.

Trudy was not going to let go until she decided to and had already decided that she would only let loose when she completely owned her.

Amanda was bucking wildly with every new wave running through her body.

Wave after wave, she had lost all touch with reality and did not care. She wanted to force her pussy through Trudy's skull.

With every thrust, there was a new wave or an increased height of the already running wave. Her body was beckoning to be released and begging to stay. Time stood still, blurred, the euphoria of the endless releases the only sensation she could now register.

Her body shuddered and shimmied uncontrollably in waves.

Fully five minutes had passed before she realized that she was balled up in a fetal position on the bed beside this beautiful girl, who was adoringly watching her body still quake from the slightest breeze across her body in the aftermath.

And Trudy was enjoying her effect, timing a soft blow across her back in coordination with the ebb and flow of the shimmering.

Breathless and sweaty, the tide within her began to subside, leaving only lightly audible coos in its wake.

Amanda rolled to her and hugged Trudy in such a unique way.

It was not love, per se, nor was it a thank you—it was more like an acknowledgment, an appreciation that someone had given so selflessly to her.

She had never experienced this feeling, and it had captivated her.

Trudy needed no explanation, as the hug was understood in a visceral plane known to just these two women—here and now—on a raw, primal, uncorrupted physio-spiritual plane.

She had given of herself without regard to thought. Admittedly, at first, it was for pleasure, but it had morphed somewhere in the moment into a oneness of sharing without regard to self.

She fully understood the clenched wrapping of their bodies in a hug so profound it escaped words.

"Trudy, I…uh—"

"Shhh, I felt it too."

"I have never felt like that before. My god, I can't help but want more of you in every way I can think of, but right now, I can't think of how to begin to give to you what you have given me. Somehow, I—"

"You already have. Just hold me. Enjoy this right now with me. Feel me with you."

"Oh, Trudy…!"

She hugged her just as tightly and as closely as ever before.

Several minutes had passed before they both began to stir.

The bed was a mess on top, but the girls had not gotten much deeper than the top cover after sliding the duvet off it, so it was not hard to remake with a new cover.

They dropped the old one near the washing machine.

Both girls were completely nude and completely comfortable in their state with each other.

It was an extra enjoyment for both to occasionally stop and cup the other one in an embrace—capturing breasts or asses or just a body-to-body embrace.

It felt crazy good.

After the bed and room had been reassembled from the destruction of the encounter, Amanda grabbed Trudy by the hand.

"I think we should complete this loss of virginity with one final thing. I have never showered with another woman, much less one that is my lover."

"I have been in the shower with another guy many times. Danny and I end up there a lot," she laughed. "But it has never been with another woman, much less someone as gorgeous as you. I would love washing you."

"I think the only other person I have showered with was Danny as well. He is fun to shower with."

They both laughed in agreement.

They entered the shower room, and Amanda took charge, as it was her idea.

She started the water, warmed it, and then stepped in, pulling Trudy with her.

Trudy appreciated the hotness of the water—it was exactly to her preference—and noted that maybe girls appreciate hot water more than boys.

Trudy loved the caresses on her body and was taking in the total enjoyment of being pampered, laying back into Amanda as the water danced on their shoulders and chests.

The feeling of breasts on her back excited her a bit, but it was hidden by the heat of the water and her standing nipples.

She could feel Amanda's nipples react to the closeness as her body was cleansed by wonderfully soapy, slick, and wandering hands.

She had closed her eyes and was enjoying her treatment when a hand took extra care in cleaning her patch of hair. It was just starting to pull a bit as the soap had been rinsed away. The hand that had been washing her cupped her full vulva. She sucked in a breath unexpectedly, her stance widened, and she leaned perceptibly more into Amanda as the hand took its time in a slow, deliberate massage of her womanly parts. She felt one finger go in, followed easily by a second.

The attention she was getting had awakened her inner being once again, and her body was responding in kind. The hand made deliberate headway and did all the right things to cause her breath to hitch and catch. Less than a minute later, she had the most luxurious release—not exactly a utility come, but one that was gentle and fully complete, satisfying, and direct. A statement of appreciation that was fulfilling and yet still weakened the knees.

The hot water helped extend the ride as Amanda sensed just the right time to stop her manipulation and simply kissed the back of Trudy's neck. She was completed, satiated, and now completely relaxed.

Both girls finished washing each other's bodies, enjoying the uniqueness of what they knew was a first experience for both. This knowledge somehow made it all that much more special as they shared it together.

They dried each other purposefully, without reigniting any flame, and walked hand in hand to the bedroom to dress.

They traded panties just for the novelty of it, like a souvenir that served as a wonderful reminder of the other. After helping each other with bra clasps, zippers, and buttons, they both worked together to fix the makeup that had been destroyed.

With a final pass to make sure the room would pass inspection, they walked out into the clean, crisp air under a cloudless, star-filled sky. A sky devoid of all light noise, as the countryside often was.

They took a moment in a shared embrace against the front fender of the Cherokee, enjoying this time together without a care in the world.

As they turned to go, Trudy stopped, captured Amanda once more, and gave her a soft, beautiful, caring kiss that was received and returned with the same care it was given.

Trudy spoke.

"I am glad we got to this point. It was wonderful. I'm so glad it was you as well because I have always liked you."

"I feel the same way. I tend to hold my friendships very separate and sacred in a sense. That is why I said I could never be upset with you or Danny. I like you both in such wonderfully separate ways.

"I won't lie and say that I don't miss pieces of having him around and being with him, but being with you was amazing tonight. I want you even now, but as much as I loved what you have done to and for me—and what you let me do to and hopefully for you—I still miss Danny's dick."

She continued, "I haven't really been interested in other boys because I hear how they are disappointing all our other friends. It seems like the boys at our school are total dicks in that regard. Some are even rough.

"You would think that the more mature boys would know how to treat a woman, but they seem to revert to the old Neanderthal ways. I'm really going to miss having Danny around next year."

"What are you doing Sunday? Would your dad let you get out?"

"After he conducts the services at nine, he spends the rest of his time well into the afternoon visiting with the new members and the older set. Why?"

"I had a thought that could involve you if you would like. How do you get around if your dad is gone all the time? Does your mom drive you too?"

"I drive…duh…just not to school. My dad doesn't trust the other kids to not dent the car…even if it is a beater. It's his way of having a little more control over me.

"It's just an old Volkswagen Jetta. I would have driven tonight if we weren't going out with a bunch of other girls."

They both laughed a bit.

"My mom divorced my dad a couple of years back, which was a good thing because they were fighting all the time. She tried to get me to live with her, but things got ugly and nasty between my mom and dad.

"Long story short, Dad got full custody, and Mom gets to visit every other weekend. I would rather live with Mom, but for now, I'm stuck with Dad until I'm eighteen. Praise Jesus," she said in a dismissive, mocking voice.

They got into the SUV and headed back to town for a collective milkshake and fries.

After they killed the fries and shake, Trudy dropped Amanda off at her house at eleven ten—enough time to make it home under the curfew limit herself.

Chapter 22 - The Guys Cook

Danny had mentioned to Sam and Bill that he had been studying culinary arts on the side, after school at home. He had taken over a good portion of the cooking at home to help with his mother's changing work schedule.

After describing some of the elaborate meals he had cooked, an idea had formed. It was not clear whether it was Bill, Sam, or Danny who first suggested it, but the notion became one clear voice with a specific objective.

They were going to collectively cook Sunday lunch for everyone as a thank-you of sorts.

They wanted to pull out all the stops and shoot to impress.

This meal was going to include Sadie, Sam and his now-girlfriend Jessie, Danny and his mother, along with a friend of his, Dave. Bill had also mentioned he might bring a guest, to Danny and Sam's surprise.

They planned to decide on a menu Friday and spend Saturday morning gathering everything they needed to make it all just right.

Danny knew that they were looking to him to pull it all together and coordinate what had to be accomplished. He was up to the task, but a small element of fear tagged along as a sidekick.

Friday, they all met at the office as agreed upon and decided that the meal would be prepared there and served banquet-style on the long tables used for breaks in the office and work bays.

Danny had downloaded a couple of menus from sites ranging from high-end to medium fare and laid them out before the others as an example and primer for ideas.

The first suggestion was to keep the appetizers simplistic so they could concentrate on the main dishes and get them right.

It was agreed upon to serve jumbo shrimp cocktail and hot yeast rolls, with a choice between butter, honey butter, cinnamon butter, and apple butter.

They all agreed that this would be a great start—most of it could be prepared early and left to stay chilled, except for the rolls, which would be brought out piping hot as soon as everyone arrived.

The men were going to hand-print the menu on white poster board so everyone would have an idea of what to expect. Since it was clear that Sam had the best penmanship, this duty fell to him.

After the appetizers, there would be a round of soup or salad.

The salad was to be a mix of butter crisp, spinach, and arugula, with shredded carrot, sliced radish, chunked orange, red, and yellow bell peppers, sliced celery, and halved grape tomatoes. It would be topped with craisins for sweetness.

There would be French, Ranch, and Italian dressing available, as well as croutons and sunflower seeds.

Most of these ingredients could be bowled or prepped and kept chilled until it was time to be served. The soup would be a choice between a cup of broccoli and cheese or white bean and bacon, both of which could be prepped and kept hot in small crock pots.

The broiled lobster would fall on Danny, and the steak bombs only seemed logical for Bill to make on the grill. The maple pecan-infused asparagus, also bacon-wrapped, was just a matter of timing—after being prepared, they could share oven space and temperature with the lobster tails. The cheesy mac and the mashed sweet potatoes with walnuts and marshmallows could both be made a day in advance and heated in crocks.

And for dessert, a small contingency of double chocolate brownies for chocolate lovers, as well as a pineapple upside-down cake with evaporated rum drizzle, would be available.

The three of them felt as though they could manage all of this but knew they would be busy if they were to pull it off in the fashion they had intended.

When Saturday morning came, there was a buzz of activity in the office. Danny had meticulously written out the ingredients for all the offerings and the preparation instructions that could be easily followed.

Bill had gone out later Friday night, after everyone had broken up to leave, and purchased a new double set of white-on-white dinner plates and dishes, as well as service for twelve silverware sets. He also picked up two of the three-bay crock pot dish warmers to contain the soups, steak bombs, potatoes, and asparagus.

Saturday was building up to be a busy day.

About this time, Kevin Stephans, Kate Taylor's fiancé, walked in. He and Kate had decided to make a surprise run home for the weekend. Danny quickly brought him up to speed on what was going on.

Kevin was not one to be left out or shy away from a challenging task, so he asked young Danny for marching orders. Danny handed him the sweet potato and asparagus recipe cards and asked if he had any questions.

Kevin said he had it under control.

It was clear early on that when Kevin said he could do something, it would get done. All the boys were impressed with him when he had shouldered up like family when the sheriff came calling a few months back. He was now a trusted man.

The guys were all pulling off their parts in the preparations, and other than an emergency run to add lobster tails and a few more quantity-related items due to two welcome add-ons, they were all but done shortly after noon.

When they had finished, they all gathered in the bay. Danny looked just a bit tired.

Bill asked, "Are you OK, Danny? You look like you're a little ragged."

"I would have been fine, but I had a little more to do than the rest of you. And before anyone defends themselves, I want to explain that I knew it was going to be a busy morning, so I planned a little extra event.

"Why don't you all have a seat at a table and give me a minute? I'll be right back."

Danny disappeared and reappeared from the kitchenette carrying a large aluminum pan laden with wrapped something in the form of an elongated, thick oval and two bags of chips. He set it down in front of the guys.

Sam piped up, "Oh wow, I don't know what that is, but it smells great!"

"Thank you, Sam. I knew that we would be too busy to make lunch, so I planned that as my task as well. I give you my famous Philly steak and cheese.

"If you don't like onions or peppers, well then, tough—you're out of luck, because this is how they should be made."

He laughed as he pulled them out one by one and distributed them.

"And since the bun package comes in a six-pack, Kevin, you're in luck. If anyone wants more, there are two left."

Just as he said that, the door opened, and Trudy came into the bay, immediately hit with an amazing mix of smells as she looked at the subs.

"Uh, make that one left."

They all laughed.

"Lunch, Trudy?"

"Absolutely. It smells absolutely divine in here. What is it?"

Bill cut in, "Philly steak and cheese, and they are fantastic. What you smell is the prep for tomorrow.

"It is up to you to tell Sadie and Kate and the girls that lunch is on the guys tomorrow at twelve o'clock sharp."

Danny chimed in, "If you guys want something to drink, someone will have to get them. I would like a Seven Up if anyone gets the chance, please."

Kevin contributed, "That's the least I can do for lunch…three beers and a Seven Up. Trudy?"

"Lemonade, please. If not, a Seven Up as well."

The Phillies were perfect.

They were on toasted hoagie buns, the meat sliced thinly but thick enough to pick up what was obviously a wonderful marinade—delightfully tangy, layered with alternating pepper jack and American cheeses, sautéed onions, and sweet peppers, dusted with hot pepper flakes that gave off the perfect balance of flavor and heat.

They almost melted in your mouth because they were so good.

Barbecue chips and ruffled chips set the tone.

Other than the pop tops making their collective spits when they were opened, lunch was primarily silent as hunger pains were being quelled.

The rest of Trudy and Danny's Saturday had been spent on Jax's couch, watching a movie they had streaming online. It could have been any movie—the title really did not matter—as Trudy realized that Danny was fast asleep, snuggled into the arm of the couch, even with her full body weight leaning back onto him.

After readjusting a few times, it was clear he was out for the count.

Trudy carefully removed herself and covered him with an Afghan that had just magically appeared one day in the last couple of weeks.

It was a very intricate pattern—well-made, sturdy, and warm.

It puzzled Trudy as to where her dad had gotten it. She had never really seen her father go to the store to buy anything without the he-man hunter mentality.

Usually, it went something like: need this, find who has it, trek to that store only, enter, bag it, tag it, pay for it, now leave.

This wonderfully warm blanket just did not fit his style for a conquest drive.

In any event, she watched Danny curl up with it completely.

When her dad came into the room, he almost laughed aloud and caught himself so as not to wake Danny.

Bill commented, "Man, he's out cold. I guess he was up late. That would be Sam and my fault."

"Why is that?"

"We all planned the meal for Sunday last night. He brought recipe cards, and all the cooking instructions were specified to the letter. They were quite well thought out, and they saved us a bunch of time.

"We would still be in process down there if he hadn't done that. I think he is really going to become a chef—and a good one at that, based on his preparedness."

"He is a good cook. I have had a lot of what he has made. He uses me as a guinea pig sometimes. Mostly, that is a good thing, but I don't pull any punches when it's bad.

"He has a good sense of combinations—what works well with this, that, or the other.

"I'm really going to miss him next year."

She changed the subject.

"Hey, Dad, where did that blanket come from? It's really nice. I didn't buy it, so where did you get it?"

"I have been meaning to talk to you about that. Uh, I'm not sure how to do this. It's just that…."

It connected with Trudy as to why her dad was stumbling over his words, and she let it flow across her with a ginormous smile.

"Someone gave it to you. Someone nice, who knows how to make such things. Someone decidedly feminine?" She broadened her smile. "I hope so anyway. I hate to see you so lonely."

"I was afraid that you might be mad that I'm moving on in my life."

"Dad??? Really?? I'm happy for you. I know you loved Mom—everyone could see that—but even Mom would want you to move on.

"I'm not mad at all. And just because you found someone doesn't mean we will forget Mom. It is just something—or rather, someone—different after her."

"I am glad you feel that way because she is coming to lunch tomorrow. Promise you will be nice? She will be meeting a lot of the people that mean so much to me—all of you at once."

Trudy joked, "I've always wanted a step-monster. Do I have to call her Mom?" She teased further.

He started to lighten up due to Trudy's way of working him over like a prizefighter.

"No, Paula will do. Paula Crane. I met her at the Tractor Supply warehouse. She was trying to figure out what sump pump to get because hers failed in her basement. I was getting some fittings for the field pumps, and we just kind of met.

"I helped her pick out a pump. She asked if I knew any trustworthy plumbers. I told her that I could put it in for her, but I wasn't a plumber, and as for being trustworthy, that would be a little self-serving—so she would have to figure that out for herself and decide.

"She laughed, and we talked for a while. I put in the pump over lunch at her house. It just went from there.

"She used to be married to a preacher, but he was mentally abusive, according to her. She tried to fight for custody of their daughter, but he had all the money. Most of what they had—which wasn't much, apparently—he had hidden.

"She moved away for a few months to get back on her feet and moved back here to take an accounting job in town. That's everything in a nutshell."

"I'm sure she is nice, and from the sound of it, she has her head on straight. So go for it, Dad," she said, beaming another smile. "Is she bringing her daughter too?"

"No, not yet. She doesn't want to restart any fights with her ex until she is on firmer ground, but I'm supposed to meet her soon. We might go out for pizza. Would you like to go when that happens?"

"Sure. Does her daughter go to school here? What's her name?"

"I'm not sure what grade she is in yet, but I think she may go to your school. Her name is Amanda."

"I know a couple of Amandas at our school, but no Amanda Crane. I'll have to look her up on social media. In any event, if you like her, she can't be all that bad." She again beamed another smile.

Danny was embarrassed to wake up on Bill's couch while Bill was in his recliner watching Saturday football. Sam was on the other end of the couch. Trudy was nowhere to be seen.

"I must have fallen asleep. I'm sorry, guys."

Sam laughed. "Fell asleep? Son, you have been dead to the world for an hour and a half since I got here."

Bill joined the laugh. "And forty-five minutes before that. Trudy is out doing some running. She said she would take you for a ride tomorrow after lunch."

Sam ribbed him jokingly, "Look here, Loverboy. Nothing says 'I really like being around you' like falling asleep on them. You are doing just great."

"Real funny, Sam. Man, I was tired. I think I'm going to head home. Please tell Trudy I said goodbye."

"Will do," Bill confirmed.

Sunday arrived in great fashion. The air was a bit cooler, and there was a slight breeze, with the sun in full view due to a cloudless sky. It just felt good.

Danny had arrived early and was going to take Dave, but Dave had to cancel due to a family activity, so Danny was by himself when he entered the office.

Bill already had the tables out, and Sam was loading crock pots as prescribed. Kevin was moving chairs about and helping coordinate setting the table. There was a teamwork air that moved all of them along fluidly.

All the food was ready to go. The only things left were the grilling and the broiling, along with heating the rolls and timing the wrapped asparagus. It was a waiting game and a matter of micro-timing.

The ladies were to meet at Sadie's house. Trudy had arrived around eleven to find that Kate and Sadie had been home from church for some time.

Jessie showed up not long after Trudy arrived and was welcomed in.

Another car arrived, and when the occupant got out, Trudy instantly recognized her and stepped out to welcome Mrs. Veach.

Shortly after, Trudy introduced Mindy Veach to everyone.

There was another trail of dust heading their way.

When the car was on its approach to the gathering cars in the drive, Sadie grabbed Trudy and excused them both so they could step out and meet the newcomer.

Paula Crane stepped out of her car.

She knew she was in the correct place immediately, but she had hoped that when she met the ones closest to Bill, he would be with her. She was a bit uneasy and apprehensive at first, but those feelings quickly melted away when Trudy and Sadie introduced themselves with openness and friendly beckoning.

Sadie stepped forward and greeted her.

"You must be Paula. This is Trudy. I'm Sadie. It's great to meet you!"

Trudy stepped forward to greet her, and a handshake turned into a light hug.

"It is really nice to meet you both. I was really nervous meeting you by myself. Thank you for being so welcoming."

"I thought you might be a bit uneasy, so I wanted to get right out to meet you. Men…they have no sense of formality sometimes."

They all laughed.

Sadie continued, "Please come in. We will introduce you around to everyone. It is truly nice to have you out today."

"Thank you. Thank you both for making this so much easier than I thought it would be. I wanted to kill Bill when he said he wanted me to meet you all by myself."

When they reentered the house, Paula was greeted warmly by everyone.

It had been partly easier because Mindy Veach, though very much aware of who everyone was, had also only met them for the first time today.

It was new for everyone, which made for a lively gathering as multiple introductions were happening at once.

The women hit it off well with each other.

Paula was very open and easy to talk to.

Mindy Veach was floating in and out of the conversations, right along with Kate, Sadie, and Trudy.

At eleven forty-five, Sadie suggested that they make their way to the office.

Trudy began to object to Sadie because the walk was only five minutes at best.

Then Sadie gave her a lighthearted "zip it and don't say a word" look.

It caught Trudy off guard for a moment, but in short order, she caught on and understood her intention.

The gaggle of geese meandered slowly down the lane on foot. Their pace was decidedly without intent, but even so, they managed to arrive six minutes early.

Trudy had an idea of what would happen for arriving this early, as she had seen dish duty handed over for a thirty-second infraction.

Sadie announced their arrival, acting oblivious to the time.

Kevin and Sam welcomed the ladies at the door and formally ushered them to the tables that had been decked out in their honor.

What had begun as gangly folding tables had been transformed into elegant restaurant-style accommodations. White linen adorned with white bone dishes sat atop the table, garnished with multiple centerpieces.

Candles were lit in the center of the tables, and the shop lights had been dimmed to aid in the atmosphere. The serving table boasted its presentation alone, although there were still a few holes in the serving caddies.

Danny and Bill rounded the corner with the missing dishes as if on cue. Danny set down the lobsters under a metal canopy and asked for Kevin's help with the rolls and asparagus.

As they made their way to retrieve the final fare, Bill filled the center crock to overflowing with the New York strip bombs.

In short order, the rest of the food was brought forth and laid to rest, revealing a truly amazing feast.

The men put on a great show and demonstrated incredible attention to detail as they served everyone community appetizers along with hot rolls and a multitude of butters.

This was overshadowed only by cooled bowls of salad with multiple dressings, along with small cups of soup.

Danny monitored the progress and initiated the signal as the men got back up to deliver the main course.

The event came together with perfect timing. Everything had been planned exquisitely, and it all fell into place impeccably well.

There was a bit of indecision on the women's part when it came to dessert. However, one had already been decided by Danny, as he knew his mother loved both his brownies and his pineapple upside-down cake.

He had already doled out a smaller, graduated piece of both types to accommodate her.

She really loved the attention this gave her, and even more so, she felt the love from her son that teenagers sometimes forget to share.

They all had dessert and concluded that if anyone left hungry, they just weren't trying hard enough.

Danny made a "to-go" plate for Dave, and Trudy made one for later, though no one else had been expected.

As the women collectively got up to leave, Bill and Sam shouldered up with Danny taking the rear tripod position, and Bill spoke up.

"Hold on now, you can't leave."

All the women stopped to take in the guys and see if they had missed something.

Sadie spoke up. "Is there something wrong?"

Sam chimed in. "Now, Momma, fair is fair."

Bill sided with him. "That's right, Sadie…right, Danny?"

"Uh, uh," Danny finally chimed in sheepishly, making his way into the conversation. "Yes, well…yes, fair is fair."

"What's wrong? I don't understand," Trudy feigned.

Bill pointed out, "You all showed up early. We said twelve o'clock, and you were here a full five minutes or so early."

Jessie, Mindy, and Paula looked at the other women inquisitively, able to tell that the others knew what was afoot.

Sadie interjected, "Just one second, boys. I'll need to confer with our group."

The women gathered into a loose huddle as the rules of lunch were explained to the newcomers, who immediately understood the game and why Sadie had chosen to arrive early.

Paula innocently spoke up as she turned and stepped away from the on-looking group. "Bill, can't you forgive the rules just this once since I'm new and didn't know?"

She was playing the wholly innocent bystander and batting her eyes.

Bill stuttered. "Well…uh…"

Sam chided him. "Bill, fair is fair, right?"

"Shit, uh…you're right, Sam. Fair is fair."

Paula gave him an are you sure you want to pay that price look.

"Really?"

"Yeah, I'm sorry, Paula, but fair is fair," he said, defeated, like a man who could not win in any direction.

The women returned to the huddle and congratulated Paula for the deviously mean attempt.

Jessie stepped out.

"Sam, Sadie, Kate, and I, along with whoever wants to go, are going shopping. We haven't got time for games here!"

"Well, baby…uh—"

Bill jumped in, riding Sam close with an in for a penny, in for a pound tone.

"SSS AAA MMM??"

Sam, with his head bowed to hide the wince, muttered, "I'm sorry, baby, uh…fair is fair."

The women returned to the huddle and congratulated Jessie for the squeeze she had put on the boys.

Unexpectedly, Mindy stepped out.

"Danny, you are going to make the woman that brought you into this world clean the dishes at a home where I just met these people?

"I need more time to get to know them. We are going to be busy all day. You are just going to have to give up these silly rules."

"Uh…well—"

Bill caught on to their game. "That's a classic guilt trip, son."

Sam joined in. "Don't fall for it. Momma used to get me every time with that one."

Bill bolstered him. "Hold the line, Danny!"

Mindy's arms were crossed, head cocked, shoulders set. "Well?"

"I'm sorry, Mom, uh…" Danny feebly got out. "Fair is fair."

The women returned to the huddle, and everyone really appreciated the attempt on Mindy's part. It was well crafted and executed perfectly.

They all turned to the boys, and Sadie stepped forward.

"OK, fair is fair. We will do the dishes. Trudy, dear, what is for lunch next week?"

"Peanut butter and jelly or bologna sandwiches, I think. I'll have to check."

The boys collectively groaned as all the women tried their best not to explode with laughter.

"Well, what are you four waiting on? Get on out of here." Sadie chased them away.

The women stayed eerily silent as the boys filed past.

They listened to the sound of them walking away to Jax's house as Trudy peeked unseen through a window and announced they were gone.

At that moment, the women all busted up in laughter.

They commented on the expert guilt trip, the girlfriend in need play, and the newcomer argument.

They were all quite tickled at the manipulatory attempts.

The women worked together flawlessly. Even the new faces held their own and pitched in where needed along with everyone else.

As expected—and wanted—on Sadie's part, getting to know everyone there more intimately was the goal, and it was indeed accomplished across the board for the fledgling group.

Bonds were forged based on friendship and fellowship.

The dishes were just a means to an end that everyone appreciated.

The women also collectively agreed that the meal was beyond upscale restaurant quality, and the service was not half bad either.

Everyone congratulated Mindy Veach for her son's orchestration of the dinner.

They all knew and agreed that, though the other men could collectively accomplish anything, this could have only been pulled off with Danny's directorship.

They were sure that the men knew it as well.

Overall, this Sunday lunch was one for the books.

The women finished the cleanup in record time, leaving out the chairs and tables for the men to contend with later.

They lingered for thirty minutes more, sitting and conversing among themselves.

Trudy spent time with a few of the women separately.

Kate had quietly asked her how things were going, to which Trudy had explained the advancements of the hotels and how things were progressing to the point where she thought she might try to diversify.

Kate asked her if she had considered getting help with growing and maintaining the business—someone like a CEO of all her interests—as it might be good to take some of the weight off her shoulders, at least for now while she was in school.

Trudy appreciated the input and promised to put some thought into it.

When Trudy had time to spend with Paula, she started by telling her the whole sleeping boyfriend and the Afghan encounter, along with the ensuing conversation with her dad and how he had told her about how they met. She complimented Paula on how intricate the pattern was and how well it was made.

Paula just laughed a bit. "I threw that one together just for Bill. I was happy to do it."

"Dad said you have a daughter, Amanda?"

"Yes, I do. Why?"

"I told Dad she must be younger than he thought she was because I know a couple of Amandas at our school, but none of them are a Crane."

"I can see I created a bit of confusion here. Her name is Amanda Parker. I went back to my maiden name after I divorced."

Trudy smiled big—for more than one reason now.

"When Dad said your ex was a preacher, I thought of my friend's dad. Her name is Amanda, but she had a different last name. It all makes sense now—I am good friends with your daughter. She is fun to be with. I, uh—"

"What?"

"I'm not sure it's my place to talk about it, but I get the impression that her dad keeps Amanda under his thumb whenever possible.

"She has given me the impression that he wears her out at times. School is a great escape, and it seems like after-school activities are how she gets out to have fun. Like I said, it's not my place."

"No, it's alright. That makes perfect sense, given what I know of him. He wasn't always like that, but he fell into a religious group that was far to the right—the kind where women are supposed to be quiet and subservient to men and the whole bit.

"That isn't what I married into. It caused a bunch of issues, and eventually, a year later, we divorced.

"Unfortunately, I didn't plan as well as I should have, and Amanda has been paying for it ever since.

"That was two years ago, and I'm still fighting to get custody.

"In about nine months, it won't really matter because she will be eighteen.

"I'm hoping she will move in with me to finish high school—if she can tough it out that long."

"Something tells me that she has her own mind. She won't be dissuaded from anything if she doesn't want to be.

"I think I'm beginning to see where she got that from."

"Thank you. When you see her again, tell her I said hello.

"I only get to see her every other weekend, and I was going to tell her about dating your dad, but since you will see her before me, you can let her know if you want.

"No need for you to keep any secrets on my behalf.

"And tell her I love her and miss her.

"If I had the money her dad hid from me and the lawyers, I could have gotten custody.

"But as it is—if it weren't for the judge seeing what was really going on—I might not have been able to see her at all."

"I'll tell her, but from the conversations we have had, she knows already. And she is looking forward to moving in with you."

"That is so good to hear. Thank you. Let her know that if she needs anything, she can call, and I will do my best to help her."

"No problem. You know, now that the cat is out of the bag, I'm looking forward to getting to know you.

"I hope you come over a lot. It is great to see my dad smile like he has for the last few weeks.

"It is even better to meet the reason for the smiles.

"Really, come over anytime. If Dad isn't home, we can visit—if you like, that is.

"In any case, I'm glad you are here."

"I'm so glad to be here as well and to meet Sadie along with everyone else.

"Thank you for your warm welcome, Trudy."

"I was afraid that you might see me as some kind of step-monster or something."

Trudy's eyes shot wide open.

"What? Too soon?" Paula asked with a big smile.

Trudy smiled widely. "Clearly, Dad has been talking with you. I'll have to bring that up with him a little later."

She laughed.

"But for now, I think I'm just going to take my boyfriend and leave."

Paula and Trudy said their goodbyes to the group after telling Mindy that she would see her soon.

Paula and Trudy headed to the house to let Kevin and Sam know that Kate and Jessie had gone with Sadie to her house.

They forewarned Kevin that there were wedding discussions happening.

Kevin was not surprised, as he was supposed to see about using the office as a reception place the Saturday after Thanksgiving.

He had to make sure it was alright with Bill first, of course, and he had to ask the farm manager.

Bill was excited for Kevin.

"A wedding here on the farm—that would be perfect. Use anything you need, as long as it is all right with the boss."

Sam piped up immediately, "Nope. Not a chance. We are going to be awfully busy. I can't have you disrupting the flow of commerce here."

Sam and Bill started laughing as the look on Kevin's face was momentarily priceless before he realized he was being given a hard time about it.

Sam kicked in. "Anything you need, brother."

After the women arrived at the Jax house, there was a little small talk about how the women getting stuck with the dishes was an oversight—but that the men were forgiven for holding their ground.

The men were informed that the vote was close, but Sadie's final say cast the decision.

There was a general question as to whether the next men-initiated lunch would occur anytime soon, as the women felt it was a good start to build on.

Trudy and Danny met up, embraced casually, and excused themselves to head to the barn to procure a Razor.

After they said their goodbyes, they turned to head out.

Bill warned them to be careful and to let Trudy know that he and Paula might be going out for a while.

Paula picked up the Afghan and sat next to Bill on the couch.

She cozied up to him, nestling under the blanket, with the glow of the TV bouncing off the walls.

Sam and Kevin turned to go as well, to catch up with the girls at Sadie's.

Chapter 23 - Paula and Bill

Paula leaned into Bill. "She is everything you said and more. Trudy is really an amazing young woman. You should be so proud." She had a tear in her eye.

"Thank you. I would love to take all the credit, but it really does take a village at times. I want you to know that you're not alone. I can see what is going on with you right now—at least, I think I do. You're thinking about Amanda, and it is tearing you up inside. Am I right?"

"Yes," she admitted in a soft and muffled voice.

Bill continued, "We haven't known each other for a long time, but I think it has been long enough for a good read on things. I've always been good at getting a handle on situations quickly. You might get mad at me, but I have got to tell you something I've done, and I'm not sure how you will take it."

Paula became concerned. "Because of me? Did I do something wrong?"

"No, no, no, it's nothing like that. I might have done something you won't like, but it was for a good reason. I talked to Kate. She knows a lot of the lawyers here in town and nearby because of the internships she did through high school and college. From what I gather from talking to several of the lawyers in town, she is well respected. I asked her to find the best family lawyer she can find and hire him for you. What's more, when she finds them, she is going to put the next three best on retainer. Your ex won't stand a chance of keeping custody."

"Bill?!? I will never be able to repay you. I can't afford that."

"I'm not asking you to. It's a gift. We could break up tomorrow, but I will still follow this through because it's the right thing to do. A young woman needs her mother. I know. It's got to have been tough on your daughter, just as it has been tough on you.

"It was tough on Trudy—still is—but I was so lucky that Sadie came into our lives." He laughed just a bit. "By the way, I want to go on record here saying I don't want to break up tomorrow. I think I really like you being around too much to do that."

He had a look of love in his eyes while face to face with Paula, giving time to let all that register.

"Oh, Bill." She started to cry, sobbing tears of joy, overwhelmed by his gift and lying on his chest.

"How about we go on a drive, catch a movie, and maybe dinner later?"

She stood up as if to get ready to go. "That sounds great, or…" She stood there with a thoughtful look as if she were contemplating alternatives.

Bill stood as well and naively replied, "Or what?"

"Or you show me around the house," she feigned innocence. "Could we start, maybe, with your room?"

"Uh, well, uh…" He stammered and then initiated a big smile. His smile met and matched Paula's. "It might be a mess."

"If it is not, I'm sure we can find a way to mess it up." She winked at Bill.

Bill took her by the hand and led her up the stairway and down the hall to his room, which had been immaculately maintained—predictably, by the maid service. They both stepped into the room.

Paula hesitated. "Is this truly OK with you? I mean, I hope I'm not crossing any lines here."

"No, no, it's fine…that is if it doesn't make you uncomfortable."

They both were avoiding the use of Sarah's name for the moment.

"Uh, it's been a while."

"I was promised a messy room," she said, stepping backward just a bit to catch the edge of the door and swing it shut. "Let's see if we can't remedy that."

Bill smiled.

It had been a while for both, but they figured out each other's tempo just fine. Bill stepped forward to take Paula into his warm, bear-like embrace, hugging while kissing her. Paula loved his approach and embraced him passionately. It had been a long time since someone had wanted her for her.

There had been others who clearly wanted a random hookup, but that just was not her speed. Now, it seemed that this speed might be a tad too slow for her at the moment. She wanted to feel Bill next to her—skin on skin—to absorb his essence and elate at his loving touch.

What's more, beyond that, she also felt a growing need to have him in her, to be one with him. She had only felt that way one other time—when she had married Nick. This was somehow more intense, deeper, almost holistic in a primal way.

His big hands held her in just such a way that she felt like she was being honored, coveted, wanted, and appreciated for being there. What's more, there was a simmering fire below that was threatening to explode into an uncontrollable blaze. These feelings in her—some familiar, others new— had her filled beyond desire.

When his hands' caress floated soft and featherlike along her sides and across the side of her breast, her eyes closed, and she struggled but could not hold back a moan of wanting desire. He noticed as she perceptively arched forward in response to his touch, and he felt a stirring within himself.

It had been a while since Bill had allowed himself to think this way. There had been a few discreet women on the side; he had hoped to make a connection but had ended up with only the benefit of a needed release. There just had not been enough interest to pursue anything beyond those brief physical encounters. The partners he had were genuinely nice and well-intended all the way around. The problem with the others was that he felt there was no real connection to take it to the next level.

Paula scared the hell out of him because he felt the same as he had with Sarah. More in some respects and less in others, but just the same— completed. Wanted. Needed.

It had not been about his money when they had met; Paula had not even heard of the Jax's. He liked that they got to know each other on a totally neutral field. He was suddenly feeling that maybe the playing field was now lopsided, as Paula seemed to have control of all his cards.

And he liked that.

He liked that very much.

It was finding root deep within himself, and he loved it.

This is what scared the hell out of him—and, in the same measure, exhilarated him just the same.

Bill had released Paula long enough to walk to the door and lock it. He doused the light, and through the glow filtering through the curtains, Paula watched him as he pulled back the sheets for an easy entry—all of this before he turned to gaze back into her eyes. Bill stared at her for a long moment with loving, caring eyes. When they locked gazes, it was as if an unspoken plan had been set in motion. He stepped forward and gently began to unbutton her blouse—one button after another until it just hung loosely on her shoulders.

She felt something inside her—something she thought had long since died—resurrected. It had come to life, absorbing all the colors she was feeling: elation, sensuality, respect, and desire. This wonderful soul was taking a deliberate, calculated, slow route to her disrobement. It was wonderful to feel this specialized attention directed solely toward her.

Bill dipped down and kissed her long and hard before breaking off just long enough to venture to her neck and shoulders. She loved it when he sheepishly nibbled the back of her lower neck. She let the shirt glide effortlessly off her back and down her arms to the ground where they stood.

He stepped behind her and deftly dispatched the clasps that held her ample breasts in place. She leaned forward, letting the bra slide past her hands before turning toward him. He stepped back to admire her. He could not help but stare lovingly at her 36-D bosom for a long moment. Gravity had been mostly defied—though some of nature had taken its toll. She was very fit, and he was mesmerized by the whole package.

He had to stoop down when she wrangled the tails of his pullover, loving her brief struggle to pull it free. He felt a natural ease with her.

She had already kicked off her sandals, so when she bent down toward her feet, he realized she was reaching for his bootlaces. He sat back on the bed, watching as each boot took its turn being removed. In between boot removal and placement, he took advantage of the time to remove both socks. When he stood back up, she stepped behind him and lightly ran her nails down his bare back. It might as well have been a bolt of lightning because it set every molecule within him ablaze.

He was caught off guard momentarily when she grabbed his fly from behind, realizing that she was unbuttoning the first toggle on his jeans. She grabbed the zipper and guided it to the bottom of its travel. He was relishing her approach when she grabbed both sides of his jeans and, after a few brief tugs, figured out how to navigate them over his buttocks and down his legs, well past his calves. Standing there in just his white underwear, he almost felt naked in a non-physical kind of way.

She snagged the edge of his waistband and freed his body from any confines that remained. He sat back on the bed, and she again stooped down to remove the jeans from his legs, summarily discharging the briefs as well. Now, he truly was naked in more ways than one—and he just did not care. It felt natural and good. He felt natural. She felt natural.

When she stood, he was at the perfect height to help her remove her slacks in turn. It took no time at all for her clothes to join his on the floor. She was wearing what looked to be dainty and delicate yet sturdy and inviting panties. Their chances of staying in place had not even been contemplated, as she had them off in a flash.

He scooted under the covers in the semi-darkness—only to see her walk to the door, flip on the light, turn back to the bed, and, with a strong grip, catch the corner of the sheets and bedspread, sending them careening to the ground. She walked to the foot of the bed, where his view of her well-maintained body was only interrupted by his one and only team member straining to get his own view.

She took a moment to take him in, like the first drink of a person lost in the desert. There was a flash of something across her eyes—he saw it, but it had no audible voice. This only left him guessing.

Much like a cat, she entered the bed from the foot, silently, as if stalking prey, moving slowly and deliberately up the bed. She hovered over his erect dick, only inches from its head, and blew a stream of breath on it.

The change in atmosphere caused it to twitch violently beyond his control. They both half-smiled, half-laughed.

After teasing him just a bit in this manner, she continued to climb her prey. She had barely managed to clear over his hips when the head of his cock met her belly button. Her skin seemed to sear into his rod, causing yet another twitch. To his dismay, as well as her pleasure, a droplet of pre-cum surfaced.

He felt like a kid, and she knew she was driving it on—and that made her smile.

She moved further, still up his body, and he watched in awe, feeling his head drag right into her fur. It traveled just a bit more and stopped. The heat surrounding him was exquisite. She lined up, moving slightly forward and backward. This happened several times—maybe as logistics, maybe as a tease—but one thing was certain: his straining prick was now immersed in wetness shared with the air of the room.

Without warning—no precursor, no facial tic, no preamble—as she stared directly into his face, absorbing each other's presence, she sat down on him fully, completely, and with no hesitation.

They both moaned in delight.

She pulled up halfway and sat down again, the result even more complete—better fitting.

Once again, she pulled him almost free and, with some speed, sat down completely again.

This time, they just stared at each other in euphoric disbelief, knowing by feeling alone that they were both on the exact same wavelength.

She sat there, drinking him in as he consumed her every essence, letting the centers of his brain catch up with the rest of his body.

As she sat there in a glow, bits and pieces of her life flashed before her.

She had never been this happy.

She had never felt this good.

He was so much more of a man than Nick was—fully three inches taller, fifty pounds of muscle beyond Nick's best workout weight, a fit body. He had a profound sense of humor and a wonderfully even-keeled personality. Not to mention, at least two inches in length more and a fullness that required all three refittings to properly seat him within her.

There was nothing she could find fault with Bill over except, maybe, it taking so long for them to have found each other to meet. Maybe everything truly did have a purpose. The only negative thing she could muster was a twinge of jealousy for Sarah, but in a twisted way, it was more of a compliment to her than anything else. It was easy to see why any woman would fall for this man. She could also see the depths of his love and knew that for him to think about moving on, there had to be many nights that the demons would come to call. To persevere past the loneliness, the loss, and the emptiness took courage. Beyond everything, she loved this about him, too.

He looked up at her in awe. There seemed to be a glow about her, the same kind of thing that had happened to him when he met Sarah. Now, here he was in their bed with Paula. It was as if Sarah had walked through the room momentarily unseen but took the time to whisper in his ear.

He could hear Sarah say, "I love you too, but it's time. Time to move on, time to be happy, time to let go and become more."

A tear struggled to maintain its position in his eyes. How one single, solitary tear could mean two separate but fully rational conversations was beyond his comprehension. There had been so many nights he sat in the stare, waiting for Sarah to arrive again in vain. One conversation was of love and devotion, the other of letting go and remembrance. It was inside this one single tear that the DNA for both had been made possible. They embraced each other, and she pushed him back to his new love.

Neither Paula nor Bill moved a muscle. He was engulfed by her, sheltered deep from harm inside her fortress, her embrace and cocoon that promised, without a word spoken, that this was true, safe, and real. He could trust again. He could dream again.

He could love again.

She had been holding back something in herself as she sat there, feeling his every heartbeat within the throb captured deep in her. She realized that it was the last wall she had built inside of herself for her own sanity, her own safety. She realized that it was not actually the wall per se but rather a remnant of it. How this man, without a single tool in hand, was able to sneak ever so deftly, unnoticed inside her, and dismantle what she had built over the years for her protection was beyond comprehension.

She had been holding on to the last of the wall, her last vestige of safety, the smallest of safe places that she alone controlled for no reason at all. It simply did not matter anymore. It was not needed anymore. She saw a glint, a tear in his eye, and felt the rest of the world disappear from around them both. There was only one thing that mattered now, and it was right in front of her. She knew she ought to be terrified sitting there—raw, naked, exposed on the inside and out—but there was a spooky, almost eerie calm about her. There was a special something that let her know there was nothing left to fear.

What clinched the deal for both was the timing. Neither one was willing to move a muscle and chance losing this total feeling of weightlessness from their freely given love. There was a desire to capture this moment and die instantly inside this once-lost but now welcoming bliss. Without a word, for what seemed like an eternity, they finally both began to move in tandem, in unison. It was a lovemaking of the slowest, most sensual kind. She took him in just as easily as he embraced her need. Perfect motions and angles were found as they rolled on the bed, lost deep in each other.

It had been a day or three since either of them was where they were now, but just the same, their bodies were able to anticipate and coordinate each other's wants and needs perfectly. If ever there was a storybook of endings, they both began to release simultaneously while wrapped around each other. Paula became fairly audible as an all-encompassing wave crashed over her, deeper than she had ever known. Maybe it was the longing, maybe it was the timing, but it really didn't matter. When the head of his cock began to swell, she felt his fullness grow in every dimension, and that feeling launched her body into almost epileptic-like convulsions with a profound depth her body had never experienced before.

Her coming was explosive, undeniable in its magnitude, and the animation from her body deep within her squeezed and pulsed along his shaft. His cock, his essence, was being pushed to the precipice. He had felt the beginning of the end. That almost forgotten swell that was now happening had initiated something that started a cascading reaction deep within her, causing his shaft to be treated to a squeeze that was spasmodically milking him. The whole of it all pushed him, yet one more fraction to the edge, like begging or a summoning was taking place inside himself.

It was epically glorious as he tried to hold himself back to extend this excursion of undeniable pleasure. His struggle was to no avail, although it did not seem to matter to either of them, as his penis throbbed out its load and joined into the dance that was playing out quite dramatically and physically inside each other. His was a horrendous release as he bucked forward and joined her audibly as they both loudly came as one.

He stroked at a much slower pace until she stilled him. Her inner waves still occasionally, rhythmically kneading his still-hard shaft. They were once again in the same position they had started out in, but this time, they were both sweaty, mutually satisfied, and wonderfully spent. They both rolled to each other's side, parting only in the union but not in touch. They wrapped around each other and drifted off to a mid-day afternoon delighted nap.

Chapter 24 - Payback

Trudy and Danny had made their way to their cabin by the lake and began to walk to the door. Danny entered the code, but just as he started to push the door, Trudy stopped him.

"What?"

She laughed. "Do you trust me?"

"Yes, why?"

"I mean, really trust that I wouldn't hurt you in any way?"

"Now you're starting to scare me, but I trust you completely. Why?"

Trudy reached into her back pocket, pulled out a blindfold, and hung it in front of him. "Your turn, lover boy. I'm in control now. You will do as I say when I say. What is your safe word?"

He laughed. "OK, OK, your turn. Lobster. That will be my safe word. Lunch will guide the way."

Trudy tied the blindfold, opened the door, and steered him to the same chair that she had used and told him not to move. Danny could hear Trudy coming and going as long as she was near, but now he was straining to hear what was obviously a preparation for his happy internment. When she arrived back, he felt cold steel wrap around his wrist, a familiar set of ratcheting clicks on one arm, then the other. Trudy now had a set of handcuffs of her own—or so he thought.

He was directed to the bedroom and backed against the familiar bed edge. Trudy unbuttoned his shirt and let it fall clear of the cuffs, then unlatched his belt. When she pulled his pants beyond his hips, she found that he was commando and full. She pushed him to a sitting position on the bed as she removed his shoes and socks. He was directed backward and upward until the exact spot he had chosen for her had been achieved. He did not think anything of being told to lie back on the bed nor having his arms cuffed to the bed. He liked where this was heading. He liked the touch of the smooth ropes that had been bound to each leg. She was efficient in lassoing his appendage. She left the bed as he could feel the empty air.

A finger slowly and lightly began to trace a vein on his cock, and this prompted a blood flow that quickly brought his full dick to firm and his firm cock to hard. He felt the bed move as she got on it. He still was not exactly sure how this was going to play out, but he was still liking her direction. She straddled him with her hips and sat on his stomach, then reached back to fondle his balls warmly and gently. The contact only encouraged his cock to protest more. When she quit caressing his manhood, he went into full anticipation mode. He was now wanting, hard, and straining, so he reached for her out of habit and found only six inches of movement available. Trudy laughed aloud.

"I wanted you to experience what no movement was like, but now, I have something much better in mind if you can be good?"

"I can be good, I promise."

"OK, here is what is going to happen. I'm going to loosen your legs, uncuff you from the bed, and you are going to get on your hands and knees right where you are, and I'm gonna tie you down all over again. Do you understand?"

"Can we just have some fun instead?"

"Do you understand, or are you calling lobster already?"

"No, no, no, it's your turn. I'm sorry. I'll be good and do as I'm told."

"Now that is a good boy."

She uncuffed him and untied his legs as he complied with her prescribed position. He was reattached in this kneeling position, unable to touch his hands and knees together, and had little movement except for leaning forward and backward. He felt a drag along his spine and heard a simple question.

"Remember this item?"

"I…ah…I…well…yes, I…"

Before he could finish his acknowledgment, there was a slicing through the air and a brutal thaawwaap, a snap on his ass that almost caused the entire head on his dick to erupt through a fissure on its throbbing convulsions that was directly connected to that very spot on his ass. He let loose an "uuuhh" as he collapsed forward.

The glorious pain coupled itself with a moan, but he was not able to complete the entirety of the thrill audibly before the next snap. It felt as though it was ripping his skin off his body in the most wonderful way. He could only manage a guttural moan and an attempt to flee forward, only to find that he was indeed trapped by the ropes.

"Where are you going? You didn't ask if you could leave. That is a very bad boy."

'Wwhhhiiiirrrreeeerpp.' The crop planted hotly and wholly in the flesh of his ass cheek once more. Two more equally brutal and successive lashings were unceremoniously unleashed on each ass cheek. He jumped forward, in small part due to unanticipated pain but mostly because of the sheer ecstasy of it on his skin.

"I told you not to move. Now stand still and take it like a man."

"Yes, mistress!" He let the moan that was trapped inside of him escape.

"I have a few things planned for you, slave, but I can't move on until you stand still. Do you understand?"

"Yes, mistress!"

"Swwiipp, ttthhwwat, ppphhheeewwwip."

There were eight hard lashings doled out in all, spaced at intervals to let each and every stinging arrival have body and take shape. In between each stroke on his now-reddening ass, the crop danced on his cock and balls. There was another whip and another. Danny screamed out in extreme pleasure from the blows she delivered to his cheeks. He writhed and danced in place between each contact. Each of the punishing snaps was a full-body swing that turned patches of his ass cherry red. Each landing was a new height in pleasure for Danny, but he finally managed not to move from where his knees were planted.

"Now that is a good boy, and good things happen when you're a good boy. Would you like me to reward you by pegging you now?"

"Oh yes, please, mistress."

"Do you want me to lube up my girl dick and fuck you right now?"

"Yes, please, mistress."

"When you feel me against you, you will push all the way back to me when I tell you to and thank me for my dick. Do you understand?"

"Yes, mistress." He was still blindfolded, but he could hear Trudy rooting around and some shuffling noises that he assumed were Trudy putting on a strap-on harness. She had delighted in dominating him several times before. She fucked him incredibly well, but being blindfolded this time made everything so different. His ass cheeks were throbbing in the most wickedly wonderful way. His cock was orchestrating the throb somehow. It was keeping everything at its pace. His mind was straining to hear for a clue as to what Trudy was doing, and he began making up sounds to compensate for the loss of sight. When the bed moved as she got on it, his excitement built.

Danny felt her hands gently spread his cheeks a little, and he felt the pressure of the artificial cock press up against his asshole.

"I want you to slowly lean forward."

He complied as the cock moved forward with him, resting against his bung. They traveled only inches before being commanded to stop. He could feel the cold lube contradicting the hot wave coming off his still, highly reddened ass.

"Now push back on my girl dick and tell me you like it."

He started to push back slowly, and as he concentrated on it, his sphincter relaxed to accommodate the intruder. He moaned in wanting.

"Oh god, yes, I love your dick in me. Oh god, that is so good!"

When he bottomed out, she spoke.

"That's a good boy. Now forward again and back onto me harder."

Danny did what he was commanded to do, moaning in pleasure the whole time he was moving.

"Again, but faster this time."

Danny complied, but after a few strokes, he was commanded to stop.

"You will not move, no matter what I do. You will not say anything at all until I say you can speak. Do you understand?"

"Yes, mistress!"

His ass was delightfully full. His ass cheeks still hummed a stinging song delightfully, and his prostate began to get massaged as Trudy's life-like girl dick started to stroke him wonderfully, causing him to moan loudly. He hoped that moaning sounds were not a punishable offense. All the while, he was building up to a most pleasurable place to be.

As his ass was being deliciously stroked, he tried his best to maintain composure and position, but something very strange happened. The bed moved but near his head. His ass was being serviced in a manner he loved, but how could the bed move in front of him?

He felt a set of legs slide under his chest from the head of the bed. Danny's mind began to reel. He wanted to say something, but he could not. He was not allowed to.

He had to risk it.

"Uh…Trudy?"

"I warned you not to talk."

There was a series of brutal whips landing on his ass, reigniting the hum in his buttocks and making his asshole clench delightfully tight on…her dick. Something that just made no sense at all.

He felt someone push his head down toward what was now clearly a set of wide-open thighs. He could smell the sex in front of him. His face was pushed forward and into it.

"Eat my pussy, slave."

Danny began to lick the pussy in front of him, though his mind was spinning. He considered yelling LOBSTER, but he traced the conversation back to the door when they first got here, now understanding the true nature of her declaration.

Trudy would never purposefully hurt him, so he enthusiastically dove into it.

There were questions that had questions upon questions that he was prohibited from asking—that is, if he wanted to be able to sit anytime soon. The inquiries were beginning to take shape, but they all had to take a back seat to a new realization.

He was clearly tasting come.

There was a creamy flow of come filtering out of the pussy he was sucking, and it tasted great. He had liked the taste of come from the first time Dave had let loose a torrential flood in his mouth during his very first excursion with a cock.

Whose come am I tasting now? That was his question now.

He was contemplating asking anyway at the risk of jeopardizing his already tender ass when he felt the head of his cock enter a mouth. His manhood was completely consumed all the way down to the balls.

There was a change of direction, and the mouth had relented just far enough up the shaft to get the full effect of the deep-throated blowjob.

He heard a smack of skin on skin, but it was not on his body. He figured out that it was a signal of some sort because the strokes to his ass became slower but more forceful in the manner of total length that rocked him forward.

He felt a hip smash into his ass that propelled him forward again, which in turn pushed his cock to the hilt in the mouth on him. Along with the resulting push, his face slammed deep and hard into the pussy he was cleaning.

There were six long, glorious, full-on hammering thrusts forward when he heard another slap.

His body was beginning to spin out of control, and he was having trouble comprehending the symphony of erotic chaos that was splitting his being.

He could not keep track of the three others connected to him, giving him such extreme pleasure, but he felt the beginnings of what he knew would be a magnificently horrendous release that was on the way.

This slap had indeed been a signal to the owner of the pussy in front of him as they removed the blindfold from his head.

Once his eyes had been uncovered, the hands that freed him cupped his head, and the hips attached to them arched upward to his mouth just as his eyes adjusted to the light.

All at once, the silence that had been dutifully observed ended, and everyone there became audibly alive.

He stopped only briefly and looked up and saw, to his surprise, Amanda.

This excited him even more as his cock voluntarily engorged ever so slightly, tightening up his already tensed balls.

He looked behind him to see Dave grasping his hips, plowing his real meat into him at full speed.

He should have known that the ass treatment was all but perfect, and he was the only one person who would know how to do that for him.

He looked down, seeing his full length at the front of Trudy's mouth. As Dave's stroke pushed forward, slamming into his hips, it pushed his cock down her mouth and neck.

It was almost more than he could handle—almost.

He closed his eyes and let everything fall into place as he lost himself to nothingness and came harder than he ever had before with a back-arching roar.

His come was hard and voluminous. Some went down her neck, but she caught the last half in her mouth, and as he opened his eyes, he watched Trudy slip out from under him and share her prize with a full mouth-to-mouth kiss with Amanda, who hungrily took what was offered. He could not tell what turned him on more—how it happened or watching Trudy and Amanda kiss so deeply, much less sharing him. If he was capable of coming again right then and there, he would have.

He could not reach forward, only lean, but it did not matter because Trudy pushed his head down into Amanda's wet gnash.

Danny only got glimpses of Trudy while he was down on Amanda, but he could tell that Amanda had her face buried in Trudy, and she was enjoying the heavenly treatment that Amanda was giving her. She had the crop in her hand and would, on occasion, punish him.

Trudy would lay into his ass hard and use one word that had the result of inspiring him. Every time he heard it, the same thing would happen, and all it took was the word "Dave."

When she said this, Dave would not miss a stroke but would, however, lean backward a bit, exposing an open field view of a target.

She commanded her lash on the sweet, soft part of Danny's ass without remorse, tanning his ass over and over.

Dave had been stroking for quite a long time now, and his whole demeanor had changed. His breathing quickened, he was becoming more audible, and he was closing in on his second come of the day when Trudy said aloud, "Now, Dave? You know you have to share."

With that said, Dave pulled fully out of Danny, peeled his condom off carefully, and stepped up to where Danny was furiously working on Amanda's pussy with his tongue.

Hard and pent up but ready to release, Dave centered himself between Amanda's crotch and Danny's face. Trudy leaned forward and grabbed his cock, stroking him several times.

It did not take much before the convulsions pushed up through Dave's cock and landed unceremoniously on Amanda's vulva and the side of Danny's face.

It was hot, thick, and white, and for his second come of the day, it was quite a bit in terms of volume. She was watching as the pulses erupted and spurted at least a foot as Dave's seed freed itself.

Feeling his convulsive pulses in her hand as he came, he turned Trudy on just that little bit more than she had needed to push her over the edge. Amanda was tongue-lashing her perfectly as Dave pulsed away, and Danny had a front-row seat in the middle of her directorial debut.

She had a raging, magnificent release flooding Amanda from ear to ear. Amanda tried her best to keep up, but her own orgasm had gripped her deeply, and as she came, she lost all semblance of control. Her juices mixed with Dave's, and they both met up at Danny's face. Danny had to wait for all of them to finish their post-coital bliss to hopefully free him. He was still dutifully doing as he was told.

When things had calmed down, Trudy extracted herself from the entanglement of body parts, found the handcuff key, and released Danny to his own recognizance. They all fell to the bed in a heap, only moving long enough to group up in the correct alignments as a sweaty mass on the bed. One by one, they each slipped away to the shower.

Trudy joined Dave, who was first, and while she washed him in the most complete and wonderful fashion, she thanked him for "missing" lunch and for going to Danny's house to retrieve Danny's box for her to use. It was an immense help to have everything sitting out and ready to use as he had done for her.

She ribbed him for having dessert before they arrived but admitted a good load inside Amanda really was a nice touch for Danny to contend with. He had laughed at that and conceded that it was Amanda's idea. He had quipped that putting it there was a fantastic experience for him—and for her, as it turned out. He could not believe how much Amanda had changed in just a few short months. He had left the shower just as Amanda arrived.

Trudy happily addressed Amanda, "I am so glad we could make this work out. I'm so glad you are here, and I think Danny is happy too. He was not expecting what would happen today. We totally surprised him for sure. For a guy that claimed to have done everything, we just added a plus one to his list."

Both girls laughed.

"I really appreciate you asking me to be here. I really missed Danny in this capacity. Uh…you think I could borrow your boyfriend every once in a while?"

"I honestly meant it. We are incredibly good together and go by boyfriend and girlfriend from the outside looking in, but really, you can be with him all you want. Uh, wait a second, when I'm not with him, that is! Uh, well, unless we all want to be together, that is."

They both laughed at that, and Trudy relaxed as Amanda took over hair washing and body cleansing. Her touch was silky, electric, and unbelievably soothing to her.

"I could do this all the time. I love your body. I really like you, too," she laughed. "I just like being with you like this. Hopefully, I can get away from my father more often."

"Weeell, I guess you might like what I found out today."

On cue, Danny turned the corner and traded places with Trudy. He began to "service" Amanda by lathering her auburn hair as Trudy commanded the conversation.

"My dad has been seeing a lady for quite some time now. She has a daughter who goes to our school. Anyway, my dad asked Aunt Kate to find the best family law lawyer out there to help her with custody. I told her I didn't know her daughter. Have you ever heard of an Amanda Crane at our school?"

"You have got to be shitting me. There is no way. Really? Are you being serious?"

"I didn't believe it either, but if your mom is Paula Crane and your dad is Nick, I'm totally serious. Given how my dad was looking at your mom and how she was looking at him, it is quite possible that we might just become sisters."

She laughed, trying her best to be serious.

"And if we do, I want to be clear on one thing."

"Yeah? What's that?"

Sternly and as serious as she could muster, "No matter what happens, you cannot stop showering with me."

They both burst out laughing as Amanda began to exit the shower, leaving Danny to take his shower alone.

"Oh, hell no, that's not going to change. I hope you have a big shower."

Trudy towel-dried Amanda, taking her time to make sure every inch of her body had been accounted for. The two naked women pressed their bodies together during a long and passionate kiss.

Danny watched on. "Keep that up, and we are going to have to start round two!"

Calming him, Trudy replied, "Idle your engines, lover boy; this is for her only."

"Lover boy? You have been talking to Sam, haven't you?"

"Absolutely, families that talk together get along better, don't you think?"

Dave had already opened all the windows in the cabin because the smell of sex was incredibly strong. He was in the middle of picking up what needed to go back to the box when Trudy strolled out of the cabin to the Razor, buck-ass naked, and came back with two plastic containers.

A naked Trudy and Danny set up lunch—although late—for their two friends and sat them down, also naked, to eat after microwaving what needed to be heated. Danny and Trudy finished cleaning up and started laundry while Dave and Amanda finished their meals.

Danny noticed that Trudy and Amanda had been checking out each other while they dressed. The thought of them together was brutally hot in his imagination. Two incredible bodies competing to satisfy each other right in front of him stirred a considerable amount of angst mentally.

They all eventually and reluctantly dressed to leave. Trudy knew that she would have to make a return trip to dry the bedding, but wow, was it worth it!

Dave followed Amanda until she neared her house to make sure she got home after "meeting up with some friends" in town. He changed directions and headed home.

Danny and Trudy rode across the farm to the barn and put up the Razor. She had walked with him to Danny's truck.

Danny observed, "I can't believe Thanksgiving is right around the corner. Man, I'm going to miss you guys when I leave for college."

"You are going to be fine, and we can visit. You are going to be busy meeting so many other people you will forget about us in a month or less."

"You know that isn't true. I don't think I can ever forget you guys, even for a day. I can promise you one thing, though. I understand just what you are doing for me. I refuse to squander it. Watch me; I will get my business degree in three years and be one of the best students in culinary school. If you need a restaurateur for your hotels, I will be the best there is to offer. That much, I promise. And Trudy, I will never forget about you."

She hugged and kissed him. "I have no doubt you will be fine, and I am going to miss you too. At least until the first dance at school anyway." They both laughed.

As Thanksgiving approached, several things happened. Sadie had requested that Danny spend some time with her privately. Danny would not say why, and Sadie gave no hints.

Trudy had been asked out on a date by senior quarterback Ryan Phipps, and she had accepted.

Bill asked his daughter out for a dinner date the day before she was to go out with Ryan.

Chapter 25 - Coming Together

Trudy said she would meet her dad at the restaurant he chose, but he seemed a little off. It was hard to describe—he was not off, but he was certainly mentally elsewhere.

When she arrived at the restaurant and asked for the Jax party, she was led to a table that already had three others at it, all of whom she knew—her dad, Paula, and Amanda.

She was quite sure what was coming and was indeed happy but tried her best to look inquisitive and lost as she sat down.

Bill and Paula were visibly trying to put a very fresh face forward. Bill tried to speak. "Uh, we want to—"

Trudy cut him off. "What do you think, Amanda?"

Taking the cue, both girls had a very plain and ordinary, matter-of-fact conversation as if their parents were not even there.

"Well, if it's marriage, I refuse to wear pink. It's horrible with my hair color."

"I will absolutely need a new dress. Who is going to pay for that?"

"I know, right? We are going to have to do some serious shopping."

"What a burden—the travel, finding just the right ensemble."

"I will help you through it. Together, we can do this, OK?"

"And if you're moving in, I am not giving up my room. You can have the one next door. It's not as big as mine, but I think it will do just fine for you, especially if we have a door put in so we can get to each other's rooms easier."

"Fine, I'll take the smaller room, but I've seen your bathroom. Pick a side. A double vanity is for two people, not for just one person to spread out everywhere. You are going to have to learn to share some space."

"Well, if I have to do that, you are going to have to help with chores around the house and the farm. I'm not doing it all myself."

"I don't know how to drive a Razor like you do, so if you want help, you are going to have to show me how. You're going to have to show me where you keep everything so I know where to put things or to get things."

"That's an easy one to teach. And as for the house, will you politely tell your mother that I'm tired of having to maintain every thought of how each room should look? She is going to have to decorate the house herself."

"OK, but if I have to go that far, you're going to have to get your dad to paint my room the color I want. I'm not doing that."

"Fine. I have him wrapped around my little finger. That shouldn't be a problem."

They paused on Trudy's cue as she looked at her father. "Don't I, Daddy?" She batted her eyes with the same eyes she had always used, momentarily getting serious and straight-faced as she looked at Paula. "I would request that a certain few pictures of my first mother remain if you can see your way fit to do that."

"Oh, we're sorry, we didn't mean to ignore you guys. So, what were you two wanting to talk about?"

Both parents looked like they were following a ping-pong ball the whole time the girls were having their conversation. They looked at each other, and Bill nodded to Paula. "We were thinking about getting a dog together. What in the world were you two talking about?"

There was dead silence for a long second, and Bill and Paula held the deadpan as long as they could until Paula started to crack a smile, and both started laughing in unison.

Bill started in, "We were thinking about moving in together starting next week, maybe around February, a wedding?"

The two girls visibly digested the time frame and looked at each other.

"February is good. But not on Valentine's Day. That would be very uncool."

"I will clear my schedule." She looked at Amanda. "Hey, sister, if something changes, have your people call my people, and we will work it out."

She looked at Paula. "When was Amanda born?"

"June third. Why?"

"June, that's great. I was born on July 9. I have an older sister." She turned to Bill. "You know what that means, don't you, Dad?"

"What?"

"If something goes wrong around the house, it is Amanda's fault. Amanda gets the blame. She's older and should have known not to influence me so badly. Older sisters, what are you going to do?"

"Mooom, Trudy is doing it again… Make her stop." Both girls laughed aloud as Bill and Paula shook their heads in mock disgust and laughed along.

Chapter 26 - Ryan

Since Trudy had talked about her upcoming date with Ryan, Amanda asked if she could help her get ready. Trudy was happy to have her near and accepted her offer. Both parents were visibly relieved that their new joining was going to go so well.

The next day, the girls organized an event by doing hair and makeup and picking out the best outfits and shoes. While combing through Trudy's jewelry, Amanda picked out the perfect complement to tie it all together. When Trudy was finally ready to go out the door, she was absolutely stunning in a classy way.

Trudy inquired, "What do you think?"

"Well, turn to the left." Trudy turned. "Now to the right." Once again, Trudy pivoted. "Oh, wait, one small thing."

"What did we miss?"

Stepping forward, Amanda captured her face just as she did that first time in school and kissed her slowly, softly, sensually on the lips and stepped back.

"Yep, just as I thought, too much lipstick. You're good now."

Trudy just smiled at her.

"Ryan is really cute. Don't hurt him tonight," she said, laughing.

"Quit it. It is just a date, nothing more."

Bill and Paula were in the living room as the girls came down the stairs. They both commented on how good Trudy looked. Trudy was visibly happy with her looks and accepted all compliments but reminded them it was mostly her big sister's doing. Everyone liked that reference.

Trudy left to meet her date in town. After connecting with him, they went out to eat and watch a movie. She said she expected to be home around eleven-thirty.

Everyone else was going to work on transitional things around the house, like bedding and clothes, deciding which furniture was to migrate, and so on. It had already been decided to spend the nights at Jax Farms until the full move was complete.

They were not ready for the call that they got from Sheriff Roger Burns.

Directly after the phone was picked up, a man addressed him. "Hello, this is Sheriff Burns. Is this Bill Jax?"

"Yes, it is. What's wrong, Roger? Is my little girl hurt?" There was extreme concern in his voice that was picked up immediately by Paula.

"Everything is fine, Bill. Trudy is fine. I do have her at the station, though. She is in good health; there are just a few bruises on her hands and nothing else. She is fine. Her date, however, is currently en route to the emergency room for minor injuries. I couldn't in good conscience send Trudy home by herself. I'm betting you would want to come get her."

"Absolutely, we are on the way. Thank you, Roger."

By this time, Amanda had heard some of the conversation and was already heading out the door, followed closely by Paula and Bill.

They all piled into the GMC Denali Sport Crew Cab that was Bill's daily driver and headed to town. When they arrived at the sheriff's station, they were met at the door by a deputy and were escorted to Trudy, who was immediately wrapped in a tight hug by Paula.

Paula did a cursory inventory and asked, "Are you OK? Are you hurt anywhere?"

"I'm fine. My knuckles hurt, but other than that, I am good."

Bill inquired, "Roger, what happened?"

"Let me give you the story from the top as I know it. First, I got a call that there was some sort of domestic disturbance on Vine Street, south of Third Street. It's kind of dark there. Sometimes lovers hang out on that stretch, so I have had patrols stepped up to ease some of the complaints we have been getting, so I figured something went south."

Bill quizzically looked at Trudy as Roger continued. "When I got there, Ryan was laid out on the ground, groggy and half loopy and moaning, and Trudy was sitting in a deputy's car."

"Was there an accident?"

Roger chuckled shortly and continued, "Well, you might say that for Ryan anyway. According to Trudy, the two of them went out to eat, and as they were driving around killing time before a movie they were going to, Ryan decided to park out there for dessert. Your daughter wanted no part of what he had in mind and got out of the truck they were in. She started walking toward the square. Ryan got out and told her that she was going to satisfy him, or he would take what he wanted. He grabbed her by the arm.

"When he pulled her around, all hell broke loose for him. Your daughter grabbed the arm he was holding her with and did some kind of twisting thing so forcefully that I'm fairly sure she gave him a spiral fracture. As he pulled away, she kicked him squarely in the nuts, and when he keeled forward, she kneed him in the face, sending him upward and busting his nose. There was a flurry of punches to his face and body. He went down like a sack of potatoes, which was when my deputies drove by. They didn't know how to respond to this, so they detained everyone and they called me. I called you.

When Ryan came to and was alert enough, he was threatening to sue you, but your daughter told him that would be fine as she would bury him in sexual assault charges. Ryan won't be finishing the football season for sure, and gauging by how he was walking and looking, he won't be feeling too good for several weeks. Now you are all caught up."

"Trudy? Are you OK? He didn't hurt you, did he?"

"Nope, but Dad, as soon as he put his hand in my crotch and grabbed my chest with the other, I got out."

Paula quipped, "Thank God you didn't get hurt."

Looking at Roger and at Bill, Trudy said, "Isaac and Thomas were with me, Dad."

Bill grew a smile that could beat the band.

Roger perked up. "This is the first I've heard about someone else helping you. Who are Isaac and Thomas?"

Bill laughed aloud, confusing Roger as Trudy continued.

"It's a simple methodology, per Thomas. Never half-commit. Full in, full on. No half-attempts—fully commit and control the action. You might take a hit or two, but the action will be yours to direct. And Isaac requires a full-on, brutal, no-mercy attack. When assaulted, expect no leniency; therefore, offer none. Superior moves, superior control, exacting placement, and effective techniques. No nice guy. When the battle is won— punctuate, punctuate, punctuate," he said. "No one gets a second run at you, ever. Make sure they are down, and they stay down.

"So yeah, Isaac and Thomas Taylor were beside me the whole time. They both had said I was as good as any of their trainees. I guess they weren't just saying that to make me feel good. I just wish they had told me that hitting someone in the ribs and face that hard would bruise my knuckles, though. My hands really hurt. I hope you're not mad at me, Dad. I just reacted. Isaac calls it muscle memory."

Roger interjected, "Damn, Bill, every father's nightmare ending with every father's dream. Do you want me to press charges?"

Paula cut in. "Let his parents know that he isn't welcome anywhere near my family and that we will pay Ryan's medical bills only, but if they want to push it, we will not be so forgiving. Other than that, we are going to take Trudy home now."

"I'm sorry, ma'am, but who are you?"

Bill spoke up. "Roger, meet Paula Crane, my fiancée."

"Paula, it is nice to meet you, obviously not under these circumstances."

He looked at Amanda. "And you are?"

"Amanda Parker, Trudy's sister," she answered.

Roger looked at Bill with a big smile. "Looks like you are surrounded by some tough and strong women," he continued sarcastically in a light, airy tone. "Good luck with that."

That comment lightened the mood all around and drew lighthearted chuckles. The entourage gathered themselves and left for home.

On the way home, Bill stopped, and Trudy handed the keys to her Cherokee to Amanda for her to drive it home. Upon arriving home, everyone recapped the night and made sure Trudy was truly OK.

Everyone made their way to bed. Amanda hugged Trudy closely as they both shared an embrace and the warmth of each other's skin through their pajamas. It was clear there was a meaningful feeling of love on many levels.

The buzz at school had ranged completely across the board, from a drug deal gone bad to a lover's quarrel and everything in between because Ryan and Trudy were seen as being detained by the police. It was not until someone managed to pull up the actual police report from the public record and it made its rounds that the true nature of the incident was revealed.

There was still disbelief that little ole Trudy could manage to hurt Ryan after all the hits everyone had seen him take in practice and on the field.

The extent of her damage was self-evident when Ryan made it to school three days later after better than half the week of calling in sick. Ryan walked in with a limp, sported a cast on his arm and a rib brace, along with two split lips that were still slightly swollen and scabbed over, and the nastiest black eye anyone could recall in recent memory.

A fantastically bluish-black bruise covered half the upper portion of his face. It looked like Ryan had taken a gang-style beating—all from little ole Trudy Jax.

Stories started to filter out about Ryan and his other exploits with other girls and how this may not have been an isolated event on his behalf. It was also clear that he paid a hefty price for his impropriety.

This sent a message rippling through the school to all the boys. It was also clear that the football team needed a new quarterback. It was equally clear that their old quarterback was not going to be dating anyone for the rest of his tenure at the school based on the talk around town.

Many girls, some of whom Trudy barely knew from all grades, asked her how she managed to defend herself so well. All the questions inspired Trudy's thought process.

There was suddenly an anonymous donation that paid for any high school girl who wanted to get life-defense skills from a local dojo.

The dojo that had been chosen had two main interests—a martial arts program that taught a structured taekwondo, jujitsu, and karate as a belted award avenue, and now a life-skills vein that taught a more visceral response to a potential assault and how to go beyond just surviving it.

Lessons that could be easily gained include knowledge of how to respond in a short amount of time as life skills.

The grant would be administered through the philanthropic arm of TJC and would be evaluated randomly by Thomas and Isaac, who had already agreed to spot-check the efficacy of the teaching for survival purposes.

They both were ecstatic to learn that their skills helped Trudy so profoundly in her time of duress. They were thrilled to hear about her total domination of this boy, who was clearly eighty pounds or more than she was. They were both equally impressed that she had found a company and had convinced them to issue the perpetual grant based on her experience. That was something they would be proud to be a part of and, if possible, help to teach along with the spot checks.

Trudy was almost as happy that it would give them one more reason to come home—one more reason to see Mama. Both "boys" shared their young protégé's experience with much enthusiasm with their troopers as an example of a clear-cut definition of dominance through training.

Chapter 27 - A Dual Wedding

Thanksgiving came in the blink of an eye, or so it seemed. Everyone knew that Sadie and Danny were putting something together, but other than the women and Danny, it was a mystery.

It turned out to be a feast fit for royalty. Sadie and Danny had planned it; Danny stepped the fare up a notch, and Sadie maintained quality control while the women filled in where needed. Danny had again made the instructions so simple and complete, with the fare so elegant, that the women were in awe. When they were done, a finer table could not be found.

There was some confusion, quietly absorbed with knowing smiles by the cook crew, when the men showed up at twelve o'clock. The usual time was indeed twelve, but Kevin and Sam were told to tell the men to wait until twelve-thirty due to the size and complexity of the meal. They were supposed to tell the guys the night before when the men all took Kevin and Sam out for one last night of single freedom. In the midst of the revelry, the instructions were not passed on.

Kevin and Sam, along with Jessie and Kate, were excited to have a double wedding at the farm. It was going to be a small family affair with only a few extra guests. Danny, Trudy, Dave, and Amanda, along with Bill and Paula, were going to cater.

The girls had gone out the night before as well and were moving a little slower than usual, but there were plenty of womenfolk, so there was not an appreciable slowdown in the kitchen.

Kevin and Sam showed up together at twelve thirty-two and made a point of showing their watches to prove it when Isaac and Thomas asked why they were so late.

"Late? We are right on time," Kevin said.

"Mama said no earlier than twelve-thirty this time. Why are you…" Sam was following up with the question before being interrupted.

Looking directly at Sam, "Shit, didn't you tell them?"

Looking back at Kevin, "I thought you were going to."

From beyond the dining room, in the kitchen, heads poked out looking at the guys, and all the hens were cackling with laughter. The men caught on to why they were being so quiet at first, and there was a collective audible groaning as Kevin and Sam tried to turn and slink out of the door.

Thomas was the first of the men to speak. "I don't think so, little brother. You're in it now, both of you. Hey Bill, I know you can't do anything about Kevin, but can you do me a favor and fire Sam? Isaac, you're in charge of digging a hole in the woods for Kevin."

The men were looking forward to laying back with taut bellies and watching the game. Now, the first order of business would be cleaning the dining room and kitchen after one of the biggest meals of the year.

The game was going to have to wait for a final seal of approval from Sadie. The only guy not on dish duty was Danny, as it was accepted that he was part of the cooking crew.

Everyone that had been invited and had made it—the Veaches (Danny's mom, who was continually impressed with her son's abilities),

Dave's mom and dad, the Tuckers, the Martinezes, and the Stevenses—enjoyed a great time and conversation.

The most succulent dinner anyone had had in a long time was slowly dwindling on their plates.

The women exaggeratedly fluffed out their "bellies" as they mock-strained while rising from the table, all full and tired. They made it clear that they were going to try to make it to the couch, let the food settle, and catch a catnap.

The men groaned audibly during cleanup as they could hear the big plays on the television and the women's purposeful overreactions.

Danny stepped in to help. "We're all brothers in arms, right?"

They knew they were missing a great game but were already forgiving the two grooms-to-be for their slip-up. It was not that long before the dishes were done, and the leftovers were housed in their containers. The first cans of beer were opened and mostly finished by the time the men made it to the office—man cave. It had been a wonderful day, all in all. Saturday officially added two more to the family list, as well as many others by extension.

Surf and turf was the theme, and Bill paid for everything for the reception, which was intimate and close, with all of the families represented. The food was once again beyond expectations for the wedding reception. Danny was continually outdoing himself to great acclaim.

This time, he had enlisted the help of several of his friends to perform the serving functions and act as a cleanup crew—all for the price of a premium meal and twenty dollars an hour apiece. Barbecued ribs, Texas brisket, lobster, crab, and large shrimp flown in from the coast, along with a host of trimmings to round out the meal, were prepared.

Though there were only a little less than sixty-five people in attendance, the meal was a daunting accomplishment that Danny once again pulled off with premium style. The "staff" ate well, and still, there were leftovers to feed the layover crowd for the next two days.

Sadie was enjoying being able to sit back and watch her children marry without a care for the food requirements that she normally would have undertaken, thanks to Danny's prowess at planning and cooking.

What pushed everything beyond all expectations was the double cake presented as a central shared layer, with two sides of the cake, each having a stair-stepping layer of smaller cakes leading up to a three-tiered round with a bride and groom nestled into the icing on both sides of the masterpiece that was presented.

The piping and decor of the cake were so expertly and exquisitely done that many people had trouble believing this too was Danny's creation. It even spawned a cake-making side business that Danny was happy to take on.

Chapter 28 - The Business of Business

Over the next four months, all the Athena Inns were up and running with comparable results. Based on the short- and long-term projections worked out by the accountant, all the bills were being paid; wages were easily covered—even with them being ten percent higher than other hotel wages. The renovation budget was almost recaptured and would be nullified within the next month. The initial investment, at the current rate of return, would be recouped within the next eight months, and the current value, based on projections and capital assets, showed that the Athena Inns had a real-time value approaching sixteen million dollars.

Although there was a flurry of activities, travel, and coordination, Fred was in his element and wielding excellent control inside this environment. Fred was reigning over all the necessary vendors with alternate backups. He had lawyers on retainer through Kate Taylor, benefits that were far above the standard of the area, and enough employees to have a decent amount of sway to get good group prices for health insurance.

He was often busy traveling to various locations to spot-check, verify, modify, and improve each venue. Fred was also keeping an eye out for expansion opportunities and, with her approval, had already acquired four more hotels that were currently being renovated under the supervision and guidance of Terry Wise.

Fred had mentioned that there would be a large expense soon for security-related services—from video surveillance to door lock readers and other things that he felt would bring the hotels further to the front of the pack in terms of safety and desirability.

Trudy was all in for this and wanted to do a little research to understand what was involved. She went to a local security store as a starting point.

At the security store, she met Carl Wyn. Carl was the owner of a local shop and two satellite stores—one in Mt. Vernon, Illinois, and one in Evansville, Indiana. As it turned out, Carl was supremely well-versed in the tech side of surveillance and interactivity on cloud servers and networks.

At first, he was confused as to why she was asking for things on the scale she was involved with. When she explained that she was an intern for a hotel manager and was doing research for an upcoming purchase for an upgrade to a hotel chain, her inquiries made much better sense—as well as intrigued him.

When she had asked every question that even Carl could think of, he expressed to her that, for him at least, all the upgrades were academic, as the manufacturers of the equipment he would endorse required a build fee of three-quarters of the total price. This requirement alone made it possible for only a few select companies to be able to bid on large projects.

What's more, the installation fees reflected this as well. On top of that, the current economy had companies tightening belts and sharpening pencils for the smaller projects the big boys would not touch. As a result, the small fish were all competing heavily. The market at present was truly a dog-eat-dog environment for survival.

Trudy asked him if he had the resources to bid on larger projects and if he would be able to manage the specs and workforce required to follow through.

He told her that, after the right crew had been developed—two crews for a rest-regimented rotation and family time requirements—it would be easy. But again, finding an investor to take on the risk would be the downfall.

Trudy asked if she knew an investor that was willing, would he want to know about it? What would it take for him to consider that?

To which he said he would gladly partner up with the right person and lightheartedly asked her if she had about half a million dollars lying around. They both laughed together. Trudy thanked him for his time and left.

When Trudy got to her car, she started it and sat there long enough for her phone to connect to the interface and cell towers, then had Google call Kate Taylor. Kate was surprised to hear from Trudy in such a brief time and was concerned that there were problems of some sort, but she was pleasantly surprised that everything was going much better than expected.

When Trudy expressed her desire to get into the security business, Kate was momentarily confused, but when the reason for it was explained, it became clear. Kate was up for the task and praised Trudy for her forward thinking.

Again, Trudy gave Kate a free hand at negotiations and expressed that she wanted to make sure Carl was given a large hand at the table with an opportunity to buy back equal equity as a partner.

Kate felt that she understood Trudy's desire and said she would be calling with the details as soon as they ironed them out. When Carl Wyn was contacted by Kate Taylor from Kovach and Associates out of New York, he was wondering why they would be calling. Kate explained that she was friends with a young lady who was currently an intern and had contacted her to talk about an investment opportunity in his security business.

As Kovach and Associates had varied clients always looking for investment opportunities, she was inquiring as to whether the intern was correct about his desire to compete with the larger companies. She explained that she believed she had a client who was ideally suited for a partnership if he was interested.

Carl was taken aback. He expressed that his dream was to grow to the point of being able to do just that, but at the current rate and in this particular economy, he was going to have trouble securing the funding to be an equal partner—which amounted to selling his business and becoming an employee.

He had told her that there had been times the thought of reverting to being an employee had been entertained, but that usually only lasted just long enough to remember how previous employers had treated him. Based on this, he felt he was not the opportunity that it appeared to be from the outside. As for the technical ability, he felt he had no equal, as he was up to the cutting edge of his business, and he told Kate this. He was about to thank Kate for her interest and regretfully declined when Kate stopped him.

Kate expressed that her client was extremely specific about making sure that whatever deal was worked out, she was to ensure that Mr. Wyn had a clear and viable path to "buyback" to a near fifty-fifty arrangement with the investor. "The end game of the investor is to have you equally concerned with the welfare of the business; after all, the investor will be mostly silent. The investor, however, will be able to give you an inside track to a strong beginning, as they have an interest in a hotel chain that will be upgrading soon. From there, that ought to seed your combined company with the income to compete with any other company out there."

Carl was now not only surprised but also supremely interested in such an arrangement, so Kate went to work. After equalizing Carl's physical assets with a cash infusion—providing Carl the ability to spin up a qualified crew roster and establish accounts with the best suppliers—his path to equal ownership was given working credit and credit for running the business. He could accelerate his buyback at his discretion with his part of the profits that were not designated to refund the business and its needs. It was a dream for Carl.

Kate told him that the investor was keen to meet him, which he welcomed wholeheartedly. Kate had one stipulation—Carl had to sign a disclosure form requiring anonymity whether he signed the contract or not. It sounded a bit weird, but he understood that some people like their security—after all, that was his business. He gladly signed the stipulation and sent the disclosure back.

The intern returned to the store the same day the contract was to be signed and was welcomed by Carl enthusiastically. Carl apologized that he could not remember her name but was so thankful that she had relayed his name to her friend. He also apologized in advance but explained that the investor she was responsible for setting him up with was also coming in to meet him that afternoon to finalize their partnership. He told her that he would regretfully have to break away when they arrived. Trudy chuckled to herself and let the whole thing play out a bit longer.

Trudy reintroduced herself to Carl as an intern for Athena Inns and explained that they were indeed going to be upgrading to a new system throughout their chain. She wondered if she could, someday soon, introduce him to the CEO. Carl was doubly excited that this day was going so well. Trudy asked if there was someplace they could talk more privately but promised she too would listen for the arrival of his investor. Carl had not noticed that Trudy had flipped the "Closed" sign outward and quietly turned the bolt when his back was turned.

Trudy was offered a seat inside the office and started to open her leather binder. She pulled out a copy of the signed disclosure and her driver's license and handed them to Carl. He did not know how she had paperwork that was privately made between him and a lawyer in New York. When he heard Trudy's explanation and realized that his benefactor was indeed exactly who she claimed to be, she was sitting directly in front of him.

Trudy went on to explain that, as a company, she was committed to working out an ROI of fifteen to twenty percent of profit as opposed to the twenty-five to forty percent expected from the "big boys." Furthermore, she wanted to pay better than the competition and expect a higher quality and more expedient job completion turnover with better customer service than anyone else. She wanted to offer a value unmatched and unobtainable by the current competition. She wanted potential clients to have no legitimate reason not to embrace them. She wanted to drive the competition out through overwhelmingly superior value. She wanted to maintain that level of service to make coming back to them repeatedly a no-brainer, whether it was a retrofit or a new install. She asked Carl if this was possible and doable.

He indicated that if the correct funding was there and the thrust was quality service and not maximized profit, within a month he thought he could be set up and ready to outperform all competitors to a degree that even if they could match price, their quality would be suspect. He had people in mind already, some of whom he knew were unhappy working where they were currently for the exact same pitfalls she was wanting to avoid.

Carl set himself up with the needed war machine to do just that. Trudy introduced him to Fred Deursh as a potential supplier and asked if he could entertain his bid but made it clear that he was in no way obligated to use him. Fred happily agreed, so Carl released his estimate to compete against other security businesses. It was so much lower than the nearest competition that Fred was understandably nervous and decided to release only one hotel for refitting. He awarded it to Carl to see if his timelines, abilities, and the quality expected could be delivered at the given price.

Upon completion of the job, two weeks later—five days under the deadline—Carl delivered his results, which Trudy and Fred evaluated on the weekend together. Fred assured her that he could inspect the setup by himself, but Trudy told him that she wanted to learn it as well. They met Mr. Wyn for a run-through of the completed system, which was running flawlessly. Aside from the bid, Carl had set up remote access to the system, administered by himself until he could turn it over to the corporate head of security at no extra charge as a bonus back to Athena in appreciation for the opportunity.

Fred was duly impressed and asked if Carl was ready and able to take on nine other upgrades. Carl assured him that he would provide a timeline that would reflect total billing and start and completion dates for every setup and ensure the same connectivity with corporate headquarters. Fred and Carl shook hands, and Trudy stepped in.

Trudy addressed her hotel CEO. "Fred, I know you are familiar with Carl and now his work. What you don't know is that I have financially backed Carl, and I am also in business with him. I didn't want to tell you until now for several reasons, but it is time you knew this. He is also aware of my age and my ties to this business. I assure you, he made no special prices and had no inside information. I wanted to see our business model in action and wanted an opinion that was unbiased as to the quality and the level of your satisfaction without skewing the outcome because of my own involvement."

Fred replied, "If this is the level of quality anyone can expect, after the completion of the project, there won't be much idle time for your business as the quality is better, the price is better, and the value is fantastic—more so than any other company I have ever been involved with. Is security all you do?"

Carl responded, "We are offering full-service door entry programs, security, strategic lighting and controls, and emergency indication services. If it involves a key, a card, a camera, or lighting to see around the complete exterior, interior, and parking, we will be able to offer the best services around. I'm already getting résumés from the competition's best people. They like our model and want a new, appreciative environment. Soon, the competition will be vastly outperformed and technically hamstrung because of their inefficiencies and greed. It is all word of mouth right now, but this sector is getting a new standard that the good ole boy institution will not be able to weather."

True to his word, Carl met or exceeded timelines and price quotes with unparalleled quality at the next build. His workers were efficient and well-paid for their expertise, and they were appreciated for their hard work and skills. With a boss who had been treated horribly in the past as a mere employee, he knew how to properly treat his workers. Being half-owned by the same entity, Carl worked out a deal for the benefit of his men. Soon, human resources would be tied to Athena in terms of benefits.

Carl was busy with other bidding for all sizes of chains and all levels of price points within the hotel community. It would take just under a year and a half before he would be able to reclaim "half" of his company at forty-nine percent and do so while living comfortably in the interim.

True to her word, Trudy had made it easy for Carl to excel and step right into the role that he not only wanted to accomplish but, as it would seem by his passion and productivity, excelled in. He truly was in his element and was efficiently and profitably growing the business at an exponential rate. Starting with the Athenas and a three-state region, he was now bidding on jobs across the country to the bane of his competition.

He had only one partner to satisfy—himself—enabling tight control over the profit margin. This fact alone meant he could starve out the competition as he could bid for less of an ROI and with a much better price point, which was already easily better than the next closest bidder. Never shirking quality, he could bid a job dead flat as a sample and pick up the rest of a chain on quality points alone. When his prices were at normal bid strength and another bid would cut themselves to the bone, he would still get the job when an example was looked at and his history was observed— under time and under budget with the highest of standards.

Upon reflection on how well the security business and its peripherals were doing, it occurred to Trudy that to go full circle on controlling expenses in the hotels, she thought that having a presence that catered to sheets, towels, and amenities such as coffee, tea, soaps and shampoo, letterhead paper, writing utensils, and the like might also have a spot in her portfolio. If she could profitably control the costs with an eye toward the upper end of quality, that too could become a very profitable proposition. She began searching for the candidate to approach and, in doing so, found Cindy Mathews.

Cindy was the Acquisition Specialist with a midsize regional cleaning supply company. Research showed Trudy that she was exceptionally good at her job, so she approached her with the idea of starting a business initially to cater to her hotels and to branch beyond as an all-inclusive hotel products supplier. Cindy was excited about this. She had been in the business for six years and found it hard to advance while fighting the good ole boy environment that was, in many ways, unavailable to her. She had constantly fought the constant innuendos and suggestive remarks, all under the transparent roof of the glass ceiling for women. The thought of being her own boss intrigued and excited her. Putting a dent in her former employer would just be a bonus.

Cindy stated that she had no money to invest beyond a saved-for-emergency bank account that she felt would bridge four to five months for rent, food, and gas. She was willing to risk her complete savings to be able to get on the ground floor of such a company. She had worked up several real-world quotes at Trudy's request to demonstrate the true nature of potential savings. Even at a modest quantity buy-in to find better price points, the profit margin was approaching thirty-five percent. Cindy felt she could do better if there were the possibility of larger quantity price breaks. She let Trudy know directly that she wanted it so badly she could taste it.

Trudy explained that she would be backing the entire endeavor and explained how she structured the deal with Carl at ASC and wanted to arrange one with her that was similar to his. Cindy realized that her wildest dreams could be coming true and almost cried.

She told Trudy that she excelled at ordering, customer relations, and supply lines but was weak at the bookkeeping side of things and was nervous about being able to properly manage everything. Trudy assured her that the help she needed would be on the way. She would be contacted soon by Kate at Kovach Law to set up the particulars, and her accountants would be in contact to arrange for the financials to be taken care of along with the training to keep the accounting software in line.

She wanted Cindy to concentrate on supply lines, inventory requirements, and personnel needed to make the whole endeavor work. Cindy was maxed out in terms of a learning curve, as Trudy knew she would be, but she was learning quickly and becoming more proficient in her abilities across the board. By the time of the first bid for the Athenas, she came in under forty percent less than the nearest competitor, passing on ten percent savings to the customer. It was a win-win all the way around.

Cindy gained confidence and prowess as she began to master the art of the schmooze and the deftness of a savvy businessperson. Cindy was becoming an expert in her environment. What had her doubting herself before was now gone. She was stepping out in many directions, including initiating a separate commercial arm catering to businesses other than hotels. This idea alone was pulling in a twenty-seven percent ROI in this business sector while still underbidding their current suppliers. There was no holding her back.

Kate again strongly suggested to Trudy at Thanksgiving that she should get help before her business interests overwhelmed her. Trudy had listened to Kate and took it to heart the first time when she had suggested hiring a CEO to run the daily grind for the business. She could see she was going to need help maintaining this growing entity that was the TJC consortium, as it was becoming more difficult both keeping things anonymous and keeping on top of things in a timely manner.

She knew she had great people in place, but great people often needed answers and direction on the fly. She knew that often, she was unavailable. Even though her business associates were very capable, she had decided it was time to find a CEO for TJC to coordinate their efforts under one roof to grow more efficiently and consistently. She put out an advertisement that was just a bit basic and vague, but to remain anonymous, she felt she needed to walk someone into the position and find that special someone who could roll with the changing times.

Chapter 29 - Finding A CEO

TJC Inc. was currently headquartered out of Evansville, Indiana, by all associated appearances. This happened to also be Darell's home. It almost felt like karma to him that he saw the small ad when he did. He had always told people that Evansville was the biggest small town in southern Indiana, saddled up next to the Ohio River. City life if you looked for it, and a hometown feel if you embraced it. He decided he was going to apply since it appeared that he could remain near his family.

Evansville was an easy drive from Trudy's home in Illinois, and it had a decent airport with major carriers. It had been her current stepping-off point up until now to any place she could desire to go. She liked the anonymity of Evansville, as she had no ties there, no one to accidentally bump into. It was also central to her short-range plans. Fortuitously, it provided the beginning of her expansion—Evansville just felt right for her.

Darell had been excited when he had decided to throw his hat into the ring and put his best foot forward to garner an interview for TJC. Though there was limited information to study up on concerning their footprint, he felt he had done well. He had rehashed his resume with the latest format while updating it as well, so it might stand out just a bit above the rest. The thought of being **the** manager instead of **the** managed held a certain appeal for him, given his knowledge of the ones he presently worked for.

It was a bonus that there was an implied promise for the use of his degree and a chance to become more than his current dead-end job could ever offer. He prepared an introductory letter, his resume, and a theoretical idea of his long-term goals. He pressed send and continued to look for other opportunities that might be out there. All Darell knew was he could not remain in the thermoforming business, as its toxicity was leaching into his demeanor. He needed a change, and though he was not desperate, he was willing to take some chances.

Trudy had given her CEO posting a two-week lifespan and discontinued it. In the two weeks it was up and running, she had received a multitude of resumes but only eight viable options to really consider. She was not oblivious to the understanding that a mature-looking seventeen-year-old was deciding the fate of people twice her age. She felt there could be some resentment associated with that unchangeable fact. She knew that she was going to have to take extra care to vet the pool carefully while avoiding points of contention. She had decided to look and function as a fortunate mid-twenty-something female in business.

Of the eight initial candidates, two turned out to be unqualified; two others had salary requirements that were beyond what she had envisioned. One simply just felt wrong. If pressed, Trudy would not be able to tangibly tell anyone why—just a sense for a bad fit in general. There were three, however, that showed promise, and of the three, Darell Cromwell piqued her interest the most. Trudy called Carl at ASC and acquired the name of a private investigator to do thorough background checks on her three candidates. When the background checks were more in-depth than a standard summation—a deep dive really had been completed—there were only two candidates left: Mike Davis and Darell Cromwell.

Trudy arranged to be "at a friend's house" on the Friday of the interviews. In reality, she had hopped in her Cherokee and made her way to Evansville. She stopped at what once was an Evansville staple that had gone defunct. It had been resurrected and now was known as The Athena Inn. When she arrived, she parked in a reserved spot for hotel management. She unloaded her small suitcase and made her way in, all under the watchful eyes of the counterperson. When she arrived in the lobby and saddled up to the reservation counter area, the clerk, Sandy, attended to her.

"How may I help you?" She had an air of an elitist attitude.

"Yes, thank you. I have a reservation under Jax."

"Let me see here." Her computer keys started clicking and clacking as Sandy deftly worked the keyboard.

Trudy looked around the lobby and was happy to note that it was clean, sharp, well-lit, warm, and inviting. She smiled to herself, knowing who she hired as the manager of her hotel interests was the right person for the job.

"Here we are. Can I get a credit card and ID, please?"

"Certainly." Trudy started to open her wallet when Sandy spoke up.

"Hold on for a second. I'm sorry, but we might be experiencing some computer issues here because it looks like we have somehow booked you for the penthouse suite. I am so sorry; give me a minute, and I'll get this resolved."

Trudy laid her driver's license where it was easily readable, and Sandy quickly caught the birthdate and stopped what she was doing.

"I think there may be more than one confusion here, young lady. Your ID says you're seventeen. Are you sure you're in the right place?" She had a most severely condescending way in her inquiry. "I kind of thought there was going to be some confusion on your part when you parked in the manager's spot." She gazed past Trudy, obviously staring at her Jeep.

"I'm sorry," Trudy purposely overreacted to reading Sandy's name tag, craning her head and feigning a squint. "Sandy, is it? Can I see a supervisor, please?"

"I'm sure I can manage anything you're going to need here."

"Obviously, you can't, and I would expect more from greeting staff, Sandy. Can I please talk to the supervisor?"

"Miss, you are going to have to leave. This is a place of business, not a playground."

"I'm sorry to have inconvenienced you, Sandy. I'll oversee this myself."

Trudy pulled out her Samsung Android and quickly thumbed through her contact list, pressing dial on the name Fred Duersh. After two rings, Fred answered the phone. The smile on his face was bleeding through to his voice.

"Trudy, it's great to hear from you. How are you doing?"

"Fred, I'm fine, thank you for asking, but I am having a problem checking in to The Athena in Evansville. Sandy, the counter clerk, doesn't like my credentials, so I'm stuck standing here at the counter with bags in hand."

"Trudy, do you mind putting me on speaker for a minute or two for Sandy?"

"Sure, Fred." Trudy held the phone up in the air in front of the counter and pressed her screen. "You're on speaker, Fred."

"Sandy, can you hear me clearly?"

"Why, yes, I can… Fred, is it?" Sandy played along with the ruse mockingly and with an overly smug voice.

"Sandy, according to my personnel screen I'm currently looking at, your last name is Cline. You were hired in with us eight months ago. My computer shows that you have two out of two favorable evaluations. Sandy, if you look under the counter to the left of the reservations window, per company policy, there is a book of standards. Pull out that manual for me, if you would, please."

"Uh, OK?" Sandy was confused about how a stranger knew what he knew and was starting to connect the dots at high speed, beginning to cave inward, realizing she may have poked a hornet's nest. "I've, uh, I have got the manual."

"Great, I want you to turn to the last page. It will be titled 'Emergency Contacts.'"

"I'm there, uh, Mr. Fred?" She realized she had just stepped out of her depth.

"The last entry should say—and I'll do this verbatim, Sandy, so there is no confusion on your part—'In the event that local managerial contacts cannot be reached, regardless of the type of perceived emergency or time of day, call Fred Duersh.' One line below that is the name Fred Duersh and the verification ID of 'FD ten, six, seventy.' Do you see that, Sandy?"

Sandy quickly realized how deep the pool had gotten. "Yes, sir, I see that, and it is exactly as you said it was, Mr. Duersh."

"Do you now believe you are currently talking to Fred Duersh, Athena Inn CEO?"

"Yes, sir, I have no doubt."

"Good, good. Now, could you please page Stanley Boze for me and let him know that I'm on the phone at the front desk and waiting for his company as soon as he can muster it?"

Sandy was already on the front desk phone. "Trudy, I'm very sorry. I will have this corrected, I promise. To be honest, we haven't even addressed these types of scenarios at any other place I have worked. I don't know why, but we will, I assure you. There will be a better training scenario developed to prevent potential issues like this going forward."

No more had she finished saying that to Trudy when a man showed up at the counter as if he were nearby or had gotten there in a hurry. Either way, he was intently alert.

Stan inquired, "Fred?"

"Stanley, this is Fred Duersh, security code FD ten, six, sev."

"Fred, I recognized your voice. How are you doing?" Stanley nervously glanced at Trudy with inquisitive eyes, thinking that his staff had somehow insulted a niece—or worse yet, a daughter or even a family friend.

"Standing before you is Trudy Jax. Trudy is having some issues checking in. I want you to oversee this personally. Understand that Ms. Jax is MY boss and the owner of Athena Inns."

Sandy's smugness now looked more like an "Oh shit" pie-eyed revelation as she tried to remember where all her personal belongings were for the inevitable firing that surely must be on its way.

"She will have nothing less than all of what our hospitality offers—without issue. Please get her on her way and brief all the hotel and restaurant staff as well. And, uh, Sandy? Are you still there?"

"Yes, sir, Mr. Duersh."

"What do you think I want from you?"

"I'll have my stuff out within the hour, sir, and for what it is worth, I will be apologizing to Mrs. Jax, and I apologize to you as well, sir."

"Sandy, here at Athena, we don't operate like that. I want to know if you can look past this situation and draw a picture that could diagram everything that has been done incorrectly here today—expand that picture to a larger, all-encompassing viewpoint of all possibilities and different scenarios. Are you capable of doing that, Sandy?"

"Sir? Uuhh…"

"I've been reading your file here while we have been on the phone. I see you are educated in hospitality services—excellent grades and resume. We don't like losing good talent, Sandy."

She had sheepishly replied, "Uh… Yes, sir?"

"If you are up to it, I want you and me to develop a training module for this type of occurrence and any other potential situations for our corporate guidelines. We have made a mistake here with one of our treasured guests that I want to avoid at all locations. Are you capable of getting past this misstep?"

She had been bewildered, going across the spectrum from thinking about being fired to being drawn into the higher corporate atmosphere. "Ye-ye-yes, sir, I think I can."

"Great. I'll look forward to arranging your arrival here in Louisville in about two weeks. My secretary will work out the details with you later. Stan, you're going to be short one person for a bit—I hope you can manage."

"No problem, sir."

"In the meantime, let's see about getting Mrs. Jax into her room."

"Her key is programmed already; I'll make sure there are no more problems personally, sir."

"Sandy, thank you. And thank you for the attentiveness as well, Stan. Your location is doing an excellent job, in no small part from your efforts, I suspect. Keep up the excellent work. Trudy?"

"Well done, Fred. I'm looking forward to our next meeting. Tell Mary I said hello."

"She will be glad to hear from you. Is there anything else I can help with?"

"I think you covered everything. Thank you so much for your help."

Fred very purposely and professionally addressed her, "You are very welcome, Ms. Jax. Have a great day."

They both hung up, and Trudy put away her phone and turned back around at the edge of the counter. Five minutes later, she was standing in a well-groomed and wonderfully color-coordinated hotel penthouse suite. The room itself was warm and inviting with a soothing undertone. She again felt good about the wonderful people that were in place.

Trudy was aware of her age. She understood how to dress up or down. She had access to nice clothes thanks to the internet—because of the net, she had direct connections to Saks, Louis Vuitton, Gucci, Prada, Dior, and many more. She knew she had to look the part, be the part, and exemplify grace and presence to counteract her actual age.

She had pulled up street cams at Wall Street, outside the D.C. Capitol building, the financial district in Boston, and several other cities on a purely educational trek to find an upscale "average" style of dress along with an attitude and presence to emulate. She already understood well the magic of makeup and had successfully conducted a test run of sorts in downtown Carbondale.

Carbondale was not a large city by comparative standards, but it was growing. She had entered three different bars over the course of two weekends—seventeen years old and looking mid-to-late twenty-something. She had never been carded and had received several "courting" drinks for free, again without a doubt about her age. She nursed these drinks while meeting several people and maintaining a persona that was clearly accepted. She paid heavy interest in the actual twenty-something crowds for pertinent mannerisms, etiquette, and behaviors. She had contemplated going home with one of the suitors but thought better of it due to curfew restraints.

Trudy was confident in her look and felt sure she could interview in the office area of the penthouse suite as the HR director of any company. Today she would be Trudy of TJC Investment Holdings, the talent acquisition manager.

She answered the knock at the door as Trudy, the talent acquisition specialist for TJC, and mentally noted that he was about five minutes late. Mike Davis introduced himself as she invited him in to join her in the office outcrop. Both she and Mike sat and began a conversation that was geared around an informal interview process. Mike looked to be in his mid-to-late thirties, well-fit and confident. He had been just a bit too confident, she had thought, and he was just a bit presumptuous. Trudy got the direct impression that he may have been a little disappointed that he was not going to meet the owner during the interview and had made it clear that he was looking forward to meeting him, though he did appreciate meeting the owner's girl. He quickly backtracked and corrected it with the owner's representative.

It was clear that he had a certain perception of male domination in the workplace. Trudy smiled inside. She felt that, as a CEO, though he was capable, across the organization she wanted to build an inclusive workplace in terms of pay and opportunity. Women would have the same advancement avenues for the same pay. That was a core belief and was going to be included in TJC's organizational mission statement. She was convinced that Mike would not be capable of fully embracing this. Even more so, she suspected that he might be resentful to eventually answer to a woman.

She thought if the next interview with Darell Cromwell was worse than this one, she would have to decide whether she was going to work with Mike or re-enter a new search. Mike graciously thanked her for her time an hour later and headed back to the lobby and left. She had watched him leave from the window and noticed a handsome young man sitting in his car in the parking lot. She turned away from the window because she had to prepare herself for the next interview in forty-five minutes. She wanted to tidy up the office cubby to its former neatness and freshen up a bit before the next "show" time.

When Trudy answered the door once again with her spiel, she had a smile on her face that was just a bit wider than she had for Mike because the handsome man she had seen from her window forty-five minutes earlier was the same young man that stood before her, introducing himself as Darell Cromwell in a most respectful yet commanding and confident way. He was five minutes early for the appointment and had expressed that if he were too early, he would be happy to come back in a bit if she needed. She immediately liked him. There was a flow and an ease about him. She invited him in.

He was just a bit short of six feet tall compared to her almost five foot nine. He had piercing green eyes, and if she guessed—judging by the cut of his suit, the way it hugged him in all the right ways—he was about a hundred and eighty pounds. He perfectly exemplified the upper business class, and she could tell from his demeanor alone that he could easily blend into any type of after-work bar crowd as well. There was an elegance in his mannerisms, an unrehearsed charm about him. The fabric of his shirt was just a bit slack below the chest, but his buttons, though not stressed, were pulled tight. She could tell there was an athletic build camouflaged behind his business world attire. His thick neck was bound by the restraints of his beautiful silk burgundy tie. He was well put together and clearly had good taste to boot.

"Thank you for coming, Mr. Cromwell. You're not too early. I'm Trudy, Trudy Jax, talent acquisition specialist for TJC Investments."

Trudy had a free-flowing conversational interview just as she did with Mike. Twice she thought that someone had switched her highlight prompt cards out or had told Darell what was on them. Not only were Darell's answers so much more compelling than Mike's, but he also anticipated what might be asked much better than Mike in conjunction with any question in general and gave insights before it was asked. He was refreshing to listen to. He walked in and out of his qualifications, touching on his education, aspirations, and goals and incorporating them with the surface direction that Trudy, the talent acquisition specialist, had expressed.

She knew that it would be inappropriate to jump up and down in happy disregard for social norms, but she wanted to. She knew offering him the job on the spot was also not normal, but she wanted to—her mind was made up at once.

Even more exciting was that he was on the low end of her salary range. He had cited being younger at the helm and wanting to prove himself to the owner—whoever they were—and earn their support and give his loyalty to them while growing the company. Somewhere along the line, he would see about adjusting his salary commensurate with his proven performance.

Trudy was sold. They ended the interview with a handshake, and Trudy reconfirmed his contact information, expressing that there was a short list that would soon be narrowed down to an agreed-upon candidate based on her report. Regardless of their decision, TJC would contact him in any event when a decision was made, and they truly appreciated his time.

Darell thanked her for her time, shook her hand, and turned to the door. Trudy caught the door and watched him make his way to the elevator. More directly, she watched his tight ass through his impeccably tailored suit and mentally noted how she liked the way his suit pants rode him just so.

After closing the door, she timed out about the same amount of time it took Mike to appear out the front, and on cue, Darell made his way out to his car and closed himself in. She watched as he put on his seatbelt and started the car. The car didn't move—Darell just sat there. She saw him pull himself inward, stretch his shoulders back along with his neck, and, as if he had taken a big cleansing breath, lean forward. Below the seat line, he gave a victorious fist pump, which, due to the angle of the room to the ground, she had full view of.

Directly after, he composed himself a little and became self-conscious that someone might be looking. He cautiously looked around. Trudy backed away from the window just in case he looked up, but she knew.

She knew she had Darell if she wanted him.

She wanted him; she wanted him in more ways than one.

Trudy picked up the phone and called room service, which was promptly answered without a room reference but with, "Hello, Ms. Jax, how can we help you?" She told the woman on the phone that she was thinking of something simple and wondered if the chef had a good cheeseburger, a side salad, and a Sprite to help it down. She was assured that her order could be accommodated, and room service inquired about the level of doneness she wanted for her cheeseburger, to which she responded, "medium." She was assured that it would be delivered shortly.

Fifteen minutes later, a covered plate with a covered side salad and a glass filled to the brim with ice and a carbonated, still-bubbling liquid, along with a cold, unopened bottle of Sprite, was wheeled into her suite after she had opened the door. The fare was unloaded in the kitchenette.

Trudy had been famished. It was surprising that the interviews took so much out of her physically, and in doing so, worked up a profound hunger in her. She realized she had not had lunch. It was a duh… moment.

The side salad bowl was cold, and the lettuce crisp, clean, and inviting. All of the ingredients looked just-picked fresh—tomato, onion, olive, radish, celery, carrot shreds. It was all crisp. There were side cups of bacon bits, sunflower seeds, craisins, and one for croutons. She pulled the cover off her burger and noticed it had come with fries that were piping hot and golden brown—perfectly done. She bit into the fully dressed burger, and before she had chewed three times, she just stopped, savoring the tastes she was now experiencing. The best burger she had ever eaten thus far in her life.

To be fair to all the other burger joints she had ever eaten in or at, she conceded that she was currently starving, which may have some bearing here. She laughed to herself and mentally said, "No matter, this is a damn good burger!" She devoured the burger but left half of the fries, as she was now sated and full.

Trudy re-dressed in her arrival clothes, packed her things, and went to check out.

When Sandy saw her with a bag in tow, she was momentarily concerned that something was wrong, as it was clear she was leaving.

"Good afternoon, Ms. Jax, how can I be of assistance?"

Trudy had a pleasant smile. "Good afternoon, Sandy. My business is concluded, and I have another appointment in Illinois later this evening. I won't be staying overnight; I would like to check out."

The appointment was with her alibi, Britiney, where she was supposed to have been all day and was going to spend the night after they went to a movie.

At about that moment, Stanley appeared. Clearly, he had instructed that he be prompted in the event Mrs. Jax was at the check-in counter.

"You're leaving us, Mrs. Jax?" he asked, having heard part of the conversation.

"Yes, unfortunately, I am. I just came up to settle the bill."

"Mrs. Jax, per Mr. Duersh, your money's no good here, today or in the future. We want to thank you for gracing our halls. I hope you have enjoyed your time here."

"Thank you, Stan, everything was better than I could have hoped for. I appreciate you asking."

She got out her wallet and pulled free two twenties. "Please send this to room service and the cook. Tell them everything was beyond wonderful."

Trudy turned to leave when Sandy spoke up. "Ms. Jax."

Trudy pivoted back around to face her.

"Ms. Jax, I again want to apologize for earlier. I will help develop that module for a training aid—something I hope you will be proud of. Again, I am terribly sorry for my behavior."

"Sandy, we all have a bad day occasionally. I am looking forward to reviewing the module, and I'm also looking forward to seeing you again as early as next week."

With that, she turned and left.

Chapter 30 - You Are Hired

Two days later, she placed a call to Mr. Cromwell from Trudy in HR Talent Acquisition. Darell enthusiastically took the call, as he knew it was TJC with a yes or a no. He liked the idea of a binary existence instead of the constant waffling and grayness in his current position.

"Hello, this is Darell Cromwell."

"Mr. Cromwell, this is Trudy in HR for TJC. Do you have a minute?"

He was on pins and needles as he felt the head of the matter coming to the surface. "Sure, I do. How can I help?"

"My report was well received at the highest level within the company. I want you to know that we had multiple responses for the position."

Darell's heart started to sink just a bit.

"Of all the candidates, we vetted eight very qualified hopefuls," Trudy was lying just a bit for effect. "Of the pool, you made the short list. After considering the entries, including you and all the qualifications…"

Darell sunk further, as he had clearly admitted during the interview that he had no actual experience as a CEO—just a drive to be one and the self-assigned belief in how to be an effective one.

"We have decided to extend the offer to you. Should you decide that we are a good fit for you as well, we will look forward to you onboarding."

He felt a bit like a jet on an aircraft carrier—sitting back with nothing happening and then accelerating to a gazillion miles an hour and taking flight.

There was silence on the line.

"Mr. Cromwell?"

"I'm sorry, Mrs. Jax. I'm here. I was absorbing your offer and reviewing my feelings from the interview. I've got to say, I am happy that you have made me the offer. Yes, I'll accept the position. We are indeed a good fit. Truthfully, I was concerned that my lack of experience may have left me out of the choosing. May I ask what your deciding criteria were?"

"On the surface, you are right—there was a concern about the amount of experience you have. But after contemplating your education, your background, your drive, and your stated goals, it seemed to us that this was an exceptional opportunity.

"We are on the verge of breaking out. We want someone who understands the cutting edge of technology, the business sense to operate and manage a multi-faceted business, the flexibility to change direction when an opportunity presents itself, and the self-awareness to question best practices and break from the norm when called for.

"We believe you will be an exceptional fit within our criteria. I personally think you will find us far from the traditional company—progressive and, in many ways, innovative. We believe you are well suited to embrace our values and goals going forward."

"I still don't really have a handle on exactly what sectors TJC Investments is concentrating on. There was truly little available publicly. Can you explain where the company's interest lies?"

"Yes, we know that we are a bit of an enigma when it comes to an online presence. This is much by design—one that you will be directly in charge of changing as the needs require it. All this secrecy will become clear to you after you have read our prospectus, glimpsed our books, and understood the parameters that you have to work with. That is, if you are still interested at that time. We want you to have a full understanding of our company walking in."

"I am most definitely interested, but now I am intrigued as well. How do you propose we go forward from here?"

"Our lawyers have drawn up a few non-disclosure forms. After they are signed and recorded back at the office, I will be able to hand you a full prospectus package, at which time you will have several days to decide if you intend to continue forward with us. Would Friday, at the same venue, work for you, around five? Dinner there at the hotel?"

"I'm already looking forward to it. I will see you a little before five."

The next Friday, Trudy again created an airtight "alibi" for her dad and set off for the hotel. The Athena was in a heightened state of awareness when she arrived, as her reservation had been flagged. From the time she parked in a managerial spot to the time she was in her penthouse suite, less than five minutes had passed. Sandy was nowhere to be seen, but Stan had already prepared her key. When she arrived at the counter, Stan introduced "Molly, our newest counter clerk," to the Athena owner, Ms. Trudy Jax.

"Thank you for anticipating my arrival. It wasn't really necessary to create such a fuss."

Stan replied, "It's our pleasure, Ms. Jax. Please let me know if we can do anything to improve your stay."

"I'm glad you asked, Stan. Would it be possible to talk to the restaurant manager in my room later?"

"I'll send her up to your room at her earliest convenience."

Trudy knew this was best thought of as, I'll give you about twenty minutes to settle in, and she will be there. Just as she thought—though she was five minutes later than Trudy had anticipated—there was a knock at the door.

When Trudy opened the door, her luggage was still on the king-sized bed, mostly empty, with a couple of outfits hanging in the closet and her makeup bag's contents neatly spaced across the counter in the bathroom in front of a wall-to-wall, floor-to-ceiling mirror.

"Hello, Ms. Jax. I'm Francine… Fran. Mr. Boze said you wanted to have a conversation with the restaurant staff. How can I help?"

"Thank you for coming up so soon. I was hoping you could help me a little later tonight in the restaurant."

"How may we be of assistance?"

"Would you instruct your staff to bring me a whiskey tumbler with two bourbon ice cubes and water only from the bar anytime they ask if I want a drink and I say, 'just my usual, please'? And anytime I am low on water, to do the exact same routine with a new tumbler? Is that possible?"

Fran looked quizzically at her. Trudy continued, "I don't want a business colleague to know that I don't drink."

Fran's look became one of confused understanding.

"We can certainly do that, Ms. Jax. Do you have an approximate arrival time?"

"I'm anticipating around five-thirty, give or take ten minutes or so."

"We will be looking forward to your arrival."

"Thank you so very much, Francine. I really appreciate it."

"You're welcome, Ms. Jax. We are always happy to help. Please let us know if we can do anything else to make your stay better."

Trudy dressed for a high-end power lunch. Her outfit would have been at home in any business conference or boardroom in any city in America. Again, looking in her mid-twenties, she was completely ready for her meeting. She had a bottle of champagne that she had put on ice and two flutes she had acquired just for this occasion, which she had brought from home. Stepping back and eyeing herself in the mirror, she thought she looked upscale and on the leading edge of professionally dressed—not to mention hot to boot.

Trudy answered the door after a little self-prescribed waiting time following Darell's knock.

"We are so excited to have you back. Won't you please come in?"

"Thank you." He looked around and saw the champagne. "Are we celebrating?"

"Well, that really depends on if you're ready to sign our non-disclosures."

"Absolutely. I'm looking forward to reading the prospectus and seeing what we are working with."

"Let's not waste any time."

She walked to the office, where there was a pen and three sheets concerning non-disclosures—one about the business and its confines, another about company personnel names and functions, and lastly, one about the financial abilities of the company. All aspects of the business—lock, stock, and barrel—had been completely locked down. If Darell had changed his mind for any reason, he was legally bound to remain silent in all matters involving TJC.

When the papers were signed, she made a call and verified—to someone, which was actually her own voicemail—that all the forms were signed and that she was going to scan the sheets with an app on her phone and send them on. She scanned the forms and smiled.

Trudy walked to the "bar" and struggled a bit until the cork relented and pressured out from the bottle of Dom Pérignon. She poured them both a glass, leaning heavily on Darell's flute. It was smooth, and both had finished their glass in short order.

"We have reservations downstairs. I hope you have an appetite?"

"That is excellent. I definitely could eat."

They made their way to the elevator and traveled down together. When they got to the restaurant, Trudy asked for a table for two for the Jax Party, and the name itself elicited an immediate and effective response. They were seated in short order, and a waitress asked if she could get them any drinks.

"I'll have my usual. Actually, make it a double. We are celebrating a bit."

The waitress looked at Darell. "And for you, sir?"

"A Maker's Mark, please—four fingers, neat."

"Certainly, sir."

Their drinks arrived and were set in front of them. Trudy's drink looked like vodka on ice.

"Have we had an opportunity to look at the menu?"

Trudy ordered lobster thermidor, asparagus, and a baked potato. Darell ordered prime rib, medium, honey-glazed carrots, and a baked potato. The waitress commented on the excellent choices.

Darell had carefully paced his drinking with Trudy's. He wasn't that far from his frat days—even now, his Saturday evenings were still reserved for some of the guys. His liver still got a regular workout, but this was not a frat night.

He was, however, wondering about Trudy's tolerance, as he was on track for a slightly faster pace than a good night with the boys. She finished her water, signaled the waitress, and requested another one, again asking to "make it a double." Darell ordered his again, but this time on the rocks. They were almost done with number two when the waitress came by and let them know that their food was almost ready. Trudy looked at Darell.

"Another round for dinner?"

"I'll follow your lead, Trudy."

Trudy requested another round for both, and the waitress headed off to the bar once more. Their food arrived in short order—it looked and smelled fantastic.

Darell's perspective on all aspects had started to be heavily affected by the bourbon. Up to this point, he was holding his composure. Through dinner, Trudy had one more, and Darell kept pace. When the table had been cleared, Trudy declined dessert, as did Darell, but Trudy asked for one last drink. Darell matched suit.

The waitress asked how she wanted to pay, and Trudy said to just put it on the room. The waitress said she would be happy to do so and brought out the ticket to charge it. After signing and tipping heavily, Trudy slammed the last shot worth of her "vodka," as did Darell with his bourbon. They both got up to leave and headed for the door.

Trudy was steady and clear-headed, and though Darell was not staggering by any means, he was very much aware that it had been a while since he had been this influenced—ten shots in just over an hour and a half. The shots had begun to take their toll, even with a full stomach. When they reached the door of the restaurant, he said, "Ms. Jax, I believe I'm going to need to call an Uber, but I want to thank you and TJC Investments for this opportunity and for a wonderful dinner. I'm looking forward to collaborating with you in the future."

"You are welcome. I really enjoyed your company as well. We can call you an Uber from the room."

"Excuse me? Uh?"

"I assumed you were not leaving without the prospectus?"

"Oh my goodness, I can't believe I almost walked out of here without it. I think I may have had a touch too much bourbon. Yes, by all means, let's get the prospectus."

Darell entered the elevator first. Behind his back, two buttons on Trudy's shirt became undone. She knew that the lace fringes of her bra would be seen at certain angles. She had also undone the lower fasteners on part of her skirt, revealing more of her thigh under the table while sitting at dinner. After three buttons, up to mid-thigh was now free.

She saw Darell take better notice of her—partly because of this change in wardrobe status, partly because of the alcohol. She saw him definitely casually look at her with different eyes on the reflective surfaces of the elevator as she remained oblivious, feigning not to notice.

After opening the room door, Trudy led Darell into the foyer. Darell stopped at the bedroom foyer intersection as Trudy walked on. At the far end of the office cubby, Trudy intentionally passed her briefcase, which consisted of a large leather-pocketed sleeve that was zippered on top. She turned so she could purposefully face Darell. She knew there were multiple ways to retrieve the paperwork, but she had something in mind that she was going to implement just for Darell.

She half-squatted, half-stooped, and partially leaned forward all in one graceful, fluid motion. She was concentrating on taking her time locating the paperwork. There could have been much more efficient avenues for prospectus retrieval, but she was playing a very intentional game.

For his part, he could not help but watch Trudy's smooth and graceful transition from standing to, well, showing. He felt a little like a voyeur and knew he should look away. Whether it was the booze, the amount of time it had been since finding temporary barroom love, or Trudy herself, he could not stop himself from sneaking a peek from his peripheral vision—though he thought he was being very discreet.

He knew she had no clue that her innocent retrieval of the prospectus had revealed more of herself than she could have wanted to, but still, he could not force himself to turn away just the same. Her thigh was exposing itself at just a bit above halfway. It was tanned and buttery smooth, tight under the strain of the squat and muscular pose. The way her skirt was riding up—he wanted to see more.

Locking down his desire, angry inside at himself—this was the head of HR, not a good thought at all. He became angrier still at himself because his inner animal was acting on its own volition. He locked it down, but even so, he could feel blood starting to shift positions within him, causing him to firm up uncontrollably. He realized it wasn't just the thigh anymore—he was all but looking down her shirt as it hung open, inviting, welcoming.

Darell became angrier at himself that he had allowed himself to see another human being as an object.

The little fucked-up portion of his brain, that thing that resides in all men's brains, said it's OK to just, well, just a peek, and so he did. Her lace bra captured her essence in a firm embrace, at least on the bottom side, yet his hazy brain still wondered if her breasts, cupped and straining as they were in their confines, would be better off free. It was almost as if her left nipple was doing reconnaissance as to whether the escape would be successful or not. It was on the top side, visible in the gap created by the squat, and her right areola edge was looking as if it were the moon coming up. He briefly thought he could get lost there if given a chance.

All of this had happened in the time it took for this innocent HR manager to squat and rifle through her case and find the prospectus binder in her case. It had been thirty seconds, forty-five seconds at best. Darell was not hard yet, he was not standing up, but there was a tension developing underneath him that threatened to make it officially known if this continued much longer.

When they had entered the room, Trudy had sensed his position while following her. She had heard him stop at the corner of the bedroom space there at the edge of the office cubby and knew exactly where he was in relation to her as she passed her briefcase by a step and a half on purpose.

On her way there, she very covertly had pulled her blouse forward on her shoulders and, just as discreetly while walking, pulled the left side of her bra down just a bit with an imperceptible tug. She thought that she had tugged a bit too hard as she felt her nipple break free of the lace on the left. She felt her nipple still caged on the right side. She knew there was going to be something to see if he looked, and though she wanted to be just a bit subtler in her display, she was OK with the result.

Darell was a bit tipsier than she realized, as he had hidden it well. The transitions were made while she had been walking; because of the angle and the mental fog, he had not noticed her making the adjustments. Trudy was, however, very much aware that Darell was trying hard not to notice all the while indulging himself at the same time. She knew this because searching for a prospectus in her briefcase was a moot point—there were exactly three non-disclosure forms in there and only one letter-sized paper binder and nothing else. Her search was the slowest retrieval of a known location she could muster, all while "searching" the confines of the brief for an elusive prospectus. While she looked for her paperwork, she had been concentrating on her peripheral vision. She saw him look, she saw him fight the gawk, she even believed she perceptively saw a micro amount of movement from just below Darell's beltline.

She declared, "Here it is, Mr. Cromwell."

She pulled the binder free and rose from her position. A full minute had passed from the squat to the stand—Trudy had hoped it was enough. She went to give the binder to Darell but changed directions with her arm and set it on the nearby secretariat edge. "Officially, you are not employed with us yet."

Stepping forward to almost adjacent but by his side, the front of her hips and pelvis were ninety degrees to his right hip and ever so slightly in front of his center. "I don't want to regret wondering, so I'll just ask."

She could see a slosh behind his pupils, that heavy-eyed alcohol haze that occurs when a person is supremely lubricated. He was mentally completely there, good for decisions, but gone enough to not make the best of decisions in retrospect the next day.

"Do I interest you?" Simultaneously looking him in the eye and feeling forward with her right hand to cup his crotch. In doing so, her hand wrapped around the front of a completely heavy cock. His dick received her hand and responded by opening his internal let's fuck valve for the blood that was already moving toward his groin to fill the rest of the void areas at double time. His dick rose in her hand, hard, throbbing, and standing. All Darell could muster verbally was, "Shit!"

His eyes closed in that instant, willing his cock to shrink and go away, only to be overridden by that same menacing let's fuck valve and the portion of his animalistic brain that was screaming, It's time, it's time, it's been too long, let's fuck and let's fuck now!

Despite his best concerted effort to backtrack it in, the Neanderthal inside his brain took over. All he managed effectively on his part was a guttural moan as he closed his eyes and relished her touch. "Uhmmuugh!"

Darell opened his eyes and could not say no. He wanted to, but her dark, deep brown eyes begged him forward. He knew he was capable of saying no, but he just did not have the ability at that particular space and time. He gave in to the moment.

"Yes, I… I want you."

His eyes closed briefly, and another pleasing "mmmhhmm" escaped him, partly because it was there but also partly because his now blue-veined, standing member had just received a full-on shaft-surrounding, through-the-slacks squeeze from Trudy's hand—a hand that, even through the trousers, felt searing hot. It had indeed been a while since he had been this interested in anyone.

Trudy freed her grip on his member and moved in front of him, wrapped her arms around his neck, and met his lips with a wonderful kiss that was, in turn, wonderfully received. It was the perfect first kiss—the kind of kiss that spoke volumes in a few brief seconds. Warm and inviting, wet with just the perfect amount of shared tongue, an exchange of silent information that defined a secretive blueprint on how to treat the other.

She kissed his neck and began to remove his tie. When it was free, she threw it carelessly, not really tracking the toss. As he watched, she began to unbutton his shirt one button at a time while kissing the skin under each location of the individual buttons as if they had caused a boo-boo where they were stationed. Darell had been caressing her back all while she was exposing his chest and stomach, thankful for continuing his core exercises from his college days. His washboard abdominal muscles posed an obstacle that this hot woman before him tried very intently to contend with. She had been doing well with hot, wet kisses as she made her way over the washboards, back up to his chest, while alternating sides.

When she arrived at the smoother areas above the abs, things changed a bit. It seemed that the lack of obstacles was replaced by proceeding right on to his left nipple, where she had sucked it in expertly. This gave him pause. Not even his ex, Jenny, had taken the time to please his nipple in such a wonderful way. The perfect amount of wetness blended with the perfect amount of suck and lick, causing him to catch his breath a couple of times as she moved and varied the intensity of the onslaught.

It was hard to describe, but the erotic effect of it had him wanting more. She nibbled his nipple hard but, well, not too hard. She sucked it in hard but not too hard. She knew well what she did to him. His level of being turned on was beyond what he could have expected and had only been equaled by the thrill of when she moved to his other nipple. When she bit down on it, the bite had been harder still—a test. If it were indeed a test, she had found his tolerance and stepped on it and all around it. He winced just a little bit verbally but also half moaned too.

She rose and kissed him full on the mouth. His hands aimlessly roamed her body, clumsily bumping over one obstacle after another until he gathered himself and began to concentrate on the woman before him.

He wanted to grab the top of her blouse and just rip it open, popping buttons all about the room, throwing the garment wherever a random toss would take it, but he had tried that once with Jenny in what he thought was a wonderfully spontaneous and sexy moment, only to have the spontaneity and brutality misread. This had caused him to miss any action whatsoever when she got pissed about the blouse being ruined. He thought better of it for now.

He started at her top button, which had started at four buttons down. He kissed her neck while he located number five. Number six did not make it through the end of the sensual French kiss. Hot and wanting, their tongues met, and there they fought, neither side wanting to win as if a stalemate was being sought and earned. When he started to kiss down her chest, she arched backward, giving more of herself to him. It was a quick flip and a small tug to free the tucked tail end of the blouse, revealing the treasured number seven button. He released the jailor and eased the garment backward, letting the lightweight, airy fabric slide free down her arms and to the floor.

Her nipples had retreated into their hiding places, but he knew full well they were just taunting him because her two newly formed thumbs hiding beneath her bra were telegraphing their GPS coordinates to the world.

Briefly, he smiled when a joke he remembered flashed through his mind—the housewife that had waited for her husband to get home only to yell from deep in the house, "I'm naked and I'm hiding." Husband yells back, "When I find you, I'm going to fuck you but good." Upon hearing that, she yelled back, "I'm naked and I'm hiding… in the hallway closet."

Yep, he could tell that her nipples were hiding alright—in plain sight. He was inwardly amused for a moment.

He kissed her cleavage high on the breasts. Both of her breasts strained against their white lacy confines. He kissed both fabric-laced nipples from the outside. As he tried to suck her right nipple, he could swear he could feel it pulse yet bigger through the material itself. He began by moving across her chest and onto her shoulders, kissing a path as he went and caressing her amazingly soft, supple skin.

He could feel his own heartbeat meet up with the head of his dick, seemingly getting harder with every beat pounding through his body.

Stepping behind her, he cupped her breasts in a combination hug and embrace, his thumbs grazing her hardened nipples through the bra. She laid back into him with a subtle, inviting arch. He turned his attention to the hardware that was preventing him from truly being skin to skin as he set his fingers to work. The clasps were no match for his wanting; they released one clip at a time until her bra fell forward past her shoulders and on past her arms to the floor.

He slowly dropped down behind her while softly dragging his fingers down her back to the convergence of her spine to her panty line. He started there and half-kissed, half-licked his way up her back, taking extra time where the awful restraints had dug into the flesh of her back, leaving their brand as they did. She was again slightly arching back into him, skittered occasionally, and moaned approval all the while.

Standing behind her, he once again wrapped his arms around her and cupped her breasts. It was so incredibly different this time as his fingers delighted in their new environment. No lace, no exclusion, no barriers—it was genuinely nice. Genuinely nice melted away to unbelievably incredible when he cupped both breasts fully with each hand. Both hands were delightfully full; her breasts felt as if they were searing his hands with her body heat. It was a heat that could have only come from more blood being brought forth. He knew it was true because somehow her nipples were now ever so slightly larger and even more heavenly in his grasp.

He turned her toward him to get a look at his newfound joy, only to be met with a sobering truth: her nipples and breasts together were the most beautiful, impressive appendages he had ever witnessed. Jenny's tits were spectacular, unequaled, but now his one and only thought when the comparison again crossed his mind was, Jenny who?

Trudy's breasts truly were a vision—a sight shunning all comparisons. Her tight areolas supported her fantastic nipples, which were all supported by wonderfully, perfectly round, symmetrical, perky mounds of heaven.

He bit the base of her left breast at the underside. Turnabout, he thought, was fair play, right? She moaned in approval. As he made his way up the breast he had just accosted, her breathing had shallowed, and her head was tilted back, clearly enjoying his skilled advance. Without touching any part of it beforehand, he sucked her left bare nipple into his hot, wet mouth deeply and with a fair amount of suction pressure, hoping he had not been too aggressive in his assault. She just moaned and pulled his head—really, almost smashed his head down further on her solid standing mound amid her wanting. He sucked it harder yet, which yielded more verbal delight. He licked the extents and perimeter of it before moving on to her right breast.

When he sucked in this nipple, he had a firm grasp of her left nipple in his left fingers. Sucking his face ever firmer down the right nipple and areola, he squeezed the left with a fair amount of pressure. As the pressure from his hand raced through her body, Trudy gasped, and her nipples pulsed back at him.

His raging hard-on had been listening to the play-by-play as relayed by his animalistic brain and was trying desperately and physically to eye the situation for itself—standing as tall as it could, straining to do its own investigation. But for the moment, Darell continued on as a solo act.

She had moaned louder, pulling him forward deeper. One last time, he sucked her nipple yet harder, squeezed harder still, and when she moaned even louder, he added a bite to the right nipple, trying to gauge his pressure. Apparently, he accomplished a good grade because the resulting pull inward and the audible, on-the-verge-of-a-yelling moan outwardly coupled up together and blatantly screamed approval to him. When he relented momentarily, Trudy pulled free.

She freehanded his chest from the front for a moment, filtered through his chest hair as she moved around behind him. She cupped his breasts in a quasi-mirror-like action that he had done. For a moment, he wondered what she had in mind, but suddenly, her cupped hands on his breasts turned into individual nipple eradicators simultaneously.

The start of it concerned him heavily, but when she found the most incredible amount of pressure in the squeeze—beyond what he thought he would like—he laid back into her a little with delight. She squeezed just a little harder. His cock pulsed, just once, but it pulsed uncontrollably, half rocking his hips upward. A moan of pure, unabridged ecstasy left his lips without asking for any permission from him.

Letting loose and filtering down his ample but lightly haired chest, she stopped her hands at his belt, undid, unbuttoned, and unzipped him in what was such a fluid motion he thought it was one event. She held his trousers there, almost as if it were a teasing game. She slightly lifted them, with the crotch of the pants pulling gently into his balls. She dropped them free, and they slid off his ass cheeks and down his legs, bunching up on the floor around two leg posts.

With two small steps forward, as she guided him, he stepped free of the leg holes. Grabbing both hips—one hand pulling, one hand pushing—she spun him around gently to face the front of his current underwear of choice, bikini briefs. His back was to the foot of the bed, but there was no sign that she wanted him to use it, so he stood there for a moment. She squatted down and found the edge of his left sock with a single finger. She hooked it and peeled it off his foot, doing the same with the other foot just moments later.

Expecting her to pull his briefs off, he waited with bated breath, desire, wanting, and a pulsing dick drive begging to do its thing. She reached up to the front of his briefs and started to pull them down to his delight but stopped at mid-hip. His rock-hard cock stood full-on at attention.

His erection was not straight up like a kid with a piss hard-on. It was not straight out like someone with issues or early-onset ED. It was hard, pulsing, angular, turgid, and solid. Trudy looked at his member adoringly. She wanted his cock in so many ways, so many positions, so many places. She wanted to thoroughly enjoy his cock—from touch to come and beyond.

She let a finger trace up the side of it, chasing the cock's involuntary pulses that were trying to help it escape her touch. With such pleasure, it shimmied up and back, and up still again. When she circled his glans with the soft tip of her finger, Darell let loose a singular prayer—at least she thought it was a prayer because it started with, "Oh God." He must have kept the rest of it to himself because his head tilted back, looking to heaven, his hips flared ever so slightly forward, and his breathing hitched.

When she stopped circling, she gave him a moment to find himself and to find her again. She looked up into his eyes with the biggest I wanna fuck you, I wanna suck you, I wanna please you, I am begging you please cow eyes. Somehow, this made him harder still, which he honestly did not think was possible at this junction in time.

She looked down, as did he. There his beautiful rod stood, vertical at her beck and call, with a huge drop of pre-cum boiled up onto the tip. It had not been the first pre-cum to escape, as there were two trails down the sides of his meat where some had escaped down his shaft. She started with the mid-portion of her pointer finger and used it to edge up into the coitus drop. Simultaneously, she dipped into it and pulled her finger alongside it, harvesting the glistening love juice on her finger.

Once again, she looked into his eyes and smiled, then slowly sucked her finger into her own mouth, sucking the harvest of him off it.

His muscle twinged while he watched and healthily replaced the juice, the head of his pulsing love joy threatening to disintegrate through an actual physical explosion. It had become increasingly more difficult to stand still, although through some force of will, he maintained his spot. His will was being actively oppressed by her actions. She was purposefully making it more difficult yet to hold still when she leaned forward and sucked the head of his cock expertly into her hot, moist mouth.

She sucked him in, all but consumed him in what seemed more like a loving want on her part rather than an obligatory, means-to-an-end mechanical action. This vision burned his brain and stained this picture indelibly deep in his mind. Trudy took him in as if she were savoring him, savoring this moment, savoring the experience. It made him feel special, like he had been the only one. It made him want her more. It made him want to know more about her. He was captivated by her now. She all but owned him through her actions and could do anything as she pleased.

He might have been able to articulate just what he was feeling if they stopped right now, but right now, she was sucking her way down his shaft slowly, and his body was straining to appease her. He did not have the ability to suggest a stop even though he knew they were crossing a line that could not be uncrossed. Right, wrong, or otherwise, he could not give a flying shit about protocols.

He was more than grateful for the home his prick was now enjoying, even if it was temporary. Darell was fully seven inches, almost eight long. He knew from experience she was about at the end of travel. He knew he was thicker and longer than a lot of other guys. It was his size that posed the problem. His ex had a dildo that claimed to be one and three-quarters in diameter, and he was bigger than that. He knew the way the parameters were going to be played out. At this moment in time, it was all right with him because he was in total bliss.

He waited for the change in direction in the same manner that all the girls who blew him did, but his mind was ripped from his skull. Trudy had gotten to the back of her throat, somewhere around four inches as usual— the direction change area of all those who blew him—she turned her head just a little bit and sucked him in, further and further and further still. Trudy's "further" stopped when her lips met his belly. It was somewhere in that seven-inch-plus distance that he had lost his mind.

He had never been deep-throated. Ever! It was always a size thing; he had never been deep-throated. Ever!! His balls were resting under her chin. He had never been deep-throated. Ever!!! Every girl said he was too big, too long. His mind was blown, and when he thought about himself fully in her, the singular notion in and of itself could not be paralleled.

She pulled up the shaft slowly but stopped, still retaining his head in her mouth, and slowly proceeded down again—all the way. After four full-on strokes down his shaft slowly, she picked up the pace, shortening the arrival time with his balls under her chin with each wanting mouthful. She was full-on deep-throating him completely. He was being face-fucked, or was she? He could not tell, nor did he care.

When Trudy first saw his cock, she had wanted it. She wanted it badly. When she wrapped her hands around his shaft, she knew that this was the girthiest dick she had ever felt. She had plenty of experience with Danny, and as compared to this—well, Danny was big, but this was a touch bigger and almost a full inch longer. She could not wait to describe the feeling of it to Danny.

When she took the head in her mouth, his pre-cum made it that much more delightful to her. She massaged his glans with the tip of her tongue, not only to make him feel good but to coax out more of his juice. She had loved the taste of pre-cum. She had loved the taste of come in general, though she conceded that occasionally, it did not taste all that great. When Danny had eaten a lot of garlic, no blowjob for him. But Darell's pre-cum tasted good to her. She could hardly wait for the main event.

She got just a bit wetter with the thought of draining Darell's balls completely. Her mouth was the fullest it had ever been, and she was loving it. She was good at deep-throating, as she had plenty of practice with Danny and Dave, but the size of this might pose a serious challenge, she had thought. When he bottomed to the back, she drew in a long breath, prepared herself mentally for gag reflex control, and pushed herself forward and beyond. At first, she was not sure it would even go down her throat, but then it did, and she loved it more still.

She felt his shaft fill her neck fully, almost bulging her neck, and felt her lips meet a forward barrier in his belly. Her chin was surrounded by his nuts. Her mouth being this full, her neck occupied like this—something in this combination had her eyes watering to a point she could hardly see, but she had him full in, and more beyond that, she knew she had him for as long as she pleased.

She changed direction and decided the next couple of strokes would be slow, as saliva was your friend while deep-throating. This was a lot of dick, a lot of long dick, a filling dick. It was going to require some exceptional care in handling. Down she went again and then up. She repeated it again as she consumed him, and she now could feel her saliva glands in full bloom.

When she started to full-on face-fuck Darell, she felt his enthusiasm rise. Her mouth was almost stretched to the limits, but it was glorious. His member started this exhilarating feeling just at the tip of her lips and moved slowly into her mouth, with the wonderful head filling quite a bit of the void. As more dick entered and found the back of her mouth and down her throat, filling her neck quite deeply, it was clear that there was officially no more room at the inn.

The feeling of cock totally filling her orally was setting her pussy on fire. Why the feeling in her neck was communicating with her inner flame, she did not know. What she did know was that his cock down her mouth was spectacular. She could not give two fucks for the reasonings that drove her; she just knew she liked his fullness there.

After what had to have been fifty strokes or more in her mouth, she pulled herself off him and pushed him—barely able to stand—backward, dick hard, onto the bed in a sitting position. She put on a show of sorts for him while she undressed. He drank in her every loss of clothing and was in awe as her goddess-like body was slowly revealed.

She knew she had a tight body; she knew her body was phenomenal. She worked out and maintained a great physicality. She knew she had what was a "perfectly rounded" ass. She knew all of this not out of smugness but because the ones who had seen her naked often told her so. Danny had expressed this early on, and he was direct and usually honest to a fault with her. Dave had, unprompted, repeated much of the same praise. Amanda was not coy or shy about it either; she made it clear that she was spectacular. She knew from their testimony that she was well put together. She also knew how to use these truths to her advantage when need be.

She guessed for the general population, her 'truths' mostly held true, and by the way Darell was transfixed as she removed her skirt—the way his eyes never left her body even as she threw the skirt somewhere in the room—he also believed it to be true. Darell was on the edge of the bed. As she approached him, his cock throbbed and strained upward. She stopped just inches away from him. He could feel her body heat; her breasts still stood there like dutiful soldiers, pikes at the ready. He could smell her sex, and he could see that her panties were wet. He wanted to attack her badly but held his ground.

She had bought the panties she was wearing hoping to be able to use them. She was smiling on the inside because she was right where she had envisioned. She bought them not only because they were a fantastic fit on her body but also because they were an insanely delicate lace. She reached forward, grabbed Darell's hands, and put them on her hips.

"These darn panties are in the way; do you think you would be able to rip them off for me?"

He knew he could, and when he violently ripped them free from her body, his prick strained against its dermal confines just a touch harder. His balls were at the front end of being sore from the strain. Tearing her panties off her body turned him on in the most phenomenal way, enhancing the problem rising with his balls further still.

She pushed him backward, following him as he army-crawled on his back up the king-sized bed. When they got to the pillows, she pushed them away and allowed him to stretch out fully, unobstructed on the bed. Straddling his legs, she started to work her way up his body. He could feel her soft, hot thighs on his legs and occasionally a tickle of hair. He looked down as she moved up. She was a vision to behold. Jenny now was a very distant second.

Her tight body flowed, fluid as she moved. Her nipples stood out hard and straight on top of wonderfully firm but now upside-down mountains, and beyond that, her pussy was clean-shaven, although there was a patch of hair just above where her clit would be—a small triangle, short, trimmed, and beautiful. He thought about reaching forward for a second to touch her, but just when he was about to do so, she leaned forward and sucked him into the hilt one more time, both moaning with delight. His toes curled, and his head and body arched back.

She sucked him full-on for several strokes again, bringing his cock to new heights of awareness. Still lost in amazement at being deep-throated, he barely detected that she had stopped sucking him and was moving further up his body.

For a moment, he envisioned a new onslaught of nipple play, but she bypassed that completely and firmly grabbed a hold of the headboard. Pinning his arms to the bed with her knees, she pulled her dripping wet pussy up to his face. There was no question, no asking if he would like to lick her, no nice concern—just a presentation coupled with an expectation that he would not deny.

There was no question needed. His tongue dove as deep as the length would allow. Trudy arched her wetness into him and moaned loudly. He easily picked her up as she felt light as a feather. His endorphins were in overdrive, and his adrenal glands were pumping excitement into him for the last twenty minutes or more. Regardless of where the strength and energy came from, he was able to free his arms and cup her ass with his hands. He helped her wave her clit over his tongue and create the best spot possible to lick her honey pot dry if he could.

She tasted sweet, and although his face was getting sticky, he did not care. She began to face-fuck him, writhing and moaning as he worked. He loved eating pussy. He loved cunnilingus and everything about it—hell, he loved all things sex. Somehow, this was all that and more.

Just when he thought it could not get any better, she stood up and off him and turned around. She sat on his chest and worked her wet slit way back to his face once again. He had just stuck his tongue in between her hot, wet labia when he felt her mouth encompass his cock head. She spent more time on his head this time. It took a short minute to connect the dots, but he figured out the game. If he lashed his tongue, so did she. If he sucked her clit, she sucked his glans.

He wanted to come badly. His balls were wonderfully aching and sore, and judging by the wetness forming on the bed past his ears, so did she. Darell did what any rational man would do in the situation. He reached up, firmly grabbed her ass, and thrust his tongue as deep into her as he could. She took him to the hilt fast, hard, and deep, rocking his core and shivering his body.

He set to work licking her pussy and clitoris like a carny worker hurriedly setting a tent stake. He lashed big and deep and with unrelenting, continual determination. She sucked on his penis in kind, bobbing on his cock, removing his mind from his body in the process.

He felt his balls calling from somewhere deep inside him, so he began sucking her feverishly. Both moaning, both writhing, both getting close to what would have to be a massive release. He let out a barrage of the evillest intent he could muster on her clitoris, and she answered him, moaning louder and arching into him as she went. She came hard, flooding him and pounding downward into his face.

He had heard the jokes about looking like a glazed donut when done eating pussy, but she was clearly glazing the whole dozen, and he loved every little bit of it. She had stopped blowing him long enough to enjoy her come that presented itself more like a tsunami. It forcibly washed over her, completely stripping whatever control she had left, leaving her shuddering and with mini convulsions for each subsequent wave that passed through. He was lost enjoying her come as well, reveling in his ability to own her so completely. He was lost so much inside himself momentarily that he did not notice at first that she had recovered and had started down on him again.

That was when his heightened awareness kicked in, and he heard that familiar calling inside him. Strangely, though he had heard that calling hundreds of times, this was different—more in-depth. Being deep-throated had changed things. Maybe it was just mentally, maybe it was physically. All he knew was that it was fast becoming a singular, blinding event commanding every ounce of his concentration to hold it off. Trudy was determined to destroy his resolve.

His vision narrowed as she picked up the pace. It was like she knew he was close and that she was now driving with all the control he once had. Point of fact, she did know he was close, mostly because she liked sucking dick. She liked sucking Danny's dick in particular and had learned from him how to tell the telltale signs—the breathing changes, the type and depth of the moan, head size and swell, hip inflection, that last vestige of a whisper that gave men away. She absolutely knew he was close and was going to suck every last drop from him when she set it free.

His toes curled as she was pulling his cock up her inner neck, and when his glans met tongue, he arched and almost yelled, "I'm going to come." She was already in tune with him and wanted that first explosive load in her mouth. Darell did not disappoint. His ass cheeks scrunched in tight, his six-pack strained and roiled, his hips bent forward, and he let loose with a mighty, "Uuuuhhhhgghhh!!!"

His first shot from the depths of his spasming balls was raggedly dry as she felt the rippling convulsion of the meat through her mouth as the completeness of the first contraction roiled through him. This wonderful dick had over seven inches to travel before any come could be freed, and though Darell enjoyed the first jolt as if it were completed, Trudy's prize was going to have to wait until the next pulse of his cock. Half a second later, her patience paid off. His second pump was long, thick, and hard. It shot deep into her mouth, hot on her cheeks. He tasted spectacular.

She swallowed and dove at the same time, pushing the third spasm's bounty along with the head deep down her throat. This act alone sent an incapacitating wave down his spine—incapacitating in everything except for the singular sensation of every jetting pulse of his juice in her throat. He was moaning, writhing, and reveling loudly with every shot spurting from his penis tip. She held him fully down her throat for five full pulses and then pulled off to mouth-only level, still sucking him. She was licking his shaft while coaxing the remaining remnants up and into her mouth as a consolation for the work she had done. She swallowed the leavings and turned her attention back to Darell.

She spun her body back around and straddled his legs once more as if she was going to go down on him again. She could well have continued to face-fuck him as he was still hard—because sensory overload would not let him deflate—but she had something else in mind.

For Darell, he rarely had trouble maintaining a hard-on. He had plenty of alcohol in him still, and it was helping to bolster his granite-like tubular flesh. Trudy smiled and moved forward. She was heavily anticipating, with glee, having his manhood deep in her. She was glad she sucked him off. She was glad she swallowed him. It was a delicious flood in every way and every sense. Now she wanted to ride him because she knew it would take a fair amount of time for him to come again. She was committed to making him come at least once more, and in the process, she was going to steal one or two orgasms for herself.

She inched his head into her wet gnash and felt the heat searing from his skin. Slowly sitting down on his standing meat, cowgirl style, she felt herself get spread just a little more than she had ever been spread before. The last part of the spread was reminiscent of when Danny first carefully entered her, as it was touching some of the same muscles. He filled her up fully and completely. She loved it and made him aware of it too with a wanting moan. The pressure this time was wonderfully exquisite. She was much wetter than the first time she had taken a dick in her, but now she knew how to best take what she wanted. She rocked her hips forward at the bottom of the stroke and determined it all would fit. Though she was maxed out in terms of depth, it felt divine.

He started fucking from underneath. Her vagina was wrapped tightly on him, as he all but knew she would be. Flaccid in the shower house, he rarely noticed anyone near his size—not that he was looking, but guys noticed things. In jest, his friends all joked about him not being allowed to fuck anyone they intended on dating because he would stretch them out too much. To an extent, he partially had virgins all the time, as he would invariably go deeper and wider than most girls ever had in them, so to an extent, they were partly right.

He knew that a pussy would stretch, but his dick was nowhere near the size of a baby's head nor as long as its body. But if the girl he was with had not had a kid before, odds were he was going to feel old muscles strain anew. The wonderful thing about it was that through the tightness, he could tell the differences they had experienced, and that in and of itself was amazing. He could tell Trudy had not had anyone quite this size, but she was taking him quite fervently. She must have had something close at one time or another.

For him, this was better because he did not have to pay as much attention to hurting her by accident—going too fast inward before her body was ready for it or too deep—as she controlled that. Trudy fucked on intently, and he was starting to feel a strain, a reload, a replay. She pulled up and off him and moved to the edge of the bed, all but commanding him to connect to her doggy style, which he was happy to do.

He stepped out onto the floor and lined up behind her at the foot of the bed, facing the headboard. The bed elevation was perfect for him—or she adapted. In either case, her man cave achieved perfect placement just for him. He aligned the head of his dick to her pussy. Because he was now raging so hard, he had to push as she moaned again, and he pushed his shaft slowly into her depths.

He knew that occasionally, he would bottom out some girls in this position, so he had learned, especially with doggy style, to push in three-quarters of the way and let his adversary come hunting to him. He started to stroke Trudy with long, even but short strokes at first, but she could feel the lack of depth that she had from him before and pushed herself to him deeper. As he picked up speed, he found that she had been taking him for his full length and had backed into his territory, making him do all the work.

It was glorious work. He had stepped up the pace and was full-on hammering her hard. He leaned back and halfheartedly slapped her ass between a stroke. It elicited a moan and a, "God, yes."

So, he did it again just a bit harder. Trudy moaned for the whole forward stroke and said, "Harder!"

He pulled back and slapped her ass once again, harder still. She moaned the full stroke and groaned out, "Fucking harder."

The next stroke was a full-on ass slap. She gleefully moaned. He repeated this twice and really laid into the next slap, which met with a euphoric, wanting moan and a heightened pushback that excited the hell out of him. He pulled back and, without remorse, turned her once white ass into a dark shade of red, alternating the ass-cheek abuse in between strokes.

He resisted the urge to look behind him because he had realized that he had been here before—sort of. This time, he was on the front side of the television screen, still marveling at luscious curves, wonderful skin, and the red ass that he was commanding. Momentarily, he considered calling and thanking good ole Joe, but he lost the notion, deeming it in seriously bad taste, as he smiled somewhat deviously at his own inside joke.

His next stroke and subsequent slap were almost brutal. He thought maybe he had crossed a line, as he had heard these boundaries often had tenuous edges, but Trudy bucked into him wildly. The bronco was raring up, and he felt her sugar walls clamp down firmly on him as her already tight vagina started to convulse.

He pulled back hard and slammed home, no longer taking time to slap her ass. He stroked fully and feverishly as her moaning reached new heights. Slamming home one stroke after another relentlessly was at first a conscious, willing act, but now his balls had taken over and were driving the whole show. What a wicked driver his balls were. He stroked harder and harder, thrusting her physically forward each time as his hips collided violently with her ass. He was unconsciously hauling her hips with his hands back to him until the motion became a burn in the back of his mind.

He felt it build, and she felt his head swelling through her own orgasm, causing hers to reach even new and dizzying heights. With one last massive thrust, he let loose something guttural and animalistic in nature yet verbal—

albeit unintelligible. He strained into a hip-mashing arch and released his offering deep, spasming inside her.

Thinking the event was over, he pulled his now barely waning member out of Trudy. Whether it was the tightness from his large dick, the assault to her depths by the head of his penis and his length, or just the massive overload of the hard coming mixed with the wonderfully brutal ass slaps—possibly a combination of all of it—when he pulled his dick free, she squirted hard and drenched the floor in front of the bed, propelling her juices well past and all over the edge of the bed for several mind-boggling pulses. There was a healthy residual flow down her legs.

He had never made a woman squirt before and was in awe of the whole event. It was a massive turn-on for him. She had never squirted before and was having trouble processing this bonus—an indescribably, amazingly delicious feeling from this flash of a come. Regardless of how it arrived or how it manifested, she knew she not only liked it—she loved it. This took on a new level of completeness, check-marked in a book somewhere she did not even know existed.

For now, it was all she could do to fall forward and curl into a shaking, shimmering, and whimpering ball. Darell laid in close and had pulled a sheet over them both, watching her through the occasional shuddering in post-coital bliss.

Twenty minutes later, Darell invited a half-asleep and half-mesmerized Trudy in to take a shower with him, and she accepted. The water was comfortably hot, welcoming, and endless. They washed each other down, avoiding any possible sexual overture. They dried each other off, and Darell offered her a shot from his champagne flute he had just poured as a mouthwash substitute, rinsing with some and drinking a little.

It felt good to sleep with a woman again for the night. For Trudy, it felt good being with Darell as well. She had many nights with Danny under the stars, in the back of his truck, at one of the cabins, and tent camping, but this was new. It was new, and it felt good.

Trudy had been watching him sleep when he came to life at 6:30 AM. She smiled at him, and he smiled back. And he said, "That was one hell of a night. I really enjoyed myself. Thank you.'

He looked around and said, "Shit, when they see this room, they are going to ban us from this hotel."

Trudy laughed and said, "I didn't think so."

Darell sat up and back against the headboard. "Why do you say that? Look at this place. It looks like we bombed it."

"That may be so, but TJC owns this hotel, and seventeen others just like it."

Remembering why he was at the hotel in the first place, "I need to get a handle on that prospectus soon, huh? That is, well, if we are going to be OK, I mean, working together?"

"I think we will be OK, but I guess that really depends on you."

"I am just worried about the owners finding out about…uh…our…uh…"

"Fucking?"

"Yes, us fucking. Aren't you concerned about what they might say or do?"

"I'm pretty sure they won't mind."

"Won't mind?! Surely, you're not going to tell them. Shit, sweet Jesus, you're going to tell them, aren't you?"

"I AM their HR person; I believe they need to know. Actually, to be truthful with you, they already know."

"How? Did you call them last night or this morning?"

There was a knock at the door as Darell's head and eyes flung in the direction of the door, taking on a panicked look.

"Are they coming here? Is that them?"

"Oh, they are already here, but I suspect that is room service. When you started to wake up, I ordered breakfast. Not knowing what you liked, I ordered a bit of everything. I hope you don't mind; I was hungry too."

Trudy tucked the sheet over and under Darrell's naked torso. Naked, she walked toward the door with Darell; even in mid-fear, he was delighting in her tight ass and body again. Trudy stopped at the bathroom, grabbed a large towel, wrapped it around herself, and made her way to the door and opened it.

"Please bring it just inside; I'll take it from there."

The busser obeys. "Yes, Ms. Jax."

The busser wheeled the cart into the entrance and saw the room in total disarray. It almost looked like someone opened their suitcase and flung the contents in every direction. He momentarily went wide-eyed while scanning the room until he saw Darell. Darell and the busser locked eyes just for a second, and the busser smiled a smile that all but conveyed he knew precisely what had happened here. The busser turned to leave.

"I'll leave the cart here as well, Ms. Jax; we hope you enjoy your breakfast."

He finished his turn and left. Trudy turned to the bed, pushed the cart over some clothes and a towel, stopped near the kitchenette, and backtracked to the bed.

Darell nervously continues, "If they are here, where are they? This could be big trouble for both of us!"

"Darell, look at me."

Trudy was standing in front of the bed, still in her towel. She untucked the "tab," holding her towel up, and dropped it to the floor. She was a tight-bodied vision that immediately drew his attention back. Because of the shower the night before, she was supple, glowing even though her hair was mussed up.

Being clear-headed and panicked now, "I get that I may have ruined my chances here with TJC, but I don't want to ruin my whole career as well. More sex won't change that. Aren't you afraid they will come to you for a report from last night?"

"They already have the report. Given your performance and willingness to go the extra mile, I'm one of your best advocates."

"I am, we, we are so fucked right now, and you seem so damn casual about it."

Laughing lightly with a mild chuckle, "I have left you hanging for long enough, Darell. I am not worried about what 'THEY' will say because I need you to listen to me closely here. I am 'THEY.' I own TJC, and I am looking for a viable face of the company."

"Wait, if you own TJC, why do you need me?"

"I need your expertise; I need someone to guide my company when I can't. I need you to be the outward face the public can see. I also need someone with vision, and I believe that someone is you."

"I'm missing something here; you want me to run it when you can't? Why can't you run your own company?"

"OK, here comes the hard part for you, and I'm going to apologize upfront for deceiving you. I'm sure I know what you're about to feel and how you might react, so again, I'm sorry. But I also want you to know that it is one hundred percent legal. I've checked; I've had my lawyers check. I want to apologize again upfront. I needed you to believe me and take me seriously, so I hid a few parameters from you."

Trudy walked to the secretariat where her purse was sitting; she pulled out her wallet and thumbs through it and retrieved a business card-sized item, cupping it in her hand, still stark naked and radiant, walked right up to the side of the bed, sat next to him and casually reached under the sheet and wraps her hand around his member. It twinged, twitched, and started to think about being heavy; she stopped and handed him the card as she watched his cock slowly press against the sheet and began to raise the circus tent upward. Darell turned the card over and saw that it was her license. He was confused at first and suddenly sat even more bolt-upright in bed in sheer panic.

"Holy fuck, oh Goddamn, Fuck me! Fuck me! Fuck me! Oh fuck. You are only seventeen?"

"I want to at least one more time, and yes, I'm only seventeen."

"You want what? One more time?"

"You were saying fuck me, fuck me, fuck me, and yes, I'm seventeen."

"Fuck me! What about last night?"

"You were very good; I really enjoyed your dick and how you fuck," she said, laughing just a bit because she knew that was not what he meant.

"Not that! The restaurant, the drinking. Do they know you're seventeen, that we could be fined for that and lose our business licenses?"

"Yes, they know I'm seventeen, and I would never jeopardize our businesses. I was drinking water all night. The only alcohol I had was champagne—champagne that some kid smuggled in from elsewhere, not served. And I would also like to point out that now that you just referred to it as OUR business and WE as a business, I'm happy to hear that."

"Oh fuck, tell me your kidding."

"Not kidding here, and I'm trying extremely hard to get you past a simple number. Are you taking the job?"

"Shit, I thought you were at least as old as my ex."

"Nope, Jenny is about seven years older than me, by the way. She is pregnant now. She doesn't know who the father is, but I assure you it isn't Joe. She has been fired from two jobs as well. I think you really dodged a bullet there."

"Wait. What! How do you know all of that?"

"It was paramount that I knew everything that could affect my new CEO. One of my companies is in the security sector. I had you checked out very thoroughly. My offer is real, Darell; I know a lot about you, and I'm willing to trust you with a multimillion-dollar company and give you unprecedented access and reign. There really is no direct comparison to," She jokingly finger quoted, "thermoforming is us." "They haven't even begun to see where my league plays."

"Oh shit, you are for real, you really have multiple companies?"

"All above board, all tax-paying, all needing attention I can't give them right now."

"Why not?"

"Well, high school, of course."

She let that hit home and ruminated for a long second.

"Only a few people know about my business; I want to keep it that way. I want to grow this company more, and I want this company to be more. I can't do that if I'm wading through people while trying to maintain my grades. It's a simple number; I am hoping you can get past a simple number. Can you be more?"

"But you're seventeen."

"The way I fuck, the way I act, you couldn't tell. Do you know what has changed in the last eight hours? Nothing. We ate, we drank, well- sort of, and we fucked. For the record, we fucked well, I loved it, you loved it, and it's all legal, every little bit. Only eight hours have passed. Nothing else has changed."

"But you're seventeen."

"When was the last time you felt this good?"

From on top of the sheet, she stroked over his cock. She grabbed him with her hand and palms her hand around the shaft and felt the blood begin to flow once again, making him harder still.

His head rolled back, and his eyes closed. "Seventeen? Oh god, I can't believe I'm going to say this: seventeen; seventeen could be a good number." His dick began to strain, "I'm starting to think seventeen is a really good number."

Trudy still had her hand wrapped around his shaft.

"Oh god, yes." He was losing his breath incrementally, "Shit, Seventeen?"

His Cock was pulsing hard and using the sheet as a mini pup tent.

"I think I can get past it, but? Seriously, you are seventeen. You were absolutely incredible, you, you are incredible. Are you sure you're only seventeen? Oh shit, all of this is a lot to take in." His eyes closed again as he again hitched in his breath, "Uhmm, yes, I think I can get past it."

He was beyond hard and started to throb in waves; she squeezed him firmly, encompassing his shaft once more with her hand.

"It may take a while to get comfortable about all of this, but" He smiled directly at her, "I think for the moment, seventeen can be an excellent number."

"Great, now there is only one thing left for me to do."

"What?"

She got up, still hot-bodied naked, and took her ID from his hand, walked it back to her purse, dropped it in, turned around, grabbed the sheet, and ripped it free and clear of the bed. Darell was still sitting up against the headboard naked and hard, watching Trudy with new eyes.

Trudy glided her hands up his legs while crawling up the bed; she grabbed his rock-hard shaft and started to work his shaft up and down until she bent forward and sucked the head in. He closed his eyes and moaned deeply as he felt himself go down her throat, not caring about the number seventeen anymore in the least.

Once again, Trudy deep-throated him for her own pleasure for about thirty strokes and pulled up and off him. She embraced the headboard with a two-handed hold and hovered her juicing slash directly over his begging cock; he reached under her and helped guide himself in her as she sat fully down on him.

She was hot and wet, and his shaft welcomed her down. She began a slow glorious trudge, sensually rising slowly and falling even slower, feeling his engorged cock filling her completely to her depths. Clenching him as she pulled up and again slid deliberately and slowly to the base all the way down on his cock. His balls begged for relief amid her slow torture.

His heightened awareness started to kick in as it reminded him that he was technically fucking a minor, but now he was all out of give a fucks.' Her intensely slow, insanely delicious, inching pace was driving him to near madness. Somewhere, his body started to gather all that was required to explode with abandon. When his body found all those requirements, it sent every ounce of energy left in his body tunneling through to the end of his meat. His cock was a bit sore but also longing for salvation which came as an avalanche of convulsing muscles and a pulsating rod with thunderous release.

As Darell came, he was arching upward for all his worth, feeling a gloriously slow fuck culminate in the most complete and satisfying physical, mental, and stress-quashing release. She raised inches and fell back onto him in between each pulse of his dick, draining his every drop. She lowered herself and kissed him fully on the mouth.

His faithful friend had defended his partner to death but now was just spent, so Trudy just lowered herself deeply on him and relished the position. His fullness warmed her; the pleasure his heartbeat was giving her made her feel whole. There were little butterfly sputters that were so sublimely splendid inside her depth with his every micro movement. She was happy that he once again was satisfied, happier still as she felt the expulsion deep in her sending every fiber in her to a new and wonderful plane.

He looked directly into her eyes and smiled a smile that warmed her. He was spent and done, physically, mentally, and, maybe most significantly, emotionally.

"Seventeen?" Half statement, half question, fully conceding, and beginning acknowledged acceptance. Trudy rolled off him, began walking to the shower, stopped, and turned to Darell.

"Darell, you are officially hired."

Darell thought about following her to the shower but got the sense that was not what she had wanted him to do. It felt like she was giving him a space to collect his unencumbered thoughts. He was truly spent once again, still grappling to get on top of all his heightened senses and endorphins for this most unusual start to his morning. He was also famished, and being mentally exhausted and physically spent made the food smell even more incredible and inviting.

He was worn out but felt like he had to eat; he was sure that eating would help put things in perspective. He was unsure if it was a Darell thing or a guy thing, but he gave it no more thought as he plucked the first piece of bacon from the tray.

Wrapped in a towel, Trudy joined Darell as he was drinking coffee. He watched her take a seat with brand-new eyes. She turned to him while reaching for a bagel,

"I'm not sorry for last night nor this morning, but at the same time, I am sorry for the deception. You need to know that I will not solicit you for sex again unless, of course, we both want it. I really enjoyed being with you; however, it is not part of the work plan or any work plan in my, uh, or our company ever. It is not, nor will it ever be, required as any condition of employment at any level within our structure, regardless of position or tenure in our company. Anyone found to be holding a position over someone in this manner will be acted upon and dealt with severely across the breadth of our company's reach, no matter how large we get.

"From this day forward, you can expect complete and full honesty from me. We will need to be able to trust each other implicitly and explicitly. If you are capable of beginning anew right here and forgive the omissions of the past few days, I welcome it. If that isn't possible and you want to go now, I will understand that too. What has happened here will not follow you in any way.

"But if you stay, the conditions here will be self-described and reliant on how you want to proceed in our business, as we both agree on the basic tenets. I have some ideas on an actual values statement, not just a feel-good boilerplate quote but real direction, real conduct, and a real embrace of business and people at its core. I'm looking forward to your contribution as well.

"I'm sure by now you have seen the good, the bad, and the unsavory that a person must navigate to get by in the working world. My Father raised me basically alone, as your mother raised you alone. I was lucky in that my father had no discernable struggles except the loss of my mother. On the other hand, you have seen the struggles that your mother had to endure just to get by.

"Less pay than a man for the same work, no upward mobility, discounted because of stature. This will not be accepted. One of the first things I will require of you is to put forth a living guideline of how to succeed in business here and within our business for all races, creeds, colors, or sexes. We will truly be an equal opportunity-based company driven by ability.

The prospectus is real. The offer is just as real, and after you read it fully, see the books, and understand the nature of the company, I think you will want to join me in creating a solid direction and destination for TJC. I hope you can embrace this as I believe that together, we can do anything."

There was a giant pregnant pause, a giant smile, and a tilt of the head before she continued. "As the talent acquisition specialist, I know what I'm talking about."

Darell half-laughed and half-smiled at her comment but said nothing while gathering his thoughts and hoping the coffee would clear his head sufficiently.

With that, she dressed under the watchful eye of Darell, who stole more than a gratuitous look or two while she slipped into her jeans. She packed her belongings from around the room and bath while he ate his breakfast silently. She could tell he had listened to her and had been seriously considering his options. She had decided to give him time to collect his direction and drive. Getting ready to leave, she turned to Darell.

"Everything here is taken care of. I requested a late checkout at one-thirty. You can still get a nap in if you try. Lunch will be delivered if you call room service. It is all covered. I happen to know the owner; I can make that happen."

She smiled big at him; he accepted the smile and returned a nice, warm one back to her.

"I must be home by ten, or my dad will ask questions. I look forward to hearing from you soon; you have my number."

"Trudy, wait, I do want this opportunity, this chance to stretch; if we have a solid relationship, a good structure, and positive direction, there is nothing we can't accomplish. Though we started out in a most non-conforming manner, I understand why you decided to go this route. When I found out how young you were, I immediately started to doubt your ability and resolve, so I get it, and I won't make that mistake again. I want this opportunity on so many levels. I believe today can be a good beginning, and every tomorrow will be a new day, so let us see what that brings together. I am going to take that nap as you suggested because this is a really nice hotel, and you have worn me out on many levels. I'm going to digest everything that has transpired. After that, I'm going to get to work on our vision statement and have it for your approval within the next week, right after I sign my resignation letter."

He was smiling broadly, "No more, uh, how did you say it? Oh yeah, 'thermoforming is us' for me."

He disappeared within himself for a second, pulling out a new expression of acceptance visible on his relaxed face. "You know it is just one among an infinite set of numbers, right?"

"What is?"

"Seventeen is. I think if I had good fortune early, I too might have stretched out and learned to enjoy seventeen more as well. We will talk soon, Ms. Jax."

With that, Trudy smiled a big smile as she felt she now had a firm and good direction for the company to grow with.

"I'm glad you can see past the simple numbers; welcome aboard, Mr. Cromwell."

Trudy turned and left the room, saying nothing more.

Trudy's mind was abuzz on her drive home. She had just hired her CEO and felt like there was not a better choice to be had. She smiled when the rogue thought passed through her myopia of the present when a voice inside her added in and lord does he know how to fuck. She chased the thought away but vowed to relive it with Danny soon and, if possible, recreate some of the proceedings.

She called Kate and thanked her for suggesting she hire a CEO. She described Darell to her as a matter of qualification and likeability, letting her know that she would be getting all of Darell's bona fides soon. She asked about Kevin and how they were getting along and more. After about twenty minutes of catching up and talking on the phone, they ended the conversation with Kate looking forward to "meeting" Mr. Cromwell.

Chapter 31 - Bill and Paula Slept Late

Trudy arrived home at nine-fifteen, and as she parked, Amanda was arriving as well. Both girls had spent the night with their friends.

Trudy said, "I can't wait for coffee. I could really use a pick-me-up."

"I think I'll join you. Clearing out this brain fog would be a welcomed event."

They both laughed.

"I hope it's not too old. Dad usually starts the pot around five thirty or so on Saturdays."

"I'll take whatever I can get," Amanda replied.

The girls entered the house and found something odd. The house was dark, and the coffee pot was cold and hadn't been touched.

Amanda asked, "Are they even here?"

Trudy started her way up the stairs and was about to call out when she heard familiar noises from down the hall—the same noises she and Danny had made before, and for that matter, she and Amanda as well. This put a smile on her face as she quietly backtracked down the steps and, in a lower tone, said to Amanda, "You start the coffee, and I will get a Sharpie and a Post-it note."

She explained what she had heard to a broadly smiling Amanda. After having the pot pulled forward and loaded, set to brew, she started the cycle. Trudy placed a Post-it note on the pot tank that said:

"Going to the Diner Bell without you two sleepyheads. The coffee started at nine thirty-five. Be back later. Love, A&T."

The girls quietly left.

"Let's take my car. There's something I want to tell you about. But first, what have you been up to last night?" Trudy inquired.

"I would love to tell you all the lurid details of my night of debauchery and fun, but the truth is, I was at Sally Wheaton's house. She just broke up with her boyfriend after he cheated on her, so a couple of us stayed over bashing guys all night. She will be OK, but Jesus, guys are such dicks sometimes."

The girls talked about random idle topics all the way to the diner, and Trudy suggested getting their breakfast to go.

"Must be serious if you don't want to talk about it in the restaurant. Shit! You're not pregnant, are you?"

"No, no, nothing like that. It is a good thing, I swear."

Still listening to the radio and idly chatting, Trudy headed for the back roads, one where Amanda knew a cabin was at the end of. She waited until they got there to press Trudy for more. Both girls carried their breakfasts to the porch table and chairs. It was cool on the porch, but the coffee and the hot food more than compensated for the chill.

"OK, Tru, spill it."

"I know you can keep a secret, and this is a big one. Only a very select few know what I am about to tell you."

"Danny knows?"

"Yes, but only recently. See, I have been doing some aggressive investing, and a few things just fell into place. To make a long story short, I now own several businesses. I want to do the same for you that I am going to do for Danny and Dave. The only difference is that Dave won't know about what I'm doing, just you two."

"Businesses? Like what? And what are you doing for Danny and Dave?"

"My businesses are in multiple areas, and I'm growing—so much so that I just hired a CEO to run things while I'm in high school, in college, and beyond. He was just officially hired this morning. That's where I've been all night."

"Wait, start over, and go slowly. What businesses? Multiple? In what type of business are they?"

Laughing lightly, Trudy said, "Hotels, security, cleaning supplies, apps for business—for now. I am hoping to grow that."

"Wait, you're messing with me, aren't you?"

"Nope, totally serious right now."

"And what do you mean by what you are going to do for me?"

"I know you have been applying for scholarships, and I have no doubt that you will land one or two. You are too smart not to. I want to take the pressure off you and your mom. I also know that, realistically, my dad will most likely help in that regard, too, without even being asked—if I know him. But I will be paying whatever else you need along with a spending allotment at any college you desire."

"What? How much money are you making now?"

"I'm not exactly sure at this moment, but I can tell you that at last check, it was well over eighteen million in total assets. That was a few months back, and things are really fluid at this point. I have two upstart apps that are trending well in the security sector in terms of both ad revenue and app sales. My hotel manager has been eyeing a small chain to buy. My hotels are under the name of Athena Inns. I stayed in one last night. I spent the night with the man I hired as my CEO this morning."

"Shit?! You're not kidding me, are you? Start over from the very beginning. You must tell me everything. I mean everything from how you started until now."

Trudy laughed at that and began to tell her about how she started the first investment up until this point. She then began to explain her night in between bites. Amanda finished her breakfast and was nursing her large coffee. She left out none of the lurid details, especially taking Darell's size and how she enjoyed herself right up until his last come. Her detailed account had Amanda riveted. The Diner always had great coffee with legs and by the time Trudy had finished recapping her night, the coffee was waking up both girls wonderfully. Trudy looked at Amanda and laughed.

"What?"

"Me too."

"Huh? You're not making sense."

"I know it's chilly out, but that isn't it, is it? Just talking about it again is making me horny too."

Trudy reached over to Amanda and placed a single pointer finger on the center of Amanda's nipple and swirled her finger around her rock hard nub on one side and caressed the other breast with the back of her hand to a wonderfully received moan as Amanda arched back and half closed her eyes. Trudy stood up and took a pace to the door and punched the code, smiled at Amanda, turned the corner, and disappeared. She knew that Amanda would follow so she made a direct line to the bed preparing to disrobe as she went. When Amanda turned the corner of the bedroom door, she was buck naked with her nipples straining outward as if to say I need attention.

She had intended to surprise Trudy with her nakedness, but the tables were turned when she entered to find Trudy laid out, gloriously bare, with her head at the side of the bed nearest the door, looking upside down at her. Her breasts were in total deference to gravity yet stood firmly in place, with her nipples reaching still higher. Amanda bent down and French-kissed Trudy, then slowly kissed her way down her chest, her stomach, and her inner thighs. She had been receiving as good as she was giving on her travels across Trudy's body in the form of warm kisses as well.

When their tongues set about to probe each other, it was clear there was no lack of wanting on either of their parts. The only difference was that Trudy had a flavor left over, a tang that still lingered—the remnants of flavor left from Darell. Amanda decided she liked Darell's flavor and licked any hints away, then set about scolding Trudy's standing nub, defiantly exposing itself through the labia. She might have stopped a while to admire it more thoroughly, but she was currently struggling with maintaining her composure as her crotch was now on Trudy's launch pad, and a countdown had been initiated.

Both girls gently sucked and licked each other with one singular goal in mind—make the other person come and come hard. They had each cultivated a thought to the point where cautious optimism turned into wonderfully nurtured, completely satisfying orgasms. Afterward, they turned to be in line with each other. They hugged and kissed, their breasts nestled together. The heat and placement of their bodies kept their nipples comfortably cradled and warm.

They lay there for twenty minutes or so, their bodies intertwined, each holding the other close. The girls had been living under the same roof for a short while, but the benefits were amazing. One of the best benefits by far, besides the awesome sex, was showering together. They both delighted in washing each other's bodies. More than once, the shower had led to the bed and the bed back to the shower. This time, it was a one-way trip, but on feather-light steps, as both were sated sexually—for now.

It was eleven thirty when they arrived home to find Paula and Bill, thankful for the coffee but wondering why the girls had not woken them to go to the diner with them. To save embarrassment, Amanda spoke up.

"We didn't want to wake you, and since we had just got home, we decided it would be nice to share some sister time. But tomorrow, we will be knocking on your door bright and early—that is, if Mother will buy us breakfast?"

"I think I can manage that. If not, Bill might be able to help me with the money needed to feed you two."

Bill joined in. "Absolutely!"

Trudy interjected, "Hey, is anyone hungry? I was thinking about making lunch soon. Do chicken tenders, tots, and baked beans, all with a simple side salad, sound good?"

That sounded great to everyone, so they collectively started getting everything out and ready. More than once, Bill caught Paula taking in her new family, and he could tell she felt deeply about all of them. He snuck up behind her and whispered in her ear.

"I love you, Paula. You have made me the happiest man alive again."

There was a tear streaming down her face. "I never thought I could feel this way again either, but here we are. To be honest, I feel better than I have ever felt. I love you, Bill." She beamed a loving smile at him. "I wish every day could be like today—right here and now."

It felt right to spend the day together. They had not been together in the same house for long, considering the grand scheme of things, but due to the twists and turns of life, they were already becoming a cohesive family unit. It felt natural, unassuming, free, and good. It was as if a void in each of their personal lives was not only being filled but the fit was being tailored to them alone—as family dynamics are. There was an ebb and flow to their interactions that was hard to describe but could not be denied. They were truly a new-age family, warts and all.

Danny met the girls to make Sunday lunch at Sadie's. Sadie had begun to really enjoy the side seat as she got to watch the youth energetically move about the kitchen, talking all about the latest trends or baubles, the gossip in town, and the things that keep life interesting. Only occasionally would she interject her influence on a meal—mostly because Danny had asked for a distinct perspective on how to accomplish a look, texture, or taste.

She conceded that the young man was really an exceptionally good cook. She enjoyed his fare and the panache he gave it. Today, however, she was not as confident in his choice of Mexican chili, but she was willing to give it an honest try. When Sam and Jessie arrived shortly after Bill and Paula at twelve o'clock and some change for good measure, the chili was ready to be bowled. The cornbread the girls had made under Danny's direction was pulled out of the oven piping hot and perfectly done— upgraded to perfect after the butter was slathered on top of it and the cake cut into squares. When Jessie looked in the pot, she looked at Danny, who was smiling back at her.

"Have you been talking to my mother?"

"I talk to all mothers. That's where the best recipes are, and yes, your mother told me that this was your favorite fall dish. She wrote it down for me at the wedding. I may have changed it a bit so I could call it mine, but it is essentially the same."

Sadie smiled, hearing this, and gave a little more hope to the dish.

Jessie asked, "And just what did you change?"

"Well, your mother's recipe called for some seriously hot peppers, and I know a lot of people don't like extra spicy," he looked directly at Sadie with eyebrows raised. "So, I have created a side pepper sauce that a person can add for sensational heat in any amount they desire."

Jessie conceded, "Mm, good idea. Let's see how it tastes."

Before anyone else had a chance at commentary, Sadie spoke up as she had already been tasting her bowl full.

"Danny, this is a fantastic young man. I didn't think I would like it, but now I know why it is Jesse's favorite. It just might be my new favorite chili of all time. Crumble in a bit of your cornbread, and I don't think it can be beaten."

Jessie complimented, "Yours is better, Danny. This is beyond what I remember, but if you tell my mom I said that, I will totally deny it."

They all laughed at that.

Paula and Jessie joined forces after the second helpings had been finished and took claim to doing the dishes. It was a wonderfully simple meal and easy for two to clean up. Sadie said she was a bit tired and might nap, which was a bit out of character for her. The two men decided to stick around and help with the cleanup of their own volition. Amanda and Trudy suspected their help was more to stay in good graces than anything else.

The young crowd excused themselves for the count and disappeared to Danny's house for some gaming. They brought a bowl for his mom, who welcomed it as she had not had time to fix herself something and be ready in time for the shopping hiatus as she had taken a late nap and let the cool morning carry her beyond the wake-up time she anticipated. She had all but finished eating when the horn sounded, and she excused herself to leave.

Trudy recapped her Friday night and Saturday morning to Danny with an eagerly listening Amanda digesting it all again. There was nothing left out as she made a point to try and describe the details involved in the squirting event and how wonderful it was. By the time she hired Darell once more, Danny was visibly hard, and Amanda was poking through her bra. Trudy would have pointed this out and mock ridiculed them except for the fact that she was reliving the telling as well and subsequently was panty-wet badly as well.

Danny suggested that they do a little porn research on the squirting phenomenon, so they did. After several videos and a few 'how-tos,' leaking all around was an understatement. There were techniques described in painstaking detail, so Danny decided to try them on one of the girls. They flipped a coin, and Amanda won.

Gleefully, she stripped down to her birthday suit and got comfortable on the couch. Danny went to put three fingers in her slowly to not hurt her but found she was so wet the point was mute. He started to internally message her just as prescribed, and Trudy began to lick on her clitoris and labia as had been done in the video. They had been going at it for about ten minutes when Danny questioned aloud if he was doing something wrong, but as if that were a cue, Amanda arched violently skyward.

"Oh my god."

Her body clenched every muscle she had from her ear lobes to her pinky toes, and she yelled.

"I'm going to…"

Nothing more had to be said; there was a drenching spray hitting Danny, Trudy, and all areas caught in front of her thighs. Danny fluttered her pussy with his fingers hard back and forth, and she sprayed again. He pulled his fingers free, and Trudy waved her fingers over the labia and clitoris along with the vaginal opening just like in one of the other videos and elicited the same spray but in a more violently upheaving motion from Amanda. She was writhing as her body sprayed. Her pleasure center in her brain checked out and went crazy. She bucked wildly multiple times as it slowly began to subside.

Danny decried, "Oh hell no, you don't!"

He had already shed his clothes and centered up on Amanda. There has never been a more complete contraction of pussy muscles ever recorded like the one when, in one brutal stroke forward, he pounded his cock completely and fully, deep in her. With that one animalistic thrust forward, her body detached from her brain and came alive. The magnitude of her release was almost indescribable; she looked like she was in excruciating pain, and for a moment, Trudy and Danny both thought she was. Her mouth connected to her speech center only momentarily, long enough to make a pleasurable moan, and half yelled, "Oh my god!!!"

Her body started to quake as if some unseen seismic event were taking place that she alone could feel. A virtual stream of fluids began to shoot from around his cock as it had blocked the easy egress.

He was like a restriction in a hose, causing the pressure to turn up several notches and spray with velocity. When he started to pump her hard and furiously, her body began exploding with his every draw and push. Her whole being flushed red, and the comes she had been experiencing melded into one blinding event. Trudy watched in amazement as Danny shifted from one motion to the other with a grind and a push, slamming brutally and deeply.

Amanda screamed in pleasure and whimpered all at the same time as her body betrayed her by not letting her control any aspect of her release. Wave upon wave crashed over her with blinding regularity, with only mere seconds in between neurons firing in successive order, driving the events. She was nearing pass-out status when Danny slammed home even harder, eliciting her last arch forward to receive his flooding release of victory.

He fell backward and pulled out. She fell to the side of the couch and either passed out or immediately fell asleep. Whichever it was, it lasted for about five minutes. When she came to, the floor was drenched with her come, and she flowed a mixture of him and her onto the couch. She was absolutely soaked from a mixture of sweat from her and Danny. She barely had the energy to speak. Looking groggy and trying to be devilish, she turned to Danny. "More please." She managed to giggle a bit.

"I can't, I, I, I just can't. I don't have the energy to move, but oh my god, that was so unbelievably hot. I want to do it repeatedly if I could, but I just can't."

Trudy spoke up, "You may not have the energy to stroke anymore, but you're still hard, and I need to come, so just lay back while I use your dick; I'm going to show you what I did yesterday morning."

Danny sat back on the recliner of the couch and scooted his hips forward just before the edge because he knew from experience that this would allow her to sit on him fully and give her the best penetration possible. Trudy straddled him and braced herself on the couch back, and lifted her ass up to sit and engulf Danny's meat.

Amanda watched her first slide down Danny's turgid shaft with awe and longing. If she had not been so spent, she would have been behind Trudy accosting her nipples, but as it was, she was doing well to just stay conscious.

Watching this incredible scene up close like this helped her stay awake. She savored the view. Trudy lined up on Danny just as she did on Darell, but to be extra mean, she intentionally and with concerted effort clenched the muscles on her pelvic floor and sat down on Danny at a snail's pace. To Danny, she was insanely tight and felt incredible. Her muscles begged a response from every nerve ending in his dick. He shuttered, and this caused Trudy to smile because she intended to destroy him with every stroke.

Further and further, she forced herself down on him, never releasing the clench until she was sitting directly over his balls. She could feel his balls with her labia as she had bottomed out; that was when she released the clench and shifted ever so slightly down more. His foreskin that had been stretched downward rebounded up him when she released her grip with an incredible new sensation.

Her man-animal bit him again with equal force, threatening to try and cut off all his blood supply at the base of his granite-esque meat. She began a slow, arduous journey in the other direction, knowing exactly how she was tormenting Danny as well as herself, for that matter. Her silky fall onto Danny may have strained his contact with reality, but the cost of her determination was that it threatened to release her own grip on the real world, too. Every sensation he felt and shuttered sent a new wave through her body that was building up to something outrageously epic inside her. She was not sure how many strokes she could manage at this rate before she came, but she was willing to narrow it down, if not for science, then for her own personal knowledge.

Her muscular stamina was barely maintaining its original grasp, but she could tell it was having its desired effect. Danny started to swell just a bit somewhere around the eighteenth stroke; she was not sure of the count exactly as the sensations were blurring her mind as well. A few more strokes later, Danny's breathing ticked up as she could tell he was fighting to maintain his control, a resolve she was determined to steal from him.

She doubled down on her clench and increased her speed ever so slightly, and that was when he lost it. His hips started an involuntary tic, dipping forward and back just a fraction of an inch. That fraction ruled his world for a brief moment in time as he began to release for the second time.

"Oh, shit Tru…. I can't, I can't hold it. Tru."

When the head of his prick started to swell, Trudy's inner walls gave way; the clench failed her, only to be replaced with a rippling convulsive reaction throughout her pussy. It traveled out in every direction, enabling her to thrust wildly downward onto her post. He came while she was coming, and she had no clue he had nor cared when he did. She was banging him wildly with Amanda looking on. Her body came in waves from Danny's hard dick in her. It was beyond what she had known from this position before, but she looked down and smiled.

Amanda had a hand perfectly perched on her belly with fingers that were boxing her clitoris around with every up stroke and down. The accosting of her clit was pounding glorious pleasure through her brain. She hammered until she could fuck no more, and with the last ounce of the energy she had left, she stroked once more and collapsed in orgasmic bliss, lying forward on Danny.

Somehow, he managed to pick her up and off him to lay her on the couch. They all were piled up in their makeshift mosh pit. They all lay there sticky and sweaty, with no one willing or with the ability to move.

When the strength to stir back to life came to them again, they tried to work out who would shower and who would clean up; in the end, both girls showered together and, after they dried, came out and re-cleaned what Danny had wiped down and had finished the clean up before Danny was dried off. Trudy and Amanda swapped panties for fun as they now often did and helped each other dress. When Danny came out of the shower, he stopped by his room, partially dressed, and met the girls out in the living room.

"Damn, that was good. Let's do it again, who's ready?"

Amanda shook her head, "Danny, you are such an idiot…. men are so clueless."

Trudy rang in, "Just so you know, and for the record, you are OUR clueless idiot."

Acting childlike on purpose, "Just so long as I belong to someone."

Danny suddenly became serious. "You have no idea how much I'm going to miss you both next year."

Amanda posed philosophically, "About half as much as we will miss you since there are two of us." Danny just shook his head.

Trudy joined the philosophy discussion at a much baser level. "I am sure that once word gets out, and believe me, word will get out, girls talk…. Well, most of them do."

Sharing an eye smile with Amanda. "They will be knocking on the door. Your only concern might be your involvement with guys. Some women don't like that kind of competition."

Amanda added, "If for some reason you feel like you are being neglected, just call us, and we will come visit."

"You have a deal!"

Danny picked up his phone and started to fiddle with it; Amanda's phone began to ring.

Without looking at the caller ID, "Hello, this is Amanda…"

"I'm feeling neglected," It was Danny who had called.

Hanging up the phone, she scolded him. "Shut up !!"

They all had a good laugh, but all of them knew there were bits of truth throughout, referring to the upcoming days all too accurately.

Chapter 32 - A White Christmas

Christmas was a grand time for the whole family. Kate and Kevin were expecting their first child and had announced at the gathering that she was just past her first trimester. Julie brought home a date, but Sadie had told Trudy that he felt more like a stray than a forever man to her—time would prove her right. Isaac and Thomas both brought home dates. It took about two-point-three seconds flat for Sadie to notice the rings even before they announced it. Isaac introduced Dana Linton, and Thomas introduced Tracy Adkins.

Sam dropped the real bomb of the season—that Jessie and he were well into the second trimester with their first child. They had waited so long before telling anyone because of an unfortunate string of miscarriages and did not want to jinx their child. It was a happy Christmas indeed. Trudy could not recall seeing Sadie any happier.

Christmas morning was a slow-paced awakening for the whole crew at the Jax house. Both girls' bedroom doors were locked, and Trudy and Amanda were laced in each other's arms in Trudy's bed. This happened about twice a week, as the girls would fall asleep while just visiting or talking and occasionally when the desire hit one or the other after a night of indulgence.

Trudy was the first to wake and had deftly removed herself from Amanda's entangling arms and legs, slowly, without waking her. She dressed in country-girl jeans and a soft T-shirt and quietly let herself out of her room, relocking the door behind her. She made her way to the kitchen and started to make coffee when she noticed that a thin layer of snow had fallen. She smiled, remembering how much her mother loved a white Christmas. Because of that, white Christmases held a special place in her heart. The dusting brought back fond memories.

Paula surprised Trudy. "It's beautiful out there."

Trudy spun around to find Paula had joined her in the kitchen.

"What are the tears about?"

"It's silly. I was thinking how much my mother loved Christmas, and for a brief moment, she was right here with me."

"I'm sorry for interrupting. I'll give you some privacy."

"No, no, please don't leave. You are my family now, too. It's just a special time, and if it doesn't bother you, I don't mind sharing at all."

"I am here for you always, Trudy, and I love hearing about you and your mother. I can look around and see how loving she was by the little touches throughout the house still. I'm here for you anytime."

The coffee pot sang out its final attempts to pull water from the reservoir and filter it across the coffee bed.

Trudy offered, "Coffee?"

"Oh, thank you, yes. But not more than a gallon, please."

Trudy half smiled, half laughed. "Maybe we can build a fire in the living room and talk about you. You know, in many ways, you remind me of my mother, but there are also many ways you are different. For me, it all comes together beautifully. That's why I am so glad you and Dad found each other.

Honestly, I think if we could ask and get an answer, my mother would approve of you as well. You and Dad have what they had, and it's really quite beautiful. If I could only get my older sister to be nicer, this whole family thing would be perfect."

With a big smile and a wink, Paula laughed. "You know, a warm fire would be nice this morning."

Both women set about working in harmony—gathering kindling and small starter wood, setting the damper for a good draft, and igniting the fire. Within fifteen minutes, they had fed medium-sized wood into the flames, which were diligently consuming themselves, warming both them and the room. They settled back and enjoyed their morning coffee.

They heard rustling and banging around in the kitchen and made a wager as to who it could be. A bleary-eyed Bill turned the corner as Trudy claimed victory for guessing correctly. They had all just settled in for the quiet consumption of the first cup when they heard rooting noises once again. Paula playfully challenged Trudy to another bet, which was refused because she felt as if she were being set up.

The two women were still chuckling when Amanda rounded the corner to find a spot on the couch between her mother and Trudy. Shortly after the morning ritual of silence—which usually happened at least once a weekend—had ended, Paula officially retrieved cup number two, and their family unit began to converse openly beyond caveman waking-up grunts.

Gifts were exchanged. Trudy gave Paula her gift: a picture of both her and Amanda in a beautiful silver frame inscribed with a decorative scroll around the edge that read, "A mother isn't just the one that gave you life."

Paula cried tears of joy, especially after her morning talk with Trudy. It was directly from the heart, and she knew that.

Bill received the same gift from Amanda. He had been quiet and reflective while watching Paula open her gift, smiling approvingly when he read the inscription because he knew then and there that Paula was everything he had hoped for. But when he read the inscription on Amanda's frame—which was the same except it read "A father"—he had to get another cup of coffee.

Paula followed him and found that the big lug had tears streaming down his face. He looked at Paula and said, "I love you. I love our kids. You make me so happy, Paula."

It brought on another round of tears from her as they hugged.

Both girls had followed but decided to retreat, not wanting to invade what they suspected was a powerful moment for their parents.

It was the best Christmas experience for everyone in a long time. It was a good day indeed.

Chapter 33 - Bill and Paula Wed

January was a flurry of detail-oriented confirmations, double and triple-checking vendors, and reevaluating whether everything was accounted for. The upcoming wedding was set to be one of the biggest events in the area for a very long time. February 19 was fast approaching, and all the plans were coming together in grand fashion. Bill was a practical man, but he did not want to shy away from a little extravagance for this marriage.

When he first got married, things were tight financially, but now there was plenty of financial space to not only wiggle but outright walk. The farm had done exceptionally well, all due to the meticulous groundwork and business savvy early on. The Drax Hotel had one of the biggest restaurant and bar areas around and had been contracted to shut down its dining facilities and bar to hold a private event—the Jax wedding.

Six months before the ceremony, and only directly after a hefty deposit was made, the Drax announced that it, along with five other sister locations, was being acquired by Athena Inns. There was concern as to whether there would be any problems with the transition when it came to the expectations of the new owner.

Trudy told Paula that she had a good feeling about the new company, as she had heard they were a top-notch hotel, but she would call and try to get through to management to see if she could get assurances. She called Darell Cromwell immediately, who in turn called Fred Duersch, who connected him straight through to Terry Wise.

"Hello, Terry, how have you been?"

"Mr. Cromwell, I have been doing well. And yourself?"

"Please, Terry, call me Darell—you make me feel old otherwise." Chuckling.

"Old habits, Darell. How can I help you?"

"There is a wedding booked for the Carbondale Athena, which is currently being remodeled, and I've been asked to check if it will be ready on time for the lucky couple."

"You wouldn't be talking about the Jax wedding now, would you?"

"The very one."

"I'm afraid not. I think you're going to have to call them and cancel the venue."

"You have got to be kidding! Are you sure we can't get it done in time?"

"I'm absolutely sure I'm kidding." He laughed and let his 'joke' set in. "Jax isn't a common name, so I did my research, and I believe that Ms. Trudy Jax is involved, yes?"

"Yes, and thank God you're kidding. I didn't want to have to call Trudy and be the bearer of bad news on something like this."

"Not only will the remodel be finished, but the new addition of the sectioned-off meeting rooms will be completed as well. And though Miss Trudy isn't the one getting married, I'm having my crew go all out on decorations as my gift to the newlyweds. I was really impressed with that young lady—I wouldn't want to be the one to let her down after she breathed new life into this old man. I really enjoy the on-again and off-again; it suits my needs."

"I'm sure she will be glad to hear about this."

"My decorator is scheduled to call and coordinate with the bride as a 'thank you' for their trust and patience tomorrow."

"That is fantastic. Always over and above, Terry. I can't thank you enough. Do you want to call Trudy, or do you want me to?"

"No, you go ahead and call her. In the meantime, I will take a look over everything once more and make sure there are no surprises waiting in the wings."

"OK then, I like bringing good news. Please thank your crew on my behalf."

"Will do."

Darell hung up with no more concern, as every one of Terry's projects always came in under budget, under time, and over quality in workmanship. He was excited to relay the good news to Trudy, who was, in turn, excited for Paula and her dad. When she relayed the news to Paula, just by happenstance, Amanda was nearby, and she gave Trudy a big glowing smile. The next day, Paula excitedly explained to her girls the contents of a call she had just received.

"You will never believe what I just found out! The decorator in charge of the Athena remodel and facelift just called me personally to tell me that they thought a new start for a new start was great karma, so they are sending someone over to coordinate decorations for the whole area to be used for the wedding. On top of that, they wanted everyone to have a great start, so they are reducing and refunding the venue fee by fifty percent and offering every room used for the Jax wedding at fifty percent off as well. This is such great news! I can't wait to tell Bill."

She hurried off, beaming a smile.

Standing next to Trudy, Amanda swatted her lovingly but firmly on her ass.

"Good job, sis."

Smiling hugely, "It just so happens that I know someone who knows someone. And just for your information, if you smack my butt like that again, big sister or not, I will confine you to a cabin and punish you until you are remorseful."

"Is that so?"

Amanda stepped in closer and smacked her other ass cheek hard, eliciting a half moan from Trudy.

"That's it, I have had enough! You're grounded. You go sit in the Razor and think about what you have done. I'll be there in a minute—I have to get a, uh… a toy bag."

She smiled a devious smile at her.

"I'll be waiting in the Razor to be punished."

The wedding went off without a hitch. The hotel was literally at capacity on the day of the wedding from all the family and friends that came in for the affair. Comments about the decadence put forth by the hotel, the wait staff, and all the hotel employees were overwhelmingly positive.

Whereas the bride and groom were happy for the day, Trudy ran a close second in happiness as she recounted all she had obtained for her business. She counted herself incredibly lucky to be graced by such wonderful acquaintances.

Her smile started from deep within her core.

Chapter 34 - The End of School Fling

The end of the school year was fast approaching, and Trudy decided that a last-breath-of-school event would set the tone right for the summer. Her plan was simple—because Danny would be leaving soon for college, one last big fling was in order. She even told him that it was his responsibility to find "a piece of ass replacement" for her—someone that he thought might be able to fill his shoes at least halfway.

She gave him three weeks to find someone, as she had already reserved the penthouse suite at the Carbondale Athena. He smiled when she presented her challenge to him and started racking his brain to find a junior with the ability he wanted for Trudy.

With one week to spare, he told Trudy that he had found just the ticket and believed that Amanda would agree as well. However, he admitted that the guy's experience level might require a little coaching, as he was often quieter and more subdued than "the other guys." Danny had told the new guy that there was a get-together that was more than likely going to end up with everyone naked and that where it went from there was anyone's guess. The guy had liked the idea and wondered if he should bring a date. Danny told him absolutely—but only if she could truly keep a secret. That made Trudy a little uneasy, but she agreed to it.

Trudy arrived at the Athena in the morning and parked quite visibly in a manager's spot under the watchful eyes of the desk attendant. She pulled her suitcase behind her and made her way to the lobby, crossing over to the counter.

Carol Spenser, the desk clerk, spoke. "Good morning, miss; how can we serve you today?"

"I have a reservation under Jax."

"Oh, I see it here. Looks like you are booked for the Penthouse?" There was an unsteadiness in her voice as if a question was developing. "I'm not sure if that is right. I'm sorry, miss; I just want to make sure you don't get charged for an unintentional purchase. Are you expecting the Penthouse, or have we made a mistake? If so, I can correct it right now."

"No, Carol, there has been no mistake. I reserved the Penthouse."

"Thank goodness. We have a new computer system that is completely integrated with security doors, the restaurant, the pool, rooms, and more. It is all very seamless and all very new. I have yet to see it make a mistake, but I wanted to be sure for your peace of mind."

"It's all good."

"I just didn't want to be the one to call corporate and tell them of a system failure. Our training chief told us about a time she didn't have such resources and made a bad assumption about a guest that turned out to be one of the owners. She said the name Jax could have been the end of her…" She stopped dead and looked up. "Your name is Trudy Jax, ma'am?"

"Yes, it is, Carol. And I'm so happy with the way you have handled yourself here today. I'll personally call Sandy myself and let her know how pleased I am right now." She was smiling inside. "I'm going to need six room keys as well."

All while processing room keys and a credit card, Carol hesitated. "I don't actually know her personally. When I said, 'my training chief,' this was in a training video. I didn't mean to imply—"

"No, no, no. I understand that, but I want her to know her efforts have paid off tremendously."

"Well, Miss Jax, welcome to Athena Carbondale. Obviously, you can leave your car right where it is, or if you'd like, you could park next to the far entrance. The rear elevator is right there and lets out just down the hall from the penthouse. It would be much more convenient if you so desire."

"Thank you so much, Carol. I'm going to go up to the room for a moment, but I'll remember to park there, as well as tell my guests so we don't congest the lobby. You really have done a wonderful job, Miss Spenser. Thank you."

"You are most welcome, Miss Jax. Please enjoy your stay."

"Thank you."

As she turned to the elevator, she caught a glimpse of Carol looking at the elevator while on the phone—undoubtedly talking with the manager about their VIP.

Trudy dropped off her suitcase and left using the back elevator, walking across the parking lot to her car. Once inside, she called out to Google to dial Sandy Cline. The phone began to ring on the other end.

"Hello. Sandy Cline, Director of Training and Customer Relations."

"Sandy, this is Trudy Jax. How are you today?"

"I'm fine." She was laughing just a bit. "I was half expecting your call, as I just got off a call from a manager at Carbondale. It seems you excited one of our newer recruits there."

Trudy laughed. "That is exactly why I'm calling. She was excellent—professional and courteous. She was making small talk while processing me when she realized to whom she was talking. She was—rather, your training was—spot on. If she is what we can expect everywhere, I can see great things for us all. Thank you so very much."

Sandy offered, "The feedback is wonderful. Thank you so very much, Miss Jax."

"Sandy, please call me Trudy. And let Carol know I was impressed with her presence. I'll let you get back to what you were doing, but I just had to call you about this. Thank you again."

"Well, Miss… uh, Trudy, thank you again for calling. I will get in touch with Carol Spenser personally shortly. Thanks again, Trudy. Have a wonderful day!"

"You too, Sandy. Goodbye."

Trudy drove to the Diner Bell, where she was to meet Amanda, Dave, and Danny for lunch. They all had cheeseburgers and fries with sweet tea. The Diner Bell's cheeseburgers were simply the best, and the fries were always hot and crispy. The combination there could not be beaten—at least by Trudy's standards.

Danny was impressed by how such a simple fare could please so well when done right. He took mental notes, as always.

The night was set—Dave was spending the night at Danny's, and Danny at Dave's, which meant their night was now free. Amanda and Trudy were going out with the girls and, afterward, heading to a pajama party for the night. The group collectively was not expected home until about nine or so in the morning the next day.

When they had finished eating, Trudy dug into her purse and gave Amanda and Dave a key card, then handed three to Danny, as he was going to meet with his replacement after lunch—although he still would not give any details as to whom he had selected.

She explained where the best place to park was, as Carol, the clerk, was indeed right about it being much more convenient for the penthouse suite.

They all went their separate ways, as everyone had some running around to do in one form or another, but each had expressed anticipation for the night.

Trudy returned to the hotel around three-thirty, intending to settle in and relax until everyone arrived. She had not really looked around the parking lot when she arrived; she had just gotten out and entered the building. She rode the elevator to the top floor of her building with a smile on her face while thinking about how she got into the hotel business and how well it was working out. When the elevator door opened, she was still on autopilot, lost in business thoughts, noting to herself that she would touch base with Darell soon, if for nothing else than an update on how things were going.

She scanned her key to the lock, and there was a green flash and a barely audible beep as it greeted her and released the latch. She opened the door and pushed her way in, ready to lay back on one of the king-sized beds for a rest. When she turned the corner, she saw Dave with his face tucked in between Amanda's thighs and her head in his lap, and upon closer inspection, it turned out to be his dick down her throat. They had not heard the door open and were totally engrossed in each other's pleasure. Trudy stood very still and just watched for a bit, enjoying the show. As she watched, being a quasi-voyeur, the whole scene started to get her hot.

She could tell that Amanda was about to come from all the familiar sounds and movements she was making; she knew because, far too many wonderful times to count, she had brought Amanda to this exact moment. She enjoyed watching her release; Dave was clearly skilled. It was also clear that, much beyond the foursome with Danny at the cabin, these two had kept on seeing each other. Trudy thought, "Well, why not? They are good together - not to mention that a double date with Danny and her literally could go any direction with reckless abandon. From the outside looking in, the only thing that would be apparent to anyone else was two traditional couples hanging out. She liked the symmetry of it."

Amanda stopped blowing Dave for a moment. She arched hard into Dave's face, and Dave looked like he had shifted gears to overdrive. His face was moving side to side, and his tongue up and down and all around; his cunnilingus skills, she noted, really were phenomenal. Amanda came and then came again, and just because she had done this many times with Amanda, she knew that Amanda was entering into what she called an orgasmic wave. After the first come, the second come was not hard to find.

Once the second one was found, all that was required from that point was sporadic, well-timed touches, and she would drift away into orgasmic bliss, soaking whichever direction was down.

Clearly, Dave had gotten the multi-orgasmic wave memo because he had her legs jacked firmly in his biceps and was eating her like a water-starved dog with a fresh bowl of water. Amanda was clearly Dave's muse to do as he pleased. After what appeared to be about six or seven fantastic rolling orgasms, Dave relented and relaxed to let her ride the euphoria down.

Trudy went and sat on the other bed directly across from the two writhing bodies, which was when Dave noticed her and smiled. A minute later, a half-breathless Amanda opened her eyes, saw Trudy, and smiled.

"Hi, sis; sorry we couldn't wait for you."

"No, no, that's quite alright. I really enjoyed the show, but now I'm sticky because of you two."

Dave spoke up playfully, "I would apologize, but I'm just not sorry…. Uhhh…"

Losing his breath because Amanda took him fully down her throat in one fluid motion.

"Oh fuck…"

Amanda started literally humming a song; Trudy was not sure of the tune but could tell that the low notes had a devastating effect on Dave. His eyes were half rolled back in his skull, and his face looked tormented, and rightfully so because Amanda was really sucking him well. His fellatio began at the very tip of his rod upward, never quite breaking contact with the tip, followed by her tongue that would circle his glans, and as she would suck in his whole head and cradle the under-shaft with her wet tongue, she pushed herself down his shaft right on into her throat bumping lips to belly before doing it all over again. Dave was not going to last long at this rate, but she was quite sure that at this junction in time, it was not much of a concern to him.

Amanda was incredible going down on him and watching this performance from the sideline was nothing short of inspiring, erotic, and molten hot. She was taking Dave down her throat in glorious strokes, one right after another; it was hotter than watching Danny take Dave for the first time in front of her. She was almost envious of her sister's cock sucking skills. About seven minutes later, the tell-tale signs of the end were telegraphed. Amanda gave no respite, but she was now looking lovingly into Trudy's eyes. She was incredible to watch, and Trudy was getting wetter by the second, watching Amanda engulf him so expertly. Dave released; Amanda moved to the top of his shaft and caught his full load in her mouth. Trudy could tell she was torturing the poor boy by circling the oversensitive glans right on through the end of his very audible body-twitching release.

Amanda looked at Trudy with questioning eyes and was answered with a yes by Trudy, so she pulled up off Dave and, with a full mouth, moved from one bed to the other and kissed Trudy with a huge French kiss, sharing Dave with her. Their kiss lasted a minute or more as both girls kissed each other and used Dave up. When they were finished, Trudy was completely panty-soaked. A very sweaty Amanda got up, grabbed an equally sweaty Dave, and pulled him along to the shower. Trudy disrobed and opened her suitcase, pulled out a rose, turned it on, and satisfied herself with a nice orgasm while Dave and Amanda finished their showers. Afterward, Trudy stepped into the hot water to rinse off. She joined the others on the bed to lay back and relax while waiting for the others to arrive.

They lay together on one bed with Trudy on the edge and Amanda and Dave on the far side of her. Trudy was facing up, just relaxing; Amanda had her back to her as she faced Dave, who was on his side looking at Amanda with his hand draped across her and his fingers gently caressing Trudy's vulva and occasionally flicking past her clitoris. They all fell asleep for a nap. An hour had passed as they all blissfully slept. Dave rolled to his back; Amanda was half lying on him, and Trudy was spooning Amanda when Danny came in. No one heard him arrive as they continued their slumber until Dave abruptly jolted in bed. Danny had watched them all sleep for a while, enjoying his friends sleeping so soundly, but he decided to wake Dave, sort of.

Danny started to gently stroke Dave's member as it was dressed right and flaccidly laying there. He slowly and softly traced a vein up his dick which started to bring it back to life. He traced another vein that clearly had a better relationship with the blood control valve making his flaccid dick slowly but steadily go from limp to filling to full right on through too hard. Danny softly caressed his shaft, causing Dave to moan in his sleep. It was not until Danny had slowly sucked Dave into his mouth and down his throat that Dave jolted awake, stirring the girls to life. Danny pulled up off Dave and spoke.

"So, you guys started without me?"

"Not really…. I mean, I didn't really do much, but…??" Dave replied.

Amanda piped up, "Yes, we did, and I have to say, for your information, at least for today, I was the first one there."

She was pointing at Dave's dick and shooting a questioning glance at Dave, who was nodding yes wide-eyed in answer to the question.

"I'm sorry to tell you this, buddy, but it is quite possible that Amanda can suck a better dick than me and possibly better than you as well."

"Now I'm hurt."

Danny was holding his heart, feigning pain, and looking at Amanda, squinting with a mean look.

"I'll have to make you pay for that."

Beaming a smile, she retorted, "Promises, promises, promises."

Just when she finished saying that, she rolled up to her knees and cradled Dave's balls with one hand and the lower part of his shaft with the other and, staring directly at Danny with a "top this grin," lowered herself to Danny's glans, circled it, and slowly took in the head just a little better than she had before and orbited all over the head while humming in delight. With steadfast determination, she hummed herself down his shaft and didn't stop her slow, arduous advance until her lips touched belly, all while massaging his nuts; she quickly changed direction and made her way to the tip only to break contact to look at Danny in the eye with a "what do you think about that" look.

"Damn Amanda, that was so fucking hot, but I guess I'm really going to have to discipline you for sucking MY cock without asking permission. But before I do, can you show me that orbiting thing you did again?"

Amanda gladly started down Dave's cock, and right when she was going to start the main part of her orbiting, Danny said, "Not on him, on me."

His pants were unzipped and down to his hips as he saddled up to the edge of the bed.

Danny, Dave, and Trudy all laughed; it was possible that Amanda had laughed too, but her mouth was too full of cock to tell. Amanda pulled off the last laugh when she rose up off Dave, who really liked the feeling, and she gently grabbed Danny by the balls.

He thought that he had gone too far for a moment and was about to pay for it, but Amanda just leaned forward and wrecked his world. She took him in even slower than she had Dave and wound around his glans in her orbiting fashion; it was as if her tongue had decided to trace every vein it could find before she would move further down. By the time she had parked her lips fully at his belly, he was fighting to maintain control. She hummed her low-note tune all the way up, and when she pulled free of him, he was trying his best to stop shaking from the feeling he was experiencing.

Amanda confronted him, "Well?"

"Holy shit, I will remember how you did that, but I have to agree, you can suck a dick better than me. Uh. how about…??"

"Not a chance …. I'm not sure if I will accept your apology. Help me out here, Dave." solicited Amanda.

Dave pulled Danny up the side of the bed and leaned out, and began to suck him furiously while both women watched in awe. Less than a minute later, Danny arched forward and came hard into Dave's mouth, so much so that some come dribbled out of his lips as he was trying to swallow the load.

Amanda chimed in, "Well, shit, Dave… I meant, what was your opinion?"

They all laughed as Amanda licked a large dollop of white creamy sauce off Dave's chin and kissed him deeply. It was not long before Danny was naked and in bed with everyone. There was a train of sorts that developed with Dave laying on his back and Trudy straddling his face, half-face fucking him while he probed her with his tongue. Amanda was on her hands and knees in a reverse cowgirl and rocking back and forth with Dave's dick buried deep in her, and on every forward stroke, Danny's cock was making a full journey down her throat.

They had barely just started and had found a rhythm where the whole train rocked back and forth, accommodating everyone's desires, when they all stopped because someone said, "Damn Danny, you weren't lying." There, at the foot of the bed, were a girl and a boy; Danny introduced them both to the group.

"Everyone, this is Mickey Leeds and his sister, Nora Jenkins."

"Did you just say his sister?" Trudy asked.

Nora interjected, "Actually, his dad married my mom; we are step-siblings."

Mickey continued, "We are the same age, two months apart.

Danny was a little surprised, "I thought you were going to bring a date? Not your sister."

Mickey was looking at his sister, who gave him a discernible nod, "You said to bring someone that I could trust to keep a secret; we may be "step" brother and sister, but we have been sexing each other down for about a year and a half now."

Nora backed him up. "With all the bullshit at our school, it's just better this way."

Looking at Trudy, she said, "Thank you. By the way, Ryan tried to rape me, too; he would have succeeded if some other couple had not pulled up; I got free and never looked back. He deserved everything you gave him and more."

Mick continued, "So instead of trying to work it out in the dating scene, we just turn to each other for our desires. There is OUR secret for YOU to keep. Your secret is safe with us."

Danny asked, "So, what are your boundaries?"

Nora began, "Well…"

Stepping forward and dropping to her knees, she started sucking Danny deeply in and pulled off him with everyone looking on. "I guess we will figure it out."

Trudy walked over to Mick and lightly grabbed his crotch, only to find a heavy bulge trying to free itself. She smiled at him and raised an eyebrow, and he smiled back. She made her way around the back side of him and caressed his body from his ass up to his neck. He was broad-shouldered, and his physique had muscular overtones throughout. She reached down to the tail of his shirt, grabbed both sides and peeled it up and off him. He was tanned all over.

She pushed a hand down his pants and found a hand full of pulsing cock; she could feel his heartbeat in his shaft. Trudy pulled her hand free, undid his trousers, and pulled them downward along with his bright blue bikini briefs. She spun him around, pushed him back to the other bed, and kneeled in front of him to untie his shoes and remove them. She grabbed one pant leg and then the other and pulled them free, leaving him naked with nothing but his socks on, which she thought for a moment would make for an excellent picture. She reached one sock rim and pulled it free, then the other. She worked her way up his muscular legs and frame stopping to look at his cock.

She noticed he had NO tan lines and quickly worked out he had a natural tan tone to him, and he was gorgeous. She grabbed his cock with a hand; it was firm, almost fully hard. She always compared a dick with Danny's. Why she did this, she was not sure, maybe because he was the first, maybe because his dick was just so fantastic; in any case, a guy better come well prepared to earn a good rating.

If Danny was her ten and Darell her 11.5, Mick would easily have garnered a 9.5 right up there with Dave. She loved the look of his cock, circumcised, straight, not curved in the least, well proportioned. He was easily six inches, maybe more, and his hair was thicker than Danny's. She would have to give it the neck test to be sure. She stood up to face him, leaned forward to the bed, and planted her lips on his left nipple. It was clear that this had not been done to him before, but he adjusted and let the feeling float free; she changed nipples and sucked it in hard. He arched into it this time.

Trudy bit his nipple lightly at first, but she added pressure when he gasped and pulled her head to him. With her hand, she pinched his other nipple hard, and his cock twitched to her, letting her body know he was fully hard by knocking on her belly. She released his nipples and moved downward, and for some reason, she felt it was just right, so she took his dick in her mouth without pomp and circumstance and sucked him completely down to his belly. This sat him bolt upright as he also tried to arch his hips into her and muttered, "Sweet Jesus."

He had never been deep-throated by anyone, not even his sister; she gave excellent head but never like this. He looked down and saw Trudy's lips just leaving his belly and watched as she engulfed him slowly five more times, and when she shifted her speed to enjoy herself more, his writhing made it all that much better. She could tell he was methodically being destroyed; he was loving what she was doing to him. His breathing hitched and became shallower, and his prick in her mouth seemed to harden perceptively more; on the next upstroke, she could feel his head gaining in size and knew he was close.

She was going to take him for all he was worth. He cried out, "Oh god, shit, shit, shit."

It was loud enough for the others to momentarily look at him; his sister was in awe seeing Trudy so deep on his root. She pulled up to the top and attacked his glans, and he came hard, arching into her. His cock was spasming and sputtering his juice in her mouth. She had planned to capture him and savor it slowly and maybe even share him, but his come volume was incredible. He filled her mouth; she went to swallow about the same time his cock spasmed once more and lost a bit down her cheek and chin. She swallowed again and regained control.

He tasted heavenly. She did not know if it was him or just a new dick; it did not matter to her one little bit as she absolutely loved going down and more so enjoyed her prize for her hard work. He spasmed a bit more even after he had finished coming and looked at her and said,

"Trudy, that was incredible. My sister is good, but that was on another level. I have never been deep-throated, and it was amazing. Nora is going to have to learn that."

Laughing, Trudy said, "Well, you might be in trouble because there is at least one person here better at giving a blowjob than me, maybe more."

"That isn't possible; that was the most insanely wonderful feeling I think I have ever had."

He became just a little self-conscious when he realized that everyone had watched him come; they were all impressed with the amount he had mustered up.

Nora inquired, "Somebody is going to have to show me how that is done because I have never seen him come that much. If it's that much better, I want to learn it."

Before Mick had such an audible release catching everyone's attention, the others had the most incredible train of their own on the tracks. Because she was already on the bed, Danny had slid in beside Amanda, and she took over and rolled him to his back, grabbed a firm hold on the headboard, and straddled his face. He started to lick her without being asked, and as he was doing so, he felt a warm mouth encompass his dick and start to suck him.

He could not see that Nora was bent over the edge of the bed, leaning forward and sucking him. He also could not see that Dave was at the end of the train, but he knew. He knew because Amanda was on his face, and the mouth being rocked back and forth on his dick was slamming forward rhythmically. He knew that Dave was fucking the newcomer, and judging by the violent way the bed was moving, he was pounding her hard.

He had been right on every account. Dave had entered Nora with ease as she was very wet, and he and Mick were about the same dick size. It was only when Mick came so loudly that the whole train had wrecked. Mick had laid back on the bed, thinking for a moment that everything was fine, but Trudy had other plans. She pinned his shoulders to the bed with her knees and slammed her pussy right in his face, he had no choice but to eat her, and she wanted it badly after getting so worked up seeing him through to completion.

Mick could not see who was playing with his dick, but it felt good. Danny worked his way up beside Mick and Trudy and watched Mick's tongue accost Trudy's labia and standing nub. He noted mentally that Mick was doing well; he leaned forward and whispered something in Mick's ear as Mick nodded while licking. Danny retreated to the foot of the bed.

When he got back to the foot of the bed, he caught Nora's attention and said, "Watch and learn, get up close, and ask anything you want to."

"What do you mean?"

Danny just leaned forward and took Mick's cock in his mouth, balls deep. Nora was caught off guard as she had never seen a man suck another man in person. She had seen porn videos but figured it was mostly contrived bullshit, but when Danny started down for the third time, she was completely enthralled. Danny pulled up and explained to her how to breathe past the gag reflex and how to best take a cock deep, balls deep, and kiss a belly. He moved to the side and told her to try it on Mick.

Nora struggled at first but was able to get him down her throat. She almost puked twice as she fought with the gag. She got in the right groove and found it actually easy to do. After she was deep-throating her brother for about twenty strokes successfully, Danny pulled her back and sat on the foot of the bed and lined her up with his cock. She could see he was visibly larger and longer by a little in both regards and was not sure about the bigger size, but Danny assured her he would help her, so she took him in her mouth.

She struggled with the new size just a bit, but she got into the groove again and had him balls deep. Danny praised her and told her to let him know when she was comfortable and that he would show her the rest. She was confused but got into a rhythm that was comfortable and started to hum with delight. She was very happy with her newfound skill. Danny told her that she looked comfortable, and she hummed, "Uhmm huhmmm." He grabbed her head, cupping behind her neck, and proceeded to begin to face fuck her. She was taken aback for a second but found she really liked it.

Being force fed dick was incredible; she worked out how to breathe and how not to gag. Danny stopped, pulled out, and led her to the bed. He had her lay back with her head just over the edge of the foot a little; she did not understand the position until he walked around the bed and lined up with her mouth again. This time Danny really face fucked her hard, but she loved it, and to top off her experience with it, Amanda had gotten into place and was destroying her clit and cunt with her tongue until Dave being the odd man out, walked by the suitcase and saw it was full of all kinds of toys.

He found a dildo that was a little bigger than he was and handed it to Amanda, who wasted no time sinking deep within Nora's' pussy. She worked the dildo hard, and Nora responded incredibly. She was approaching maximum sensitivity when Amanda hit the on button, and the faux dick came alive in her. The combination of dick in her mouth and dick in her twat while her clit was being licked sent her over the edge. She started to come so hard that Danny pulled out of her to let her ride her own wave.

Danny moved around the other side of the bed to watch and join in with Mick, who was eating Trudy well now, and when he did, Mick caught him off guard by reaching out and grabbing his dick. Danny just stood there and only moved to give better access when Mick started to stroke him. Trudy saw this and decided to roll off Mick to give him complete access.

No one had discussed whether touching Mick by another guy was OK. Certainly, there was no way to tell if the other scenario was part of Mick's plan either. So, everyone was pleasantly surprised when Mick took this level of initiative; they all watched as it escalated.

Danny quipped, "I didn't know you were bisexual?"

Mick replied, "I don't know what I am, but I heard you talking Nora through it, and I thought I would like to try it. When you went down on me, that was amazing. I appreciate you asking beforehand if you could suck me. I was wondering if I could suck you now?"

"If you're sure you want to, yes, please do."

Danny was standing in between the beds, so Mick rolled off the bed and made his way over to Danny.

"I am not really sure what I'm doing or want to do, so let me know if I'm out of line."

"You will be fine with me; I'll make sure of it."

Mick sheepishly cradled Danny's face, gently kissed his lips, and broke contact. He thought about it, kissed him harder with just a little tongue, and pulled away yet again. Danny let him be the full aggressor, knowing he had never done this and would have a lot to process later. Danny did not want to be part of the problem.

Mick moved down and kissed both of his nipples in succession and stopped to suck on one for a bit. After a minute, he knelt in front of Danny and looked his cock over for a bit and grabbed his shaft and stroked a couple of times and leaned forward, and gently sucked the head of his dick into his mouth. Everyone was watching at this point. His sister was amazed to learn that a side of her brother was there, and she had not even guessed it was there.

Mick sucked himself deeply down on Danny and stopped at the back of his throat. He forced himself to push on down, feeling Danny's cock in his throat. He pulled up and out quickly and gagged for a bit and then did it again, but this time, he did not gag at all. Mick started to suck, stroke Danny, sometimes going to the hilt, other times just to the top of the throat. Mick grabbed both of Danny's hands and put them on the back of his head and mimicked him pulling forward, so Danny started to fuck his face.

With being deep-throated by Mick's sister and a new mouth, a virgin at that, he knew he was not going to last long at all, which was both good and bad for Mick. For a first-timer, this was going to save his jaw from being so sore, but on the other hand, he was about to get a really big face full of goo. Danny warned him with an extra amount of time, "You're going to make me come."

Further, he announced to everyone, "I'm going to come soon."

Mick only picked up the pace until he announced, "I'm coming!"

He felt his prickhead swell hard, he had been holding his come back to give Mick every possible moment to not catch a load in the neck and mouth, and when he could fight no more, he released a torrent.

Mick stayed down for the first pulse to go down his neck and, after, pulled up to mouth-only level and let him finish completely there. Trudy moved in close and kissed Mick deeply, and they both shared what Danny had spent. When there was none left, she pulled away from Mick.

Nora was amazed," Damn, bro, I never knew."

"Neither did I, but I was here, and I had to know what it was like. I almost didn't do it twice, but I'm glad I did. It was an incredible feeling knowing I was the reason your cock was pulsing in my neck, and after I got past the fear, you tasted good. I liked that a lot; it kinda surprised me. Since we are here, there is one more thing I want to know.

Nora asked. "What is that?"

Looking at Dave, "You're gonna need a condom, Dave, that is if you're willing?"

Dave followed up with, "And some lubrication. I can talk you through it slowly, but there is a better plan if you trust me?"

"Dude, I just asked another guy to fuck me in the ass; I'm pretty much as exposed as I can be for you right now, so show me."

The others let it become the Dave and Mick show, with Nora on the verge of disbelief. Dave got out a vibrator that was about three-quarters his girth, he put a condom on it, lubed lightly, and had Mick move to the edge of the bed and kneel face forward with his head downward on the bed. He turned on the vibrator, centered up on Mick, made contact, pushed gentle pressure forward, and said to Mick, "On your pace, push back to me."

Mick slowly pushed back until about half or more of the vibrator disappeared. Dave told him to just relax for a moment. Mick visibly lost tension, and Dave took that as a cue to move. He slowly worked the vibrator in and out of him as he learned to relax with every movement and stroke. He pulled the vibrator slowly out of him and removed the condom by pulling it inside out and dropping it into the trash. He lined up behind Mick, applied a small amount of lubrication on his condom, and pushed up to Mick with a little pressure.

"When you're ready, push to me."

Dave held his ground as Mick pushed backward and encompassed his dick about halfway. He stood still without moving a muscle. After about forty-five seconds, Mick again visibly relaxed, and Dave pulled back slowly and went forward again. There was a long pull backward, and allowing some time, he let some lubrication dribble from the bottle to his shaft. When he pushed forward slowly this time, he went completely in. He did not pull backward because Mick leaned forward and slid backward, and he made the same motion again.

There had been a few moans of discomfort, but now it had changed to something more delicate. Dave started to move slowly now, and Mick stood still and moaned aloud,

"More please."

Dave picked up the pace, eliciting a moan of ecstasy, and Mick whispered, "More, please." Dave Increased the stroke length and speed.

Because he knew this was new to Mick, he drizzled just a bit more lube on his cock while stroking him; this really did the trick because Mick asked, "More, please." Quite audibly.

Dave was stroking him at a good pace when Mick moaned, "Please fuck me, Dave."

Dave started fucking him intently. Danny could see in Dave's eyes he was about to bust his nut at the same time Mick moaned, "Oh god."

He buried his head in the bed and came. When he came, the tensed muscles in Mick's ass were more than Dave's resolve, he could not hold back, and he came along with him. Afterward, he gently pulled out again. Carefully, he pulled off the condom and threw it away. Mick was in a shimmering ball on the bed.

Nora leaned forward and softly, with concern, asked, "Are you OK, Mick?"

"Shh… Oh god, yes, just leave me alone for a minute, please."

He shuddered as his body was quaking.

Dave suggested that he shower because of the lube and offered to shower with him but Mick said he was good. Slowly and weak-legged, he made his way to the shower. A couple of minutes after Mick had been in the shower, Amanda slipped away from the group and joined him in the hot water. Amanda and Mick lathered each other with hotel soaps and shampoo while taking special considerations and time near the sensitive spots.

Amanda exited the water to dry off. When Mick got out, Amanda was lying on her towel on top of the sink space face down, bent over the countertop. As he dried, he noticed that she had something stuck to her, and upon a closer inspection, he realized she was wearing a butt plug. He walked up behind her and lightly patted it inward. He was about to say, "What is this?" but when his hand hit the exposed end, it whirred to life with a pulse, and it shut off when his hand broke contact. He lightly swatted it again, and it pulsed once more to life, beckoning a moan from her. After that second pulse, Mick caught on and understood exactly what his role was here.

He had experienced his first prostate come and had not fully recovered from it, but he was still hard, so he lined up behind Amanda and, with one long, smooth stroke, pushed into her fully. When his belly met ass, the plug roared to life again, coaxing a moan from her. He slowly stroked, and it responded in kind. He started to step up the pace and had the toy sounding like a broken, unending turn signal with every stroke.

He realized that he could control the duration of the buzz by the duration of the bump with his belly and set out to break her in any way he could. He was thrusting her with long, violent slams inward, arching and holding his ground up close, making the whirring prolong at every contact. Amanda, for her part, half regretted pushing in the plug because she was systematically being destroyed by her own device. She just went with it and came hard and continually; she had just gotten out of the shower, but her thighs were now wet again down to her knees.

Mick continued to hammer her until his own ejaculation became evident, and his stride altered. Amanda felt the change and struggled through each subsequent wave to clench her pelvic floor and let her pussy help jack him off. His volume was not as before, but the effect was still the same; deep in her, his meat was spasming uncontrollably to the point where he did not want to pull out because of sensitivity overload. Amanda had taken the brunt of his hammering right through several massive orgasms that he relished by hammering her hard and holding the rocket in her ass in the on position; there was no way he was going to get any relief from her.

Her pussy clenched in waves, and he pulled inward and out; he had trouble standing. She saw the strain on his face in the bathroom mirror; she was fucking back into him furiously as she looked him right in the eye.

"You better not fucking quit on me now, boy."

He was barely able to mutter, "I'm no quitter!!"

Amanda bucked back into him so profoundly that he went to the floor and curled into a ball. Satisfied with her assault, she straddled him, dripping on his shoulder and side.

She beamed an "I definitely won that round smile," 'Are you OK?'

With a mix of giddy sarcasm, "I'm just peachy, why do you ask?"

They both started laughing, and Amanda stepped into the shower, which was now a convenient step and a half away. She had extracted her toy and had all but cleaned up when Mick managed to join her once more for a quick clean and rinse. They had stepped out of the shower and dried each other. When they turned the corner from the bathroom, they were met with a site to behold.

Trudy was lying comfortably on her back, propped up with two pillows at the head of the bed, and Nora was on her knees with her face buried deep between her thighs. Danny was behind her doggy style fuck slamming her with long smooth strokes, and Dave was on his knees at the head of the bed, cradling Trudy's' head and skull fucking her from tip to hip. Amanda looked at Mick as she had held up her bump buddy with a "should I?" look at him.

Mick answered her, "Oh hell yes."

Amanda walked over and retrieved the bottle of lube and slicked up her little friend, and got in between Nora's ass and Danny's waist. Danny arched back to accommodate her space, but Nora could not see anything. She felt it when it touched her ass, and it came to life in Amanda's palm. Amanda just pushed pressure forward, and Nora pushed back until the bulb sunk into her. She took it in stride; Mick was all but sure she was not ready for what was to happen next. Even so, he and Amanda laid out across the other bed with pillows under their chests in a perfect position as if watching TV and began to enjoy the show.

Danny started to plow Nora, making sure that the bump was now prolonged, and it was easy to see that it was threatening to take control of her. That was when Danny laid down the law.

"Hey, Nora?"

She barely turned her head and had to moan through a forward bump to reply, "Oh God," She drew a ragged breath. "What?"

"I'm going to fuck you until Trudy comes hard, you better start eating her right because I'm going to destroy your ass."

"How can I make her come when you are…"

Danny picked up the pace, pounding Morse code to her brain. She understood at once that this was going to be challenging. She started to come, and Danny took off like a sprinter; she was thrashing around like she was in the middle of a train wreck, all while trying her level best to bury her face in Trudy, who was getting the benefit of every thrust from Danny. Trudy was sucking Dave beyond any expert expectation, and he was getting close.

Danny let loose a barrage of thrusts like a sprinter coming out of the blocks just as Dave came. Trudy had been thrust backward just as Dave released but managed to swallow most of him; a stream that escaped on her cheek was the only thing she missed. Dave pulled out of her, leaned forward, licked himself off her in one pass, and French kissed Trudy, who shared the remnants of what was left. Dave joined Amanda and Mick for the show.

Dave commented, "Mick? Your sister is in big trouble."

"Why do you say that?"

"She has started to come, and Danny can stroke for an hour just like that. He has amazing cardio stamina."

Nora heard the conversation, "Oh fuck!" She buried her face hard and doubled her efforts on Trudy.

Between her attacking the cunt before her and the forward thrusts, Trudy began to breathe hard.

Amanda spoke up, "Mick, if you want to help your sister, go suck on Trudy's nipples and pinch the one you're not sucking. That will set her off."

Mick slid off the bed, dutifully, stationed himself at Trudy's side, and began to nurse on her feverishly; he reached across and pinched her other nipple hard. Trudy let loose a wincing moan causing Mick to jump away, thinking he went too hard, but Trudy caught the back of his head and pulled him in forcefully to her tit, assuring him that everything was all right. When he bit the nipple, Trudy arched up and bucked wildly face fucking Nora, who was lapping and sucking for all she could muster.

Nora stopped sucking when she saw the flood on the bed roll forth. At the beginning of yet another orgasm, which was coming faster and more intense each time she looked up at Mick.

"Thank you," Was all she could muster for the moment. She looked over her shoulder, and as a crazy challenge, she said, "I thought you were going to fuck me? What are you waiting for?"

Danny adopted an evil smile as if it were a personal challenge to deliver. He stroked on at the same pace, which was mostly unbelievable. He had been stroking this way for about twenty minutes, yet he didn't slow or speed up; it was as if he were waiting for something. Nora began to orgasm once more, and that is when they all saw Danny visibly smile.

No one could hardly believe it, but just as Nora spasmed forward a bit, Danny captured her hips with his arms and hands and locked firmly onto her as if they were welding her in position and doubled his already blistering pace. Nora screamed out in ecstasy. Her body was convulsing, trying to escape his grasp; every time she hauled away and began to contort, she was snatched back right in time to feel the next brutal pounding she was to endure.

The bed was soaked under her, half from the sweat pouring from Danny, half from all the juices combined. It was truly reminiscent of a rodeo, but this time, the bull was trying to escape the rider, and the rider would not submit. She began to wonder if she had made a critical error in challenging him. Danny suddenly stopped his thrusting and let her attempt to push away. He slammed one more thrust home, hard, raw, and deep. She came hard from the singular assault violently and had a series of mind-numbing out-of-body experiences when he held tight up close to Amanda's little bump buddy snuggly in her ass, causing an endless whirring buzz.

She convulsed in midair with her molten confines twitching deep within her. Danny let loose just fractionally and, with a massive "hhhuuuuuught," arched forward and came. He pulled out of Nora just after he finished and rolled to the side, breathing deeply on the edge of the bed. Nora lay there destroyed, shaking and whimpering; she was in a sticky mess, balled up beside him. Nora convulsed about every minute or so for about ten minutes afterward. The show itself was spectacular.

Dave and Trudy shared their shower together; there was no touching beyond mutual bathing. They were both deeply satisfied and physically beat. Ten minutes or so later, Dave and Trudy got comfortable on the other, mostly dry bed.

Danny helped Nora to shower and bathe her, but hardly a word was spoken. His touch was more like a lathered caress than simple mindless contact. When they made it back to the bed, they had pulled the covers back on the bed they had just left to get to the dry base sheet underneath and laid down buck assed naked as well.

Nora tangled her body into Danny's half for warmth, half out of the comfort of a touch.

In disbelief, Nora spoke, "I had no idea. Mick and I fuck all the time, but," She looked at Mick. "I'm sorry if this hurt your feelings, little brother, but I have never been fucked like that."

Looking at Trudy.

"I see you two around all the time but never suspected somebody was getting more than Mick and me, much less getting fucked so well. That was incredible."

Mick chimed in, "Uh, well yeah, I watched it from here, and you, sir,"

Looking and talking to Danny. "I bow to the master." He half laughed, "I'm pretty sure I'm going to be sore tomorrow."

Dave piped in, "I tried to be easy, but you kept asking for more."

"I know, but now I know. Honestly, I loved it all. There are a few things I'm still processing and more than a few questions to answer for myself, but all in all, I'm good. Thank you."

Nora addressed Mick, "You sure surprised me," Her hands were up in submission. "No issues here, but damn, you were unbelievably hot to watch. I wouldn't have believed that I would like to see two men together, much less like you and Dave were, but you were begging for more, and I couldn't help watching how much you were into it. You were so damn exciting and raw, and Dave? Damn."

They all fell silent, basking in the sexual decadence until the silence was broken.

Amanda asked, "Is anyone else hungry? I could eat a horse."

Danny added, "I could drink a gallon of water and then eat a horse."

Everyone laughed and agreed on one part or the other as it applied to them.

Trudy suggested, "Let's go to the restaurant downstairs; I hear they have great food here."

They all dressed from gym bags they had brought for clean clothes and went down to dine. It was going on seven thirty when they got there, but the kitchen was still in full swing, so they ate incredibly well, especially after Trudy told them all that she had gotten a gift card from MasterCard and that the sky was the limit because everything was on her. Danny and Amanda smiled knowingly at each other. Three of the group had not noticed how well they were being attended to, but two of them now saw the constructive collaboration as the restaurant employees rotated through and ensured there was no need for want.

Trudy had requested two more sets of bedding for her room; there was no problem getting them without a single question as to why. She was sure that Carol had amply spread the word that one of the owners was in-house for the night. The Jax name was noticeable, and all positions associated with the hotel and dining facility were on full alert. Ownership was a good thing, indeed.

Nora, Danny, and Trudy shared one bed, and Dave, Amanda, and Mick the other. Between the sex and the food, everyone was fast asleep by eleven thirty or so.

Trudy was always the early riser; the next day was no different. Nora stirred awake but was unmoving when Trudy had untangled herself from her and Danny. Nora watched in amazement when Trudy gently raised the sheets from Danny's hips and slowly and lovingly caressed his cock. It grew all the while Danny slept. When it had gotten fully hard, Trudy began a most wonderful slow deep blowjob on him. She watched for a while and realized this was more than a sexual thing.

Trudy was blowing him in the most loving way, consuming him as being a part of the whole together. It was at that time she understood the nature of the love between them and smiled. She flushed warm inside when Trudy locked eyes with her and slowly took Danny deeply and slowly to the hilt. Danny again woke up in mid-cum and had a knowing subsequent smile. This was not the first time he had been woken up in this manner, although every time he did, it always seemed better than the last time.

"Thank you, Trudy." He caressed her hair and head in a loving way. Nora leaned over the top of Danny and kissed Trudy full on the mouth, sharing what was still left, and gently pulled away.

"That was beautiful to watch; I get it now. Thank you for letting me share that."

The three of them "accidentally" made too much noise, and the other bed began to stir. Amanda was the first to sit up, and then Dave made his way off the bed and was the first to the bathroom; Mick followed suit. By the time the last of the group finished with their needs for the toilet, Mick was on his knees in front of Dave. He asked Dave if he could find out something with his help, and Dave agreed. Mick asked him to the side of the bed and went down on his flaccid cock. He began to use his newly found skills as Dave began to grow in his mouth. They all watched as Mick deftly put into action all of what he had done or heard. Less than ten minutes later, he was wiping Dave's remnants from his chin. He looked at Nora.

"I'm in big trouble, sis. I think I really like sucking dick."

They all laughed.

Trudy breached what everyone was thinking, "Who wants Breakfast? I'm famished."

They all went down for a big breakfast. The food fare was excellent, and the service was unequaled. They all had their fill and returned to the room to gather their stuff. Trudy and the others had brought their things to their respective cars. Mick and Nora made their rounds, saying their goodbyes.

Nora took an extra moment, thanked Trudy for inviting them along, and kissed her on the cheek in appreciation. Danny accompanied Trudy to the lobby to check out mainly because he knew they were aware of who she was and was curious to see how she was treated in general. Carol happened to be at the counter as her work cycle had her working this weekend.

"Ms. Jax? How can I help you today?"

After freeing her black credit card from her wallet. "Good morning, Carol; we were just going to check out. But since you are here, it is a great chance to thank you again for helping to keep things running so smoothly.

Everything I have seen for the last two days was excellent. I will let Fred Duersh know he is doing well."

"Oh wow, a good report card to the CEO from one of the owners; I don't think it could get any better than that. OH! By the way, soon after you left yesterday, Sandi Cline called me personally to thank me! I really do appreciate your kind words."

As she was punching up the bill. "Well, that's different; I've never seen this before."

"Is there a problem?"

"Oh no, ma'am; to the contrary, your account has been flagged as paid-in-full and has instructions to send the bill to an email at corporate headquarters. We are all done here then. I'm so glad you had a pleasant stay with us; we look forward to serving you again."

"It has been a very enjoyable stay. The service was excellent, and the food was unbelievable. Please let everyone know that I really appreciate everyone's hard work."

"I will spread the word, Ms. Jax. I hope you have a wonderful day!"

"Thank you, Carol, and I hope today goes just as well for you."

Danny and Trudy turned and headed out the back corridor to leave.

Danny commented to Trudy, "Just like that, the bill is paid. It is nice to be the boss, no?"

Laughing, "It is, but, for the record, it also comes with some tough decisions to be made. I got lucky and made the right ones."

"Somehow, I think where you are concerned, luck may play a part, but not as much as you let on. You forget I know how smart you are; it is a big part of why I love you, but you already knew that, didn't you?"

Looking directly at him and smiling, he said, "Flattery will get you everywhere."

Arriving at their cars. "See you at Sadie's tomorrow?"

Danny replied, "Wouldn't miss it. See you there."

Chapter 35 - It Is Good to Be the Boss

Trudy made a mental note to thank Darell Cromwell for once again covering the bill for the weekend next Wednesday when they were scheduled to talk. Wednesday had turned out to be the most appropriate time to have a conversation about the state of the company, as it was midweek and provided a good recap of the previous week—especially the weekend when hotels saw an uptick in business. This allowed for an assessment on Monday, a gathering of facts and figures on Tuesday, and by Wednesday, accurate projections could be made and new business addressed with enough time to act on any necessary decisions.

This was not to say that Darell was being micromanaged. On the contrary, and as promised, he had been given free rein to function as necessary when he saw an opportunity and felt he could exploit it for the betterment of the company. It was clear, after speaking with Fred Deursh, Carl Wynn, and Cindy Mathews, that their collaboration with Darell was very much welcomed, as he truly helped each business capitalize on the resources at hand. He had already opened many opportunities on multiple levels for business and expansion. The hotels, which Fred was now overseeing, had grown to three times their original investment number and were still growing.

Darell performed flawlessly as both a symbiotic partner and an adept financial advisor in procurement. They were rapidly closing in on one year since Darell had taken the helm, and Trudy was prepared to triple his onboarding salary based solely on performance. His nurturing of both the advertising and app development divisions was becoming a stable revenue source with no signs of slowing down. He had also begun to analyze other possibilities in service industries that typically catered to hotel chains as well as the private sector. There were potential partnerships in the pipeline.

When Trudy had wondered aloud to him whether there was room in the boutique airline industry, he picked up the ball and ran with it. He slowly allocated funds to the acquisition of twin-engine turboprops, as well as light and medium-sized jets. He also developed a pipeline for pilots and flight attendants. Now, pilots and attendants were reaching out to him because of how well the employees in his service were being treated. Word of mouth was spreading.

TJC now owned three twin-engine turboprops, two light jets, and one medium-sized jet, with plans for future expansion. The small jets remained the busiest, and the returns on the others, even after maintenance and operational costs, were still well above twenty-five percent. This allowed for expansion at a steady, controllable rate. Because the rate of business share was gradually increasing, he was able to keep up with the necessary pilots and crews to maintain readiness with sufficient availability overlap.

He had his sights set on becoming a player in the rental business. As an added bonus, he named it Boutique Air, borrowing the name from Trudy's original request, as he thought it summed up their offering well and worked effectively as an advertisement. He was also overseeing her pet projects and had assured her that the scholarships would be set well into the future.

Chapter 36 - The Army and The Navy Marry

When Sunday rolled around, Danny was already at Sadie's house. They were discussing the upcoming weddings and the food fare. They talked about the wedding cake, and Danny mentioned his ambition to outdo anything he had done so far. He was looking forward to the personal challenge.

Sadie made a strange request when she asked if she could look over Danny's personal recipe book for ideas on the final serving choices. This was only odd to Trudy because, usually, Sadie was very decisive when it came to direction and always thought three steps ahead of everyone. Mama rarely missed a step, no matter the reason. There was absolutely no distrust between Danny and Sadie when it came to the kitchen, so he agreed without hesitation.

The June fourteenth wedding was very apropos for the boys, being Flag Day. The motifs of red, white, and blue were easy to achieve. Both Dana and Tracy came from small military families and had moved frequently while growing up. Their ties were few, so their guest list was limited to a small number of family and friends, mostly family.

Again, as luck would have it, the Athena was in the process of updating its seasonal decor and felt that it could incorporate its main room along the same lines as Flag Day to accommodate the lucky couples. Because both couples were willing to allow the hotel's decor to influence their ceremony, Athena also offered a special room rate for all wedding attendees.

This time, Trudy had to call Fred Duersch to pass along the word that she wanted to remain anonymous with the staff, meaning that if they recognized her, she requested that they keep her presence among the staff only and not make any acknowledgment of her being there. Fred understood her concern and assured her that he would oversee it personally.

The food from the restaurant was unbelievable. They had prepared an array of finger foods for appetizers, followed by a choice of T-bone steak, lobster, lasagna, salad, or any combination of them all. Everything was prepared according to recipe cards and instructions provided by Danny.

At first, the in-house chef was aggravated that someone had altered his offerings—until both a call and the recipes arrived. The first call was a direct discussion with Fred Duersch, who explained the magnitude of their guests. The chef took a deep breath and explored the suggestions before him. Once he reviewed the recipes, he became excited by the sheer simplicity yet extravagance of the dishes. He was wholly impressed when he finally met the person responsible for the menu's inception.

When a double four-tiered cake arrived in a van—connected by intermediate layers that stair-stepped between the two spires, holding the bride and grooms in their separate spaces—the chef gave up on normal altogether. Each cake side reflected the flavor choices of each bride and groom. Red velvet, chocolate, lemon, strawberry, and white cake were connected by different levels of sheet cake, with two sides featuring

German chocolate. Meanwhile, the outer layers were coated in white coconut cream with shaved coconut icing. The entire display was truly spectacular in its layers and presentation.

The only hiccup of the night occurred when Julie's water broke near the last quarter of the evening—but no one even considered it a hiccup, as everyone was too excited for her and Sam.

Sadie gained two daughters and a granddaughter in one evening. At ten forty-three that same night, Sadie Monique Taylor—carrying names that represented both of their families—was introduced to the world.

Everyone was more than happy about the events of the night.

Chapter 37 - Danny Goes to College

By the end of the summer, Trudy had become sullen. She knew that in just a week or so, her best friend and confidant was going away, and though she had Amanda, Nora, Mick, and Dave, it just wasn't going to be the same.

Danny had chosen to attend college in Austin, Texas. Upon graduation, he would enroll in an esteemed culinary program there. He felt the city offered him many benefits—no wintry weather, a great business campus, diversity both within and outside of school, and a booming restaurant industry. There was growth, and there were people looking for diverse offerings in the culinary arts. He believed his Midwest-inspired cuisine would be well received.

Thanks to landing The Young Businessperson Scholarship at school, he was able to go with a full-ride scholarship. It was easy to tell that Mindy Veach was relieved—her son's scholarship had lifted a huge weight off her shoulders. Danny had yet to learn that his flight to Texas was going to be courtesy of Boutique Air.

Sadie was putting together a gathering to wish him well—barbecue ribs, coleslaw, green bean casserole, and, for dessert, his favorite: German chocolate cake with ice cream. Sadie wasn't prepared, however, for the number of people who RSVP'd. Reluctantly, she asked Danny if he would be willing to help "cater" his own party. Danny was excited and gladly pitched in.

Bill had to scramble to find two large smokers, in addition to the one they already had and was more than happy to source enough ribs to fill them all. Danny had touched quite a few lives—through his daily interactions, favors for friends, catering, and cake baking. Nearly seventy people, plus their families, showed up.

Nora, Mick, and Danny volunteered to work the food line while Trudy played hostess, and Sadie supervised the food prep with a helping hand from Danny.

Everyone was having a wonderful time when Bill Jax took the mic on an improvised PA system. He recounted his first meeting with Danny and how impressed he had been with the young man. He praised his work ethic, his abilities, and the hidden talents they were all currently enjoying— prompting a round of applause that made Danny blush.

Bill called him to the "stage" on top of the farm wagon, shook his hand, and, uncharacteristically, pulled him in for a hug. Then, stepping up to the mic, he clearly—and very purposefully—addressed Danny with a name shift.

"Dan."

He let the name change hang in the air.

"I wanted—"

He was joined by Sam, who stepped up to the mic.

"Dan, we wanted—"

"We," Bill said, glancing at Sam, "wanted to thank you and send you on your way. Please accept our gratitude for all your hard work over the last couple of years."

Sam added, "And thank you for the friendship and camaraderie."

Bill continued, "To Dan."

He raised his drink, and everyone followed suit. Directly after the toast, Bill handed him a card.

Sadie took the stage next, and the crowd quieted. She commanded presence and was highly respected in the community.

"When I first met this young man, he told me he was going to be a chef one day," she began. "Kids talk and dream out loud, so I didn't put much weight on it. Then Dan"—she looked right at him, emphasizing his new moniker—"cooked me a meal for the first time, and I was amazed by his skills. After that, he continually impressed me—meal after meal after meal.

"He catered our family's weddings and made quite a few cakes for others in the community—usually at-cost, with a donation to his gas money fund."

Everyone either laughed or clapped.

"The cooking world has someone to look out for."

She held up a book.

"His book of recipes and mine, Dan, they are yours now."

When Sadie borrowed his recipes, she photocopied them and artfully printed them onto individual placards, placing them in an expandable recipe book. She handed it to Dan and, out of earshot of the microphone, told him:

"Dan, the ones of mine are yours now to do with as you see fit. Give them life and make them yours. Be true to yourself, and save me a spot at your table when you can."

Dan had a tear in his eye. "Yes, Mama. Every day," he promised, pulling her into a tight bear hug but being careful not to squeeze too hard.

The microphone was opened for anyone who wanted to speak. Many thanked him for his cake services and fantastic food.

Near the end of the party, Sam approached Trudy, holding the baby in his arms.

"You're really going to miss him, aren't you?"

"I really am, Sam. I wanted to be more prepared, but we've been almost inseparable for the last two years. Then—poof. What do you do with that?"

"School will be starting up soon. Hopefully, that'll be a distraction for you for a while."

"I'm sure it'll help, but there's going to be a big space to fill. Hopefully, we'll find a way to visit."

"He leaves tomorrow?"

"Yeah, I'm driving him to the airport in Evansville in the morning."

"I guess you two are gonna say your goodbyes tonight?"

"Yeah, not sure what we're going to do, though."

She already had plans to visit the cabin one last time.

"Well, I made sure the refrigerator at the cabin is stocked."

He looked Trudy in the eye and winked. Trudy gave him a half-panicked, half-worried look.

"When your dad made me the farm manager, I had perimeter alarms installed to protect from vandals. The razors are GPS-tracked in the event of theft. Don't worry. It isn't my job to babysit you or be your overseer.

"Your dad doesn't know, but if he ever asks, I'm prepared to answer honestly. I know you're too smart to be dumb, and I know Mama wouldn't let you be dumb, either. So, your business is your business. Just make sure you turn the A/C back when you're done, OK?"

"Uh… I don't know what to say other than thank you. And yes, we're being safe—with help from Mama. You never let on. Thank you, Sam."

She half-hugged him and rested her head on his shoulder, careful not to disturb the sleeping baby.

"Older brothers can really be cool, you know?"

Laughing, Sam said, "Go on and get out of here. We'll clean up the mess."

"Thank you, Sam! You really are the best."

Everyone had dissipated, and Trudy grabbed Dan by the hand and announced she was going to take him for one last ride around the farm and that they would see everyone later. Both headed for the barn and were heard driving off in a razor. Dave, Amanda, Nora, and Mick all had a good idea of what was going to happen next but were part of the cleanup crew that had formed impromptu around them, so they joined in.

Trudy parked the razor on the beach, almost in the exact spot they had parked in that first day. Both kicked off their shoes and socks and walked out to the edge of the water. Neither one of them spoke but just held hands. Danny bent down, picked up a stone, and skipped it into the water. Trudy laughed and found one of her own and skipped one more time than Danny's rock.

"Oh yeah," Looking for a rock and locating and retrieving it, he gave it a zing, and it skipped the same number of times as Trudy's.

"How is that?"

While Dan was throwing, she was looking and found the ultimate stone, flat, weighty, and just the right physical size, and whizzed it just as hard as she could, causing it to get two more skips beyond the recent best before sinking out of sight.

"What about that?"

"Give me a second."

He migrated down the beach in search of an optimal choice; finding one of similar size and flatness, he reared back and let it fly; he watched as it managed to barely get yet one more skip in but, just barely, leaving room for the mock argument he knew would come.

"Beat that!"

There was no answer, no witty rash reply, so he turned to look at Trudy. There was a pile of clothes on the beach and a very naked Trudy standing in the doorway, just like the first day.

"Well?"

Leaving the question hanging there just like the first day. Danny smiled, stopped by Trudy's' pile of clothes, and disrobed right there. He was still every bit the sight she had remembered from the first day, and she flushed wet while watching him make his way to her. When he reached her, she grabbed him by the hand and led him inside to the bedroom, both of them completely silent. She pulled back the covers, pushed him onto the bed backward, and crawled beside him.

"Dan, not Danny? I am going to have to get used to that, but I like it. Dan, out of all the things we have done right here, I am about to give you my best. You know, from that first time, you have always respected me and liked me with or without the sex. I have to say that I have felt the same way about you. Right now, I want to mix them both together, so let me do this my way. I have always been your Tru. Nothing has changed; nothing is going to change."

Trudy smiled at him and reached down and pulled the covers over them to combat the AC. She reached under the covers to find what had been full was now fully hard. When her hand caressed gently under his sack and up his shaft, any sign of not being fully hard had been eradicated. She rolled up to a straddling position and pulled the covers up over her shoulders; she lifted herself ever so gently and without hardly any struggle due to familiarity. She carefully aligned on his rock-hard dick and sat slowly down to his depth fully and completely and leaned forward and hugged his chest and nestled into him, wrapped in each other's arms.

They lay there unmoving for five minutes or more, neither saying a thing while absorbing each other's heartbeat through their connection. They throbbed a silent message of longing and oneness for the other. It was Trudy who broke the calm when she slowly and with mediated determination pulled up until his head was shrouded in labia, and she just as slowly and determined sat back down and repeated this. She kept her action steady and slow with a dogged determination to bring him to climax without him moving a muscle.

She, on the other hand, was working her pelvic floor, clenching him on the upstroke and releasing for the down every so often, reversing and clenching on the way down and releasing on the way up. He came with a flood in under six minutes. When he came, she sat on him fully, deeply, completely, feeling every strained release as he spasmed and ejaculated deep in her. She waited for his cock to quit convulsing and, like a tantric queen, began to pull at his root with her vaginal muscular control.

Her muscles started deep inside her and clenched his glans and, in a wave of squeezing muscles, worked their way up to the base of his dick. By the third time she did this, the sensations were causing him to shimmy and shake with her every contraction as her muscles moved along his shaft. He could hardly take it; as he fought to control himself, he swelled in a matter of seconds and came hard again. His body thrashed him about with every little micro movement of a muscular change, yet she had not moved physically from sitting there staring him right in the eyes.

When he finally regained his composure, he realized that they had connected beyond a physical plane and that he had his first emotion-driven orgasm. She stopped moving both inside and out and folded herself into his arms.

"I really am going to miss you too."

He felt a few tears drop onto his chest, so he held her tighter in their embrace. They stayed inside this bare, intimate space with each other for a long time.

The next move was from Dan. He lifted her to a kneeling position and, from below, began an arduous trudge bottoming out in an upward motion; changing direction, he took forty-five seconds or more to make a complete stroke. His stroke was meticulously slow, and it was imperceptibly speeding up. By the time his full stroke had been completed in three seconds, her labia were incredibly engorged, her clitoris was begging to be touched more frequently, and her insides felt as if she were aglow. When he crossed over the one-second per stroke line, her breathing was noticeably more ragged and labored. Still incrementally increasing in speed, when he passed two strokes per second, her body was building into a massive reaction. He crossed three and a half strokes per second, and she knew she was about to launch in a fashion that they really had not adequately explored. He felt the changes in her as well as heard them, too.

At first, it felt like a beautiful come getting ready to be released, a very satisfying encounter, but as her first wave signaled its arrival with the beginnings of a clench, Dan released the throttle to run sensually deep and balls out. His balls were flailing her at more than four strokes a second from the bottom; she was crying tears of incredible elation, and her body was convulsing. The muscles deep in her vagina were spasming at an unbelievable rate and being pushed further to their limit with every thrust driven gloriously deep in her.

She thrashed in unbridled ecstasy, thumping and pounding downward on

his advancing cock. She lay forward and whimpered as her lower torso moved on its own volition. Dan stopped his movements suddenly, but she quaked on for two minutes or more. Just when she felt toleration being within her grasp, Dan thrust forward without a word and fucked into her as if his only escape was pounding directly through her.

Her body convulsed and tightened up so tight that her face began to turn

red under the uncontrollable onslaught. Her pussy sprayed around his shaft as she came hard and destroyed whatever sanity she thought she had left. He pulled out of her hard and fast as she continued to squirt for three hard blasts, soaking everything around her. Both breathlessly fell together in a sweaty mass, tangled with each other once again. They drifted off to sleep, physically and deeply emotionally spent. They were awakened an hour later when the AC overcame the heat of their bodies.

Dan ribbed Trudy, "We should have recorded that…for…uh…reference later."

She jokingly replied, "You are such a perv."

"Tru, I really will miss you, the cabin, the lake, everything. Do I have to go?"

"I'm going to miss you too. Now shut up and come wash my hair and body one last time."

"Absolutely!"

Danny had made his rounds on the farm, saying goodbye to Bill and Paula, followed by Sam and Jessie, along with Sadie Monique. His hardest goodbye by far was unexpected by him, but Sadie's warm embrace and love cut him deeply and, for some reason, shook him to the core. He had said his goodbyes and, with very unexpected tears, promised he would stay in touch.

He met the gang at his house. Dave and Mick were stoic about it, but everyone could tell it was not easy for them. Nora shed quite a few tears of joyful remorse. Mindy hugged him tightly and made him promise to call once a week. Trudy reminded him that there was a "wayward" group at his college that raised funds for financially strapped students to fly back home every so often and that he better join the group when he got there, or she would kill him.

Dan was lost as to what she had been talking about and was on the verge of questioning it when he caught a "look" from Trudy, and the lights came on, and he promised he would join as soon as possible. Trudy threw him the keys and headed for the passenger door. Dan kissed and hugged his mother one more time, who watched the Jeep pull away. After they were out of sight, she openly cried as a mother often does. She was comforted by the group who accompanied her inside. No more had they gotten inside and settled back in; there was a knock at the door.

Melinda answered the door to a pizza boy with five large pizzas and breadsticks with various toppings. They had a card taped to the top of it. Confused, she said we didn't order…. The pizza boy cut her off and said, "We know you didn't order it, Dan did. He is a friend of mine, too, and it has all been paid for. Enjoy. The pizza guy wouldn't accept a tip as he said it had already been handled, so he turned and left. Mindy opened the card. "Tell them all to eat up. It's not as good as my pizza, but it's close,' Mindy dropped the card and balled. Amanda retrieved the card off the ground as everyone else comforted Danny's mom; she finished reading it aloud, "I love you, Mom!"

Two empty lines later, it began again, "Tell mom to stop crying, it'll be alright."

Directly after that, there was another brief knock as three ladies let themselves in; it was Mindy's shopping group two hours early. They had each gotten a wonderful request in the form of a card to lend support to his mother on this day at this time. She hugged her friends for their care. The kids killed three pizzas, and the women finished their lunch and left three-quarters of a mixed pizza combined into one remaining box. The two groups said goodbye to each other, and the shopping group helped Mindy get ready to go out.

The road to Evansville oftentimes can be boring from the backroads of Illinois. There are long patches of road when you see no other cars for miles, and today was no different, except there had almost been a wreck not even ten miles away from Dan's house when Trudy had unzipped his pants and freed his cock to the open air. He stood full, but when she leaned over and sucked him into the base, he became hard in a New York second.

Her head had bumped the wheel on an upstroke and caused a swerve. With one hand, he pulled backward on the switch, and the seat floated backward an inch to give her more space to use. He had to concentrate on maintaining his road awareness, often using about half of the other side on the narrow two-lane.

He was doing a decent job holding on even though she was doing her level best to make him succumb to her charm. She had taken a cue from Amanda's playbook and was "orbiting" his head in an incredible floating circle, accosting his glans. With her tongue, she was caressing the undershaft by cupping his meat with a warm embrace just before slowly and methodically taking him down her throat, all the while massaging his balls in a rhythmic fashion gently with her hand. Just as slowly as she had when she went all the way down, she teased his manhood, pulling the full of the meat forward as she rose until his shaft skin cleared her throat and rebounded.

The torture would begin once more when she orbited the glans again and sucked him in with the most incredible negative pressure that almost slurped him in slow motion. It sent electric shocks through his system, starting at the tip of his rock-hard erection, straight through his jewels and onto his brain in microseconds. Driving had become intense.

A half of a mile from the Wabash River bridge, he could not hold out any more as her will and expert cock sucking abilities started to get the better of him. On the approach to the bridge, he felt it begin; she had felt it too; there was no need to warn her, nor was he inclined to. Since she was destroying him systematically, he was going to fight back any way he could, and no warning at all seemed like the best option at the time. She had been sucking him well for about the last twenty miles when he busted his nut, coming in a molten torrent, hard and fast.

The volume surprised even him when the first spasm broke loose; he had just reached the pinnacle of the bridge. He thought to himself, it was all downhill from here, and he was right. His shot was forceful in her mouth, but she knew it would be and was ready for it. This was not his normal release; this was somehow different as the first jet made a slight pressure bulge in her mouth; she struggled at first to keep up with the first two jets of his juice. After she had caught up, she captured the remaining spurts easily. She tasted him with delight and only wished she could make him double his output, but as it was, for the last event with him for who knows how long, it was perfect.

As they made their way off the bridge, it was, in all practical terms, over. She knew there was no more to extract from him but stayed down on him to finish her cleaning and to tease him just a little bit more, which ended up teasing herself twice as much as it did him. She wanted to straddle him while driving and feel his manhood buried in her dick home but knew that was not going to happen.

She made a mental note to warn Amanda of how horny she was and that she was going to need a little extra attention when she got home. Five minutes later, she took the wheel and let him hump upward and put everything away and get as comfortable as he could until he deflated. The rest of the drive was sexually uneventful but great for reminiscing and extending their friendship.

When they got to the airport, they bypassed the commercial lanes and headed to the private hangars. Dan looked inquisitively as to what was going on and slowly realized he was flying privately. Trudy delighted in explaining Darell's prowess in acquisition and explained that there were opportunities to come home more frequently than he had anticipated. They got out of the car and walked into the private line counter. She met up with Boutique Airs' pilots Ian French and Clay Waters.

Ian came from the Navy as a fighter jet jockey with three different airframes under his belt. His family life had taken a beating due to the amount of time separated from them, so he had retired at his earliest opportunity with a full pension. Through a fortuitous encounter at an airport, Darell and he had met, and a relationship was born. Clay was in the Air Force and answered a professional request for an application to a professional affiliation website. He was a widower with three grown children scattered across the country.

Salary and hours were worked out, and most importantly for Ian, family time was enhanced even though he was away at odd hours. Clay enjoyed the motion of it all and the opportunity to visit his kids through work assignments. The hours were well telegraphed, and the "air traffic control" at Boutique Air was being expertly choreographed by the new corporate scheduler, Jeanie Campbell.

All the pilots referred to her as Genie C. because she had the ability to foresee issues in front of their assignments and, like a genie, solve them before they were an issue. It made their dealing in and out of the airports and hotel stays seem like a dream. She took it for the compliment it inferred.

The fourteen pilots in the queue were treated with the utmost respect. More importantly, their availability was diverse and varied, so finding a pilot for any given run was not really a challenge at all. There were many overnighters due to the nature of the runs, and if there was not an Athena Hotel available, the expediter had already made arrangements for a flawless stay in a five-star hotel. If there was an Athena, they were treated like royalty. Often, they rubbed shoulders with their passengers in lobbies and restaurants. Their proximity to potential clients had been ultimately good for business. As it was, the boutique travel business had taken off and had shown no signs of waning.

Trudy was just as excited to see one of TJCs' jets. They owned three now, along with two turboprops. Darell had done his research and was able to buy two of them at a ridiculously lowered price from the government as narcotics confiscations and one from a corporation upgrading their fleet. The turboprops came from the private market and were acquired with favorable pricing after negotiation. Overall, the fleet was worth more than thirteen million dollars at face value, but Darell had invested a commitment for six million and change, using the fleet itself as collateral, and there were only two million dollars of actual capital involved.

The boutique nature of the business kept the planes busy just from the personal private market. There were also corporate agreements that were being developed that would further enhance their cash position. It turned out to be an excellent investment that was already paying for itself fivefold.

Both pilots welcomed them cordially and invited Mr. Veach and Mrs. Jax aboard. Dan was in awe of the accommodations, and Trudy made a mental note to renegotiate Darell's' salary in his favor yet more still. Dan and Trudy kissed inside the jet and reluctantly parted. Ian and Clay both thanked Ms. Jax for using Boutique Air and boarded as she cleared the tarmac to the private counter desk. Trudy was excited and sad all at the same time as she watched Dan lift off and bank out toward Texas. Dan was in total blissful disbelief at the accommodations. In flight, one of the pilots left the cockpit to welcome Dan.

Ian inquired, "Mr. Veach, would you like to have a seat up front?"

"Please, call me Dann…uhh…Dan."

"Well, Dan, are you interested?"

"Oh, hell yes, I can't believe Trudy owns this plane; it is so cool."

"Trudy?"

"Trudy Jax, that was her back at… Shit."

"Is something wrong?"

"I kinda spilled the beans; she is going to kill me; she wants to keep her name clear and free until."

"Until what?"

"Until she gets out of high school, at least; she is really gonna kill me if this gets out."

With Clay listening in, "Ms. Jax back there owns this plane, and she is still in high school?"

"Technically, her company, TJC, does, but yeah. Can you guys please keep this under your hat? I don't want to die young. She will most definitely kill me if she finds out."

Loudly, "Clay?"

"I didn't hear anything, did you?"

Ian continued, "Mr. Veach…Uh Dan, would you like to sit up front for a bit?"

"Oh, hell yes." Beaming a smile of understanding like they just rebooted.

The direct flight to Austin was incredibly smooth and enjoyable, and not once did he have to take off his shoes or get strip searched. The pilots reassured him they heard nothing and thanked him for flying Boutique Air. He was met at the other end of the airport by the 'scholarship facilitator' who drove him to his new domicile on the edge of campus, within walking distance from the main facilities. The house was set up as well as anyone could hope for.

It had been an incredible day for Trudy, one that signaled changes in the extremely near future. Her emotions were all over the place: up because her friend was going to college, down because he left, up when she was able to physically walk into the fruit of her endeavors, down because she could not leave with Dan, and up because she had a wonderful family and friends.

Overall, she felt like she could not complain, and yet she felt like she had a hole in her heart.

Chapter 38 - Making Waves

When Trudy arrived home, Amanda was waiting for her. She had passed up going out to eat with Bill and her mom, knowing Trudy would be home soon, and out of earnest love, care, and concern, she wanted to be there for her. When Trudy walked into the door, she was met by Amanda at the bottom of the stairs, who was wearing a silken nighty top and boy-style panties. Not a word was spoken, but when Amanda wrapped her in her warm and loving embrace, she cried heartily on her shoulder for a long minute. When she had recovered herself, Amanda led her up to "their" room and locked the doors. She lovingly stripped Trudy, and as she stood there bare naked, she stripped herself and led Trudy once again, but this time to the shower. The hot water was barely tolerable, just like she liked it, and Amanda took her time washing her hair and conditioning it.

While she let the hair treatment set in, she gently washed her face and her back, followed by her stomach and breasts. She followed up with a cleaning of her patch and lower torso, making her way down to her legs and feet. When she had cleansed every part of her body, she stood and dipped Trudy's' head back into the stream and began a rinse that encompassed her whole body, leaving her clean and refreshed once again. After she had finished rinsing her, she hugged Trudy in a loving embrace under the water, saying she all but knew her pain. She kissed her deeply and passionately to express her feelings to her.

Trudy stepped out of the shower first and retrieved a towel, but instead of drying it off, she received Amanda on her way out and dried her.

Amanda's smile of appreciation said volumes between the two sisters. Grabbing another towel, she returned the care and concern, leaving only two wet-headed girls standing in front of the mirror.

Amanda stared Trudy right in the eyes through the mirror and wrapped her in a loving embrace that resulted in her arms being crossed over each other and the respective hands cupping Trudy's breasts. Her nipples were already hard from the sheen of water evaporating from her skin. Her nipples stood out further in response to the fire-like heat contained in Amanda's palms that were now supporting her. Amanda leaned forward a bit and half sucked, and half kissed the middle of her neck just above her shoulder, all while her left hand drifted down to her sex and cupped her vulva, while the other teased her nipple that she still had captured.

Trudy arched back into her, eyes closed but clearly now in a different space than she had come home with. She let herself flow into the stream and followed Amanda back to the bed as she led the way. Amanda was all the sexual being anyone could want if they let her be their desire. She was fearless, strong, and passionate. She exemplified what it meant to own your own person. Trudy felt her strength when she asked her for support in coming out to her mother. Trudy had waited silently in the wings in the event she needed that support and was in awe as she expressed herself to her mother.

She confessed that she did not think she felt like the other girls in her class because she liked to kiss the boys, but she felt kissing a girl was equally fulfilling. Paula hugged her and simply said that she had always been a strong young woman with her own direction, that it did not matter what the world thought as long as you do you. Her love would never sway in any regard, and she was always available for a talk on any subject. When she noticed Trudy nearby, she beckoned her in with her arm for a group hug. Things went quiet when Bill entered the room.

"I'm fairly sure I've done nothing wrong, but as a measure of safety, I'm going to retreat because three women going silent when you walk in can't be a good sign. I'm not gonna wake up beside a hole out in the middle of the farm somewhere…am I?"

Paula spoke up while laughing, "You don't have to worry about that; I mean, really, you think you would wake up?"

The girls laughed aloud, "Really, it's nothing to be concerned with … we were just." Amanda finished the sentence. "Actually, uh…Dad."

Using the word DAD captured Paula and Bill's attention as she had never actually referred to him this way. "I was telling Mom that basically, I think I'm …well, bisexual."

A long minute went by in silence while the girls tried to gauge Bill's non-reaction. After another eternity, Amanda broke the silence. "What do you think about that?"

Furling his brow and pursing his lips several times as if he were conjuring up the right words, they all watched for about thirty seconds pensively in anticipation as to how he felt on the subject. After a long moment of silence, he spoke.

"I was wondering when this conversation would take place. To be honest, I was more concerned about how your mother would take it. We had never talked about the subject in general, and I didn't want to bring it up for obvious reasons."

Paula looked at him incredulously, "What obvious reasons are you talking about?"

"Paula? Really?"

He looked at Amanda and Trudy as if they would explain it all to him, and he continued. "I have known our daughters were bisexual for about a year now."

Everyone's eyes went wide in a combination of surprise and disbelief.

"If you can't see the way those two look at each other at times, it's more than just a sister thing. I had my doubts at first, but there were a few other signs."

"Like what?" Paula asked.

"Ok, what sisters want a door between their rooms before they even get to know each other well? And some other things."

"Biiilllll??"

"When I hear a noise that isn't right, I slip out of bed, check out the house, and check on the girls to make sure everything is safe. More than once, I have found one or the other of the girls in the other's bed."

"Girls do that. They get to talking, and if they fall asleep, the other just leaves them be."

"Yeah, yeah, that's what I thought too, but then there are also the monthly bills."

"This one has got to be good. So, Mr. Detective, how would the monthly bills indicate anything?"

"Actually, they really don't directly indicate anything, but when the power consumption in a cabin is much higher than it ought to be, an investigation is warranted."

Both girls looked nervously at each other.

"So, I did some checking in my free time."

"And just what did that prove?"

Looking at the two nervous girls, he stepped forward, drew them into a close hug, and said in the most loving voice, "It's OK, but both of you need to know that it's best to close the curtains when you're on the first floor of any building. So, I have known our girls were bisexual for about a year now."

"But that may just mean…"

He cut her off. "Paula, dear, they were not alone."

Both girls flushed red. Bill turned to them and finished, "I saw enough to know there wasn't a power problem, just a glimpse and nothing more. That is your business. If there was a problem, I'm sure Sadie would have told me. Nothing gets by her; she is sharp as a tack, and nowhere near the prude her daughters think she is. Afternoon talks with her are just wonderful."

"And you didn't think to tell me?"

"Wasn't mine to tell. I knew they would be right here where they are now when the time was right. I'm just hoping that Trudy isn't mad that I outed her as well. I am sorry, baby, but there really isn't any way to talk about Amanda without you as well."

"Oh, Daddy, I'm not mad. I just didn't want to disappoint you."

"I could never be embarrassed about you, and I certainly could never be disappointed as long as you do you."

All the girls laughed in unison, confusing Bill.

Paula was still laughing as she informed him, "I just told Amanda those exact same words. I guess great minds truly do think alike."

Turning to Trudy, she said, "How long have you two… uh?"

"Much by happenstance, two weeks before I met you."

Looking at Amanda, she said, "She was so scared her dad would find out."

Paula quipped, talking through an acknowledging laugh, "Yep, his head is gonna explode."

"But we will be right there, so there is nothing for you to be afraid of—not now, not ever. You both are safe here. And Dave and Dan?"

Trudy asked, "Just what exactly did you see?"

"Nope, it's not like that. It was just the occasional same look you two give each other from a distance when you think no one is looking. I was confused at first because you and Dan were so tight. I figured you two had been together."

His forehead raised along with his eyebrows as if to say he already knew that. "I mean, really, I'm not dumb… but at first, it was a curveball. It was like a light went on when everything, all of it, just fell into place in my head. I figured you would come and talk if you needed to. And since I'm not really good at this, I just waited for you to come to me.

"I figured only a zebra knows if it is black with white stripes or white with black stripes. I'm sure it only matters to someone on the outside looking in since he couldn't change himself even if he wanted to. It is exactly what it is, and nobody can change that. That is why I just left it alone and saw it for what it was. Like I said before, you two do you."

Bill turned to head for the door as if nothing significant had happened. "Is anyone else hungry? I'm going for lunch."

The trio looked on in half amazement as Bill walked to the door like he had just completed an easy task. Paula felt even closer to him than she had before, learning just how big of a heart her big dumb galoot had. She was smiling on the inside to the depths of her core as she followed the girls to the truck because she was starving as well.

Chapter 39 - School Restarts

The five in the tight-knit group became even closer as the school year started. Dave and Mick hung out quite a lot but also made a point of being around the others. Nora was happy because she had a source for her dick in the form of Mick and Dave collectively and had absolutely no qualms sharing either of them—or both. Whether it was as a group, one-on-one, or her personal favorite, two-on-one, her hardest decision when it came to threesomes was which combination she liked better. She finally settled on whichever one she was most interested in that day. Amanda and Trudy had free rein with each other but kept to an unspoken agreement to keep it self-contained.

They all found that the hard classes they had taken as juniors were the most difficult they would experience for the rest of school, and that was already behind them. They weren't sure if they had matured, making things a little easier to endure, or if maybe the scholastic plan was to let up on the seniors just a bit. No matter the cause, it all just came easier to them.

They had all made a commitment to befriend three incoming freshmen as a project of sorts, remembering how tough it had been for them. They turned heads when they collectively left the "senior" corner of the world in the cafeteria and parked themselves as individual islands intermingled in the "lost" section, opening up for questions.

Their friends all watched on, afterward asking, "What the fuck?" The answer they got helped them understand what they had done. Most of their friends thought it was cool. The next day, a quarter of the seniors had moved to new positions. By Wednesday, half of the class had been displaced, shifting the dynamic. By Friday, almost all the seniors had adopted a freshman friend for a month. Some doubled up, but the whole freshman group had a wing over them. Many of the relationships would turn out to last all school year.

Trudy was seen as a legend of sorts among the incoming girls, as the self-defense program had been disseminated and embellished. After all the exaggeration about what really happened that day had settled, the new story was outlandishly good.

Ryan had recovered from the coma she had put him in, but he had to move schools to accommodate his wheelchair more comfortably. And although he still needed help using the restroom, he was getting better. There would be versions and embellishments to this story for years to come.

Regardless of the story, the football team did not like the reputation they had received and wanted to clear things up. During an after-practice brainstorming session—where the weirdest to the most solemn suggestions were made to improve the team's reputation and image—one realistic option stood out for the team to pursue.

By the end of the following week, an unofficial club had been started. Posters were made, and the My Brother's Keeper network of students was initiated. The basics were simple and clear. If you followed Ryan's Rules, you would be fine:

No means no.

Upon a breakup, a no-touch and no-call requirement took effect for one full week.

Whether you are a guy or a girl, if you feel threatened in any way, find a senior sponsor who will shed light on the options to the offending party, backed by a wall of human monitors across all areas of the school.

Hurting anyone to gain sex will result in a wrath yet unknown.

If you cross any line after a social trial, the police will be called.

At first, some of the guys felt this was beyond what they had to comply with, but after a complete explanation by many more than just the football team's guys, the recipients of the friendly advice usually decided the rules were more than fair. My Brother's Keeper remained at the school as a solely student-controlled quasi-club run by and for the students.

By the second year of My Senior Sponsor—which had been started by Nora, Mick, Amanda, and Trudy—it was embraced by faculty and became a beginning-of-the-school-year tradition. It was introduced in the cafeteria in week one. No other school had the interclass relationships that theirs did. The two programs together were cited numerous times as reasons for school transfers and district moves.

The principal and those to come after him enjoyed better attendance, smoother school relations, and better funding due to student participation—all thanks to the initial commitment by four friends to better the school.

Chapter 40 - New Blood

About halfway through the school year, Mick asked Nora if she had liked Dan's cock that much better because of his size. Nora was afraid her answer was going to be offensive, so she responded that she loved how he used his dick and that she would always enjoy him being in her. After her assurances, she continued telling him that, for her, occasionally, more was better. He laughed and assured her that he was not offended. He had asked her the question because he happened to see something today that might be of interest to her. She was intrigued and asked him to explain.

"Two words, sis—Larry Dill."

"The football center?"

"Yep. Not that I was particularly looking, but he might be bigger than Danny. I thought of you."

"Really? Why?"

"I know we have a good time, and I can give you good orgasms, but with Dan, you were unhinged, so I thought, why not him?"

Nora told him she would think about it.

The next day in the hall, she caught up with Trudy and Amanda and relayed what Mick had said, asking them what they thought about it. Everyone was concerned about what Larry would say and how much he would keep to himself. Amanda was the first to come up with the idea, and as she passed it on, the other girls agreed that it was a viable route.

It was a simple idea—they were going to triple-team him and wear his dick out. Afterward, they would make it clear that if he said a peep, they would express how terrible the experience was. One girl saying it was a disgruntled relationship, two bad luck, but three saying it? There must be some truth to it. They felt like it just might work. It was up to Nora to put things in motion since she had him in her next class.

Nora accepted the challenge with delight and unbuttoned one more button on her blouse, asking Amanda to help her with her bra clasp. Through the fabric of her shirt, the clasp was released, and she worked her arms in and out of her blouse, removing it from the front. After she readjusted herself, she deposited the bra in her purse to put it back on after class. The freedom and the fabric made her nipples begin to stand, but the shirt type allowed decent concealment even without the bra.

Trudy saw what she was after, as she could almost see her nipple through the side, and warned her,

"You need to go now before we have to skip class altogether."

Nora smiled. "I must be ready, then." She turned away to go to class.

She sat next to Larry in Economics, so her access was assured. She had accidentally bumped into her desk so that it slightly angled, then sat in her chair just a little crossways and purposely leaned forward just a bit.

The view from the side was spectacular. From a lower angle and from the side, her complete nipple was in view. The best part was that the only one who had a view of it was Larry. From the front, it was hardly noticeable, as she had leaned forward so her blouse bagged outward. Out of the corner of her eye, she could tell that Larry was more than a bit distracted. Without looking directly, she could see he was uncomfortable, shifting in his seat for more personal space.

There was a fine art to the show—little accelerations and quick stops—and with every "accidental" movement, her breasts snapped back to their designated space, but the sway was noticeable if you were looking. It was clear that Larry was looking and trying his best not to appear to be looking intently, but he was.

Occasionally, she casually glanced in his direction, "oblivious" to his labored position, and smiled a warm, pleasant, unknowing smile at him. Larry was starting to sweat in the midst of trying to navigate class.

When class ended, she acted as if nothing was amiss and left. She knew his locker was just two cubes from hers, so she waited—or rather, was busy doing absolutely nothing in her locker. When he arrived, she acknowledged him audibly for the first time.

"Larry, I don't know about you, but how do you get through Econ? It is so boring. If we weren't on the first floor, I would have considered jumping out the window. How do you manage?"

"I just let myself daydream or look for a distraction, but yeah… boring."

She had already caught him trying to steal another peek. Her nipples pressed hard through the fabric while she was standing upright and facing him. He had already gotten into his locker and half-turned his hips away. Nora knew she was tormenting him mentally.

"Can I ask you a question?"

"Sure, what do you want to know?"

She pulled her shoulders back ever so slightly as if begging for him to peek—which he clearly was trying hard not to do.

"You have been right beside my locker for the last three years. Why haven't you ever asked me out? What is wrong with me?"

"NOTHING is wrong with you! You're gorgeous. I just figured I wouldn't stand a chance, so I avoided it. Rejection sucks." He laughed a little nervously. "Why? Did you want to go out?"

"I'm not going to make it that easy for you. You have to actually ask."

He shifted with extreme unease. "Uh…" Feigning his best-forced smile, he continued, "Nora? Would you like to maybe go out with me?"

"Nope."

His self-esteem was beginning to implode when Nora spoke again.

"I wouldn't LIKE to go out with you—I would LOVE to go out with you."

Larry's eyes lit up, his face broke into a smile, and he beamed. "Awesome! Uh, dinner and a movie Friday?"

"Dinner sounds good. Afterward, we can play it by ear. What do you think—maybe a drive or something?"

"That would be great."

Larry was one hundred and ninety pounds of complete farm-boy muscle. Broad shoulders, gray eyes, handsome, five-foot-ten. Everyone said he was strong as an ox; he played center for the football team as well as a lineman on defense. It was a rarity that someone got around him, and when they did, he made them pay for every inch of ground. On the defensive line, the opposing team quarterback had better know how to scramble because his farm-boy frame had all but squashed the quarterback at least once a game.

It was not unusual for two of the opposing team members to be assigned to block him—oftentimes, that was not enough.

As tough as he was, Nora could see the joy, a happiness that had seeped through to the surface when she said yes. It had taken her aback. She reminded herself to discuss this with the others because he was truly a gentle giant right now, and she wanted no part in jading that.

Chapter 41 - A Night to Remember

There was an in-depth discussion about how to treat Larry. It had been decided that they would be honest with him on all fronts. Nora was still going to go out with him because she did, in earnest, like him, but now his innocent sweetness drew her in as well. She was looking forward to the date, although she was nervous about explaining their position.

Larry picked her up at six—actually, he was about five minutes early—and sat in the living room talking to Mick while they waited for her to finish getting ready. She came down dressed to the nines, and even Mick was caught off guard. Larry audibly said, "Wow!" before trying to check any over-enthusiasm that was beaming through his smile.

"You look fantastic, Nora. Are we still going out?"

"Don't be silly. This is for you—I'm all yours."

A quick glance at Mick, who had a "this boy is in trouble" look on his face.

"You really look fantastic, sis."

Looking at Larry, knowing full well they were the same age, Mick smirked. "You kids have fun now."

Larry chuckled. "Does he always give you a tough time? I could talk to him if you like. I am my brother's keeper, you know."

Mick, stout for his size—athletic and solid—but standing next to Larry, was quite diminished in stature. Nora smiled at them both, then looked at Mick.

"No need; I can take him all night long."

Larry laughed aloud. "I'm sure you could—you seem very able to me."

Catching the play on words in stride, Mick played along.

"If you try it, you'll be going down and begging me to let you up." Looking at Larry, he added, "She's my big sister by about two months, and still, she thinks she can boss me around."

"We'll see you later."

Mick opened and held the door for Nora. Larry nervously reached for her hand, and she took it, walking with him to his truck.

"I know it isn't all that fancy, but I was wondering if Applebee's would be OK?"

"I don't need fancy, Larry, and I really like Applebee's, so yeah, let's go."

After he helped her into the passenger side, he rounded the front, hopped in, started his truck, and headed to town with a smile. They talked while they ate, and the more they talked, the more she liked him.

He wanted to go to college to become a botanist. More directly, his dream was to work with hybrids to feed the world. He liked farming but felt he could do the world good by combining a love for the ground and science to grow better. After he had told her of his desires, he followed it up with a request to keep that to herself. He said he preferred to keep things close to the vest. He also admitted that she unnerved him a bit because he had never told anyone his dream like that except for some family—but she just felt comfortable to talk to.

They had finished their meal, and he paid the bill with cash. When they made it to the truck, Nora suggested a drive in the country, so she began to give him turn-by-turn directions to meander. Yet, every change in direction brought them closer to the cabin. The last turn to nowhere dead-ended at a cabin.

"Oh no—end of the road. Let me turn this thing around."

"No, wait."

She reached over and turned the ignition backward, and the truck sputtered, then became silent, still in gear.

"Before we leave here, there are a few things you should know. The first is that I'm terribly sorry for not seeing you for who you were at first, but now I have very different eyes."

"What do you mean?"

"I will tell you what I mean, but first, can I ask you some very personal questions? I promise never to repeat what you say."

"You're not some moon-crazed female serial killer, are you?" he asked, trying to lighten up a darkening conversation.

"I promise I will make better sense in a moment, but it might help to have a few answers first."

"You can ask, but I may not answer," he said, getting a touch more serious.

"I will ask you all my questions, and you can answer any way you want."

"OK, fire away."

"Are you a virgin? Are you straight, bi, or gay? Have you ever had a threesome? If you could be with more than one woman at a time, would you? Can you keep a secret? I'm sorry I'm being so blunt, but you're not what I expected at all. It is—rather, YOU are—uncommonly refreshing."

"What did you think I was?"

"I made the mistake of thinking you were just some dumb football jock. I'm completely wrong about that."

"Really?" He laughed and shook his head. "No, I'm not a virgin. As far as I know, I'm straight. Never had a threesome but have a fantasy about it… uh, two other girls, that is. And yes, I can keep a secret. Most of my teammates think I'm a dumb jock, too. I think that about covers it. Now it's my turn. Are you a virgin? Are you straight, bi, or lesbian? Have you ever had a threesome? Do you like dumb football jocks? Why are we outside this cabin? And why did you really want to go out with me?"

"Fair is fair. I'm not a virgin. I am very much bisexual. I have had more than a threesome with boys and girls. I like my men with a good smattering of intelligence. I asked you out because my brother noticed something he thought I would like about you. And there are two naked women inside the cabin, hoping you will follow me in."

"Wait, what is it your brother noticed? Who is inside? Am I going to be a laughingstock at school on Monday? Do you really like my mind?"

She liked the method and candor of the interaction. It had an air of playfulness yet was astonishingly efficient.

"My brother… uh, well, he knows I like a man who is, well… hung. You only get to know who is inside if you come in. I—we, for that matter—would never kiss and tell, regardless of if we do anything or not. Tonight—tonight has me wondering if I want to share you at all."

"How do you and your friends keep something like this quiet?"

"It is a small group who keep to themselves; mostly, we have what we want but have lost something that we were fond of. You fit the bill, and we were going to really rock your world in a blur, but we decided we could not do that to you because we would not want that done to us. It must be your decision whether we go in or not."

Larry finished putting the truck in park and restarted the truck; just when Nora thought he was going to turn and drive away, he aimed the truck at the porch and parked within a few feet of the door. He got out of the truck and walked around to the other door, opened it, and gently grabbed hold of Nora's waist, lifted her down to the ground, and took her hand.

"Thank you for the honesty; I have noticed that it is hard to come by these days."

As they approached the door, he stopped and looked at Nora.

"Should I close my eyes or something?"

"Only if you want to."

They opened the door to an empty living room space, but as the door closed, Amanda appeared from the bedroom in a sheer teddy. Her body was hot, tight, and perky in all the right places. His eyes opened wide, but there were temporary communication issues with his manhood. He surmised that it was the odd state of events. He had wanted Nora badly from the first glance and accidental view of her spectacular breast and nipple, but now here was a hotty, perfect in every way, with hardly a stitch of clothes on, and his mind and body were confused. Nora had drifted to the rear of him and wrapped her arms around his waist. One hand had drifted down, and she could tell that he was full; she was in the middle of a caress right up the center of his manhood when Trudy turned the corner in a tight teddy that perfectly showcased her every asset. That was the final straw that made his muscle twitch upward, and his eyes nearly popped out of his head.

Amanda walked directly to him and picked up a pillow that had been placed in the dining room as the trio had premeditated his imminent destruction.

He watched as she carried the pillow toward him in awe, disbelief, and a fair amount of wonder. She dropped the pillow at his feet and knelt down in front of him. She laid a hand on the most prevalent part of the bulge and felt her hand sear a message inward with her heated palm. The message was received, and an answer was given in microseconds in the form of a rise that had begun.

She unbuckled his belt, pulled it free from his jeans, and went to work on the snap. Upon its release, she unzipped the man's pants, and his member released himself into the open because he was commando. She began to pull his pants down and off him, but he lost sight of her when Nora began to pull his shirt up. It was over his head, blocking all sight when Nora just let the shirt fall loose. He had just managed to wrangle it in and pull it off when three things happened all at once. Both nipples got hot and moist, and the head of his cock was set ablaze.

When the shirt cleared his face, he was greeted with the sight of three women attached to him orally. And one was bringing a sense of immense animation within his meat.

Amanda was in orbit and humming her song; she really had perfected the art of the blowjob. As much as Trudy loved to make a man come in her mouth, she had to give credit where credit was due, her big sister really knew how to suck a cock, and at times, even she was in awe. She was damn good at cunnilingus as well, but if there was a contest for this sort of thing, she was sure that Amanda would be crowned the queen of the dick.

Nora broke contact, urged his feet from the jeans, and pulled his socks free. On her way back up, she could not help but interrupt Amanda for a few licks of her own. Amanda relented and watched as Nora took him in deeply as she stroked up and off and smiled at Amanda; she kissed her deeply and took him in her mouth again. This time, she did not stop at the back of her throat; she paused just briefly and pushed on down until she was kissing her belly; she slowly came back up. Larry was half arched backward, and his eyes were starting to roll back in his head. She pulled off him and looked at Amanda, then over to Trudy.

"It's close." That was all she said.

"I'll be the judge of that," Trudy interjected.

She led the naked statue-worthy man to the bedroom. His proportions were just incredible. She pushed him to the bed and helped him get comfortable. With the others watching on, Trudy straddled Larry, who was still playing mental catch-up. She lined up on him and lowered herself until his helmet pushed past her lips, and all her womanhood began to spread apart; she sat down fully with one smooth, precipitous fall. It was spectacular on the way down as she had been missing a big dick. Dave was close, but this dick was even better. Larry was the ticket that she had been missing. She sat fully engulfing him, nonmoving but kneading the walls on his shaft with her pussy muscle control. She looked at both girls.

"Just slightly bigger and just a hair longer."

Nora pushed at her from the side, and she took the hint and lifted free. Larry shuttered on her way up because it felt as if she could have easily picked up fifty pounds with her muscle control. She was soaking wet; the clench was palpable and drew his meat upward in a glorious hands-free stroke. Nora replaced Trudy eagerly. She sat down for the comparison and started stroking him from the top.

"Shit, Larry, you're perfect." Nora had said.

"Thanks, but who am I being compared to?"

Amanda nestled up near his face and spoke. "No need to worry about him; he was just our last victim. May he rest in peace."

Larry's eyes widened with a no-shit question on his face; it was followed by the three girls laughing, and Trudy spoke.

"He graduated last year, and now we have you, that is if you want us?"

"Who all is in your group? Are there more of you?"

"Two guys, my brother Mick and a friend Dave. I'll warn you now that you better decide what you will tolerate before you meet them."

"Why do you say that?"

"At least one of them will want to suck your dick, and one of them would love you to fuck him. And both are really good at giving head, from what we have seen."

"I get it now; am I straight, bi, or gay? Honestly, I have never thought about it. Is that a deal breaker?"

"Oh, hell no, we are going to fuck your brains out if you let us. I promise tomorrow you're going to have a sore dick. It is just a matter of communication; we respect each other's boundaries. So, are you…uh…with us?"

"I think my answer is most definitely yes!"

Nora was still stroking him up and down slowly when Amanda nudged her. She bailed off his hardened root, but his shaft never got cold as Amanda took him into the hilt and kissed his belly; he was gobsmacked with her skill and manipulation of his concrete root.

She was enamored with the mixture of three bodies; she could definitely taste all three and wanted more. Nora made the argument that it was only fair that she should get the first round; the others relented and agreed. Larry was confused at first, and his mind was spinning while trying to play catch up with the events of the night. He was still reeling in an evening he could not have even guessed would happen. He caught on quickly, though, when Nora planted her knees at the edge of the bed, hips high face down.

"Uh, Larry, could you help me with something?"

Larry's mind was still spinning a bit, but he understood easily where he was supposed to be. He left the bed, then positioned himself directly behind her, and carefully slid his cock's head inside. He took a small step forward while adjusting his hips backward to find a position that was comfortable; after he stabilized himself, he pushed slowly forward deep into her. He found she was slick and wet for the full distance, so he pulled almost out and slowly sunk into her glistening wetness again.

"Is there a problem, Larry?"

"No, no problem, I just didn't want to hurt you. I have been known to accidentally hurt a girl I was with. Actually, one girl, I couldn't even get in more than halfway before she asked me to stop, so I'm just being careful."

"See? I told you guys he was a sweet, gentle giant. Thank you for caring, Larry; I really do appreciate that."

"You're welcome." The conversation was surreal from this position, but the whole situation was becoming clearer as he went.

Nora continued looking over her shoulder, "Hey Larry?"

"Yes?"

"I really do like you, and I want to know more about you; you are not what I had expected at all. I've gotta say, I am delightfully surprised. Later,

I want to take a walk and find out who the whole you is, but right now, Larry…?”

“Yeah?”

Nora spoke with a commanding calmness to her voice, “Right now, I really need you to fuck me. And really, I want you to fuck me hard.”

Larry was catching on, so he tested the waters with a full stroke at half speed and then another a little faster but with a bit of a collision mixed in. He picked up the pace that traveled out of her to the tip and railed it home to an amazing guttural moan from Nora.

The moan was an acknowledgment of a wonderful stroke; it beckoned for more and carried with it a hint of a challenge to pound another home, so he did. Each subsequent stroke dredged new moans from her depths, spurring a shared excitement. He had never had the freedom to fully stroke anyone before because of his size. The girls he had been with never wanted him fully in them as they had never had anything this big before. It had been a hindrance in the past, but here he was being coaxed to not only give full stroke after full, glorious stroke but to slam it in hard without care, concern, or bother. He was freed to enjoy his own manhood, all the while enjoying a tight pussy that was pleading him on with overtures of more and more, and while he was at it, harder, please!

He picked up the pace and intensity. Nora was thankful for his enthusiasm in many ways. It had been a while since she had a full sheave of meat shoved in her so eloquently. It was a slice of heaven each time he hammered his hips into her ass, and the travel time from tip to hip involved just a nicely perceptible increase in distance that was feeding the "yep, that's it" bone; she was approaching climax quickly.

This type of climax was simply different; she had labeled it the full-package climax. It was not that it was better, as all climaxes were gladly accepted, it was just the climax that came with a certain itch that a full-sized cock could deliver, and Larry was scratching her every itch perfectly. She came once quite nicely. The release in her added a slick smoothness to the stroke; he felt it and was about to slow down. Nora's head was completely buried in the bed, but when she felt Larry slowing, she all but yelled, "I said fuck me, Larry."

Larry was easily one hundred and ninety pounds of pure man muscle, his boyish change had been complete, and Nora was maybe one hundred fifteen pounds of hot, perky athletic build soaking wet, yet at this exact moment, she could have commanded him to crawl naked through broken glass, and he would have done so. She bucked back into him as hard as she could, but his mass collided with her and pushed her forward and easily four inches beyond. He had already figured out he had to haul her ass right back to the edge on every reverse stroke to be able to sink to maximum depth as she was begging for on the next stroke.

He was holding on to a nut that was starting to build inside him; it lacked a certain urgency, so he dug in and started to fuck her without any concern other than to please her. The change in pace as he left all his inhibitions behind, the noticeable change in intent and determination as he learned what her body wanted was the bonus she had been wanting. She felt her next wave coming, and she knew what that meant and what would happen with it.

Amanda and Trudy heard her come the first time and knew she was about to come again; they also knew that Larry was going to be treated to what Dan had described as a pussy paradise. When Nora crossed that bridge, she began to come endlessly in wave after mind-boggling wave, and when that began, her walls hugging the shaft would have the most incredible massage from her muscular contractions. The trick and the key were for whoever was in her to not come until that happened. After she began her inner convulsions, the meat roll in her would be treated to such an incredible delight that when it came, the kneading on the head of the glans was beyond powerful and increased the satisfaction level tenfold easily.

Amanda had been going down on Trudy the whole time this was going on, and because they were so familiar with each other's body and which buttons to push, she had already come once. She found it interesting that Larry was having difficulty with where to watch. Amanda was incredible on a twat, and the show was as good to watch compared to his own show in front of him…. almost.

Nora went into full wave contorting orgasmic bliss, and it was easy to see that Larry had never experienced something like this; he was shuttering as he fucked, pumping hard, deep, and often, bouncing Nora forward and pulling her back. It looked like his mind and body had separated, and he was unrelentingly and without mercy pounding this pussy as a show of ownership. Nora was thrashing around in some mental bliss-like state; she was looking like a puppet at the end of a rod being moved for the puppeteer's enjoyment.

His eyes were fixed and narrowed, and had Nora been in any condition to communicate it, she would have described the swell before his release. She would have been able to tell the others that when he was swollen up, his cock, in particular, swelled just a little more than most, adding to the recipient's pleasure just that little more. It was the very same benefit that prevented her from passing the information on. It was the increase in pleasure that quelled the ability to communicate at all.

He roared out a come, Nora was locked by his hands to his hips, and when he arched up and back, she was lifted tight to his rock-hard cock upward into the air like a rag doll. She briefly landed back on the bed, and he arched again, and she was flailing and convulsing in the open air for a few seconds. He sat her back down, and his dick pulsed deep in her multiple times. He finished coming and pulled out of her, still dripping wet. The two girls had stopped and watched in awe the culmination of body strength, copulas desire, and the intensity of the completion, and when he pulled free, they both saw an opportunity and took it.

Larry thought he was done and had laid back on the bed spent, his dick mostly straight up, and Nora was in a whimpering ball, still dealing with the slightest breeze to cross her skin that was keeping her in super sensory overdrive. Amanda took this time to take Larry's cock in her mouth and clean him with her tongue, all the while keeping him hard and in the sensitive zone. She began to suck him in earnest. She was putting on her best performance and pulling out all the stops. Four full engulfments later, Larry was becoming unglued, "Oh my god, that is incredible, oh shit!"

He tried to concentrate on not physically exploding, though he was not sure he would get out of this alive. Amanda was sucking a dick like no other dick had ever been sucked, and he was responding in kind. He had just come, but she knew he would not last long; at the pace she was keeping and the attention he was receiving, she did not care. She was going to drain the man of anything he had left and, if possible, suck him until he imploded into a hollow crushed shell.

Trudy had taken the opportunity to not only ensure there was absolutely no mental capacity left but to remove all traces of self-identity in the process. She had pushed Nora back, still shaking uncontrollably with every micro intrusion to her body and skin, and had parted her clamped legs and really kind of muscled inward, fighting her thighs until she was licking her pussy deeply, landing devastating blow after devastating blow to her clitoris with a singular goal in mind.

She was going to make her flow until she got all of what Larry deposited back. It had been agreed that if it came to it, Nora would get his first come. No one had ever said she got to keep it. Trudy was systematically destroying her, but if Nora gave two fucks about it, there were no indicator signs. To be fair, Trudy thought she would have to be able to actually speak to object to the proceeding, but really, that wasn't her fault right now, was it? She licked on for five minutes or more, stealing her goal and sending her friend on the most extraordinary, mind-boggling kaleidoscope journey. When she felt she had accomplished all that she had wanted to do, Trudy left her to her senses, which she clearly was having issues locating. She had watched her sister extract another load from Larry with a smile. Larry laid back, completely spent. He was on the verge of falling asleep when two guys came in.

Larry sat up straight and was about to work on what to do when Trudy intervened.

"Mick, Dave, meet Larry; Larry, this is Mick and Dave."

Dave looked at Mick, "Damn, bro, he does have a nice cock, and is big."

Sheepishly, "Sorry, Larry, I just saw you in the shower room. Well, now you are here. And by the looks of things," Looking at Nora still in recovery mode, "Things went well?"

"Uh. well, kinda sorta, I guess." He had a huge, satisfied smile.

Trudy spoke up, laying the law down for Larry, "Larry is hands-off without express permission; he said he had never thought about a guy, so his pace and boundaries, please."

Dave took it in stride, "It's all good; we have each other."

Dave and Mick started to disrobe and were all but finished undressing when Trudy grabbed Amanda by the hand.

"We're going to take a shower."

Looking at Mick and Dave, she winked. "You boys, be nice; we are all tired.

"No worries, Tru," Mick replied.

Dave crawled up the side of the bed beside Nora with Larry on the far side of her; Mick walked along the side of the bed and entered upside down, flipped Dave's cock around, which was already getting hard, and took him in his mouth just as Dave consumed him as well. They both had developed into magnificent cock suckers and were sucking each other with a fair amount of gusto. After eight minutes or so, it was obvious that Mick was ejaculating hard down Dave's throat. Mick was a heavycomer, and Dave especially enjoyed the fruits of his labor. Mick never broke stride but obviously enjoyed his release. Suddenly, Dave came without warning with a hot, massive load that Mick took with little trouble. There was a bubble of come on his lip, but it was retrieved with a tongue as he finished cleaning him up.

Both guys lay there, lost in their euphoria and basked in the afterglow of a good release. Nora watched this with Larry looking over her shoulder, dragged Larry out of bed after crossing over him, and pulled him out to the shower as Trudy and Amanda returned. It did not go unnoticed that Larry, who had been spent and flaccid, left the room full, if not hard.

When the showers were done, and the cabin tidied, the group gathered and asked Larry if he felt like he might fit in. He said he did, but it was certainly a lot to process all at once. Trudy explained that they wanted to give him the full spectrum so he would know exactly what they were about. They impressed upon him that this group had started two years ago, and no one knows about them because we all keep quiet, have no bragging, or have no indications in school. He had no issues with it and fully understood the desire for secrecy.

Nora continued, "I'm glad you feel that way." It was clear she liked him. "If you want, well, anything, all you have to do is ask whomever you think would be best suited to give you your desire. I'm sure one of us can find some version of whatever it is that has caught your attention. I'm sure with a dick your size, several of us might want a full package occasionally. Also, remember, no means no; you won't be badgered about anything."

"Shit, I'm just worrying that I can't keep up with you guys."

Amanda added her thoughts, "Don't worry about that; this was kind of a one-off. Occasionally, we all get together, but it is usually one or two on one."

Nora told him, "Tonight was special. I was thinking that tomorrow you and I could see a movie, just us together. I wasn't kidding; I really do like you."

Larry smiled, "That would be great; I really like you too."

Larry drove Nora home, and everyone else left as well; they all were happy with the arrangements.

It took a few weeks for Larry to fully leave his unfounded reservations behind and ask for what it was that he wanted when he desired, but it finally found the light of day. He had been getting laid more in the last two weeks than he did in the last four months. It was novel, exciting, and fun for him; however, up to this point, his coital relations had been initiated by one of the girls eight separate times and twice by two of them.

He began to see an advantage to having this kind of relationship; however, it was also just a bit taxing until his cock size novelty wore off, and Dave and Mick were re-included in the carnal call-out. He started to experiment with his own volition and began to call the girls for various things he had heard and wanted to try. It was noted that he was really quite agile, and his endurance was absolutely delightful.

Nora and Larry had become an item and were constantly together, which initially caused some confusion on his part. He was not sure how this whole loyalty thing worked. He was not sure that since he was now serious with Nora, was he hers only, and was he supposed to stop seeing the others? Nora had sensed a hesitation and decided to see how he was doing.

"Hey babe, what's up with you lately? You seem like you have been walking around on pins and needles; what is going on."

"I have been avoiding Trudy and Amanda for the last couple of days."

"Why? Is something wrong? Did someone do something bad?"

"Not wrong, but, well, I'm confused."

"What has got you confused, babe; we can figure it out together."

"That is it exactly, us together. Are we together? And if so, what do I tell the others?"

"OH!? I get it now. You don't want to hurt my feelings? And you don't want to hurt theirs?"

"Exactly, I'm lost! What am I supposed to do about that?"

"Larry, I really like you, and if you don't get a big head and freak out, to a good degree, I love you too."

Larry's eyes open wider.

"But don't freak out because I used the L word. I won't be with someone I don't at least like a lot." Her brow furled, "Well, I might have if I had been asked by a friend to, but only as a big personal favor." She laughed, trying to lighten his mood. "But Trudy and Amanda are different. They would do as I ask because we all love each other to varying degrees. You are wondering why I don't want you exclusively, right?"

"Exactly, I feel like I'm trapped between desires; it's really confusing."

"You're going to a college in the Midwest, right? It makes sense; that is where the best agricultural universities are, right?"

"Right."

"I'm going to the East Coast, basically. Have you ever seen a long-distance relationship survive like that for more than a year at best?"

"Well, no, not that I can think of."

"Why do I want to hold you down over some bullshit notion that we are the ones that will beat the odds? So, as a jilted lover, we stop being friends over a failed love, OR as my friend and lover, my friend with wonderful benefits, we can love each other and remain friends for now, AND the next time we see each other, whether that is tomorrow, next week or next year.

You can bet that when I see you after a year has passed, I'm gonna want to ride that sweet big cock of yours for two reasons. I like to see my friends, and I will still love you. So that is why I do not want to be exclusive even though I love you and want only the best for you always. That is also why Trudy and Amanda want to fuck you as well; they really like you, they obviously trust you, and they truly are your friends who will do anything you ask. By the way, that also includes Mick and Dave. Are you mad that I still fuck them? Suck them, enjoy them for my pleasure.

Yes, we all use each other to a degree, but it is always with a loving tone. That is why it works. And in three months, we will all be going our separate ways. When we do, we may be apart, but we are never separate."

She leans in close to whisper in his ear. "If you feel like Trudy or Amanda have the pussy style you want today, go fuck them; just remember, when I call, your ass is mine."

Sporting an acknowledging big smile. "OK, OK, I think I get it. Can you explain one more thing to me? I heard the others talk about it, but I'm not sure I believe it."

"OK, I'll do my best, what is it?"

"They keep saying," After a slight pause and a big shit-eating grin. "That right after your second come, you have an orgasmic bliss that is highly susceptible to a large dick; I think I would really like to see that again right about now. What do you think?"

"Absolutely, let me give Dave a call," Feigning a need for the phone, and laughs. "Oh, you meant you want to see it from on top of me?" Acting innocently naive.

Mom and Dad will be home in an hour and a half, so you have forty-five minutes."

"I'm thinking the bliss train in twenty, and Nora, I promise you one thing."

"What's that?"

"When I get you there, I'm really going to fuck you hard. You didn't think I noticed you like it rough? I was being careful with you because you are so small, but not today. I am going to tear you up. You are about to get pounded beyond what the others have ever seen. Just remember one thing: when it starts, I'll be showing you how much I love you, too."

Nora flashed wet upon hearing the words. Larry was naked in a flash, and Nora was struggling to get comfortable when he entered her. True to his word, he put forth a stellar effort and made her come in twelve minutes flat, but he never stopped stroking. Her face was buried in a pillow when number two came along, just as was advertised in the memo it started. Her orgasmic wave was never hard to recognize, her pussy walls convulsed, almost sucking a dick on their own, it was a fantastic sensory experience, but he changed it up and owned her soul for the next fifteen minutes easily.

Every time she had reached this state before, her partner shifted gears and poured on the coal; it worked for her and worked well. Her state of bliss was never so good, but just as the full body of the bliss was introducing itself, he pulled out of her, flipped her over, grabbed her legs, and pulled her thighs up around him while at the very same time, his prick had been realigned and he slammed it brutally home setting bliss off and running. He picked her up off the bed and, holding her in midair by the waist fucked forward, rocked backward, and posted her brutally down to the root of his meat.

Everything came together as an explosion that was layered on top of another explosion and another. He post-fucked her in midair as she writhed and squirmed to try to escape his grasp but had been rendered unable to as the post was firmly secured in place with each subsequent thrust. A fountain had erupted between them, and bliss became overloaded with squirting.

The whole area was soaked by the time he came. He lay her down on the bed, stretched her right leg skyward, and flipped her over, still buried deep in her. She struggled to find her knees, but when she did, he started hard, long strokes, her body became weightless, and she damn nearly passed out; he stopped the onslaught and pulled free and watched the aftermath of his crusade. He loved her too and showed her in just the way she wanted.

He understood the logic and the reasoning; now, he also had something to look forward to, as he had never had a woman so completely in tune with him. The first time they would meet after being away was sure to be of nuclear quality. He waited for reality to mean something to her again; they both cleaned up and cleaned the room. They had changed the sheets and put everything back in order twenty minutes before her parents, who were running late, got home. They had not heard, however, when Mick came home and never noticed him, as he stood in the doorway for five minutes to watch the show in awe. They were taken by surprise when Mick's bedroom door opened; it was next to hers.

"Damn, guys, that was seriously impressive."

Larry blushed as he thought they had been alone,

"I have never seen her like that, Larry. My hat is off to you, sir. There is no way I could ever begin to hold her in midair like that, and when you were posting her, that was really freaking hot, dude. I mean, it looked like you guys were having a moment, but I couldn't help but watch for a while. Sorry."

Chapter 42 - Graduation

School had been winding down and was in its twilight for all the seniors. There was a graduation party planned, and Sadie oversaw it, so everyone knew the food would be great. Sam, however, started to worry when there were no supplies showing up. He asked Sadie if she was OK. She cheerfully acknowledged that she felt great, even more so because the whole family was going to be there, which now included the grandchildren. She was excited that all the Taylors, save one, would be there. Thomas was deployed, but his wife and child would be there.

With a week to go, Bill, Paula, Sam, and Jessie grew more concerned, wondering if there was indeed something wrong that Sadie had not told them about. She assured them that everything was under control. The day before the event, moving trucks arrived with four able-bodied men per truck. She directed them to the barn, where they cleaned the whole area and began to put up decorations. They started carrying in tables and chairs. Looking as if she were an orchestra maestro, she directed traffic and laid out locations with the point of a walking stick.

As quickly as they had arrived, they were gone, leaving the venue ready to receive guests in under two hours. Bill and Paula had taken a jaunt to Evansville to pick up a gift purchase, and Sam and Jessie had gone to the John Deere dealer for a product demo and review. When both couples returned home, they were in awe of how everything had just appeared. They quit worrying about Sadie at that exact moment—her abilities never ceased to amaze them all.

Now, they were concerned about how she was going to pull off her home cooking when she had not even appeared to have lifted a single finger to do so yet. A fair point was made about the "Sadie magic" on the tables, chairs, and decorations.

Everyone had already taken their seats or at least had claimed an area. Bill wanted to go all out and opened the list of invitees to Trudy. The headcount was high because it had turned into a "party" for her close friends. There was going to be Trudy and Amanda, obviously, but she was also greenlit for Nora, Mick, Dave, and Larry. They all had a great rapport with the extended family, floating in and out seamlessly for the last six months.

Bill wanted it to be special and had told Sadie he would foot the bill for it all, but that meant food for six families plus friends of the families. He was worried that he was asking too much of her. There was a DJ playing a good mix of songs. The only thing missing now was the food, but Sadie, curiously, was not concerned in the least.

Most people had already arrived, and Bill, Paula, Sam, and Julie had slowly gathered around Sadie, who was at the entrance. They were just about to gently wade into the discussion of the missing food when she looked at her wristwatch.

"Right on time."

The others looked up to see a dust stream heading their way. Just as before, a flurry of activity erupted when the trucks came to a stop. Jessie held the door, Sam and Bill cleared a path, and Paula made sure the food tables were clear of party debris. Sadie stood between the tables that would be the buffet and again directed traffic and placements as she had already prescribed in her head.

The food had been placed in short order—ribs, burgers, chicken strips, bacon, slaw, green beans, baked beans, salad, and a host of other finger foods, enough to feed an army.

There was a chef's hat making its way through the crowd to the center. They all converged on Sadie as Bill looked closer.

Bill saw Mrs. Veach and immediately understood why Sadie was not even momentarily concerned.

"How very nice to see you, Mindy. And Dan, I should have known. Sadie told us not to worry."

He looked at Sadie.

"You're a sneaky old woman."

"Who are you calling old? I haven't missed a step."

She stepped forward and hugged Dan.

"I can always count on you. And what are we having to eat, young man?"

"Mostly your recipes, with a twist or two."

"Mm-hmm. I can't wait."

Bill inquired, "How much do I owe you for all this, Dan?"

"Nothing. It was covered by a guy in Texas."

"What do you mean?"

"Well, a while back, I got a call from a man who said he was desperate. His daughter was getting married in a week, but his caterer, including the baker, were, uh, well… deported. He was in a full-blown panic. One of his other daughters, a nice girl, had heard about my cakes and food from some of the guys. She told her dad, he called me.

"I prepped the food, made a wicked wedding cake…" He looked at Sadie with fresh, widened eyes. "Five layers, Momma. It was epic. I have pictures for you."

Sadie smiled.

"…And I used my friends to serve. Mostly did it to get a date with his daughter, but he paid a premium that HE made up. I told him no charge. Every one of the servers left with two hundred cash for four hours of… well, if you could call it work. He paid me the catering fee plus a huge, as he phrased it, 'you saved my ass' payment.

"I told him it was nothing—good practice for cooking for my friend's graduation. He asked where, so I told him. Right before I left to come here and figure it out, he called and said he had hired a crew. I get the feeling that money was not an issue for him, so here I am."

Dan looked up.

"Oh shit!"

He was almost tackled by Trudy, only staying upright because Amanda had hit him from the other side. The party only got better from there.

Bill, along with everyone else, was laughing.

"I'll let you kids catch up. Thanks again, Dan."

"More than happy to do it, Bill."

The adults meandered off to get a plate of food that was beyond expectation, as always, with Dan's fare.

Trudy, baffled, asked, "How did…"

Dan cut her off.

"Darell sends his regards."

"I should have known."

Dan continued.

"I get the feeling he is fond of you for one reason or another."

Amanda butted in.

"I'm first."

She kissed him directly on the lips.

"I'm so glad you're here!"

Trudy planted a long and deep kiss on him that was received with desire. Mick and Nora made their way in with Larry in tow.

Nora spoke up.

"Dan, here is someone we would like you to meet."

"Larry! How are you doing, brother? And more importantly, how did you get tangled up with these losers?"

Amanda whacked him backhanded.

"Watch it, Bub. I know where you live."

Dan was holding his stomach in mock pain.

"You know I love you guys, right?"

Nora continued.

"You two know each other?"

Dan answered, "Know? Not really. If I'm thinking correctly… Advanced Chem. He was the only junior in the class. I figured he would graduate early, or something kept messing up the upper end of the bell curve."

"Good memory." He stuck his hand out to officially meet. "Glad to finally meet you. They said you are going to college in Austin. How is that going?"

"I love it there; I love college in general. You get to rethink who you are and start fresh. No old acquaintances with expectations and old ghosts hanging around. It's a fresh, clean slate, and better yet, you can relax and be who you want to be. You don't have to live up to anyone's expectations but yours. It is really liberating in many ways. Plus, the house I'm in is just incredible." He looked at Trudy with a smile. "It has become a haven of sorts with strict hours."

Trudy asked, "How do you mean?"

"Since I'm the one on the lease, school days are restricted to studies only until eight-thirty. All quiet by ten. Test days and finals are off-limits except for study. Saturday and Sunday are quite a different story—actually, Friday after five and on. The main gathering spot is in the basement. Rooms are off-limits upstairs except for the tenants unless there is permission from them. I have rented three rooms to pay for anything needed for the weekends—pizza, burgers, drinks, and the like. There is the most impressive shower downstairs that will fit four people easily. Two big-screen TVs in two large rooms. There is another smaller one in the gathering room. The bathroom is connected to both big party rooms. One party room next to the gathering space is clothing-optional. The back room is no clothes allowed. It has been interesting, to say the least. Like I said, I can be anything I want there."

Intrigued, Amanda asked, "So, you are in continuous party mode?"

"You would think I would be, but really it isn't so. There are a few regulars who like the freedom being off-campus affords, and honestly, I get to do almost anything I want. I have built a little bit of a reputation there. When I party, I party hard, but when it is work time, I put in the work. I am on track to graduate in three years. I will not be wasting my scholarship in the least."

Looking directly at Trudy again with an appreciative smile, he continued. "In fact, if things go well, I will be graduating from culinary school about the same time you guys graduate college if you are on a four-year path. That is also why I won't be here for the summer; it is just a week and a half before summer classes begin."

Larry was impressed. "Wow, that is aggressive, but really, I can see you pulling it off."

"Thanks, man. I would say I am all on my own, but I know if I needed, you guys would have my back. Plus, with my new roomie keeping track of me, how can I go wrong?"

Nora asked, "How do you mean?"

Amanda happily chimed in, "I have been accepted at Austin U. I won't tolerate him messing up, or I'll have to spank him."

Nora laughed. "Oh no, it's the briar patch for you, Dan. You are in such big trouble now."

"I know, right? Actually, it will be nice to have a slice of home. It is fun there, but everything and everyone is on their way somewhere else. Amanda's room is ready and waiting for her. I was hoping Trudy would consider Austin as well, but she insists on going to Bloomington, Indiana. Like there is something better there." He finished while ribbing her.

"Oh, I plan to visit my sister every once in a while, and if you're there, I guess I will see you as well." Laughing, "The business program is good at Austin, but Indiana has carved out an exceptional program to aspire to master. For now, let's just have a fun time. Maybe we can all get together tomorrow if we can make it work out."

The food was fantastic, the DJ was hitting every tune perfectly, and everyone was having a wonderful time. By the end of the party, the food was all but gone, and the adults had settled back, watching the teenagers wind down. The crowd slowly dwindled until there were only a few people left.

Dan made a call as the DJ closed his sound system down, and a cleaning crew showed up out of nowhere and had the tables and chairs gone, food areas cleaned, and all the trash collected. When they left, the friends and their parents were the only people remaining. They all said their goodbyes and went their separate ways after thanking Bill, who deferred to Sadie and Dan.

Overall, it was a great night.

Sunday was a bright, warm, wonderful day. Paula, Jessie, Sadie, and Trudy had an easy prep and cook day compared to when it was just Trudy and Sadie alone. It felt like a homemade bread and lasagna day, so that was what was made.

The lasagna was sitting nicely in a small roaster pan while the cake was cooling in the kitchen on the counter and ready for icing. When the men arrived with a grace of two minutes, the house had aromas that made their mouths water at the first inhale.

The fresh garlic bread was only bested by the first cut of the lasagna. Danny noted that the lasagna was his recipe. Sadie commented that she liked his better than hers.

Dan was also pleasantly surprised when the cake came out. Sitting alone with Sadie, both commented aloud once again, mocking everyone else about the lack of adventure as they poured milk into the bowl, making white moats around the German chocolate cake.

The others feigned disdain and commented among themselves how weird some people in this world were—never mentioning names, but the indication was clear.

It was all in good fun and ended as every meal at Sadie's did. They were full and ready for a sit-down for any afternoon game. What type of game it was really was of no concern as long as it involved a couch or a recliner and could provide a nap if desired.

Trudy and Dan excused themselves to "catch up" with each other.

Sadie said with a wink, "Be safe."

After a long pause, "I would hate to see an accident stop your college dreams."

It sounded innocent enough and spoke of seatbelts, speed limits, and safe driving decisions. As for Trudy, though, she knew Sadie's true intention and replied.

"I always wear my seatbelt, Momma. Promise."

They left for the barn to get out a razor and headed out. They truly did spend about an hour catching up and hearing all manner of stories.

Trudy interjected, "We have to be at the cabin at three-thirty."

"What's happening at three-thirty?"

"Well, if you don't mind, I wanted to do something for myself, and I promise it will be fun for you too—just not as fun as you might want it to be."

"What do you mean?"

"When Larry entered the group, one thing was certain—he was hung like you. I remember having a full throat and how much I enjoyed it. You know me. But I wanted both at the same time. So, unless you would rather not, we are meeting Larry at the cabin for a threesome. I want you in me deep and him down my throat—again, unless you don't want to?"

"Tru, I love nothing more than being in you, you know that, well, except maybe if I'm in you and sucking a fantastic cock at the same time." They both laughed at that.

"I would love to be with you. I can't tell you how many times that I'm in the middle of an average fuck that I'm dreaming of how well you do this, that, or the other. You are a hard standard to meet."

"Uh, hello, well-hung marathon meat. I have no idea what you are talking about. I just want you in me." Dan laughed at her description.

When they got there, Larry was sitting on the porch and said he had just arrived a few minutes ago. Dan and Larry fist-bumped a hello, and Trudy opened the door and led the way in. She was shedding clothes as she walked, and by the time she had made it to the bedroom, she was down to her panties and bra. Dan stepped closer to her, unclasped her bra, and cupped her from behind. He had missed these fantastic breasts; they just felt right in his hands, more so curiously, he thought, than any other breasts he had laid hands on. Larry had made his way to the front of her and stooped down to remove her panties. His original idea had been to caress her softly and gently, make her wet before going any further, but when he got there, she was beyond damp, heading to wet.

Both men were progressively getting uncomfortable in their jeans; with what they were collectively packing, there wasn't a whole lot of free room to be had. Trudy reached forward and caught the lower edge of Larry's shirt and pulled it up over his head. It took a little effort due to his build and height, but she had managed just fine. She reached forward and unsnapped his jeans and began to pull his zipper down, which was trying to help itself open under pressure. As his jeans were liberated from his hips, a one-eyed monster rose up to meet her.

Dan was behind her when he observed, "That is a nice dick, Larry."

"Uh, thanks?" He had said with a chuckle.

"Can I feel it?"

"Uh, well, uh…"

"His cock is a girl's only thing, Dan."

"Shit, I'm sorry, man, my bad, I didn't know. It's beautiful; now I can see why Trudy likes it."

"Thanks man…. What the hell, if you want to feel it, go ahead."

"No, I get it, brother. I didn't mean to…"

"Go ahead, I just, I just never had a guy other than a team doctor touch my junk. Go ahead; there is a first time for everything. Touch it if you want to."

"You don't understand, Larry; if I touch it, it is so I can line it up and put it down my throat until I kiss your belly and have a chin full of your balls."

"I have never had a guy, uh…fuck it, suck my dick Dan, but don't dare tell Mick, he will be so disappointed that he didn't get to be the first. I just won't tell him."

"You have a spectacular dick, Larry. Are you sure it's OK to 'touch' it?"

"Do it before I change my mind."

Trudy stepped out of the way, and Danny dropped to his knees. Larry was a little taller than most guys, but this put his cock at a perfect height for Dan, who captured his beast and caressed it gently, looked up at Larry and smiled a thank you smile and put the head in his mouth. He sucked himself down the shaft for a few strokes and, without any further warning or preparation, slid the meat right down his neck until his chin was indeed surrounded by fabulous balls that he reached up and caressed.

He started to stroke his shaft with his mouth, and Larry got harder still. He had originally closed his eyes as if to say if I do not see a dude on my shaft, it's OK. Shortly thereafter, he started to watch with some fascination. Just as he had before with Amanda, Nora, and Trudy, he put his hands on the back of his head and started to face fuck him slowly, which made Dan even harder than he was. After about five minutes of Dan's face dancing his cock, Trudy interjected.

"OK, boys, let's not forget why we are here."

Larry commented, "Well, you promised me a spectacular blowjob; so far, you have not disappointed."

After pulling free from Larry's cock and stopping to orbit the glans with an Amanda special, "Damn it, Tru, his dick is spectacular."

"I know, and today it's my spectacular dick; you get to have a spectacular pussy to be in right now. And I can promise you this: I'm going to clench so tight on you going in that you will think it is the first time again."

"Hey, wait now, what about me? What if I wanted to…"

"I'm going to suck your dick like it has never been sucked before; somewhere in there, you're going to face fuck me until you come down my neck."

His cock rose up involuntarily and strained there for a second; Trudy grabbed his shaft and pulled him next to her; she got on her hands and knees on the bed. She took him in her mouth, stopping at the head, and warmed his glans. When she moved again, she pushed fully down his shaft until her forehead hit his belly. Upon arrival, she pulled up and off as both men watched on in awe.

"Uh? Dan?" As if to say places, please, she took Larry fully in again.

"Sorry, Tru, just watching you suck him is just so damn erotic."

Dan got on the bed behind Trudy and lined up and eased forward until the tip of his cock just began to part her labia lips. True to her word, Trudy clenched her pelvic floor with a tight, vise effort that Dan was marveling at as he fought for every millimeter of depth. Her pussy parted for his dick one tidbit at a time but only after a considerable strain forward. He had been pushing forward for about ten seconds and recalled she really was easier to get into fully when they were first together. He pulsed harder at the thought as he finally bottomed out ten glorious seconds later. Her love was built just for him, form-fitting his every contour and vein. She relented in her squeeze, and he went forward about half an inch deeper, surprising them both.

She had released the intensity of the clench, but she had not released all of it, so his pull-out was nothing short of mind-blowing. She held that level of bite, and he began to pump in her. After three slow strokes, he became the conductor. His hips would flex forward, sinking his meat deep in her, and when his hips met ass at velocity, she was forced forward and deeper onto Larry's cock. All Larry had to do was just stand there and wait for Dan to haul her back with her hips and thrust into her again and again and again.

They locked in step like that for about five minutes, and then Dan slowed. Trudy could not see it, but the two guys were orchestrating her spit roast. In unison, they both pulled back, catching her a little off guard; they both slowly came together, trapping Trudy between them. They stopped short of being uncomfortable for her and pulled away once more. As if they used the first few strokes to gauge depth and timing, she began to get penetrated in earnest from both ends.

The spit roast was definitely on. Both men plunged their respective tools deep into her meeting with only moderate strain between them. They fucked her like this for ten minutes or more until the timing changed, and she felt Dan reestablish the rhythm as he again began to screw her hard now. He pounded his every stroke home, and she loved every ball-bruising slam into her depth. Larry was the first to break the silence with any sound more than a moan, or a groan, or a deep breath with two words on the edge of panic.

"Oh shit!" Just seconds later, he grunted, "No, no, no, no."

Inside her mouth, with a hum, she sucked him fervently, raising to the top and orbiting the head while licking the glans at the same time, curling his toes. She pulled up and off him just briefly to say.

"You know you want to come in my mouth, so come." She attacked his cock, sucking him to the root and up, licking his balls briefly while all the way down and sucking him all the way up. She felt his whole shaft gain a minuscule increase in girth, and his head strained against her mouth and the limits of his own skin; he threw his sweating head back.

"Oh fuck," The head of his dick had swollen up just a bit more, and he blasted out a come starting in her mouth. His first shot was unexpectedly large, so it took Trudy some time to readjust while getting a cock force-fed up her twat at the same time. When she had readjusted, she had mistimed his second shot that gushed from her lips and was now running very slowly down her chin and cheek. His third shot was deep in her neck, as were the last two pulses, followed by the finishing shake and a shutter, as his every molecule vibrated at the cellular level.

He pulled his still-hard dick out and used the end and tip to squeegee the come on her face back onto his dick and fed his shaft to her once more for cleaning, which she happily did. Being force-fed, a massive load excited Trudy beyond measure, but when he had scraped his goo from her face and stuck it back in her mouth, that nearly put her over the edge. It was as if Dan could tell she was about to come as well and had changed to a faster, more brutal full batters-up stroke, pounding her ass like no other time, clearly calling his shot to just left of center field. He had already stepped into the batter's box and dug in and now was swinging for the fence.

She came, and she came hard. Her body shuttered, and her skin became a field of goosebumps that somehow managed to accentuate every single hair on her body as it was in touch with her every nerve, and every one of those little sprouts across her was caught in a flash fire that kept traversing her body in waves. With her tremors came an unbelievable clench that finished off Dan's resolve. His load left him quite audibly as he, too, quivered and stood incredibly still as his cocks' head spasmed his juice deep in her.

He could not tell if it were a result of seeing her enjoy both men, or if he had just missed "his" Trudy that much, or the thought of having everything he could want right in front of him. Nothing really mattered at this moment in time as he enjoyed the last drop of his nectar leaving as she squeezed it from him.

They all had laid silently on the bed, limbs haphazardly every which way. Five minutes passed quietly, and that was when Dan army-crawled up the bed toward Larry's crotch. He was still very firm, halfway too hard, and he could not resist himself. Larry was half asleep when Dan stretched his mouth over his cock and softly hummed a tune on his way down. Larry had not moved, but his eyes were wide open, watching as he got harder in Dan's throat.

Danny was sensually sucking Larry's root, really enjoying this beautiful rod, when the unexpected happened. Larry pulled free and stepped onto the floor just long enough to change his direction on the bed. He had his dick right near Dan's mouth when he laid back down. Dan said nothing but sucked in his toy once again.

Dan felt fingers on his shaft and the skin being pulled slowly back and forth. He felt a tongue touch the tip and a moist whole warmth on his head. His cock pulsed harder, but he did not physically move. Dan assumed the same position on Larry's shaft and slowly sucked his manhood as he would like his sucked. He did so slowly, and Larry caught on and mimicked his movements. Dan took his time to suck him; really, in effect, he was giving himself an incredibly slow sensual blowjob just using Larry's dick and mouth to achieve it.

They had been sucking each other this way for ten minutes when Dan picked up the pace and began to go deeper a little at a time until he found the stopping point in depth. Larry had about all he could manage without getting Dan's cock into his throat. For five more minutes, Dan was content at the current level; he diverged from monkey see and monkey do and consumed Larry to the base of his shaft.

Dan began sucking Larry to find the one prize for which he had worked. It was only when Larry began to come that he realized that his cock was straining hard as well, and Larry had thrown caution not only to the wind but right out the fucking door and was sucking him in, occasionally fighting his gag reflex and getting his full-length down. He came as Larry was finishing.

He would have warned him and wanted to, but his mouth was completely full. His first spunk went deep in Larry's throat, but as he pulled up to get a breath and not gag, the next spurt was fully in his mouth. He swallowed what was in his mouth, thinking that the taste was not really all that bad. He gasped for breath and was somewhat overwhelmed. He really had not thought of catching a load, but his curiosity had gotten the better of him when he watched Dan suck him the first time. He wanted to know how it felt. He started to pull off Dan when his cock spasmed yet once more shooting a line of come unceremoniously up his chin diagonally across his lips and cheek. It caught him off guard, and feeling a hot goo spatter on his face, he was trying to figure out the logistics and what to do.

Trudy had woken up because of the motion of the bed and had been watching for a while, being thrilled at seeing Larry experiment for the first time, "I will get that for you. "She leaned forward to his face and half licked, and half sucked all of it off his face and kissed him deeply.

"That was so hot watching you suck each other. Are you OK, though?"

"Yeah, I am fine. I guess I wanted to know more than I thought. It was all on me, you were asleep, and Dan started to suck me; it was feeling so incredible that I wondered how it felt to make a guy feel that way too. It was odd at first, but I liked it; the symmetry of his shaft made it exciting and fun. And coming from a guy sucking you is very much like a girl sucking you, but it is also somehow very much different in an exciting kind of way. Don't you dare tell Mick, but I might just rock his world, or better yet, make him watch while I blow Dave."

The other two laughed at the thought of Mick getting all pent up, but they both made Larry promise that if he were to do so, he would at least go down on Mick and relieve him. Larry agreed he would, but only after he drove him nuts with it. Dan asked.

"Larry, I want to ask you a favor, but I understand if you can't."

"What?"

"I want to feel your size in me; it's been a while since I have had that feeling. It's full. Is that something you could do before I leave tomorrow?"

"That really depends on if that is a reciprocal thing or not."

"It can be if you want; I would love to be your first."

"You don't understand; I don't want that with anyone," Scrunches his nose and momentarily gets lost in a thought, returning to the present. "At least I don't think so, and even if I did, your cock is huge; I don't think I could take that in my ass and feel like walking after."

Dan Laughed, "You misunderstood, no, no, I just want you to fuck me. I don't need to give it to you as well unless, of course, you beg me for it." Laughing again.

"Clearly, I've never fucked a guy, is it that much different?"

"Kinda sorta, well, no, not really. Put on a condom, and I will walk you through it."

Larry put on a condom as requested while Trudy watched on. Dan put his head down and ass up, and Larry got behind Dan still hard. Dan told him to hold his angle more out straight and to be still while he did the rest. He did exactly as prescribed but had gotten just a bit nervous the moment his tip touched Dan's anus. He held his ground, though, as Dan pushed back into him about two inches. Larry noted how tight this felt and that it felt good. Dan had not moved for about thirty seconds when Larry felt his rectum relax. Dan pushed back another three and a half inches.

Other than a hairy ass, it was much the same as being buried in Trudy. Dan pulled forward to the tip and back in again. The squeeze was unparalleled; Larry understood half of the equation in one magnificent stroke. Dan pulled forward and back about three more times, increasing in speed and conviction each time. He stopped in a neutral position and looked over his shoulder as best he could.

"Now, you stroke slowly, please." Without a word, Larry began a slow stroke until they were tip to hip, and he changed direction and made his way outward.

"A little faster," Larry had gauged his last run and gave it a little more speed when he returned.

"Faster, please," Larry added more speed.

"Faster, please," More speed. "Faster and harder now."

Larry stepped up the intensity and speed and hitched just a bit.

"Larry, Fuck me. Fuck me like you want to nut in me."

Larry dropped caution to the wind and began stroking Dan like this was his own personal piece of snatch. Larry noticed something that changed everything for him.

"Oh god…I…I, I think I'm going to come." Larry poured on the coal, and Dan bucked back into him, their hips colliding at an astonishing pace. Trudy had noted they could crush Coke cans between them.

"I'm coming!" Larry cried out.

When he said this, his glans put on a swell that had been unequaled, causing just the right amount of pressure against Dan's prostate; he came right then as well. Larry felt his sphincter contract, and this only added to his pleasure. Both men convulsed together, joined at the hips, and Danny came on the sheet. They pulled apart, and both rolled on their backs, breathless and satiated.

"Does this make me gay now?"

Dan laughed gently and said, "It makes you human unless you have an overwhelming desire to kiss me; tell me you love me and want to marry me. Are you feeling any of those things right now, or just the aftermath of a good come?"

"Just a good come…but what a come. No desire to kiss you, though, so don't ask."

"Pretty sure you're not gay. Just open to all sorts of pleasure. And how do you feel about sucking my dick."

"I really did like it, but I hadn't really thought about swallowing before. On the fence about that."

"My approach way back when was it felt so good to make another guy come with my mouth, and after a bit, the taste was, well, just another thing, and I know when I finish in someone's mouth, it feels so much better than any other way so why not give that to whomever I'm down on. Of course, I have been sucking dick for years now; you may have a different approach, that is, if you do it again. It is kind of a personal thing."

Trudy weighed in. "All I know is I can't wait to see you two together again. It was such a turn-on. It was even better when you treated me like a fuck-me sandwich.

Both guys agreed that the spit roast was an incredibly good place to be. They took a little time to let the events so far sink in and to find a comfort zone. They cleaned up the place while taking shifts in the shower. Trudy and Dan's shower time overlapped a bit, for ole time's sake. Both relished cleaning the other. When they made it to the living room, composed and dressed, Larry was all but asleep on the couch. They roused him back to reality, and Dan and Trudy said goodbye. They watched him drive off, and afterward, they made their way back to the barn.

Though the two wanted to stay together for a while, Dan also wanted to spend some quality time with his mother. Being so far away, getting together was difficult and costly. Trudy offered to make a few trips available, but Dan cited that even though he did not like the distance, the distance itself was forcing him to concentrate on being right where he was and why. All of that, he felt, was helping him maintain focus and clarity when doing his collegiate studies. Just the same, Trudy promised to make tickets or a plane available more often.

Chapter 43 - Thomas Has Been Shot

Shortly after he left, Jessie, Sam, and Sadie rushed up to the house. The Department of the Army had called and informed them that Thomas had been wounded in action and was currently en-route to Ramstein Air Force Base. They would keep them apprised of his condition when it was possible. The worry on Sadie's face was palpable. They told Bill and Paula, with Trudy and Amanda in tow, that they would be heading to Germany as soon as they could find an available flight. Sam told Bill he was sorry, but he would have to drop the daily running of the farm back in his lap for a week or two if he didn't mind.

Trudy excused herself to go to the restroom and came back with a warm smile.

"I have a piece of good news, given the situation."

Bill looked inquisitive. "What do you mean?"

"When I approached that company for the grant after Ryan attacked me, they were glad to help. The CEO gave me his personal cell and invited me to call him personally if there was anything he could do to help further. I just called him and asked if he had any contacts in the corporate world that could help you all get to Germany. I explained what had happened, and he asked if he could put me on hold for a minute. When he came back on the line, he told me that there would be a corporate jet sitting on the tarmac in Evansville tomorrow morning, waiting to take you guys on a direct flight to Frankfurt. He was already working on a plan to receive you there."

Sadie let loose a tear and hugged Trudy. "Young lady, you are so resourceful." Looking at the others, she added, "This is why I don't worry so much about her. She is on top of her world. I am so proud of her."

Bill added, "As you should be. You helped raise her right along with all of us, more so than most. I am so thankful to you for that."

Amanda complimented, "You never cease to amaze me, sis."

Jessie addressed Sadie. "Let's get you back home to pack. We will head out early tomorrow morning as soon as we are all ready."

Just as planned, they were set to leave around six in the morning. Trudy and Amanda had set alarms for four-thirty and made their way down to Sadie's. They quietly began making breakfast. Shortly after, Bill and Paula walked in. Without breaking stride, the two girls added eggs and batter for them as well.

Amanda addressed her mom. "We tried to leave quietly. Sorry if we woke you."

"We were getting up already. I get to take care of little Sadie while they're gone. I am a bit rusty, but I'm looking forward to it."

About the time breakfast was finished and ready to eat, the others began to filter in—first Sadie with a suitcase in tow, followed by Jessie and the baby, and then Sam.

Sam was taken aback. "You guys thought of everything."

Jessie added while giving up the baby to Paula, "A godsend—the best family a person could hope for."

Sadie commented, "I took my time the moment I smelled bacon. I just knew. You two girls are just fantastic. Thank you."

Coffee flowed, and the meal was consumed with little time wasted. The group rushed out the door as the table, and its wares were being cleared and cleaned.

When the threesome arrived at the private terminal in Evansville, everything was more than promised. They were directed to park in a secured lot right next to the entry and escorted right through the office and directly to the plane, which was already in the spool-up process. Ian French and Clay Waters were at the controls. Both pilots introduced themselves on the fly as they were prepping the plane for departure.

Ian took enough time to explain that they would reintroduce themselves in the air, but as both pilots were ex-military, they understood the urgency to reunite loved ones, especially under these circumstances. Twenty minutes later, they were granted a runway for takeoff. Five minutes later, they were banking for the Germany trajectory and climbing to altitude for the nine-hour flight.

The corporate surroundings were more than adequate. The plane was outfitted for long-duration flights and had been stocked with all the amenities a person could want, as well as a full spectrum of drinks available. They were the only passengers on the plane, which made finding a seat and a place to put their luggage quite easy. When the plane had leveled off, Ian came back to the cabin.

"I am Ian French, the copilot. Your pilot is Clay Waters. We are happy to serve you as a pilot for Boutique Airlines. We will be landing in Frankfurt, Germany, in about nine hours, where a car is already waiting to deliver you to Ramstein. Clay has friends who are still at Ramstein, and they have paved the way for you to be on the base and get you to, uh… Thomas?"

"Yes, Thomas. He is my son."

"Yes, ma'am. We also have a question out there to give us an update when they can get us one. With the SAT phone, they should be able to get through at any time, so if we hear any news soon after, you will hear it, too. Meanwhile, the rear seats fold out if you want to take a nap. There is a refrigerator in the back that has several food choices and a microwave should you need it. There are no extra charges for anything on this flight, so please feel free to use them at will. Also, because of the time change and jet lag, we recommend eating soon and trying to get a long nap so you won't be too tired when we arrive."

Sam asked, "Who is paying for all of this?"

"Boutique Air, sir. We are owned by TJC. It's an investment consortium. They have very deep pockets and a soft spot for our military and other causes. Most of the time, we fly the very wealthy around. I'm told that corporate takes ten percent off the top of each flight for philanthropic ventures and other concerns. Even so, we are doing quite well, so please don't worry about the costs. They are fully covered and then some."

Jessie added, "Well, we certainly appreciate it."

Three hours into the flight, Ian walked through to the refrigerator and pulled out a hot ham and cheese plate and a Dagwood sub. He heated up the ham and cheese in the microwave and laughed as the others, still awake, watched him inquisitively.

"I'm also the flight attendant for our pilot, who likes his hot ham and cheese."

This drew friendly smiles, and a slow chain of lunch started between the three after they looked to see what their choices were. The food was excellent, even though it was packed tightly for transport—roast beef plates and sandwiches, grilled chicken plates and salads, potato salads and beans, slaw and condiments, tacos, burritos, and side trimmings. It was all familiar, good, tasty, and filling. Sodas of all varieties and canned tea and lemonade were available. They all ate, and afterward, Jessie and Sam unfolded three of the rear spaces and settled into two of them.

Sadie had drifted back to the front to avoid disturbing the two as they slowly drifted off to sleep. Ian saw her alone and invited her up to the jump seat. Sadie was initially overwhelmed by all the dials, switches, and gauges, but Clay, who introduced himself, assured her it was not as bad as it seemed. After all, half of the gizmos were duplicates for each engine. After that, it was just a matter of distinguishing between the ones for the engine and the ones for flying. He made it sound overly simple, which she knew it was not—at least to her. The view was non-existent at this altitude and over the ocean; there was really nothing to see.

"So, Boutique Air is owned by… uh?"

Ian restated, "TJC, ma'am. It's an investment consortium. Apparently into hotels, services, and obviously airplanes," he said with a chuckle.

Clay added, "We actually met the president and didn't even know it."

"Is he a nice man?"

"She, ma'am. She was genuinely nice—noticeably young, too. She didn't act like she had money - if you know what I mean—very down to earth. She just dropped off her friend to be flown to Texas. She walked through the plane and said she wanted to see what four million buys." He laughed incredulously. "She just kissed her friend, shook our hands, thanked us, and left. We were halfway to Texas when her friend let it slip that she was the owner. Hey, Ian, what was her name?"

"I think he said Trudy?"

"Trudy Jax?"

Both men looked at each other with an I think we might have said too much look. Ian started to backpedal.

Ian faltered, "I, uh… I'm not a hundred percent sure that was it."

Clay sheepishly joined in. "Uh… ma'am, I think we may have said too much. The CEO of the consortium has made it very clear that she is to remain anonymous. Could you please forget we said anything? I really like my job here. They are not going to be happy with us if you know that name because of us."

"I have suspected something for a while now. You boys just confirmed what I pretty much already knew. I do know that name—I helped raise that little girl, and she does have a big heart. Clearly, she is a little bigger than I had suspected as well. But you can rest assured that your secret is safe with me."

Ian apologized once more. "We are so sorry if we have caused a problem, ma'am."

"No, no problems. It actually clears up some issues I couldn't rectify in my mind until just now. I think I'm going to try and catch a nap now."

"Yes, ma'am. I'll sit her down so soft you won't know we landed. We are about four hours out, so please have a nice nap."

Sadie went to the back of the plane, going over past events in her mind as the pieces clicked, popped, and fell into place. She laid down with a smile and quickly let her eyes close.

Clay was gently rocking her arm when they woke her first. They were at the private jet terminal and were ready to deplane at everyone's convenience. He had landed the plane as if he were landing on a pillow. True to his word, Clay had touched down so lightly that she had not felt a thing.

Clay gently shook Sadie. "Mrs. Taylor... Mrs. Taylor..."

Sadie stirred to life with a yawn. "I'm sorry to disturb you, ma'am, but we are at the terminal. Do you want to wake the others?"

"I never felt your landing, never heard the landing gear go down. I must have really been out. Thank you. I will wake the others."

Clay smiled. "Thank you, ma'am." He took her unawareness as a compliment.

Sadie woke Sam, who, in turn, woke his wife. As they were coming to life, Ian interjected.

"We received a call from our contacts at Ramstein. Thomas is out of surgery, and everything went well. Beyond patching a couple of holes, they are expecting a full recovery."

Sam squeezed Sadie's hand. "I told you he's tough, Mama. He is going to be fine."

Clay informed them, "There is a limousine service at your disposal. As soon as you clear customs, look for your sign. We will be staying here for the next two days at least until we hear from you about your expected schedule. We will adjust accordingly to get you home."

A thankful Jessie said, "You all have thought of everything. Thank you so much."

"Our CEO was very adamant in his instructions to make sure you were taken care of. Which reminds me—this is for you." He retrieved an envelope from a storage bin on the wall. "Inside, you will find three money clips with German marks and three black Visa credit cards with your names on them. My instructions were very clear—I am to make sure you get whatever you want or need, regardless of the cost. Please do not hesitate to use them. You will have no bill. They are for you to use as you see fit, and I'm quoting our CEO here, 'At will for any desire.' As I said, TJC has some very deep pockets."

He turned a bit and winked at Sadie, who caught his every meaning.

"Our contact information is also on three separate cards, along with our controller, who is amazing at arranging anything, and our CEO, Darell Cromwell, who requested you to call personally should any issues arise. There are three Apple iPhones set up for international calls; their phone numbers are on the cards. Please don't hesitate to call us as well. We have some friends around the area if we need additional resources."

They all deplaned and passed effortlessly through customs. Halfway down the chute, they saw a card with TAYLOR on it. A formal-looking driver received them and ushered them to a waiting Audi Q7—top-of-the-line, plush, and comfortable. The ride took an hour and a half. They were met at the gate with temporary passes and an escort.

The driver gave them a card for the limo service and explained that he was at their beck and call for the next two days and that he would take their luggage to the hotel that was already booked and waiting for them. They got out of the car and followed a young lieutenant into the hospital, right into Thomas' room, where Tracy was sitting, watching him sleep. She immediately popped up to hug and greet them quietly. The concern on her face lessened just a bit with her new company to help her along.

"He is doing fine, but they have him lightly sedated to help him rest. Apparently, the special operator types don't listen to doctors too well, so they end-run them by making them sleep. They said he should start waking up in about two hours. They can let him start to move a little, then.

"He had been shot eight times in a firefight in Afghanistan, from what I have been able to find out. No one will tell me exactly what happened or where, but Tom had already told me if anything happened, this would be normal."

Major John Tally addressed them from behind the group. "Actually, ma'am, he was shot fourteen times. The others, his breastplate, stopped. The action report isn't final yet, but that crazy bastard you call your husband saved twelve lives the day he was shot—four of them after he was shot multiple times—and still humped himself out to extraction with a man on his back. And yes, it was in Afghanistan, but we have some ongoing actions that prevent me from telling you more."

Everyone had turned around by this point.

"Major John Tally, ma'am. You must be his mother, Sadie, and you are Tracy. I'm going to guess you are Sam because you don't look like a SEAL, but you have service written all over you. I'm sorry, young lady, I can't speculate as to who you are."

"Jessie, Sam's wife."

"How di—"

"I make a point to know all my operators. Sergeant Taylor is one of the best we have. If I had fifty of him, I could sleep like a baby tonight. I am sorry to have to meet you in this way, but I'm told he will be up and about in short order. Nothing vital was hit except a lung that had been grazed. They patched him up nicely. He is one tough man, your son."

Sadie, who had taken on an air of pride, said, "He got that from his father. All of my boys did."

"That, I have no doubt. He told me not to call you, but my field medics told me he looked to be a mess. Turns out that most of the blood on him was from the private he carried out on his back while still engaging the enemy. After the second chopper landed and they loaded the rest of the wounded, he was the last one to board and had been covering both helos on extract. He is one hell of an operator. I just thought you should know that. I should have called you last time, but he made me promise not to worry you."

"Last time?" Sadie was looking at Tracy.

"He has scars, but he has never told me about them."

"That would have been a little more than three years ago now… but I did not tell you that. Maybe a doctor or nurse let it slip from reading his chart. Now you can ask him about that as well. He is nearing his twenty. I'm pulling him from the field and going to assign him as a trainer. I don't want to lose his expertise—maybe he can drill it into some of the new guys." He looked at Tracy. "This was his last field deployment, ma'am. Thought you should know."

Thomas struggled to join them in a weak voice. "I figured as much, sir. I was already thinking about that path as well. I'm all right, Momma."

Looking at Tracy, he added, "Hey, baby, I'm all right. I will be fine. Sir? How are the others?"

"Get some rest, soldier. I'll take care of the others."

"Sir, I'll rest better not thinking about the others."

The Major was looking less comfortable. "The twelve you saved are all fine, including Private Bell, the young man you carried out. He is in critical condition but getting better. One KIA. Your team is just now coming out of the field. They chased the ambush down and took out underground defenses that had been responsible for six deaths in the last month. Reports of a good intel cache coming in from the field. They know you are well and that your family is here. Now get some rest—that's an order."

"Thank you, sir."

Tracy saddled up beside him, and they kissed. He whispered something in her ear, and she whispered something back, which appeased him, and he drifted back to sleep.

"What did he want? Anything we can do?"

Tracy smiled as she looked at Sadie and Jessie. "Men are men all the time."

She looked Sam in the eye. "He wanted to know if he still had his—" (she made air quotes) "—junk. I assured him he does."

Jessie piped up. "Yep, men are men," she said, shaking her head with a laugh.

By the next morning, Thomas asked to walk around and assured the doctors he no longer required a catheter. He was on crutches, with bandages on both legs where six bullets had gone through and through the meaty portions of his thighs, and a bandage around his ribs where two bullets had managed to enter the side of his body—one deflecting off his vest and into his rib, cracking it, the other bouncing off another rib and grazing a lung before departing between a rib space in his high back.

Walking was painful, but he did not show a thing to most people. Sam saw it on his face—not in a painful look, but in the stern resolve one gets toughing through adversity. He knew how his brother was from a lifetime of growing up with him and let the others know as well so they could minimize his travels, which were causing some seepage in the bandages. He did, however, make it to Private Bell's room, who was now out of critical condition and laid up in bed. The nurses told him he was going to make it just fine, so he relented, let the boy sleep, and went back to his room.

When he got there, he managed to get back in bed and promptly fell asleep himself.

After he woke two hours later, he seemed much better but was in less of a hurry to get up and about. They all visited again and discussed going forward. It was decided that they really couldn't do anything here, and since he would be moved to Johns Hopkins in the States, they would head back to the U.S. and wait for his arrival. There was already permission for Tracy to fly with Thomas, so the others were going to depart.

They called Clay, who was happy to hear that Thomas was going to be fine and promised the plane would be ready in the morning when they arrived.

Sadie looked tired as she boarded the plane. Between the jet lag, long days, and worry, she was spent and was all but too happy to lay down after they hit altitude. She was awakened again by Clay at the terminal in the

States. He had sat it down again like they were landing in cotton. She had slept the whole way home and looked rested to boot.

They returned all the items they had been given in Germany, placing everything back into the envelope it came from, and thanked the pilots for their safe flights.

Sadie took Clay aside and assured him there would be no blowback on him or Ian and that their secret was safe with her.

When they arrived back home, Paula agreed to keep little Sadie for a while longer as everyone went to bed and slept. A few hours later, they all came together to update everyone about Thomas and his condition further. Everyone was happy.

Jessie took little Sadie from Paula and was surprised at how much she missed her and how much she had grown. The two of them walked to the house from Sadie's. Sam and Bill set out on foot to the barn to catch up on where the farm was in terms of daily chores and projects.

Trudy addressed Sadie. "Dan was worried when you all took off. And he was sorry he couldn't be here when you got back, but summer classes are starting today—he had to be there."

"He really is a good young man. How did he get back if I had his jet?"

"He just took the…" she stopped mid-sentence.

Smiling with a look of knowing, Sadie asked, "How many jets do you own now?"

"Who told?"

"No one. I figured it out for myself, and with just a little manipulation, I was able to verify what I thought I knew. The weddings gave it away. There were little breadcrumbs here and there that made no sense—until they did. Why don't you want anyone to know? I would think you would be enormously proud of yourself."

"I am extremely proud. I have watched all of you since I was little—how to manage money, use it, and how to develop relationships as well. There are a few people for whom it makes no difference if you have money, but there are also many who change how they behave toward you.

"I have seen the power my dad wields when he is about to spend hundreds of thousands on new equipment. Every salesperson acts just like they are his best friend. He knew he couldn't trust most of them, but he had to play the game just the same to get to the desired end.

"I would look around and see all the people who act one way when they think you have money and a separate way if you don't. I decided not to have money all the time."

"Except for some of the designer fashions," Sadie beamed with a knowing smile.

"I thought I got away with that one. If I were ever asked about them, I would scoff and say it's a good knockoff, and that would be the end of it."

Looking at Sadie with a loving smile, she continued, "But some people you just can't fool. For the record, much of the designer stuff is more durable and comfortable, but you have to pay for it. As for not telling you all, at first, it was my secret. It was a small amount, and quite frankly, I thought I had lost all my money. But a weird string of events unfolded and was laid bare in front of me, so I took my best shot, and it took off.

"Of course, I had to get some people involved, but I chose carefully, and the right people stepped out at the right time to help me along. Kate was by far the most wonderful and helpful. Plus, I knew I could trust her blindly."

"I'm going to have to have a talk with her," Sadie asserted jokingly. "You used her as a lawyer, right? The confidentiality?"

"Yes, and by far the best decision I have ever made. She kept me on the best path. It may have helped her to become a partner, too—I was happy to be able to contribute to that in return. She pushed me to hire a CEO when I got to the point that business started to interfere with school."

"Darell Cromwell?"

"How did… of course you know, you're Sadie." Laughing, she continued, "He took what I started, and together we have expanded it quite nicely."

"Baby, how many businesses do you have?"

"Hotels, surveillance, and security, cleaning, IT, airplanes. I tend to look at a business and see all the connections that can be made. I work out whether it would be additive overall, and if that answer is a solid yes, I look at investing.

"Darell was responsible for the airlines, though, and I have to say, it has been a great move. We are constantly looking at other avenues as well. I really enjoy it."

"The weddings all had such a stroke of good luck. That was you pulling strings?"

"Not really pulling strings—more like voicing my direction. I have people that are just stellar to work with. Fred Duersh runs the hotels, but it is more than that. Through his connections, he has found several small chains that we have been able to acquire equitably.

"Terry Wise has been invaluable in revitalizing them as well as educating me for the future. There are many more, but it is people like these who have meant so much to me. They have accepted me at my age and mentored me while I have helped them live their best lives—truly gifted people. I appreciate every one of them.

"So when I make a request, it is these people who go out of their way to make it happen—not because I'm a tyrant or demanding, but because it is part of a family event of sorts, and they all value the need and desires of the whole. It just works out."

"How many hotels are we talking about here?"

"To be honest, I don't exactly know right now. I started small and got lucky. I was able to leverage them to buy more, and Fred took the initiative to keep looking for possible acquisitions. They got vetted and acted on. Right now, there are forty-three locations, but there is a chain of nine that we are in the middle of closing on, so I'm not positive right now."

"Fifty-two hotels? Planes and other businesses? I suspected you were hiding something, but I never suspected it to this extent."

"It really has been a whirlwind. I have gone from what I thought was going to be a thirty-thousand-dollar loss to somewhere north of sixty million in assets. It is a cash-rich endeavor, so we are aggressively paying down loans while expanding. Besides a few people knowing, I'm just Trudy Jax—an incoming college freshman."

"Who all knows about this?"

"Well, all my business heads know. Dan and Amanda found out recently that Kate knew from the very beginning, and now you know. I was hoping to keep it that way for a while longer."

"How did Dan and Amanda find out?"

"I am paying for anything they need in college, and it was going to be too hard to hide it all, so I told them—on pain of being killed if they talked," she laughed a bit. "Dan's mom thinks he won a scholarship. Dave, Nora, and Mick all think they won scholarships, but they don't know. All of them have been special friends to me, and I can afford it, so I helped them out.

"Someone once told me that one day I would be in a position to help somebody as I had been helped. It just so happened that I was able to pay that forward a little sooner than I would have expected back then. It really feels good. Part of my business is about maintaining a philanthropic presence. I really get to enjoy this as long as I'm just Trudy Jax, a high school kid.

"Can I keep my secret a little longer?"

"Oh, Trudy, come here."

Sadie hugged her tightly. "I always knew you were going to do something with yourself. I just couldn't have imagined it happening now and at such a young age. I am so proud of you." She took on a playful, joking air. "You know I'm going to have to visit Thomas at the hospital soon. Those nice pilots that work for you are going to need to be available for travel, you know. It would go a long way in helping my amnesia along."

Trudy began to laugh. "Oh, Momma, that has already been arranged. Darell was going to—well, is going to—call you to follow up on a potential schedule to see Thomas through recovery. Athena Hotels has a presence in Washington, D.C. They are already on alert for your name." Laughing, she added, "So you liked the pilots?"

"Yes, I did. Very respectful young men."

"They are the same pilots that Dan accidentally let slip that I owned the company. That must be a coincidence. You can let them know that they are valued employees and have a home with me as long as they want."

"I'm not entirely sure I know what you are talking about, but I will let them know what you said just the same. Trudy, thank you from the bottom of this old woman's heart."

She had huge tears and was having trouble deciding exactly why they were flowing. She was so proud of Trudy's accomplishments and incredibly grateful that, in her hour of need, she had been taken care of so completely. She felt Trudy's love pour from her.

Sadie thought of all the good she was doing for her and her family, as well as for Bill and Paula—all with the mindset of being anonymous—which made her appreciate the acts even more. She pulled Trudy in for a mother's bear hug, and after a long, hard embrace, she finally released her.

When she did, she saw tears streaming down Trudy's face as well.

"Don't cry, child. You are a present from God. I know your mother would be just as proud of you as I am right now. You are a wonderful young lady. Never let anyone tell you differently."

"I'm glad you know now. I love you, Momma!"

Lightening up the conversation a bit, she added, "There is one more thing you might want to know."

"I'm afraid to ask, but what?"

"Did you like the food on the plane?"

"Yes, I did. It was exceptional for airplane food. Why?"

"Dan's recipes. I told him I would tell you one day. He will be glad to hear you know about it and liked it."

Sadie smiled broadly. "That boy is going places."

After talking a bit more, it was easy to tell that Sadie was tired from the events of the last few days. She sat back, and in the lull between discussions, she drifted off to sleep.

Trudy took a homemade afghan from the blanket rack, gently covered her up, and quietly left.

Chapter 44 - Dan Is Outed

Dan spent the day when Sadie found out about Thomas being hurt at home with Mindy Veach, who looked extraordinarily relaxed. She missed her boy, of course, but the pressure that his scholarship had taken off her plate was enormous. She could better afford things she had previously been glad to sacrifice for Dan. Their time together was incredibly laid-back and enjoyable, though they were concerned for Sadie. Mindy could see that Dan had been a little guarded and pensive about something since he had been home, and it was clear he had been keeping it internalized.

"Danny, what's on your mind? You've been a little standoffish today, and I'm worried about you. Talk to me. Is it school, or what?"

"I have something on my mind, but I don't know when the right time would be to talk about it."

"A girlfriend?"

"No, uh, not really."

"A boyfriend?"

"What do you mean, Mom? Why would you say that?"

"Danny, there are a few things I need you to know. I love you. You will always be the most important thing in my life, no matter what, without condition.

"You also need to understand that I am not blind. I figured out some things a while ago. You have always been discreet, which I appreciated—

not for myself, but for you. Kids your age would not be so kind if you were on the record as liking guys. I, however, could not give a flying flip, but I didn't want to see you get hurt.

"It wasn't too hard to figure out that games on game day weren't the only thing being played with. I was glad that you and Dave figured things out. It took a minute to figure out Amanda, then Trudy, Mick, and Nora, but I worked it out and did my research.

"As far as I'm concerned, if you are bisexual—if you are happy with yourself—I don't give a shit what anybody else thinks. As long as you are being safe and using caution, you can be who you need to be around me."

Dan stared in disbelief as the tension slowly and visibly drained from his posture and face.

"Bottom line is, you are my son. You will always be my little boy, and if anyone has a mind to hurt you, they will have to make it through Momma Bear first. You have always been good with people and have hung around splendid examples of how to be in the real world. I couldn't be any prouder of you than I am right here and now—today—except as soon as the sun rises tomorrow.

"So, I will tell you right now that whatever is on your mind won't make a difference to how I see my beautiful boy. So, Danny, what is on your mind?"

"I love you, Mom. I was going to try to break the news while I was home that I like both men and women, but I didn't know how or what you would think of me. When did you know?"

"A mother knows certain things, and that little jewel is just the tip of the iceberg. Now, come here and give me a hug.

"I just wish you would have made it to this point sooner because I saw your stress, fear, and confusion. Why do you think I gave you all that alone time? By the way, you were never actually alone. I was always close by. Half the time, I went to the library. Despite how much I like shopping, I was also saving for your college, so I never spent much.

"My best friend, Suzy, helped to make sure I kept on schedule every Sunday.

"In the time I gave you alone, I had hoped you would figure it out and talk to me. When Trudy showed up, I could see that things changed for the better. I was so happy when she was around because you were happy."

"She is a great friend. She never batted an eye—just was my friend no matter what and accepted me as I am. I wish you would have told me you knew, though."

"Nope. You needed your own time and space, which apparently was today. I couldn't be happier for you to be right where you are, here and now."

They spent the day genuinely enjoying being together on a completely different level and plane. Danny opened himself up more to his mother as he found he had a newfound, deeper respect for her. It appeared to Mindy that her boy was breathing better—maybe easier.

They both were, however, immediately concerned for Sadie, Thomas, and his family the moment they found out what had happened, and they sent their support via Trudy and Amanda.

Chapter 45 - Visiting Campus

Early in the summer, Trudy and Amanda got permission from their parents to check out Trudy's campus in Bloomington. They were going to leave on a Friday morning and return on Sunday morning, having planned their whole trip by themselves. They told Bill and Paula that the hotel they were staying at was a four-star-plus hotel that allowed eighteen-year-olds with a credit card to book a room instead of requiring them to be twenty-one and older like many other chains. They were going to stay at the Athena Inn, much like the one where the wedding was held.

They were received at the Athena in the early afternoon when they arrived, with no fuss at all. They were almost whisked through the process at the front desk, and when keys were issued for two of the top-floor suites adjacent to each other, no one batted an eye. They arrived at their rooms and began to unpack when there was a knock at Trudy's door, and a voice said, "Room service."

Trudy made her way to the door.

While opening the door, she said, "I didn't order a room—"

"It is a complimentary bottle of champagne; we confiscated it from some kid who smuggled it in." With a Cheshire cat grin, Darell Cromwell said snidely, "I can return it if you like?"

"Who am I to refuse a complimentary drink? You can sit it over there, busboy." Pointing to the table, she laughed. "Good afternoon, Darell; how are you today?"

"I'm doing well, thank you. How was your trip?"

"It was fun, actually—some good bonding time."

This drew a look of confusion from Darell until he saw another girl enter the room from the side.

Amanda asked, "Hey, sis, who is this?"

"Amanda, meet Darell Cromwell. Darell, this is my sister Amanda Parker."

The confusion left both of their faces.

"By the way, Darell, she knows about all our businesses and connections, so there is no need to be cautious when we talk."

"You said he was good-looking, but oh my…."

Darell blushed. "Uh? Thanks?"

"Down, girl." Laughing a bit. "Darell is here to show us around a bit."

"About that, we are all set for tomorrow. The realtor is ours for as long as we want. I have five places lined up; I had several more but eliminated some for assorted reasons. The five I have ready are the ones most likely to catch your eye."

"What is he talking about?"

"I already took a virtual tour of the campus, so our walk-through today is just a formality, really—a way to connect distances in the real world. We are here to look at where I am going to base my business work, and you are going to help me pick it out."

"I thought you were going to stay at the dorms?"

"I plan on splitting my time there, but I wanted some space for myself—a private retreat where I can just be me if I want."

Darell interjected, "Two of the places are at the top of my list. If I were pushed, it would be just one, but I am not going to tell you my choices until after. I trust you had no issues getting your room?"

"I suspected we were getting kid-gloved, but I wasn't positive until now."

"All they knew was I was having some guests staying that I wanted to make sure were taken care of. That is all the staff knows as well, so yes, just a little help. I'm guessing that when the CEO of the Consortium and the CEO of the hotel group mention there are special guests, people perk up just a bit." He chuckled.

"Well, everything certainly went well."

"That's good. I'm going to get out of your hair and let you two have some time. Dinner tonight?"

"Sounds good. As long as they have plenty of vodka."

"I hear they have it on tap."

Amanda broke in, "Wait… What?"

Both Trudy and Darell laughed.

"Long story, maybe I will tell you one day."

Amanda had heard only half of the full story.

"Around six?"

"Around six it is. See you two then."

Darell left and went back to his room, and Trudy explained her night of drunken debauchery—which really was a well-hydrated evening—and how that first night with Darell came about. After connecting the dots, having vodka on tap made perfect sense, and she laughed at it all over again.

The two girls finished unpacking and set out to go to the campus. They found it to be a little more spread apart than a virtual tour had led Trudy to believe, but it was easily walkable, with some venues far enough apart that a bicycle might be appropriate depending on how a person's schedule was laid out. Overall, it was more than doable and satisfactory to Trudy.

They returned to their rooms, took showers, and were fresh and ready for dinner by five forty-five. When they arrived at the restaurant inside the hotel, they were promptly seated with Darell, who had arrived about five minutes earlier. Darell and Trudy talked shop for about fifteen minutes while Amanda listened with curiosity. Afterward, the topics became more user-friendly for all at the table.

They talked about upcoming college classes, the apprehension that came with them, and the excitement of the changes in their lives. Darell contributed his memories of his first year and recalled that it was really a time optimization change—balancing the party versus the study. Both girls already had most of the management skills that he suggested being in touch with, but they appreciated his insights all the same.

It was nearly eight o'clock when they headed to their rooms, with a tentative breakfast date set for eight A.M. They rode the same elevator up and said their goodnights in the hallway. Amanda entered Trudy's suite with her and continued to hers through the cross-connect door to get ready for bed. She told Trudy, as she walked, that Darell was much more handsome than she had thought.

Amanda continued to her room and went to the bathroom to remove her makeup. She decided to take a long, hot shower to help her relax for the night.

Trudy knocked on Darell's cross-connect door. When he answered, his tie was gone, the first three buttons of his shirt were undone, and he was wearing only socks with his trousers.

"What's up?"

"I have been thinking that it might be time for me to make a change. I can't do all of this by myself, so I was thinking about hiring a CEO for my business.

"If you have a resume that you would like to submit, I would be happy to give it a once-over and see if you're qualified. But if you are happy with your current position, I totally understand that as well."

Darell smiled, "Let me put some thought into that and see if I have a resume that fits the bill. Can I get back to you in a bit?"

Absolutely, I wouldn't want you to come unprepared, especially since I want to pump you extensively for pertinent information. My door is wide open."

She turned to undress as he turned back to his room.

Trudy had finished putting on a sheer teddy and went to the mini fridge to get a drink. She had just set the drink down on the counter when she felt two hands slowly and firmly encapsulate her waist. They slid slowly up and cupped her breasts fully. As she arched backward, she felt chest hair through the silky top and a firm member on the rise against her thigh.

"Ms. Jax, I'm here to drop off my resume; where would you like me to put it."

"Anywhere would be just fine; I guess we could start the interview over there." She was pointing in the general direction of the bed. "There is likely to be some stiff competition to contend with; your oral skills might become the deciding factor. Do you think you have what it takes to compete?"

"I will give any opponent a severe tongue lashing; when I'm done, they will undoubtedly agree that they have just met a great orator, but first, I need to tie my shoelace." As he went to squat down, his fingers hooked her barely there lace panties, and he enjoyed watching them slide across her skin and down her legs on his way down.

"Oh my, it seems I have misplaced my shoes altogether."

He stood up, and Trudy turned around to face him with a smile.

"I was so hoping you would apply for the position, uh, Darell, is it? I have one extremely critical interview question for you first."

"What's that?"

"How do you feel about the number eighteen?"

"Eighteen is one of my favorite numbers, one better than seventeen. If you have any other questions about it, I will be happy to rise to the occasion for you."

Trudy pushed him back to her king bed, and he adjusted himself to the middle with a pillow under his head. Trudy slowly crawled up the bed with roaming hands; she caressed his body. She pulled a warm hand over his ball sack and grasped his shaft while it slid through her fingers. Her hands start to caress his nipples as he got raging hard, remembering the sweet torture they endured at their last encounter. She straddled his six-pack and left one hand to trail behind her to pet his hardened cock for a brief amount of time. When her petting and nipple caress had ended, she shifted herself up to near his head.

"Good oral skills are a sign of intelligence and drive, so tell me in your own words who you are, what you want out of life, and why I should hire you?"

With that, she flipped her hips forward as his mouth caught her pussy, and his tongue went as deep as he could. He began to tell her all about himself, his dreams and aspirations, how hiring him would be a great business decision and much more. It all came out as a glorious hum as her clitoris was being pummeled with his tongue as it was in the way for him to be totally verbal.

She slowly moved her pussy on him, adjusting to the best of sensations, him noticing the cues and adjusting tactics to achieve a favorable outcome. She arched back and was about to reach back and hold his hard pole when she felt a pair of hands slide up her back and around her front, cupping her breasts. She knew they were not Darell's because his arms were currently clamping Trudy's legs in place.

Trudy felt a head of hair, damp as it hit her back. It was cool and completely unexpected, and the sensations were on a totally different spectrum. The sudden cool dampness ripped through her nervous system in an additive fashion. She knew what was about to happen and, for a moment, considered interrupting her enjoyment to ask Darell his thoughts but decided he would figure it out, and if it were a problem, he would make that known. Almost on cue, as his cock went fully down Amanda's neck, he slowed, stopped momentarily as if there were a decision being made, and then he continued and clamped harder on Trudy's thighs and buried his face deeper and ate her with yet more vigor.

Amanda slowly made her way up his meat to the top. She felt hesitation and re-engagement and considered it to be an open invitation. Right before she took him fully again, she raised her head briefly and commented to anyone who cared to listen that he had an incredible dick. She noted as billed that his depth and girth were just noticeably different than Dan's. His was fantastic, gifted, and until now unequaled, but Darell's was just what the doctor ordered. She kissed his belly with his junk fully engulfed.

She made her way up to the top once again and gave it the Amanda orbiting tribute. His cock twitched and jumped as if it were trying to detach itself and run away; his moans were contributing to the vibrations while eating out Trudy. She felt the prick of it strain as she slowly went down on it to the hilt once again. Her saliva started to flow, though admittedly, it took just a bit more time for it to fully coat this amount of dick and leave enough for future depth charges.

She set out to intentionally drain his balls as she kept a determined pace up and down the full length of his shaft. The head of his pride popped past her throat entrance; it had the desired effect that she was all too happy to deliver on pace. She was face fucking him in reverse, and both were loving every moment of it.

When Trudy sat on his face, all the memories came rushing back; they only served to make him harder. Her sweet nectar, the tight body, and those tits, those unequaled breasts in his hands thrilled him once more. He absolutely loved her tight areolas and standing thumbs for nipples. Having them all again was competing with the memory of last time, and yet both were holding their own as separate entities. In the end, it did not matter, as he was as hard as he had ever been.

To top it all off, she was now eighteen; even though at seventeen, he had knowingly plowed her deep after he found out, somehow, it still mattered to him. How this was any better, he did not know, and at this junction in time, he again did not care. She was just so damn good; he loved her taste, her forwardness, her willingness to take.

Eating her pussy was fantastic; even so, he was about to lift her up and slam her to the bed and put on a full-court press in her depths with his meat wrapped in her tight body, squeezing him once again to its total length when he felt it. He was about to move, but something changed, and he needed a second to recalculate things.

A hot, wet sensation wrapped his head, his shaft, and all his meat began to heat up, followed by a cool tingling sensation all around the extent. He hesitated and worked out that Amanda was sucking him, and she had wet hair. It was fabulously uplifting and erotic to be having a threesome like this. Two hot college-bound girls with incredible bodies. Fuck yes, he thought and dug into Trudy's pussy with the sole intention of holding off his come for his own personal satisfaction just as long as he could.

He had been wanting to be completely down Trudy's neck as she was the first and only girl to fully take him. He now knew he was in trouble when he felt Amanda's tongue lick the upper part of his balls while kissing his belly. When she withdrew, he did not know how anyone could give a better blowjob than Trudy, but somehow, she was. When she started her full-on onslaught, fully consuming him with her face, he knew that he might just literally self-destruct when the time came for him to release.

He was doing his best to hold off the inevitable, but his resolve was taking a beating. He ate Trudy even more fervently to distract himself. Amanda knew what he was doing; she had been in this exact position multiple times, joyfully contributing to her sister's orgasm while trying to steal a load from the guy under her. It was always the same: Trudy would come so hard that the men would have soaked their ears as they tried to fight Amanda's onslaught off. Always and without fail, she would eventually drain their balls completely, almost seemingly to the point of implosion, and for good measure, purely for her own enjoyment and sometimes just to be wickedly mean; after swallowing their load, she would devastate them by sucking them in overdrive with her patented orbit on full tilt. The glans would do some type of electrochemical lobotomy, and she loved it, sometimes more than her victim did.

Darell, she knew, would get sucked even harder for her pleasure. His full dick down her neck was indescribable. She loved this dick; it had now taken her top favorite cock spot.

He felt his urge to come rising and again doubled down on distraction; Trudy was clamped down and bucking faceward and working on a hard third torturous come. She arched backward hard as a wave came across her, and in doing so, her back slammed down on Amanda's head as she was on a down stroke, pushing him deeper and faster than Amanda had intended, but the desired effect was immeasurable. Darell came with a thunderous blasting release. His cock was pulsing hard, starting at the base and roiling veins to the surface as his shaft spasmed out load after load in her neck and mouth.

To Amanda's delight, his first pulse was of an incredible magnitude, but it curiously gave no reward whatsoever. She had just pulled up and off to verify what she thought she knew when his cock roiled yet again, spattering her face with an incredible shot of goo that hit her, leaving a large trail as evidence across her upper cheek and past her eye into her hair right on down her face to her mouth and chin. Amanda had just found out what Trudy already knew when a dick gets this big; it takes a bit of time to move the spooge from the ball sack to the tip. Before the second spurt could rechamber and send a euphoric contraction up his shaft once more, Amanda had him back in her mouth and was in the process of taking him down the neck when he released again.

She had not gagged on dick in a very long time as her gag reflex had been well-trained, but this was a lot of cock with truly little room left for more, so when the second shot arrived, she had to choke it down. When she choked just a bit, this caused an incredible sensation for Darell and his balls; he was almost yelling a grunt as his glans, fully swollen, tremored in rapid mind-altering contractions. The whole hour he spent in those ten seconds had been paralleled only by Trudy taking him fully the first time, but only because it was the first time. This girl was heavenly when it came to sucking a dick.

He had not noticed that his face was now completely glazed, nor did he care; his attempt to hide from the inevitable had been a glorious boon for Trudy. She had already been coming with multiple mind-numbing convulsions before his singular attention was concentrated on coming himself. She used the time to bask in the glow and to listen to her sister tear Darell apart systematically. It was a hell of a sideshow to experience. She felt his involuntary thrusts, felt the ejaculations roil through his body, tensing his every fiber to help direct him to deliver the most powerful spasms it could muster. His body did not fail to deliver; he was a singular nerve acting with a single purpose to find an equilibrium that fell just barely on this side of consciousness. He had achieved his goal; it had taken all his resolve, but he got there just the same.

Just as Trudy was dismounting and turning toward Amanda, she was just shutting down the orbit machine; she looked up and saw Trudy half laughing and half grinning.

Amanda asked, "What?"

"Come here, sis." Amanda leaned forward expecting a kiss when Trudy steadied her face with her hands and began to lick a long, thick stripe from her chin to cheek and up to her eye rim. She licked her lower forehead and kissed her, sharing the missed shot.

"Thanks, I almost forgot about that. You were right about his dick, it is incredible."

"I told you so."

"You talked about my dick specifically?"

"Not all dicks get a mention; most are nice, but yours is spectacular. Didn't you notice anyone in school not wanting to shower near you? No one wants to be compared to a monster like yours. I'm told it is a male pride thing."

"My friends always joked about it; I guess it is just a little bigger than most now that you say it that way."

Trudy broke in, "Trust me, Darell, there is a reason you had never been deep-throated; I'm betting with a dick your size, you had a girlfriend or two who couldn't sit all the way down on it much less deep-throat you."

"There were a few, I guess in retrospect, there were several that I had to go really slow at first with sex, but…"

"Your dick made secondhand virgins out of a lot of women, is my guess."

"Secondhand virgin? What the hell is that?"

Amanda spoke up, "Hold on, I'll show you."

Amanda moved forward and straddled his still-standing rock-hard rod; she lined up and slowly lowered herself on his pole. Halfway down, she stopped.

"Do you feel my muscles squeezing on you? I'm not doing that. You are the biggest cock I have ever had in me," Moving downward slowly again. "That is your size stretching my muscles. Muscles that thought they knew all about dick until now. You are wonderfully big; it really is reminiscent of the first time my walls were stretched with a dick for the first time."

She sat fully on him, her full weight in his lap, his cock fully in her, and closed her eyes as if she were savoring a flavor she did not want to forget.

With his head tilted back and eyes half rolled inward, "Oh fuck, you are so tight. I think I understand what you mean. Can you show it to me again?"

"With pleasure." She slowly lifted herself up to the top and let herself fall slowly again; she repeated this about five more times, moaning with each wonderful stretch of every stroke; she stopped and pulled off him and got on all fours at the edge of the bed.

"Now you are going to fuck me until you come again. You're going to fuck me hard. I want to feel your every stroke hard and deep."

Darell looked at Trudy, who had a look of 'better do as she says 'on her face. He got off the bed and lined up on her dripping wet crotch, cupped his fingers in the void made by her hips, folding forward, and half pulled her, half pushed himself into her slowly and fully. He changed direction, pulled out, and repeated it again. Her vaginal walls knew what it meant to have a dick in them, but this was just a little bit more; old muscles stretched anew, and it was a glorious feeling. He gathered a little more speed, and as he was pushing in, she timed a very luscious…well… well-executed push backward to find his full and total depth. Her cervix kissed his tip with an incredible tingle for both. She looked over her shoulder,

"Are you going to fuck me or what?"

Darell adopted a smile that said all there was to know. He truly was going to hammer the holy hell out of his second-coming virgin's body. She was tight, her body was tight, she had an incredible set of breasts, and to top it off, he was looking at a different body with the same attributes straddled over the head of his currently skewered interest.

Trudy was fondling Amanda's breasts and nipples while her thighs were open on either side of Amanda's head in a manner that she could bury her face into Trudy's sweetness. Amanda had asked him again if he was going to fuck her or not; his immediate thought was, "Damn straight he was."

His first thrust forward, not the stroke, but the thrust, explained a dissertation in one second flat. His powerful hips and buttocks slammed home with a ferocity he had not been able to show in quite some time; it felt magnificent to her and him both. Amanda pushed back into the advancing torpedo hard, and as her hips met his, her direction changed instantaneously with a bounce. His thrust forcibly slammed her face hard into Trudy. Darell watched it all happen from his vantage point and realized a few undeniable truths immediately.

First, watching two girls go at it while he was driving this motion was incredibly hot. Second, it was liberating not to have to worry about size, rather than his bigger size being an issue. Third, he now knew at least two girls who could take him fully in all ways.

As tight as she was wrapped on his cock, the scene before him was working on his come button in an incredibly sensational way. He was not going to last as long as he thought he would, but he would try his damndest to represent the male species to its utmost. He threw caution to the wind and let his cock rail home mercilessly hard and deep with no hint of complaint.

The bed was soaked in two places; Amanda was beyond wet and running down her legs and his as well. He had quit trying to figure out if she was coming or not. It was easily evident she had already come, but another wave happened again only minutes later. It seemed like there was a wave of juices coming from her drenched pussy endlessly. With every wave, her muscles contracted and, conversely, let loose some more lubrication enabling the inner wall contractions on his cock to lessen the degree of friction. Still the same, he was approaching a monstrous release that he could not control, and worse yet, it was threatening to turn his whole body inside out.

Trudy had no reason to complain as his every stroke put Amanda exactly where and how she wanted her. His every stroke slamming into Amanda might have been considered violent had they not been coming exactly as she had wanted and asked for. It was that 'violence' that pushed Amanda's face rhythmically into Trudy's crotch. Her face rammed into her, setting her insides on fire, only to be drenched by an automatic fire suppression system that was threatening to numb her mind beyond belief. She was coming hard in waves.

The glimpses he had of Amanda's face reminded him of the glazed donut thing again. He pulled out of Amanda and stepped up on the bed and straddled over both girls and dipped down, and shot an incredibly large load, a thick stripe of man juice starting at Trudy's midriff and up to her tits on the first pull of his orgasm, and he offered it to Trudy who hungrily sucked him in just in time to feel her cheeks puff out for the second shot.

She swallowed him with a delicious moan and started to put him down her neck as his third pulse pulled his nuts upward visibly while her mouth felt the walls of his shaft contract. Five full hard pulses later, he began to pull out of her, stopping only when Trudy's fingernails bit into his ass. She orbited his tip in the most satisfying manner, coaxing the last drop from him and cleaning his whole dick.

He looked down from the upward dog that he had performed while coming and watched Amanda lick the trail he so valiantly forged up Trudy's body. They all ended up lying in a huddle on the bed, spent but happy for it.

After they began to stir, Darell slowly made his way to his feet and beckoned Amanda to go with him; he told Trudy he would be back for her. He washed Amanda under endlessly hot hotel shower water and massaged her scalp while shampooing it. He stepped out and, dried her off from head to toe and asked her if she wanted to join them in his suite for the night.

Amanda turned him down and turned to go to her room through the interconnecting door and disappeared.

He beckoned Trudy from her slumber and again took his time through the entire process and invited her to his room; she accepted and headed in that direction. He had told her he would be there just after he bathed. When he got to the room, Trudy was asleep on the far-right side of the bed; he carefully slipped into the bed and spooned up to her. She seemed to know he was there as her body accepted his touch and melded back into him. When he woke in the morning, both girls were entangled with him.

Somewhere in the night, Amanda decided to join them; he had been so spent that he had never felt the bed move or heard a thing. It took a very concerted effort to slowly untangle himself and slip out of bed without waking them. He knew their timetable and decided to order room service for all of them. He ordered enough food for five people easily but wanted to cover all the bases for breakfast, not knowing what everyone liked, a lesson he learned from Trudy that first time.

Chapter 46 - Meeting the Realtor

The girls came to life slowly as the smells of bacon and eggs filled the air, along with the scent of sweet strawberries. When they managed to roll out of bed, they joined him at the kitchenette for the first cup of coffee, noticing his strawberry jam slathered liberally over toast. It was a good start to the day. Between the three of them, there was only enough for one small person to eat leftovers. The night of hard sex had consumed all of them, and their bodies were yearning to recapture a calorie intake to counter the deficit. They agreed to meet in the lobby at nine to meet the realtor, and everyone made it to their rooms to shower once more and dress for the day.

Page, the realtor, was right on time and, after introductions, agreed to lead the way to each potential home. She had given them all a list of addresses on cut sheets with pictures of the house from the road. It did not take long to narrow down the possibilities. The first house only garnered a drive-by, and though Trudy could not put her finger on it, it simply would not do. The second only pulled them inside for a cursory confirmation that the inside view and layout were not what she had wanted. There were three more houses on the list, but the next house ended the search altogether. The house was older and stately, regal in appearance from the road, albeit somewhat neglected. There was a three-car garage attached to a two-story house with an attic above and a walkout basement below.

The realtor had been given information that the client they were seeing was a business owner, and she had been catering to the older male in the group, who seemed to be getting told opinions on the houses they were seeing. She was beginning to be frustrated with the interference from the girlfriend until the girlfriend stopped and looked at the realtor.

Trudy said flatly and with conviction, "This is it."

Page asked, "So, should we see if the boyfriend likes it?"

"Why would he care if it is what I want?"

"I would think he would have some input on where he spends his money."

Darell corrected her misconception, "I don't think you understand. When I called you, I told you my company was looking to buy a house in the area, preferably near campus."

Page defended herself, "This fits all your requirements. Great area, less than half a mile from campus, but still some seclusion with a wooded buffer. Plenty of space, although I am surprised that this was what your girlfriend settled on. It needs extensive remodeling, and it comes with a hefty asking price to boot. I just figured you might want to rein her in."

Amanda started laughing politely but audibly. "This ought to be good."

Trudy looked at Darell. "We are going to need Terry Wise, if he is up to it, a little magic, and a good interior specialist, and this will be just the ticket. Offer fifteen percent less than asking, cite the dated appearance and the need to be updated and offer cash for a quick close. Let's get this done."

Page looked befuddled. "Darell, what do you want to do?"

"Page, I don't think you're catching on to what is happening here. I told you my company is looking for a house. Trudy owns my company. I'm her CEO and friend. I will oversee the transactions through our company, but she has full rein on how she spends her money when she wants to. You might want to reconsider how you're addressing her. She is usually pretty forgiving, but she does have her limits."

Page was red-faced and embarrassed. "Trudy, I am so sorry. I mistook you for a girlfriend to the boss. I am sorry if I have offended you."

"It's alright. I tend to let things play out like that for several reasons. I generally get left alone, giving me plenty of inside access to the facts, and I get to see what kind of person I am dealing with on a different plane. It always catches people off guard when they find out the full extent of my participation. So, let's make the offer and see if we can move forward."

"I can make the offer, but I honestly don't think they will go for fifteen percent off, even with a cash offer."

"I don't either, but I think they will see an opportunity to close this out after they offer ten percent as a counter. Anyone who has done their research will find that they are about ten percent over what they should be asking. I'm sure they know it as well. I just want to give them an opportunity to feel as if they decided the price. When they make the offer, accept it. If you can make the call right now, we can have you…"

She looked at Darell.

Darell weighed in. "Ten percent in earnest money within moments of signing the offer."

Page made the call to the listing agent and explained the client was on-site looking for a verbal offer and was prepared to sign a contract for cash and earnest money of ten percent but for fifteen percent off the price. She told them that her client would wait for a reply. The listing agent said they would make the call and get back to them shortly. After a ten-minute wait and while they explored the house further, Page received a call with a decline on the original offer but a counteroffer of ten percent if the deal could be done in fifteen days or less. They accepted the counteroffer, and Page wrote up the contract with all the provisions and sent the contract email to the CFO of the corporation, who also happened to be Trudy Jax. It was summarily e-signed and then sent back to the listing agent. Within twenty minutes, all the signatures required for a binding contract had been acquired, and the deal was in motion.

There were three months left until the end of the summer, so Darell and Trudy were not sure if even Terry Wise could pull off what they needed to, but they were optimistic. When they talked to Terry, a few unknowns were aired and easily resolved.

Chapter 47 - Meeting the Build Team

Trudy asked Terry, "I have a special project if you're feeling up to it."

"What do you have for me this time, Ms. Jax?"

"I just bought a house near campus in Bloomington, but it needs renovation from top to bottom. I can't think of anyone I would rather have in charge of the project. What do you say?"

"That sounds like a great project and a break from our norm. I would be honored to oversee it for you, but first, I need to run something by you, and hopefully, you will approve of it. And please keep in mind, I wouldn't even think of asking if I wasn't completely sure of certain capabilities."

"What's going on, Terry? What can I help with?"

"No, no problems, and we have always had a good working relationship. I have totally enjoyed it, but I am starting to feel my age more than I used to."

"I hope I am not burning you out; that is the last thing I would want to do."

"No, no, no, I am doing fine. But there is a reason I have been able to do so well and keep up with things. I have taken on an apprentice of sorts. My grandson started working beside me about nine months ago. I have slowly been mentoring him, helping him to progress. You have been so good to me, and I love working for you. You are happy with my work, yes?"

"I couldn't be happier, and I'm reminded every time I stay at one of our hotels. The quality is always over and above; I am always thrilled by it."

"Thank you for that. But as I said, I am slowing down, so my grandson has been my right-hand man and more for me. On the last three upgrades and remodels, I have only looked over his shoulder as he has run the entire operation for me—contractors, materials, people, and supplies. Everything was dropped on his shoulders. He has not missed a beat; he has even innovated a few things I hadn't thought of.

"Think of him as a younger me with an energetic eye. With your permission, I would like to assign your house to Trevor. I will still be there purely in an advisory role, but he will be the mover on record—the one to report to and get reports from. He is ready, and moving forward, he will be taking over my role in the remodels unless you prefer some other arrangement."

"Terry, I have never had a moment's doubt over you. That black credit card in your wallet has no limit and has never been questioned. I am so very thankful to have met you. I have been able to trust you and your judgment from day one and have no reason to change it. So let Trevor know that from this day forward, it is on him. Any time you want to be on any project, I will happily pay for your expertise to be there. I look forward to seeing you both there and beyond.

"But for now, I would be grateful for an interior designer and contractor to survey the house and see what can and can't happen to my home for the next four years."

"I will call Trevor and inform him of his new assignment, and if I know him, there will be a meeting within days with you to discuss options going forward."

"Thank you, Terry. I'm looking forward to meeting Trevor soon."

The weekend was ending, and the group had supper together and said their goodbyes after a long meeting between Trudy and Darell over trajectories and logistics, performance expectations, and financials. The state of the business was going well. It was proposed to see the viability of a groundskeeping business to cater to the hotels as well as local businesses in each area for landscaping, grass cutting, upkeep, parking lot cleaning, and snow removal. Darell had said he would run the numbers and see what the possibilities were. Trudy knew it would be managed in good order as Darell was always more than capable.

Keeping with Terry's prediction, his grandson called four days later, requesting a meeting with himself, their structural engineer, and the interior designer. They were going to meet at a conference at The Athena Carbondale the next day. Trevor came off with every bit of confidence she had been expecting. The engineer had already checked out the structure, utilities, and general conditions and had preliminarily met with the designer to coordinate possibilities.

They had decided on an open plan downstairs, semi-open upstairs, and the basement was going to be transformed into a noise-dampened peaceful oasis. There would be a pool inside, fencing off the basement door and patio, and a hot tub mostly hidden by the attached garage. The main drive was to be gated, and the grounds were to be covered by all angles of camera security via Carl Wynn.

Trudy had pulled the designer to the side and asked about the possibility of her running a smaller crew for a special project to be completed at her request in the "attic" space that led out to an upper balcony in the middle of the back, with two large rooms to either side. This project would be held in secrecy. Sharon Thies blushed at some of the plans but assured her that only people who had a need to know about the room's layout would have access. Whenever possible, she would use nonlocal craftsmen so there would be no local gossip.

Trudy had also asked about the possibility of an elevator from the basement to the attic with keyed stops along the way on the other floors. She was assured that all of this could be completed, but the cost might be beyond the budget allowed. Trudy contacted Darell for the add-on and asked for it to be managed. He assured her it would be.

Trudy also mentioned a special project for which the designer might need extra funding. It was to be expected and approved by herself—please pave the way. Darell had no issues with her requests. The business as a whole was doing better than ever, and his pay reflected it. The ability to provide for his mother, stepbrother, and stepdad had been far surpassed, and he was grateful for the opportunity that Trudy had provided him. He was making the best use of it and had been expanding the businesses proportionally as they went.

Chapter 48 - Summer's End

The end of the summer seemed like madness. Bill and Paula were both empty nesting, with both girls going away to college, both promising to visit when they could. Mick and Nora were already gone, both surprised at the scholarships they had received.

Larry already had a good athletic scholarship for football, but the financial grant he did not even remember applying for was fantastic. He had applied to a lot of possibilities for help with schooling. His parents were struggling to keep ahead of their bills as it was. Larry's scholarships and grants were a godsend to them.

Dave had settled in and already touched base with Trudy and Amanda.

Trudy and Amanda's last night together was both spirited and sensual. The uncertainty of change had been tempered by knowing that at any time if it were needed, with a simple phone call, a plane could have them home or together in short order. Dan and Amanda pledged to keep that under four times a year if possible. Darell had his thumb on the pulse of their travels and would keep Trudy informed if necessary.

Trudy had spent a little extra time with Sadie, who had just flown in from seeing Thomas, who was on the verge of being released from physical therapy. She hugged Sadie before she left and gave her a set of phone numbers should she need travel or support. She had taken the time to explain where all her fingers had dipped into the world of business, making

Sadie prouder than she had already been. She promised to keep Trudy's secret.

Everyone gathered around as she and Amanda loaded up and headed out. She was going to drop Amanda off at the Evansville airport and continue to Bloomington afterward.

When Trudy arrived in Bloomington, she met with Sharon Thies, who said that the last punch list had been cleared two days before. The house was, for all intents and purposes, fully ready for everyday life. She gave Trudy a tour of the house from the second story down to the basement. After touring the grounds, she led Trudy into the garage where the back corner of the nearest space to the house had been added on to accommodate a four-person capable elevator.

They stepped on, and Sharon punched a five-number code and pushed down. The elevator opened in the near corner of the basement. Without getting off, she demonstrated how to go to each floor on the way up. When she reached the attic, they stepped off, and the door closed behind them. She explained that the elevator could be called to any floor, but other than the garage, it required a code to get off.

Sharon showed her the "secret" staircase that led to her walk-in closet one floor below. Both doors required a code. She stopped to survey the three large rooms. On the far end, there was a massive shower that could easily accommodate four or more people with three heads and a large overhead rain head. The middle room led to a screened balcony overlooking the yard and woods beyond. The adjoining room had the rear wall lined with every type of sexual whip, wand, and wonder. The first room had multiple pieces of furniture designed specifically for pleasure, restraint, and comfort. The whole floor was best described as a sexual palace for playing.

Sharon admitted, "I have learned quite a bit in the last two months. Some of these things are amazing. I won't tell you how I know," She slightly blushed. "Please be assured everything here is brand new."

"Thank you for my project room; it is perfect. More than I had hoped for. I hope I didn't make you too uncomfortable designing this part of the house.

"On the contrary, my husband wants me to do more of them." She laughed a bit. "He suggested we even think about such a room for our house. I have to say it has been a thrill to design from the get-go up until now."

Trudy explained, "I had been fortunate enough to have a friend that had… well, his tastes were not mainstream all the time. I learned a few things and wanted to know more. Some of this might be new to me, but I look forward to learning it as well."

"That must be exciting; I truly hope I have met your expectations. I would love a little feedback on the whole house if you got the time in about a month or so after you have had a chance to check the functionality of all the spaces. As for here, I was thinking that this type of room isn't really something you can sit down at the local design studio and conjure up. This might be a niche market into which I could tap." She blushed a bit more.

"That is a definite possibility; I would be interested to see what you find out. You know, if you would like to give your husband a tour of the final product, I don't think I would have a problem with that."

"I think that would be something he and I would really like, but we will be leaving town tomorrow. I stayed on to walk you through it. Trevor Wise sends his regards, but he had to go to a small chain of hotels in need of renovation. I watched him work; he is a very capable man. He was genuinely nice to work with."

"Well, if you want to stay another day, we can have a late lunch tomorrow and give your husband a thorough tour. As it is now, I need to check into the campus tomorrow morning, but I will be freed up shortly after that."

"That sounds fantastic. Two o'clock? Sharon quizzed.

"That sounds great."

They made their way down to the first floor via the elevator and stopped off in the kitchen, where Sharon had a 'book of the house.' Each floor was explained in detail, and every piece of electronics was identified with their access codes. It was an instruction manual that covered security, cameras, a pool and jacuzzi, the elevator to the top of the house, and everything else.

When Sharon left, both women were jazzed, but for varied reasons. Sharon was excited to show her husband her work, not once catching on to what Trudy had intended for the tour. She would soon find exactly what the "shower house," as Trudy had dubbed the third floor, was about. Trudy was excited to visit the campus.

Trudy Jax's first step onto the campus of Indiana University might have been one of the biggest thrills she has had to this point in her young life, but for Trudy, the thrill was not the newfound "freedom" that new college students must now learn to master. It was not the thrill of creating and implementing new time management skills of their own choosing; she already was well versed in personal time management.

As for the new crop of boys, she knew she was going to have fun, but they were secondary. Danny had taught her everything she needed to know about boys and sex in general; there was very little, if anything, that they and others had not tried, perfected, and improved upon.

For Trudy, the true excitement was the adulthood of it, the multitude of avenues that sparked in her inner core, the knowledge and vision she had commanded herself to strive for, the power that she alone could wield for her. Her, herself with all her goals, her timelines, her power of self, her knowing that the person within could not be held back, HER, her mind, her body, her glory all working in calculated tenacious harmony.

She was one of those people who did not see college as an emancipator of time to go wild but rather as the path to finalizing her earlier preparations and, to a lesser extent, acquiring that overrated piece of paper that claimed the holder was qualified. She had already "made it.' She already had a business sense that many would underestimate, but few who worked with, for, and against her would not forget too soon.

Standing there, on the outskirts of the entrance to the campus where, she intentionally stopped to reset her goals with a smile, knowing the path for her future. Trudy had the path mapped and polished; it was almost an afterthought at this point. She wanted the college "experience" with all its trimmings. The boyish men, the female camaraderie, the fraternity and sorority of it, and the unknowns of college life. It was that very uncertainty that was part of what she would love about this first step because looking beyond college at this point was a foregone conclusion.

The sun beat down, warming her to the core from the deepest blue sky hanging overhead that one could ever ask for. It seemed right, it felt right, and it promised a fantastic start to a new day, a new year, a new chapter to the book she alone was going to write in her life.

For Trudy Jax, this was just the beginning!

9 781968 000721